What people ar

"Diane Josefowicz
about some of the
Sixties, love, UFOs, and strange manuscripts. 'Our need for
space does not die with us,' says one of those manuscripts.
Ready, Set, Oh explores what it means to long for infinite
space while bounded in a nutshell."—David Burr Gerrard,
author of *The Epiphany Machine*

"Tino Battuta has always pulled off miracles—including
getting admitted to medical school—but 1967 finds him back
home in Providence, Rhode Island, a med school drop-out
facing the disappointment of his family, the hopes of a
psychiatrically-AWOL girlfriend, and the imminent threat of
unwelcome draft invitation from his Uncle Sam. These
challenges form the raucous backdrop to Diane Josefowicz's
moving, authentic, and vividly imagined novel, *Ready, Set,
Oh*. Josefowicz's bygone Providence is as fresh and romantic
today as it was in the era of SDS protests. With this
compelling exploration of friendship, sacrifice, and
intergenerational conflict, Josefowicz finds the large truths
in our smallest state, leaving an indelible mark on our
broader literary landscape. A stunning debut."—Jacob M.
Appel, author of *Einstein's Beach House*

"A story this big could only take place in Rhode Island.
Ready, Set, Oh gives you the quahogs, the red gravy, the
Italian-from-Italy suits. But you also get a backyard pet
dolphin, a mysterious mechanism from ancient Greece, and
UFO sightings reported by The Good 5-Cent Cigar, the
University of Rhode Island's student newspaper. Diane
Josefowicz captures the late Sixties in tightly crafted scenes
that show how the conflicts of the era—in particular
premarital sex and the war in Vietnam—played out in
suburban living rooms and kitchens."—William Walsh,
author of *Forty-five American Boys*

READY, SET, OH

a novel by

Diane Josefowicz

Flexible Press
Minneapolis, Minnesota 2022

Print ISBN: 978-1-7364033-4-1
eBook ISBN: 978-1-7364033-5-8

Flexible Press LLC
Editors William E Burleson
Vicki Adang, Mark My Words Editorial Services, LLC
Cover via Canva
Cover boat photo by Jan Huber via Unsplash
Author photo by Howard Romero

"Winter in the Abruzzi" by Natalia Ginzburg, translated by Dick Davis, in *The Little Virtues* (Arcade, 1985) © Skyhorse Publishing. Used by permission.

Table of Contents

for Matthew

There is a kind of uniform monotony in the fate of man. Our lives unfold according to ancient, unchangeable laws, according to an invariable and ancient rhythm. Our dreams are never realized, and as soon as we see them betrayed we realize that the most intense joys of our life have nothing to do with reality.

—Natalia Ginzburg, "Winter in the Abruzzi"

PART 1: SPRING 1967

1. The master tailor

Tavio Brindisi, the master tailor, was dead. Or close to it. If the spirit was ambivalent, the flesh was altogether resolved, as if the cold metaphorical shoulder that Tavio habitually turned against life had at last become real and gone systemic. Yet the undertaker was sure that whenever he turned his back, Tavio was up to his tricks, jerking his thumb, scratching his nose, or twitching his wrist inside his shirt cuff, just enough to dislodge the link.

That was Tavio, a certified hyperactive Ants-In-His-Pants. Not even rigor mortis was going to change that.

Everyone knew the story of how, eight decades back, on a jetty nosing into the green sea, Tavio had embraced his mother, whom he was unlikely to see again this side of heaven. How, at the last moment, he had pulled back, patted her shoulder, and said, *Eh, basta. Ebbasta.* Enough.

In any other family, it might have been dismissed, or minimized, or forgotten—just another one of those mysteries that charge the world like soap on a brush, lifting the day's stubble, the better to scrape it away. It was not such a mystery, though, if you knew the Brindisis. A hair-raising family, with minds like quicksilver and feelings to match.

On the quay, Tavio's mother had stepped back, fixing her son with the trademark Brindisi dick-shriveling look. And into his pockets, quick as rabbits, went those fidgety hands—the same ones that now refused to stay folded, one over the other, even as the undertaker silently threatened him with the moose glue and the stapler.

Dom Carcieri wiped his face, surprised to find it filmed with sweat. Stitching Tavio's mouth shut, he realized that to do so was a pleasure not granted to many in this life.

There was another story about Tavio: When the immigration officer in the Port of Providence asked for his place of birth, Tavio replied, *Baccauso Natale*, which meant, in rougher words, Original Shithole. This response was recorded, even though Tavio had named not so much a place as a state of mind. *Di dove?* Where you *from?* The question was the refrain of his days. And so Tavio would dig his papers from his wallet and point to the relevant line, proof that he did hail from a Shithole, all the while gesturing at some forgettable geography over his shoulder.

The undertaker spun the lid off the container of pancake makeup and smoothed a palmful over Tavio's face. The effect was mildly Floridian.

The undertaker recalled that it was his own father who'd sponsored Tavio's passage. The ticket was a favor, the sort of thing people did back then. Being the beneficiary of such generosity didn't stop Tavio from running his mouth, of course, griping to anyone with an open earhole about his steerage ticket. Still, Tavio had more than repaid the Carcieri family over the years. Not so much in money—Dom Senior was happy to embalm everyone in town, but he refused, on principle, to be anyone's *padrone*—but in tailored trousers, waistcoats and cummerbunds, double-breasted, three-piece, you-name-it, so that the two families had been literally in each other's exquisitely stitched pockets for decades, at holidays, weddings, and perhaps especially, given the Carcieri family business, at funerals, when Tavio made sure to get everyone's sartorial details, not least the corpse's, exactly right. The hand, the drape, the pleat, the hem— these details mattered so much to Tavio that, even after the advent of the electric sewing machine, he insisted on hand-stitching the jobs that still came his way, each stitch no bigger than a tsetse fly. *What a pain in the culo you are,* Dom Carcieri muttered in Tavio's ear and, feeling a tickle, snipped away a single coarse hair. He wove Tavio's fingers together and set them with a dab of glue. He nudged the elbow; the hands stayed where they were. *Piano, piano*—he draped a rosary over them and resisted the temptation to buff the fingernails one last time. Best not to push. Tavio was stubborn, and he got attached to things. Fidgeting, for instance. Or a good suit.

Tavio, who would have been a hundred come July, was dressed in a gray morning suit cut in the no-nonsense style popular during the Eisenhower administration. He'd made the suit twelve years before, in '55, right after he'd learned that the pains in his head were due to something more sinister than the eyestrain that might be expected from a lifetime spent hunched over a needle and thread while trying, at the same time, to raise three daughters, all of whom seemed bent on murdering him with their *agita*-producing behavior. Not to put too fine a point on it—Dom Carcieri flicked a bit of lint from Tavio's shoulder—those Brindisi girls were *agita* machines, as evinced by all the chest-tightening stories that made their way around the neighborhood: the burnt Sunday gravies, the kitchen fires and washroom floods, not to mention the assorted abrasions, bangs, burns, blisters, concussions, contusions, and, above all, the operatic heartbreaks that always seemed to happen when one of the girls failed to get her own way in some matter, usually romantic. Hoping his daughters would be good, plain American girls, Tavio had given them good, plain American names—Mary, June, and, daring to be a little fancier with his youngest, Lorraine. All for nothing, or nearly so: for they were neither good nor plain, though they were certainly American in their love of home appliances, their excitement over markdowns at Shepard's, and their expressive driving—about which, Dom reflected, crossing himself, the less said, the better. Tavio had been especially undone by their antics after his wife, Emmie, had died of heart failure while hanging sheets in the back yard on the same day that the radio carried the news of Lou Gehrig's retirement. Without Emmie, the girls were Tavio's alone to manage, and they were a handful. More than.

Dom Carcieri rubbed his eyes. What had he forgotten?

Never mind. Watch the hands.

Yes: They had not moved, not even when the glue had rolled down one knuckle, a detail gone awry that Tavio, in better days, would not have been able to resist correcting for an instant. Dom Carcieri wiped the glue away, noting not just the folded hands but also the ruby glass rosary spilling from them, the gold wedding band, the makeup that lightened, but did not quite conceal, the liver spot at the base of one thumb. Satisfied, he closed the lid with a smack, which he immediately regretted. It was never good to be a sore winner, even if the old mule had asked for it, putting up a fight even as the earth was being prepared to receive him. On his way out, after he'd locked the door, Dom Carcieri had a crazy feeling: What if, while he was gone, Tavio got up and *improved* something?

He shook his head. No point getting worked up. There weren't too many of these guys left, men of his father's generation. On the one hand, you hated to see them go. On the other, well—it was just as his father always said. Nature's way.

The old man's five years gone, he thought, *and still I'm hearing his voice in my ear.* As if his father still held the keys to life and death, the way he'd held the keys to the car and the liquor cabinet and the funeral parlor's back room. But the only thing his father was holding now was a handful of dirt in the Pocasset cemetery, his wedding ring resting loose around the bone. The tombstone gave the basics: *b. 1870, Pietravairano, d. 1962, Providence.*

A world was disappearing with these guys—the old places, the old ways.

The undertaker rattled the door again and made for home, where he heated a cup of milk and drank it at the kitchen sink. When the grandfather clock chimed midnight, he padded upstairs and slipped into bed beside his wife, her sleeping face slack as any corpse's, her nightgown hiked and twisted. At five, he opened his eyes to a nightingale singing. He reached under the blankets to touch his chest, as if that damned nightingale were trapped inside. But of course, it was only his own heart. It slowed; he breathed easier. His wife murmured in her sleep.

Dom Carcieri heaved himself upright.

The hat. Goddamn it. He'd gone and forgotten Tavio Brindisi's goddamn top hat.

2. The end of the line

Tino Battuta, the younger son of Tavio Brindisi's youngest daughter, set his razor on the sink's edge and smoothed his hair with a comb, which came away full. If it was true what they said, that baldness traveled down the maternal line, by this time next year he'd look just like Poppa Tavio. Not that an undiminished head of hair would do him much good now. Death traveled down every line. Was the last stop, in fact.

You'd have morbid thoughts, too, if you had just made yourself 1-A.

In the kitchen, Tino's mother maneuvered an over-easy from frying pan to plate. She had been up to raise the sun, lashes curled and nose powdered, her apron strings looped and bow-tied at her waist. Her father might be dead, but she was unfazed—already up, already at 'em. Whoever they were. "Egg, Tino?"

"No, thanks." His appetite had been AWOL for some days.

"Suit yourself." Into the pan went another egg. She poked it with a spatula, slitting the yolk the way Poppa Tavio liked, as if she still expected him to show up for breakfast.

"Mom." Tino came up behind her and killed the heat. "Stop."

She relinquished the spatula with a look that was no match for Tino, even after the long training in heartlessness that was first-year medical school. He led her to the table where someone, most likely his father, had piled the mail. Next to the centerpiece, a cut-crystal bowl filled with Hershey's Kisses, was Poppa Tavio's gray top hat.

"Oh, for heaven's sake. Can you believe this?" She sank into a chair.

"I'm sure his top hat was the last thing on his mind," Tino said. "He *was* dying, after all."

"Oh, I don't mean Tavio. I mean that nincompoop of an undertaker, who promised he'd take care of it." Lorraine glanced at the clock on the wall. "Tino, run the hat over to the funeral parlor, will you please? There's just time. The wake won't start for an hour."

"You want me to put it *on his head*?"

"Well, I suppose you could hand it to Dom Carcieri." She sighed. "Though we all know how unreliable *he* turned out to be."

"It's just a hat."

"You're giving me an argument *today*?"

"Fine." He'd do it. Of course he would. "But will you stop with the eggs?"

She threw up her arms. "You need to eat. You're too thin."

Tino didn't need to respond; they knew their lines well enough to vitiate further rehearsals of this little feeding drama, which had been playing ever since the moment he discovered his freedom to spit out whatever she spooned into his mouth. Not that he remembered details—just the feeling of power, a can-do feeling. It didn't take much to ruin her day.

Seeking distraction, his mother sifted the mail on the table. Spying his dean's letter, Tino slipped the envelope from the pile and tucked it into his suit's inside pocket.

"What's that, Tino?"

"Nothing, Ma. Nothing you don't already know."

"What in the world were you thinking?" she murmured. It was less a question than a prayer. "Are you planning to do what the other boys are all doing, giving their parents *agita*, turning in and tuning out?"

"The last thing I have is a plan."

"I don't understand it. A smart boy like you! You signed your death warrant, Tino."

How could he tell her? The dean's decision felt less like a death warrant than a new lease on life. In St. Louis, he'd volunteered in emergency three nights a week, where he learned that he had no stomach for the nitty-gritty of medicine—the gore, the urgency, the terrible responsibility. After it was all over, he felt light and pure as oxygen, relieved of burdens he didn't even know he'd taken on.

Lorraine reached into the bowl of Hershey's Kisses. They were her go-to solace, something she dipped into whenever she was, as she said, "under a strain."

"Your father and I are discussing it." She unwrapped a candy with her nimble Brindisi fingers and popped it between her lips. "And until we've come to a decision," she said around the chocolate, "you will say not a single word. Nothing. Silence. When something needs to be said, your father will say it, and you will agree to whatever it is. Understand?"

He did. Not that he expected anything too magnificently forgiving about whatever story his parents dreamed up. His father raged hot and hard. Just this morning Tino had opened his eyes to his father's roaring over some stupidity that had gone down overnight at Reliable Button, where bits of plastic were turned into brightly colored gewgaws through a complicated process involving heavy machinery, dozens of nimble-fingered employees, and an array of glues and solvents whose exact composition was a closely guarded secret. Leon's roaring was followed by the front door's heavy slam.

Lorraine unwrapped another candy and offered it to Tino. For a moment he remembered what it was like to want to eat. The sugar needled his molars, but that was just fine. For all he cared, his teeth could fall out of his head. At least then he might be 4-F, deferred, safe—for now, anyway. "Whatever Dad wants to say can wait until the funeral is over," he said.

"That's up to your father."

"Don't I get any say in this? It's my reputation we're talking about."

"You should have thought of that before you did what you did."

"Thanks," he said, not thankful at all.

"Now don't you be fresh."

"Sorry." Another lie.

"You need to make some kind of—" She struggled to find the right word. "Well, an adjustment. An arrangement. You don't have much time."

"I know."

"Do you? Do you even *see* those body bags all over the television every night? That's how kids are coming back! Kids! *Sons,* Tino! Just because we don't yet know anyone in those bags doesn't mean we never will. They're not just for show, you know."

"Ma, I know!" And *how*, he did.

"And that girlfriend of yours—"

"You're always picking on her."

"You've been dating for two years. Her parents will have expectations." She unwrapped a third chocolate. "Not to mention she just spent two months in the loony bin."

"It's a crazy time, Ma. People go crazy."

"Not like that."

The news had come near Christmas, while he'd been preparing for the fall term's exams. Primrose had gone away, "for a rest" was how her father put it, his voice tiny over the telephone. In the dormitory's hallway, Tino crammed the phone to his ear, trying to remember the last time he'd talked with her. She had joined an antiwar group, and he ascribed her excited mood to ordinary causes—a new activity, new friends. *She has a chemical imbalance in her brain,* her father told him. There had been shock treatments, wet packs, pills. Later, over the four precious weeks of Christmas break, he listened to her newly monotonous voice and wondered about the odd, blank look that came over her face when she didn't think he was watching. She was mostly herself otherwise, steadfast in her affection, ardent on their drives. Perhaps he just imagined the changes.

Tino's mother was still talking. "All I'm saying, Tino, is that you can't always have everything your way. Sometimes you have to do things for other people."

Tino's breath escaped loudly through his nose—a skeptical noise, but also a beaten one. Under normal circumstances, a guy in his situation could come home to find steady work. Or open a business. Settle down. But these were not normal circumstances. He was free to choose between dying relatively soon in a distant jungle for *nothing*—no, *less* than nothing—and dying somewhat later doing something he would probably hate, all the while worrying about going up in a mushroom cloud or, worse, surviving the initial blast only to become a radioactive popsicle when the ashes of civilization blotted out the sun. Some freedom. Some choice. America was solid as a block of Swiss cheese, with holes you could slip through—and *poof*, that was your life, your one life.

His mother's eyes filled.

"What, Ma?"

She blinked several times, quickly, and the mistiness evaporated. Pushing her lips together, she replied through the tight line they made: "I just can't stand to see you make another mistake."

3. The watch

Tino knelt before the coffin, angling the hat one way and then another. Poppa Tavio looked ready for a fight, his chin jutting up and out, as if he were already at the Pearly Gates arguing his case with Saint Peter. Or was it a different holy bureaucrat standing there checking off the names in his book? Tino could never remember. Tamping down his revulsion, he slipped a hand beneath the old man's head. It would be tricky to lift without making a pig's breakfast of the undertaker's work.

A chemical whiff rose from the body, spiriting Tino back to St. Louis, where he'd spent the autumn hacking at a pickled cadaver. The professor had mocked Tino's inept dissections, lifting the ravaged tissues with a scalpel, a pencil point, a chopstick from his lunch. "So what do you call this one, Battuta? Gastrocnemius? Popliteal? Mickey Mouse?" All the structures looked the same and nothing like the illustrations in *Gray's Anatomy*. By the time Tino finished, he was half-pickled himself, and the stink no longer came off in the shower. When the class was finally over, he burned his lab clothes. The smoke smelled worse than formaldehyde, but unlike formaldehyde, it just blew away.

Gravel crunched in the parking lot, the noise of his family arriving, early birds getting the day's sad worm. Tino nudged the hat again. If he failed at this task, his mother would give him hell; if he got it *really* wrong, say, by losing the hat, or allowing it to be crushed after carelessly setting it on the chair where his big cousin Aldo was about to take a load off, he would never hear the end of it. Still, he saw no clear path to his goal. *Oh, well*, he thought. *I tried*. He set the hat on Poppa Tavio's chest and tip-toed backward as if his grandfather's body were a live grenade, as if the hat were its pin.

"I hate to disturb you."

Tino started. While he'd been lost in his thoughts, Mr. Carcieri had crept up on him.

"Easy does it." He rested his heavy hand on Tino's shoulder. "Properly speaking, it should be on his head." He paused, considering. "You know, I have something in the office that might help."

Mr. Carcieri left, his jacket vents flapping. On his way out, he passed Tino's mother who, seeing Tino at the casket, blanched beneath her makeup. Tino felt the assessment in his tightening chest: He was fucking up, as usual. She pointed toward the door, where coat hooks lined part of the wall. Tino hurried over, intending to catch the hat on a hook and be done with it. No such luck: The hook, missing a bracket screw, twisted in the wall and tipped the hat to the floor. Crouching to nab the fugitive, Tino discovered instead the missing bracket screw, rolling from side to side on the carpet in a dime-sized puddle of light. His mother's black pumps crossed his field of vision, and then her face appeared, seemingly younger by a decade, the effect of being upside down.

"You'd think a boy your age could manage just one simple thing." His mother's hiss smelled of chocolate. "One simple thing."

He heaved himself to his feet and backed toward the lobby, muttering apologies he knew by heart. There were advantages to a hardened one. A year ago, he would have resented his mother for all of it, from the absurd task she had set him to the insult she had just lobbed his way. But his days of petty filial grievance were behind him. He was in a new country now, beyond her good opinion.

Smartly turned out in his Army dress uniform, Tino's brother Pat was loitering by the back door. He eyed Tino with a practiced thoroughness, taking him in from nose to wingtips like a butcher considering the most efficient way to hack a carcass. By some tacit agreement this look had always been his prerogative.

"Did you actually flunk out, Tino? Or were you *kicked*?"

"None of your business." A heat rose up the back of Tino's neck.

"No use getting yourself worked up," Pat sneered, "the way you do. Regardless of what you actually did, the fact is you're up shit creek without a popsicle stick. Sayonara, deferment." Failing to light a cigarette with a single match, he tried again with several and nearly singed his eyebrows. When at last he lit his smoke, he blew the first lungful into Tino's face.

"Uncle Sam won't front you a proper Zippo?" Tino coughed into his fist, keeping the other safely balled up in his pocket so it would not accidentally connect with Pat's jaw.

"Uncle Sam is the least of my problems," Pat said. "But unlike yours, mine are only romantic."

Pat's letters home, posted from a West German army garrison, foamed over with stories of ample-bosomed local beauties bearing steins full of beer. Even so, Tino suspected at least a few of his feminine interests on the home front were also receiving regular assurances of devotion.

"Fayrene called yesterday." Pat dragged nervously on his cigarette. "She told Mom she might come."

Last year Pat had dumped Fayrene, a girl-next-door brunette with a big smile and an impenetrable bouffant, right after their mother had taken a shine to her. This was the kiss of death as far as Tino could tell.

"You'll be all right," Tino said. "Fayrene only loves the uniform."

"Says you." Pat shook out his pant legs one at a time. "Jesus Christ, but I'm nervous today."

"Seems we both got our problems."

"I'm just trying to look out for you, Tino."

"In that case, do me a favor. Don't say a word to anyone about school, okay? Let Dad handle it."

"Sure." Pat toed his spent cigarette into the gravel. "It's your funeral. Or will be."

***

Mourners passed like the cigarettes Pat was smoking, one after the other. A petite woman enveloped Tino in a fug of flowery perfume. "Such a fine man, your Poppa Tavio," she gushed. "What a craftsman. Look at this suit!"

"Can't find craftsmanship like this nowadays," the man beside her remarked, pumping Tino's arm. "Everything's made in Japan."

Tino moved them on to Pat, the next link in the chain, and the ritual continued: *So sorry, isn't it awful, we only meet at wakes,* a handshake, air kiss, who's next? The repetition numbed him, leaving him unprepared for his first glimpse of Primrose in the doorway, tugging one long black glove up one long pale arm. Her black dress, nipped at the waist and none too long, showed off her figure. His class ring with its chunk of onyx swung from a chain around her neck. Catching his eye, she smiled.

Oh, Primrose.

He closed the space between them in quick steps. His thudding heart made conversation difficult, but the solution to that problem was a no-brainer.

"You taste like bubble gum," he said when they came up for air.

"Hubba hubba," she murmured. If she noticed his transition to imbecility, she didn't let on. The gum went round in her mouth and disappeared. "I'm sorry about Poppa Tavio."

He sneezed. And sneezed again. And again. The damned flowers—every surface was larded with them, stuffed into vases and shooting from pots.

She drew back. "Stop that."

"I have *allergies*," he snuffled. "I can't just 'stop' sneezing." He pointed at a white splotch on her upper arm. "What's this?"

"Do you always have to criticize me?" She rubbed the spot until the black tip of her gloved finger turned gray. "Look, it's just paint. Despite Dr. Feelgood's zombie pills, I actually worked this morning."

Her zombie pills, which were keeping her coherent and upright.

"Did you hear me, Tino?"

"What were you painting?"

"Snow," she retorted. "Macaroons. Milk."

"I'm just asking one simple question."

"No, you aren't," she snapped as she tugged at her hem, making final adjustments. "Never mind. Apart from the smudge, do I look all right?"

Now that was a simple question. "You look beautiful."

She smiled wanly, offering détente if not exactly peace. He took her arm, and they made their way to the front of the room. Standing sentry by the foot of the casket, Pat greeted Primrose by taking her hand in both of his. On the other side, at the start of the receiving line, Lorraine fanned herself with a prayer card illustrated with Jesus wincing beneath his crown of thorns.

"Tino," she trilled, ignoring Primrose, "your father's here."

Thanks, he wanted to tell Lorraine, *for the warning.* In the lobby, just visible from where Tino stood, Tino's father was extracting himself from a clutch of nervy-looking men. They were the sort Leon privately derided as "fellas," *wise guys* being a little too on the nose.

"Lupa in fibula," Pat observed.

"Fabula," Tino corrected him, sweat breaking out along his hairline. What remained of it. "Fibula's a bone."

"You would know," Pat sneered. "Or maybe you wouldn't."

Primrose inhaled sharply, and Tino squeezed her arm. If Pat had guessed the truth, so what?

"Boys," Lorraine said warningly. "Your father has been making buttons all morning."

Tino's heart dislodged itself, a button slipping from its whip-stitched hole. The old man was finding his own way of relinquishing his dream of My Son, The Doctor, discovering the fantasy it always was. All Tino could do, at this point, was let him.

"But he's always making buttons. That's just what he does," Pat muttered. "He makes buttons."

"Don't be fresh," snapped Lorraine.

Primrose knelt by the coffin, her head bent over her clasped hands. A few wisps had escaped her chignon. Seeing them, Tino fought back a wave of tenderness. She had put in the work today, trying to look right. Lorraine reached past Primrose to fuss with the carnation in Poppa Tavio's lapel.

"Lorraine!" Leon cried out. "My God. Don't do that."

"Just a minute." She fished a toothpick from her handbag, placed it between Poppa Tavio's lips, and gave his chest a thump. "There," she said. "Much better."

Primrose's eyes were round as the marbles she'd lately been so good at losing.

Leon put his hand on his wife's arm. "You can't just jump-start him, Lorraine."

From her bag she withdrew a Hershey's Kiss, which she peeled expertly despite her gloves. "Where have you been all morning?"

"One of the painters had a conniption."

"I'll give you a conniption." She cast a final appraising glance at Poppa Tavio, just in case there was anything else she could improve. "Jump-start him, my foot."

"Mom," Tino said. "Please, Mom. Sit down."

She let Tino help her to an empty seat. Primrose followed.

"Mrs. Battuta, I'm so sorry for your loss," Primrose murmured robotically. Anxiety, Tino guessed. Or the pills.

Lorraine gazed at her, taking in everything from her messy chignon to her discount shoes. "You're such a pretty girl," she sniffed. "Why don't you trim your hair so you don't have to work so hard to make it nice?"

Primrose's snuffed-out expression knotted Tino's gut. Which was why, when his mother offered Primrose a Hershey's Kiss,

Tino wasn't surprised to hear Primrose refuse. "I don't want to get fat."

Lorraine scowled. "I can't for the life of me understand you modern girls."

Some minutes later, Tino's mother was waving the obituary around, irritated because the editor had cut a line she'd written about Poppa Tavio being from Baccauso Natale. "The gall!"

"Poppa Tavio didn't talk about where he was from," Pat said. "Why should we?"

"He was honest," his mother said. "He told it like it was."

Tino sensed a different reason for his mother's irritation. She didn't like being the subject of someone else's improvements, even if they were just on paper.

Now she started improving Tino, straightening his tie and brushing at his shoulders. She lifted his lapel and ran her hand along its length, her touch firm enough to let him know she knew her stuff. This was the essence of Lorraine's charm: If you were good enough—like a fabric with a dry hand, a nice drape—she was in a position to appreciate and, moreover, would not stint. But there was the catch: You had to be good enough, and *so few were*.

"The cloth of this suit is older than Poppa Tavio. Do you recognize it?"

"Nope."

"But I'm sure we'd love to hear all about it," Primrose interjected. The remark sounded innocent enough, even nice. But was something *off* about it? He squeezed her hand, just in case.

"This suit was made from the bolt of cloth that Poppa Tavio brought with him to America! Along with his pincushion and his good scissors. That's all he had with him when he got off the boat, right near where the sewers drain into the bay. Oh, the stink." Lorraine wrinkled her nose and fanned herself with Migraine Jesus. "All his life he couldn't believe his first impression of America was a cesspit. That's what he always said: If you're too fast to leave one Shithole, soon enough you wind up in Another."

Tino, who'd heard this all before, just shrugged. Providence was nothing compared to St. Louis, which was the biggest Shithole he'd ever seen. Well, that was his opinion. For which no one had asked. So many thoughts he was obliged to keep quiet—it was isolating, feeling like you couldn't just state the facts, the truth you saw with your own eyes.

"For Poppa Tavio," Pat said, "that Shithole line was the secret of life."

Which brought back a memory. On the porch years before, Tino had asked Poppa Tavio to tell him just that, "the secret of life." Even then, the phrase sounded ridiculous in his ears, but he didn't know any better way to say it, and he was distracted by his backside, which hurt from his father's most recent walloping. For what infraction, he no longer remembered.

All he wanted was to be on good terms with his father. But he never seemed to manage it. He wondered what he lacked. *What was the secret of life?*

His grandfather groaned as he hoisted him onto the porch rail. "Look who's getting big."

"Come on, Poppa T. I asked you a question."

Poppa Tavio moved his mouth, settling his dentures. "The first secret of life," he told Tino, "is very simple. Just make a living—enough for a nice house, a car, a son's education." He plucked his toothpick from between his lips and waved it. "Are you listening? Attaboy. Here it is, the second secret of life: After you eat the food you put on the table with your own hard work, you chew one of these, so everyone knows you ate something besides green beans."

So that was it. The secret of life was to make money—and to chew a toothpick so everyone knew what your life was worth.

***

When the undertaker returned to pay his respects, Tino overheard his mother describing him to Mr. Carcieri as "the son who used to go to medical school."

"Christ almighty," Tino muttered, scanning the room. He'd lost track of his father. Pat, also, had vamoosed—a lucky development. "You might as well call the Associated Press, Ma."

"Eh, Tino. *Staccalma*." Mr. Carcieri pressed both hands downward against an invisibly burgeoning chaos. "Your Uncle Tavio was a good man. Not many like him left nowadays."

"An *honest* man," his mother interjected. "A hardworking and honest man."

"Of course." Mr. Carcieri patted her arm.

"Don't believe everything you read in the newspaper," Lorraine said. From Mr. Carcieri's puzzled look, Tino guessed he hadn't seen the obituary.

"What are you going to do now, son?" he asked Tino. The man's breath stank of aniseed biscuits. His eyes were like old coins.

"I'm not your son."

"Eh, wise guy." Mr. Carcieri clapped Tino hard on the back. "I'm sure no matter what you decide to do, you'll make us proud with the rest of our boys. Show 'em what we're made of here in America."

"He'll do no such thing," Lorraine cut in. "If Tino goes, it will be over my dead body."

"Lorraine." Again he made the *staccalma* gesture. "Let us not speak of that."

"Please don't speak of that," Primrose said.

There was an awkward silence. Mr. Carcieri salvaged the moment by encompassing Tino and Primrose in a big, aniseed-scented embrace.

"You punked out, Tino—so what?" he whispered in Tino's ear. "You'll do right by us all in some other way. Assuming the Army don't do it for you. That's simple logic, eh?" He stepped back and leered at Primrose. "And you—you'll stay home, do your time like the rest of us. Make your babies."

Primrose smiled without showing her teeth.

"Just don't let me catch you on the television, setting fire to government property while you give your parents *agita*."

The undertaker took off, leaving his halitosis in Tino's nose. His back stung where he'd been slapped, and his mind kept returning to the same difficult places: Primrose's illness. Medical school. The war. Would he be drafted, only to be borne back to Carcieri's funeral home in a box? Was he seeing the future *in advance*? He shivered. The lilies exhaled pollen. His legs itched. If his suit was Italian-from-Italy, so were the allergens embedded in it, pricking him like so many bad memories.

"I need some air."

Lorraine shook her head. "Ants in his pants, just like my father. Not a single one of these men can sit still for an instant. And *how* does the blood run true."

"Bleed through," Primrose replied absently, her eyes glazing.

His mother subsided into her chair, fanning herself with Poppa Tavio's obituary.

4. An offer

Taking the steps two at a time, Chick Bonano attained the landing—no mean feat considering the funeral home's front steps were carpeted with Astroturf and slicked with dew. His pompadour was holding up despite the humidity, and he was a sight to see in his black leather jacket and cherry red camp-collared rayon shirt. "Nice zoot," he said to Tino. "Got a smoke?"

Feeling square in his itchy suit, Tino produced a Parliament from behind Chick's ear.

"Cheap trick," said Chick, lighting up.

"Says you," Tino muttered. This sleight of hand with the Parliament might be the extent of his Brindisi dexterity—fast fingers, a way with small objects—and not the sign of the doctor, the surgeon, he'd tricked himself into thinking he might be.

Smoke exploded from Chick's nostrils. "You're not happy to see me?"

"Well, I'm down a coffin nail," Tino said.

"No shortage of those in this joint," Chick muttered. "Primrose coming?"

"She's inside."

"You left her with the old lady?"

"Tension is normal," Tino offered, "between old ladies and young ones." Normal: like tidy houses on tree-lined streets, like chemicals balanced in the brain.

"Women," Chick commiserated.

"I left her with Erma, actually." His cousin, the family's hottest ticket.

Chick nodded. "Smart."

Erma had taken Primrose aside, and soon she had her giggling. Over what, he could not guess. A secret joke was fine by him—fine, even if it was *on* him. Primrose needed a friend in this family.

"So how'd your old man take the news?"

Tino shrugged. "I don't want to get into it."

"That good, huh. Well, I've got a deal for you," Chick said. "A line on a boat."

A tentative rain pocked the pavement. Tino's watch told noon, another surprise. His stomach growled. "A what?"

"Thirty-six feet from prow to stern, a real Chris-Craft with a genuine hardwood hull. I forget what kind of wood. Two hundred bucks, you got yourself half. What do you think?"

"It does solve one problem," Tino replied. Chick had no deferment. "Your draft status."

"And yours."

"And mine. But what about marina fees? Upkeep?"

"Until we need it, we can park it in my mother's yard."

"Your mother's yard."

"You'd hear better, Tino, if you didn't slap your dick around so much. Makes you deaf, you know."

"Oh, fuck you," Tino said amiably. "So how old is she?"

"My mother?"

"This *felucca* you're trying to sell me, jackass."

"She's definitely seaworthy."

What Chick knew about seaworthiness would fit on Tino's pinky fingernail. "Let me think about it."

"Carpe diem." Chick stubbed out his cigarette. Catching his reflection in the glass door, he ran both hands over his hair, smoothing it. "The fish is good for one day only. After that it starts to stink. *Capisce?*"

They shook on it, and Chick headed inside to pay his respects.

"Hey, Chick?"

Chick turned, the glass door at his back, and the smell of carnations poured through the doorway.

"Yeah?"

"If you see Dom Carcieri, tell him I'm looking for him. That I need to speak to him about a hat."

"Copy that." Chick paused. "Seriously? A hat?"

The boat wasn't expensive but even so, half-ownership plus upkeep would cost at least as much as he would make that summer, assuming he was able to find work in the first place. But what a picture: All four of them—Tino, Prim, Chick, and Chick's girl, Dot—on the boat on some glorious summer afternoon, listening to the ball game on the radio. They'd make sailboats of their draft notices and push them out to sea.

You could take a boat right across Lake Champlain, he thought. Haul our sorry 1-A asses to Canada. If it came to that.

Which it wouldn't.

5. On the home front

That night, after the wake, Primrose caught a ride with Chick, and Tino returned home with his family. Lorraine and Leon disappeared into their bedroom, presumably to confer about how to communicate to the family the disappointment that was, or had perhaps merely overtaken, their younger son. Not knowing how their rap session would turn out, Tino anxiously spooned up three bowls of bran flakes with stale raisins while listening to Pat snore before the television. It was the last night with Poppa Tavio above ground. There was something sacred about that, Tino supposed. He finished his cereal, rinsed the bowl, and went to bed, where he stared at the ceiling until daybreak.

At breakfast, his mother wasn't surprised to hear about his sleepless night. "That's why they call it a wake," she told him. "Because you stay awake."

Tino wasn't so sure about that, but seeing his exhaustion in his mother's bleary eyes, he sensed that now was not the time to criticize her etymology.

The funeral was uneventful, a morning service in the night-chilled church followed by a half-hour at the cemetery trying not to look too fixedly at the rectangle of opened ground waiting to receive Poppa Tavio. Primrose stood beside him, shifting from foot to foot to keep her heels from sinking into the dirt. Across the way, the Pocasset River glinted as it lapped the shore's edge. When the show was over, Tino drove Primrose back to his parents' house for the consolation meal. He spun the wheel to radio music: *Turn, turn, turn.*

"Remarkable, isn't it?" Primrose marveled. Her outfit was the same as yesterday's, and she was still mouthwatering in it. "How the radio just knows."

"Knows?"

"As if it could hear our thoughts. As if it could sense when we're approaching a turn."

Tino forced himself to smile. The day had been hard enough already. Although no one sobbed or even sniffled as Poppa Tavio's casket was lowered into the grave, something was definitely different. It changes you, burying someone. This he needed to think over. Maybe for a week, maybe forever.

The radio droned some peacenik ballad: a time for this, a time for that. A time for wearing a top hat.

Primrose flipped the sun visor down and peered into the mirror. "Jesus, Tino!" she shouted. "Poppa Tavio's hat is in the back seat!"

How he loved that shout. How he loved, especially, to produce it. His fake smile gave way to a real one. "I was wondering when you'd notice."

"You do know how to surprise a girl."

"It didn't take much doing," he said. "I had a little talk with Dom Carcieri."

"Poor you," she replied, poking around in her bag until she found her lipstick. "I can't stand the way he comes too close and breathes all over you."

"He needs to lay off the aniseed biscuits, that's for sure. I swear he eats them just to get on my mother's good side."

"She does like her aniseed biscuits, doesn't she? If only it were so easy to get on her good side," she said, her voice tightening. Tino's heart gave a sick lurch.

She slipped the cap off the lipstick and wound the cylinder until the tip appeared, a sexy red. Alizarin crimson, she called it. It was her favorite color, in her paint box and on her mouth. Staring into the mirror, she began to apply her touch-up. "*God forbid* I should walk into your mother's house looking like anything less than a million bucks," she said.

Her sourness echoed his own. He didn't have a good feeling about this dinner. His St. Louis disaster had opened a rift between his immediate family and his extended one, such a rift as had never existed; until now, the family had no secrets, as far as he knew. And since his mother had placed the resolution of the problem in Leon's hands, he was at his father's mercy.

Wearing a gray top hat, Uncle Sam burped his napalm breath in Tino's face.

Tino pulled into the driveway and jumped out to open the door for Primrose. She swung from the passenger seat in a single motion, and the sight of her bare legs was enough to banish dyspeptic Uncle Sam. Primrose smiled shyly as she took the arm he offered. Arm in arm, they went inside to face his family.

"Look sharp!" Erma cried, on a beeline for the dining room, the carving set gleaming in her hands. Tino had to move fast to avoid a forking.

"Heavens to Betsy, Erma." Tino's mother was folding napkins at the counter. "That's no way to get a husband."

Erma's mother, Tino's Aunt Mary, was tearing leaves of escarole into a bowl while Tino's other aunt, June, took them out again and tossed them by the handful into a pot. "In the husband department," Aunt Mary said, shaking wet greens from her plump fingers, "Erma will need all the help she can get."

Lorraine's gaze lit on Primrose, who clutched Tino's hand.

"See?" Primrose hissed. "She doesn't want me to marry you!"

"No one said anything about marriage," he whispered.

"Not true," she muttered, loosening her grip.

Tino's uncle, Zio Zio, arrived from the hallway and, pulling a pack of Parliaments from his shirt's front pocket, made a beeline for the door.

"You'll kill yourself with those things," Aunt June warned.

"*Piacere*," Zio Zio told her. It was the polite way to tell your wife to shut up.

Sidling into a corner, Primrose bumped the hutch, which was lined with old photographs in silver frames. She caught the largest as it fell.

"My father insisted on having my portrait done," said Tino's mother, taking the picture from Primrose and repositioning it on a higher shelf. "This was during the Depression. It cost so much, we didn't eat meat for a month."

"She was always his favorite," Aunt June called from the stove.

"Don't be silly, June. You know he wasn't like that," Aunt Mary replied. "Now, about those gloves you were wearing at the wake—"

"What about them, Mary?" Aunt June stirred the pot.

"Aren't they mine?"

"June, please." Lorraine snorted. "You haven't been able to get gloves past your wrists since Aldo was born."

"There's no need to be catty," Aunt June said. "Of the three of us Brindisi girls, I got the substantial genes. So what?"

The kitchen table was heaped with plates and silver place settings in flannel wrappers. "Erma," Lorraine called into the dining room, "come help with the forks."

Erma returned, flushed with hurry, and gestured toward the piles. "These, you mean? Jesus, what a mess."

"Your mouth," Lorraine reminded her.

"Is open. Again. Sorry, my mistake."

Primrose picked up a fork and turned it over. It was embossed: Made In Formosa. Muttering, Erma straightened the silverware.

"Tino," Lorraine continued, ignoring Erma, "run down cellar and get me a can of tomatoes, would you? And some coffee. We're all out."

Tino took Primrose's hand. If they could just escape downstairs, away from his family, then he might be able to soothe her. He could still turn things around. "Let's go," he said.

She followed, and he was moved by her docility. She really was trying.

Years before, Lorraine had convinced Leon to build a second pantry in the basement for nonperishables: boxes of cereal, powdered milk, canned fruits and vegetables. It wasn't exactly a bomb shelter, but if a bomb went off, they wouldn't starve— which, for Lorraine, was usually the main worry. Primrose shifted a can of evaporated milk, revealing several more behind it. "What kind of tomatoes does she want?"

"Contadina." Tino scanned the shelf. "The one with the girl on the label."

"The contadina," Primrose said. She glanced at him, as if there was some joke he was supposed to be getting.

Was there a joke he was supposed to be getting?

"Erma knows," Primrose said suddenly. "Pat must have told her."

"Impossible," Tino replied, sounding more confident than he felt. Pat's guess about the reason for his departure from St. Louis was disturbingly close to the mark. "Mom swore him to silence until Dad comes up with a story."

"Someone told her," Primrose insisted. "I just want you to know the squealer isn't me."

Tino sighed. Primrose's intuitions were unreliable, to say the least. But even if she was right, his father was still going to lay down the official version of events. After that, nothing else would matter, at least within the family, the only place that counted.

"Do you see the coffee?" he asked, to change the subject. "She has to have her Autocrat."

"If the shoe fits."

"Primrose, please."

"I'm allowed to be sassy. I have a brain, you know. Eyes to see."

He completed the thought: "Ears to hear."

"Don't be like that," she muttered. "I only hear things when I'm *off* my meds."

Tino slid aside several paper-wrapped tins of deviled ham to find a row of cans labeled with a bosomy girl cradling a basket of red tomatoes. "Behold, the contadina," said Primrose. "She's a good country girl."

As Tino pulled three cans from the shelf, each touched off a different hellish ER memory: a sucking chest wound, a limb hanging from mere shreds of flesh, a wild bleed from a lacerated liver.

"Hey." Primrose touched his arm. "They're just tomatoes."

They never found the Autocrat, so they went back to the kitchen without it.

"Tino, round up the guys, will you?" Erma called from behind the pass-through. "The spare chairs are not going to move themselves into the dining room."

Tino set the cans on the counter. The front door was open, framing Zio Zio as he smoked by the boxwoods. From the den came a loud, sharp snore—his Uncle Beppe, Erma's dad, who suffered from apnea—and the television blared reports from the South China Sea. Soon to come: the day's body count in integers, the day's body bags in rows. Bodies everywhere and no people anywhere. In St. Louis, he had seen enough of that. More than. *Kids!* His mother's voice echoed in his mind. *Sons!*

Tino slipped into the room and changed the channel to *Rocky and Bullwinkle*. Bullwinkle took a serious goof-gas hit, yet it left him no dumber than before. The narrator wondered: Was the null result just stupidity, or did Rocky have something up his sleeve?

Pat opened one eye. "So there you are."

"Erma needs help with the chairs."

Pat leapt up and pulled Tino back into the hall. "Forget the chairs. You have to talk to Dad. He needs to get something started for you. Everything takes five times longer than you expect."

Tino shook himself from Pat's grip. "I'll be *fine*."

"In a body bag? You call that *fine*? You stubborn *chooch*."

The television's noise roused Uncle Beppe, who snorted awake and, groaning, roused himself to flip the channel. The set disgorged small thunder: a base hit. Primrose felt for the banister, the last steady point in the galaxy. Tino caught her glance in the hallway's gilt mirror.

"I think I just got hit with goof gas," she said.

"I don't feel so hot myself. Why don't we get some air? No one's in any real rush to eat."

***

Beneath the tupelo, Tino plucked a dandelion and pressed it against the inside of Primrose's elbow. It was an old game. *Butter, butter,* he said. *Butter bus. Buss.* She parried with a dandelion of her own. *Butter. Buss.* Soon they were in each other's yellow-smeared arms, and the napalm-breathing stars-and-stripes dragon was just a red, white, and blue toy that Tino could spin round his thumb by the tail.

"If I had a job," she mused after a while, "I could buy that paint."

"Which paint?"

"The alizarin crimson." Absently she rubbed her arm where the spot of paint had been earlier. "Five friggin' bucks a tube."

"You don't need a job." He'd told her so many times. Working wasn't something regular girls did. Primrose's mother worked only because her family needed money. "I'll give you the cash," he said, though he had no idea where he'd find it. "Don't you want to finish school?"

"Of course." She sat up, frowning. "But look who's talking about school."

The back of Tino's neck prickled at a fresh exhalation from the Uncle Sam Dragon, who was not so small and toy-like now. "I just can't see you working nine-to-five at Reliable Button."

"I'm keeping all your secrets, Tino. You trust me that much. And even so, we still don't have—as they say—an official relation."

"You already know how I feel." They were too young to get married. Too inexperienced. Too broke. And then there was the war. If he was destined to die in a jungle half a world away, he wanted to go unencumbered.

Her lips paled beneath her lipstick. Alizarin crimson, five bucks a tube.

"I'm sorry." Tino chafed her fingers. "I know I keep saying it, but I am." He rolled his head from side to side, releasing the pinched muscles, and told her about Chick's deal.

"You're crying poorhouse so we can't get married, and you're going to buy a *boat*?"

"We could take the boat to Canada."

"Canada?" She had never even been to Boston.

"Don't worry. Everyone has options."

"No," she said. "Not everyone."

"Tino!" His mother was calling. "Don't make me come get you!"

They leapt up and headed back to the house, straightening their clothes as they went. Tino's mother waited by the back door, silhouetted by the light from a dangling bare bulb.

"Do I look all right?" Primrose murmured to Tino. Her lipstick was smudged on her front teeth. A year ago, he might not have seen it. Since she'd gotten sick, he couldn't help noticing her smallest flaws, as if they could forecast the next bout of heavy mental weather.

"You're fine," he said. "A picture."

"I can't imagine what you're doing out here," Lorraine said acidly as soon as they came within earshot. "What pink cheeks you have, Primrose!"

Primrose blushed to the part in her hair.

"Communism," Leon announced, a spoonful of soup paused halfway to his mouth, "has a pernicious effect on man's natural competitive urges."

There was a pause while everyone took this in. Leon was not a habitual pontificator, but he did sometimes take control of the dinner table. Tino shivered. Was this the moment? His father's announcement felt like a thesis, an article of faith that he was about to nail to a door.

"I don't know if you can just leap from Darwin to capitalism," Tino said, working his spoon around a twist of escarole, which he detested. "Competition works for chimps. But we're not chimps."

Leon pinched a crouton from a serving dish piled high with them. "Tino, your book-learning is showing."

"Oh?"

"You'll see, now that you're out in the world. You'll come to understand that competition's good for business, which is good for us all."

"Out in the world?" Erma wondered.

Pat choked quietly on his escarole. Aldo pounded his back.

Tino chewed a crouton, glad for the prohibition on talking with the mouth full. So long as he was chewing, his silence entailed no loss of face.

"Those union stiffs are gazelles on a savannah." Leon tilted his head at Zio Zio, a longtime member of the bricklayer's local. "Present company excluded, of course."

"Working for someone doesn't oblige you to make his life easy," Zio Zio replied. "Besides, Leon, you've said the same thing for years. All the repetition doesn't make it true."

"Doesn't make it false, either. Eh? That's simple logic for you." Leon scraped his spoon against his bowl. Aunt Mary moved to refill it, but he waved her away. "Next thing you know, there's a drought or a flood, and the gazelles are kaput. Sayonara, pension. Sayonara, time and a half. It's the order of things."

Babies in formaldehyde, brains in a chemically balanced soup. Hold the escarole.

Erma pushed the croutons toward Aunt Mary, who was whispering to Lorraine, who was eating chocolates from the crystal bowl.

"We need to be more like *Australopithecus*," Leon continued, "and less like gazelles. The communists say American workers are a privileged class, *and they are not wrong*." He punctuated each word with a thrust of his index finger. "Collective bargaining may get you something in the short term. But in the long term, it's not good for anyone."

"You mean, it's not good for business," Primrose offered.

"Primrose, you should know by now that when pretty girls like yourself get mixed up in business, you wind up on the Piltdown, and that doesn't help anyone."

Primrose stared fixedly at the chandelier.

"Miltown," Tino muttered. "Not Piltdown. You're still dreaming of *Australopithecus*."

"Dreaming! Who's dreaming? All I'm *saying*," Leon concluded, "is that Piltdown or no, we should get back to our roots."

"Workers of the world, unite," Zio Zio said placidly. "You've nothing to lose but your—"

"Feathers," Tino said. It had just popped into his head.

"Beaks," Aldo piped up.

"*Boys*," Lorraine warned, driving a knife into the casserole of lasagna at her elbow. "Tino, you're being awfully fresh for someone in your position."

"In my position?"

Lorraine slapped an immense slice of lasagna on a dish and passed it to Primrose, who glanced dubiously at the plate.

"Thank you, Mrs. Battuta."

"Don't mention it, dear."

Zio Zio picked up where Leon had left off. "Tino, you need to understand your father will never change his mind about working people. He doesn't understand because he's only ever worked for himself."

As Zio Zio talked, Tino felt his father's eyes on him.

"He's never punched a clock, never had a boss," Zio Zio continued. "But he's right that the unions are a mess. We haven't mustered a majority membership vote in years."

"So what if the system's screwed up," Aldo said. After a semester of law school, he was bearish on "the system," as something all too easily worked. "We could all die any minute from an atom bomb."

Aunt June cut in: "Who else is ready for lasagna?"

Everyone passed their plates except Tino, who was considering an Alka-Seltzer instead.

Erma took an extravagant swig from her wineglass. "What's the story with Poppa Tavio and *baccauso*?" she asked. "The word's not in any dictionary. I checked."

"Didn't he steal that joke from Jerre Mangione?" Pat asked.

"I don't get it," Aldo said. "What joke?"

"Baccauso," Pat said. Aldo looked at him blankly. "Backa-house, dummy. Back of the house. Where they used to keep the shithouse."

Lorraine tsked.

"'Scuse my French, Auntie."

"So what does it mean?" Erma pressed.

"It *means* Original Shithole. That's the joke."

"I'm telling you," Pat insisted. "It's Jerre Mangione's."

Primrose nibbled her lasagna, and in that moment she seemed like a miracle, the delicate antidote to his crude family. If only she would keep her mouth shut like she used to. Under the table, he squeezed her thigh.

"Ow." She pushed his hand away.

"Doesn't matter," Aldo said. "We got to stick together. My house is yours, and all that. Mi casa su."

"For heaven's sake, talk American," Lorraine said. "Only fascists speak Italian in America."

"Isn't that Spanish," Primrose murmured. "Mi casa su."

"Spanish!" Lorraine scoffed. "Don't get me started."

Primrose's shoulders rose halfway to her ears.

"Besides," Aldo said, as if the women hadn't spoken, "now the FBI is busy with all those goofball war resisters, they won't have time to come after us."

"Us?" Leon looked skeptically at Aldo. "Us fascists? Who's 'us'?"

"All I'm saying is, they've got a lot of draft dodgers to chase down."

Pat raised an eyebrow at Tino.

"*What?*"

"I don't know what you're going to do about the draft, that's all."

"What's Tino got to worry about?" Zio Zio asked. "He's fine until they take student deferments away."

"There's nothing to worry about," Tino said quickly. "Pat's just working his jaw."

"Oh," Lorraine said airily, "I wouldn't say it's nothing."

Everyone looked at Tino. Hadn't he always pulled off miracles, from catching unlikely infield flies to getting into medical school? Even Primrose was looking at him expectantly, as if he might still come up with some clever last-minute save.

"How about I just spit it out for you, Tino?" Pat said. "Let's put an end to the charade."

Staring at Pat, Tino shook his head. *Don't.*

"Face it," Pat barreled on. "You're not going back to medical school!"

Forks clattered on plates. Primrose smoothed her already smooth napkin.

"That's right," Lorraine said. "He's not."

Leon, magisterially: "I was just about to say the same. Tino has made his decision, and now he's home again."

So they had talked it over, Tino realized. The die was cast. His only job now was to agree with whatever spin Leon put on the news.

"It's true," Tino said.

Everyone started talking at once.

"What are we going to do?"

"What's *he* going to do?"

"It's *our* problem. He's one of *us*." Erma turned to Tino's mother. "Isn't that right?"

"Oh, Erma," she sighed. "Of course he is."

Uncle Beppe asked Tino, "Why?"

Why? Tino had his reasons. He didn't drink Wild Turkey or wear penny loafers. His voice, when he spoke, which was not often, had sounded harsh and wrong against the other students' bland accents. On campus he didn't even have a name. He was just "the Italian fella," pronounced with the "i" drawn out so it rhymed with *why, try. Lie.*

Oh, he had a thousand reasons. But the school had only needed one.

Leon pushed himself from his chair and wandered to the window. His lasagna lay untouched on his plate.

"He could go to Canada."

"What about getting married? Having a baby? What say, Primrose?" Aldo winked at her. At least someone was having a good time. Primrose frowned.

"It would be for the war effort," Erma assured her.

"It most certainly would not," Primrose retorted.

"Marriage deferments ended last year, Aldo."

"You could go to ed school, Tino," Erma mused. "They still make deferments for teachers."

Leon, still by the window, kept his back to them.

"It's almost July." Pat squeaked his finger along the rim of his water glass. "Too late."

"Maybe some girl will drop out," Aldo said. "They only make babies and Sunday gravy. You don't need an advanced degree for that."

"Don't be a drip." Erma prodded him with her elbow. "Uneducated women are more likely to kill their husbands. It's a proven fact."

"Is that so," Tino's mother said dryly. She'd only graduated from high school.

"Present company excluded, of course," Erma added.

"Tino has asthma," Aunt June said. "That might make him 4-F."

Tino's mother offered Primrose a chocolate. "Just one won't make you fat, will it?" Primrose shrank from her.

"Oh, for Pete's sake," Tino said.

"Tino, even if you're drafted," Aldo began, "you still might not get sent. Look at Pat, he's in West Germany. You might get something stateside."

"Pat got lucky," Tino said. "He's in the Reserves."

"Luck, *nothing*," Leon grouched from his post by the window. "Pat thought *ahead*. He got on the *list*."

"Look, Dad—" Tino began, succumbing to the old impulse to explain, to make excuses.

Leon spun around. "No, *you* look, Tino. Didn't you *see* those guys at the wake? The three *fellas* standing there all night with their backs against the wall? I pointed you out to them, you know. I said, 'There he is, my son, the doctor!'"

"Dad—"

"And now, what can I say? My son, the draft dodger? Who doesn't believe in competition. Who just isn't up for it. My *son*—"

So that's how Leon had squared the news with himself. In the grand evolutionary scheme of things, worthy sons were lions, apex predators, the fittest competitors—and Tino was nothing but a gazelle.

"Dad!"

"YOU'RE INSUBORDINATE!" Leon exploded, banging his fist on the window frame. The window rattled in the casement.

"Now don't you break my window—" sniffed Lorraine.

"Leon," Zio Zio said. "*Staccalma*. You'll give yourself a heart attack."

"I WON'T HAVE IT IN MY HOUSE!"

His father, Tino reflected, was putting on quite a show. Aunt June's *tsk* was just audible over the scrape of her chair as she rose to clear the table.

"Siddown!" Leon roared.

"You can't talk like that to me, Leon," she said as she sat. "I'm not your wife."

Lorraine clicked her tongue but otherwise held it.

"Now *you* listen *up*," Leon said, wagging a finger at Tino. "Poppa Tavio came all the way over here from that *baccauso* or whatever you want to call it, to make a better life. He succeeded where many other guys like him did not. That's right. *They did not.* They washed up, and they went back to the same stinking towns they crawled out of. Now, your generation is something else. You've had everything handed to you but the keys to the universe. You're the biggest, smartest, healthiest generation of Americans ever to come down the pike, and all you do is sit around smoking dope and spouting your malarkey." He turned to Primrose, addressing her directly. "Pardon me, Primrose. I don't usually talk this way—"

Which was bullshit. When he was mad, Leon talked exactly this way.

"Think of everything we worked for, Tino. Me and your mother, and your Poppa Tavio. Tino? Do you hear me?"

Tino scraped crumbs into a pile.

"Yeah, I thought so. Now get out of here," Leon growled. "Every last one of you beatnik good-for-nothings, get the hell out." He threw his napkin on the table and motioned for Tino's mother to clear his plate.

No one wanted dessert. Primrose trapped the untouched sfogliatelles beneath a sheet of cling film. Tino took the platter from her and slid it into the icebox beside the tray of leftover lasagna. The dishwasher hummed; hot water sang in the pipes. While Primrose scoured the sink, Tino carried a thimble-sized glass of sherry to his mother in the living room. She was stretched out on the sofa with a wet washcloth draped over her eyes. He left the sherry on the side table and slipped out without a word.

After everything was washed, dried, and stowed, Lorraine surveyed their cleanup effort. "Looks about right," she said, which was about as close she ever came to praising work done by others in her kitchen, and set her sherry glass, empty now, in the shining sink. Primrose, miffed, shut herself in the powder room.

"That was some show Dad put on," Tino said, *sotto voce.*

"Shush," Lorraine whispered. "He covered for you, and now you can do your part by letting it rest. Least said, soonest mended."

"I'm not so sure about that." His future stretched before him, years of family meals during which he kept his mouth shut and his shortcomings out of view. The rift—between the real Tino and the idealized version he was now responsible for producing—could never be mended. Not now, not without losing the illusion, and his father had clearly conveyed his position on that score. The illusion must be maintained.

And still, he might die—he might die, he might die. *Sons!*

Lorraine pointed to a can of tomatoes that had been forgotten on the counter. "Will you take this back down cellar, Tino? I don't know how Erma missed it."

"Good help," Tino said snidely as he lifted the can, "is so hard to find."

"Now don't you be fresh. Haven't you caused enough trouble for one day?"

In the basement, Tino replaced the can on the shelf beside the others and adjusted them one by one until the girls on the labels were lined up in a neat sequence of ovals, cradling baskets of tomatoes in their rounded arms. As he pulled the chain to kill the light, something *moved.* As if that Contadina girl—

Had she, in fact, *winked*?

No, that was impossible.

He pulled the chain again, flooding the shelves with light. Nothing seemed amiss. There she was, the Contadina girl with her big smile, her plump bosom heaving over her basket of equally plump tomatoes. Of course she hadn't winked. Only Primrose would see a thing like that.

But if he were certifiable, he'd also be 4-F.

What a thought: Rational, scientific Tino gets out with the crazy pass.

One by one, Tino turned each can to face the wall.

6. Foo fighters

Lupo Light was locked out. Rattling the handle on the French door, he squelched the urge to shatter a pane. His father lay horizontal before the TV, in a posture of oblivion. What a show he was putting on. During the war, his father had been an artilleryman. Though most guys in his outfit went deaf, his own bad hearing was selective. Lupo rolled his eyes to heaven, or at least the piece of it he could see unaided from this godforsaken suburban backwater, and tried to contain his irritation. His father was no help at all at moments like this one, preferring to keep Lupo on the wrong side of any door for which Lupo had been careless enough to forget the key. Would he never learn? Oh, well. Better to count your blessings, to thank your lucky stars—Lupo favored the three in Orion's belt—for his dissertation advisor, Peregrine "Perry" McKee, a professor in the department of astronomy, who had nabbed him a deferment.

"He's vital stateside, you see," McKee wrote in a letter to the draft board. That was last fall, after Lupo's deferment had been slow coming through. What happened next surprised Lupo. As it turned out, the draft board was hardly the imposing array of uniformed soldiers he had imagined but just a single exhausted-looking man, with eyes made weirdly large by his glasses, sitting behind an immense wooden desk crammed into a small, badly lit room. While Lupo stood before him, twitching in time with the fluorescents, McKee plopped a stack of astronomy journals on the table and topped the ensemble with a copy of a recent issue of *The Good Five Cent Cigar*, the University of Rhode Island's student newspaper, folded to show the headlines about the local UFO sightings.

"We're linking patterns in local cosmic ray activity to recent extraterrestrial sightings, of which there have been more than a few lately," McKee said conspiratorially, "especially in Woonsocket."

The man behind the desk raised an eyebrow.

"That's right, Woonsocket. Housewives who've already lost their husbands to Johnson's jungle adventure are ready to revolt! Let me tell you, sir, the home front will be in a very bad way, should these ladies start devoting Tupperware parties to agitation on behalf of aliens' rights."

McKee was speaking nonsense, of course, but he had the bullshitter's knack, and his starched button-down and impeccable navy jacket, gold buttons shining at the cuffs, did much to boost his case. White-haired, close-shaven, cheerfully authoritative, he was everything anyone could want in a dissertation advisor. If Lupo had doubts about the UFO research, he had no reservations at all about McKee. The guy was a godsend. It helped that he lived next door. Though Lupo admitted publicly only to feeling a glad relief when the deferment came through, he privately styled himself lucky. Lucky Light.

But McKee would be of no use now. The door was still locked, and Lupo's father was still unresponsive. What a shithead he was, forgetting his key. Fail to plan, plan to fail.

He disliked his father's voice in his head, yet there it was, louder every day.

From behind the fence came a series of high-pitched whistles. That would be McKee's new pet, a dolphin named Ted, doing laps in his specially built saltwater pool. McKee had plans for Ted—"*scientific* plans," he said—but he'd not yet shared specifics. He did point out the bump on Ted's forehead: "More cortex in there than we've got, Lupo. Pound for pound, anyway. More folds, too. The best thing is," his voice dropped to a whisper, "it's a *radio transmitter*."

McKee saw a connection between cetacean neural activity and a recent spate of UFO sightings by area wives whose husbands had been called up for the war. He hypothesized that, like dogs or dolphins, these women were picking up signals no one else could hear, and he thought Ted was the perfect instrument to test this hypothesis.

Lupo wasn't so sure, but he knew better than to run his mouth. There were just some things a guy had to go along with if he wanted to stay on track and out of trouble. All this talk of dolphins and UFOs made Lupo more reluctant than ever to think about the world outside research. At times it seemed like a horrifying machine of variably speedy escalators to which aspiring adults were assigned, as if life were nothing more or less than a game of deadly chutes and unpromising ladders. Even lovely Primrose Tirocchi seemed already marked out, destined for something terrible. Facility with a paintbrush was no match for whatever inward calamity had landed her in the loony bin.

Lupo jiggled a twig in the keyhole. He had no idea how to jimmy a lock.

He did know, however, exactly where his keys were: on the sideboard in the dining room. That morning, on his way to see Primrose, his mother had shouted from her bath, "Will you be back in time to clean my gutters, Lupo?"

The task had been languishing since November. Though she'd grown up around here, she maintained that two decades of bridge-and-tunnel living in New York City had made her an unregenerate city girl. What would she know about cleaning gutters?

"My gutters, Lupo! Are you going to clean them or not?"

"If you don't mind me cleaning them at midnight," he called back.

"If you won't do the gutters, I have other things for you to do."

His mother's ominous conditional made him too tense to walk away, but if he went to her—he knew, he just *knew*—he'd be caught for hours in her whacked-out gravitational field. The gutters were merely the leading edge of it. So he had stood there, caught between two equally noxious outcomes, sorting the junk in his pockets while his mother complained about Maple Bay— the inferiority of vegetables at Ruggieri's, her astonishment that they did not carry wheatgrass juice, and then, to top it all, how she'd gone there on Saturday morning, only to find the doors locked tight.

"It's just not New York," she sighed.

"Sweetheart." Mr. Light poked his head out from the bedroom. "New York's not even New York."

"Now that's the understatement of the year!"

"You know what I mean," he said. "Don't pretend that you don't. Sweetheart."

"Dad," Lupo observed, "you can hear."

His father scowled. "What's that you say?"

Because arguing was useless and the bus would arrive in minutes, Lupo had taken off—naturally, without his keys.

Now, reflected in the dark glass, Lupo saw his own face—pale, drawn, and in need of a shave—superimposed on the living room's relentlessly tasteful, tone-on-tone tableau. His mother's fine things were all finely arranged: vellum-colored sofas and parchment lampshades set against creamy off-white walls, the coffee table shining glass and brass. Even his father seemed a set piece, at ease in immaculate white cotton pajamas. Only Lupo didn't fit. His glasses were thick and ugly, he needed a haircut, and on his chin a pimple was erupting. He resisted the urge to pick it. It was so hard to believe that any problem, even a zit, might simply resolve on its own.

If only he hadn't stopped to engage his mother in her idea of a conversation, he'd be in the house right now, in the kitchen fixing a glass of chocolate milk and a sandwich.

Lupo banged the glass again, harder this time. *I could smash this window and open a vein,* he was surprised to hear himself think. *I could get out of this by dying.*

Lighting bugs glimmered in the boxwoods. Lupo sank down on the step. He might be out here all night. Orion wheeled above him, and he saw himself as if from a great distance. So much for Lucky Light. Having fuck all else to do, he settled in to dream a little.

In his mind's eye, Lupo conjured Primrose as he saw her the first time, at a Students for a Democratic Society meeting. He'd been obliged to attend because, thanks to McKee's intervention and a fresh rash of sightings that Lupo believed to be entirely fraudulent, aliens had made it onto the agenda.

Under orders to report back to McKee, Lupo hadn't exactly relished the assignment. Like UFOs, courtship of student political groups had exactly nothing to do with his dissertation research. But then, there she was: Primrose Tirocchi, famous all over town for her shy smile and those legs that went on for quite a while in real life but forever and ever in your dreams. She was perched on the window bench, the famous legs tucked beneath a blush-colored dirndl skirt. Next to her sat Rosemary Garrity, known for her pot-and-jazz parties and the way she kept her face hidden behind a cataract of straight dark hair.

An argument was underway: Should the group's charter extend membership to all sentient beings including those that, in theory, might someday arrive from outer space?

The argument had derailed the group, and the leader, or at least the person who talked the most about the agenda, an intense-looking guy in a shearling coat that was fashionable but too warm for the weather, was putting on an increasingly loud and desperate show of throat-clearing and pained exhalations. Lupo could relate: The argument was clearly stale, yet no one seemed able to drop it. During a lull, Rosemary piped up to say that the charter was "in general and prima facie bullshit," but the explanation she gave—something about the women being something less than full and equal members anyway—was immediately drowned out by a sudden wave of loud argument on a different topic entirely: Sputnik rocketry, the various technical specifications thereof. Shearling flushed scarlet and banged his clipboard on the desk. *Order. Order.*

What happened next was unclear; Lupo did not keep good notes. But this much was agreed: For the purposes of investigation, a subcommittee should be formed—the Rhode Island Collegiate Unidentified Foreign Objects Group, or RICUFOG. A sign-up sheet went around, and a plan was made to recruit students from other schools in the area, with a special emphasis on the University of Rhode Island, which had more resources to devote to matters astronomical. "It's the place for the space race," quipped Shearling.

"Far out," Lupo blurted. He couldn't help himself. These kids were just too much.

"Very far," Rosemary agreed. "Like fucking Chepachet."

Her reply made Lupo smile—it was so Rhode Island to mention a town just fifteen or twenty miles distant as if it were the far side of the moon—but the remark's delicate levity was obliterated by Shearling, who had chosen that same moment to adjourn the meeting. The motion passed with a roar of unanimity, and Shearling made a dramatic exit, flanked by four buddies in bombers and dungarees who exchanged a complex sequence of glances and eye rolls.

Lupo was not reassured by any of this theater. The previous semester, an SDS chapter at a liberal arts college across the Massachusetts border had actually *folded* over the same chestnut—the matter of alien status—and the chapter's collapse sparked rumors of sabotage by outside agents. Perhaps not coincidentally, someone had also emptied the petty cash.

Lupo cleared his throat. It wasn't quite too late; he might still catch the attention of those who had not yet quit the room. "Wait. Wait," he puffed. "Before we break, may I remind everyone of the events at—"

Too little, too late. It was a glorious spring day, and no one wanted to be inside listening to Lupo talk about an episode of malfeasance that was basically ancient history and had unfolded across the state line to boot. This crowd couldn't even imagine going to Chepachet. Why would they care about anything that happened in Massachusetts?

Giving up, Lupo had joined the crush heading for the door. That was when Rosemary sidled up and parted the dark waters in front of her face just long enough to ask for his number. More stunned than charmed, Lupo recited it curtly, and the curtain, miffed, descended once more. Never mind. Primrose Tirocchi's famous legs, pistoning beneath the rosy-colored dirndl skirt, were already on the move. Lupo followed, drawn on by the sort of irresistible impulse that usually presaged a stupidity.

He caught up with Primrose outside the student union.

"Coffee?" he blurted to her back. An uninspiring opener, but did not every journey begin with a first misstep?

She turned to him smiling, and the world tilted on its axis. "Sure."

In the fuggy college cafeteria, he ferried coffees to the table she had chosen by the window. Everything was so strange—the coffee, the cafeteria, Primrose sitting there with him. He got the feeling that neither he nor anything in his entire life was real but only something dreamed up, sweetly, by Primrose. Aliens included. Dolphins, too. What the hell, maybe even McKee.

That was when she dropped her bomb—the first one, anyway. Privately he called it *Little Boy*.

"I had some trouble last year. With my head."

"Your head?"

She explained that she'd lost her mind one night when someone dropped a tab of acid in her Dr Pepper.

Surely she was joking. Wasn't losing your mind was just metaphorical? Yet she spoke as if it were as easy to misplace as a wallet. "That mickey they slipped me *had* to be acid," she concluded, roiling the steaming surface of her coffee with three quick huffs, "and it had to be Russian, or maybe Czech."

Russian? Czech? "How did you know?"

She frowned. "Well, I was drinking Dr Pepper and looking at the sky, and the next thing I saw was the moon—"

"The moon."

"Don't laugh. The moon! Which was winding down, whatever you call it—"

"Waning," said he, the astronomer.

"Right. Waning. Well, suddenly it had a hammer and sickle next to it."

"Wow." Astronomy had nothing on the magic carpet ride that was getting to know Primrose. The girl was well and truly nuts.

She caught his gaze. Held it. Had she sensed his judgment? Her eyes were a striking blue. She explained how she'd wound up at Dexter Girls Infirmary, so hazy she felt she'd been trapped in a nightmare belonging either to her mother or her psychiatrist, not that she could reliably tell them apart at that point. That was when she dropped *Fat Man*: She was dating Tino

Battuta. In a flash, he understood why she seemed familiar. The Battutas lived in his neighborhood. She was the girl he saw in the passenger seat of Tino's Chevelle.

Lupo sipped his coffee and winced. The swill was basically volcanic. Meanwhile, Primrose chattered on. The boyfriend situation sounded serious—as if anything serious could be attributed to that Battuta clown. But a boyfriend was not the Berlin Wall. *Mamma mia.* Time to stop worrying and learn to love this bombshell.

"What do you do for fun?" he asked, wanting to get her off the boyfriend topic.

"I paint," she said.

"Houses?" He smiled.

"What?" She hadn't caught his drift. Maybe electroshock did that, made you slow on the uptake. "If you're not cool with that—well, my parents aren't so cool with it either."

"Oh, no," he assured her. "I was just joking. You've got to do your own thing."

There was an exhibit she wanted to see at a museum downtown. For once he managed to improve upon an opportunity, using this news to ask if she would like to go with him. To his surprise, she said yes. And even now, some weeks later, she had not yet rescinded the offer. Which was reason enough to keep hoping, despite how hopeless everything seemed. Spending the night on this doorstep looked increasingly likely. He zipped his jacket, turned up the collar. Somewhere out there, in another Rhode Island suburb, some housewife was no doubt seeing strange lights in the sky, visions that he would be obliged to track down as an official participant in McKee's mad scheme.

His father's silhouette darkened the French door. He shouted: "Do you live here?"

"I forgot my key."

"What's that you say?"

Lupo yelled: "I forgot my key!"

The doorframe rattled, and the door popped open.

"My son, who can name every star in the sky, still can't remember to take his keys when he leaves the house." He paused, his expression sly. "You don't have to shout, you know."

"Dad—"

"Where were you all day while your mother razzed me about the gutters? Talking to married ladies about foo fighters?" He chucked Lupo under the chin in a way that made him feel about twelve years old.

"I wish you wouldn't do that."

"You mean this?" Another chuck, less friendly.

"I'm turning in," Lupo said.

His father gave him a disgusted look—*some son I got* was the clear and unambiguous message—before returning to the couch. A muffled laugh track followed Lupo down the hall, but it might as well have been his father, snickering at his own misfortune, that his only son was truly more his daffy wife's child than his own. But hadn't that contempt been present from the first moments of Lupo's life, when his mother, still recovering from his birth, had recast Wolf—a family name from his father's side— into her own family's language, staking a claim that no one on his father's side, including his father, ever considered legitimate? And so Lupo was lost from the start.

In the bedroom, his mother was snoring gently over a copy of *Vogue*. As he removed it, a pamphlet fell from between the pages: *Marriage and Its Alternatives*. Although his father disapproved of *Vogue*, which he called "unregenerate frippery," Lupo doubted he would be more enthused by his wife's extramarital research. Which might explain why she was reading it on the sly. Moving back to Rhode Island had been her idea; after years away, the city girl decided that she wanted to be closer to her family. But his father was the one who, by shooting off his mouth once too often, had torpedoed his own tenure bid. Maybe she hadn't come home so much as she'd beaten a retreat from a life that had, in the end, proved too much for her—as it had, perhaps, for them all. His grandparents on his father's side, who had disapproved of the marriage from the get-go, had rebuffed all his mother's efforts to please them. Now she'd come home, only to find her own parents no more welcoming of her husband than her in-laws had been of her. But Lupo had no idea, really. For all her yapping on matters domestic, she tended to keep her own counsel on the big stuff.

Lupo replaced the pamphlet in its niche between the pages of the magazine, set the assemblage on the nightstand, and tugged the covers up around her shoulders.

"Lupo?" she murmured. "Is that you?"

"Go back to sleep, Mom." He turned to leave.

"Wait." She struggled up, blinking, one hand already scrabbling on the nightstand for her glasses. "A girl called for you earlier. Rosemary somebody."

"Rosemary Garrity?"

"That's the one." Sleepily she sank down beneath the covers. "She invited you to a party. She sounds like a nice girl."

"Not my type. Night, Mom."

7. Sore subjects

As streetlights flickered up and down Calvary Street, Primrose tugged her curtains open and peered out. In the house across the way, Norah Simpson sat at one end of a table, her arms folded across her chest, as her mother pressed a plate of something on her, probably *pastéis*. It was always *pastéis*. At the table's other end, Norah's father sat reading the newspaper.

Just the end of another day on Calvary Street, another boring domestic scene. But was there any other kind? Primrose dialed Norah's number and listened to the phone ringing both in her ear and its wall socket across the way. Through the window, Primrose watched Norah rise and leave the kitchen with the phone pressed to her ear, stretching the cord taut.

"Two dollars says you're not doing much," Primrose said when Norah came on the line.

"Are you kidding?" she whispered. "I'm very busy. It's a full-time job around here, not turning into a *pastel*."

"Mothers," Primrose commiserated.

"Meanwhile, I'm told we have a world to win."

"So they say. Let's start by going to the movies. We could see *Five Ashore in Singapore*."

"The French one? With the mad scientist angle?"

"Exactly. We could get Dr Peppers. I'll even buy."

"You know I'd love to, and you don't even have to buy me a Dr Pepper. But my shift doesn't end until nine-thirty, and that's too late for anyone to come ashore in Singapore."

For the past year, while Primrose had been taking classes and then doing time in the psych ward, Norah had staffed the checkout counter at the city library. The hours were a drag—

nights and weekends—but the work was strictly temporary, to raise money for the bills that would start coming due when she finally matriculated at college the following September. The job also allowed her to rummage for material that would help with their side project, an exploration of relations with the opposite sex. The idea behind *The Book of Love* was simple: *to tell the primitive and vulnerable truth about sex,* as Norah had written in their prospectus, *and demolish all pink-and-white lace-edged illusions.* How this could be done, with Norah still a virgin, was anyone's guess, but Primrose, who was struggling with the same issue from the opposite, non-virginal side, was assisting as much as she could, clipping columns of relationship advice from copies of *Redbook* that her mother brought home from work and sharing participant-observer reports from her dates with Tino.

"Any news about the Ovid?" Primrose asked. Norah, who had breezed through four years of high school Latin, had wanted to start with the classics. Primrose liked the idea, but she was a little afraid of it, too. Nothing about Latin had ever made any sense to her. Poetry, though, was a different story, and with his big emphasis on transformation, *metamorphosis,* Ovid was certainly a poet for their time.

"I'll be right over," Norah replied. "It's definitely time to sack Rome."

"I hope you'll use that for a chapter title."

Norah laughed. "I have every intention!"

Primrose stepped away from the window, crushing an old *New Yorker* that had slipped from a pile her nightstand. She had been keeping the issue for Tino. It contained an article he might enjoy, about a man whose weird orange complexion came from a rare condition called carotenemia, which meant he couldn't eat carrots. But now that Tino was no longer a medical student, she wasn't so sure he'd be interested in weird medical conditions, and it would hurt to be reminded of how *that* plan came to grief. Yet she couldn't bring herself to throw the magazine away. Tino's parents were also having trouble accepting his new situation. Maybe the only thing anyone loved about him was his ambition.

Well, she would be different. If anything, the disaster in St. Louis just made him more lovable, easier to relate to.

Attempting to slide the magazine back into its original position on the nightstand, Primrose tumbled the whole messy pile to the floor. Although *Tess of the d'Urbervilles* narrowly missed her typewriter, the Royal took a direct hit, squarely on the keys, from a volume of poetry titled *Equivocations* that Primrose had received as a gift from a teacher who'd seen something in her, heaven knew what, and wanted to bring her along. Miss Quinton was sweet, but what she proposed was impossible. Between *here* and *there,* a chasm yawned. More than that: It breathed. It inhaled all the moments of your life and exhaled messes in urgent need of cleaning up. Scooping the fallen volumes from the floor, Primrose wondered: Would she ever be able to put brush to canvas without feeling the nagging pull of disorderly nightstands, dusty furniture, crumb-laden floors? How would she and Norah ever manage write a book of their own, never mind a *Book of Love*? Well, if there was a solution to this dilemma, it sure as hell wasn't in her nightstand. She hurried to let Norah in.

In the kitchen, the table was cluttered with bunion pads, nail polish, hot rollers, and soft packs of Luckys. Primrose's mother, Louise, was in her usual pre-work funk, sighing at intervals while applying a layer of Paramour Pink to her nails. Her puffy white nursing shoes were at her feet, arch supports already inserted. Her shift would start in an hour. "Getting ready for work," she grouched, "is about as bad as being there."

The nurses of Howard Memorial liked to make themselves memorable. You never knew when you might meet an eligible doctor—or at least that was the excuse the younger ones used. Being married, Louise was not into doctor-chasing. She just liked to primp. The fruity funk of her perfume sliced through the kitchen's standard odors: grease, cigarettes, singed hair, nail polish. She'd grown tired of Jean Naté, which everyone wore; Love's Baby Soft, which smelled of talcum powder and was a great favorite among the candy stripers, sent the wrong signal.

Louise was no baby. She was not soft. These days her favorite scent was called My Sin.

At the Dexter Girls Infirmary, the nurses didn't wear makeup, and they all smelled of exactly nothing, which made it easier to ignore the loaded needles hidden in their pockets—though there was no missing the razors in their calm eyes.

"Shed a little light on the subject, would you, Primrose?" Louise said, scrutinizing her right thumbnail through the smoke. The sun had traveled, leaving the kitchen in shadow. "I smudged this one."

The overhead light flickered on, and a spark from the switch-plate zapped Primrose, who sneezed. She rubbed her knuckles, where the zap lingered, and sneezed again.

"Stop that," Louise snapped.

"It's probably an allergy, Ma."

"More likely it's all the dust in this shitbox, which hasn't been cleaned in a dog's age."

Primrose frowned. Dusting was her job.

"Not everyone has a cleaning lady like your fancy boyfriend. Besides, children only get allergies," Louise opined, "when their mothers don't love them."

Her mother was alluding to something the psychiatrist, Dr. Addleman, had said: Nervous breakdowns were caused by mothers who didn't love their children. This remark had shocked Louise, who believed that a nervous breakdown was just what happened to girls like Primrose, who slept with their boyfriends because they did not love their *mothers*. Filial impiety caused premarital sex, which was a pathogen, and that was that. The psychiatrist, who seemed unsurprised by Louise's theory, had only looked sadly at Primrose and said something about recent advances in genetics.

Louise ground out her cigarette.

"Everyone knows only neglected children develop things like allergies."

Tino had allergies. This, too, was a dig.

"I suppose they sneeze to spite their mothers?"

"Don't be fresh." With fingers splayed, Louise capped the nail polish, shook another cigarette from the pack, and peered into it, counting how many were left. The doorbell rang. Primrose left to answer it and returned with Norah who, like Louise, was also dressed for work: cardigan, knee-length skirt, sensible shoes.

"How's it going, Mrs. Tirocchi?" Norah pulled up a chair.

"Nice to see you, Norah," she said, though her tone suggested otherwise. Louise didn't like to have people over while she was getting ready for her shift. "Though I have to say, I don't love your librarian's get-up. You'll never find a husband in those not-so-glad rags."

Primrose burned, ashamed of her mother and angry on Norah's behalf, but Norah just smiled. "I suppose not, Mrs. Tirocchi," she said mildly. "But I'll get paid."

"Primrose told me your boss was an old prune."

"That's not what I said, Ma!" Why did her mother always have to turn everything into a vulgarity? "Norah's boss is always trying to make her go to the pharmacy or the grocery store. But running personal errands is not part of the job description."

"Is she an old maid?" Louise asked. "She sounds like an old maid."

"She doesn't have a husband or any family that I know of," Norah said.

"What did I tell you, Primrose? She's a real dry vagina."

"Ma!"

Using just her fingertips, Louise peeled a bunion pad off the plastic sheet.

"Maybe she didn't want to get married. They call it a nuclear family for a reason, you know," Norah said slyly. "Sooner or later somebody goes critical and has a meltdown."

Primrose hooted. "That's a good one!"

"Hmph," Louise said, applying the pad to her little toe. "I doubt it."

Primrose peeked at the clock. Every afternoon, as soon as her mother left, the kitchen grew cool and quiet. Even the curtains hung easier on their rods. On nice days, Primrose liked to open the windows and let the curtains blow out, to hell with the neighbors and anyone driving by.

"You young people," Louise lectured as she taped another bunion, "with your little in-jokes and your boy-crazies, you don't know how lucky you are. Tonight there will be no jokes at all, and while you're brushing your hair and talking on the telephone instead of making yourselves useful around this filthy house, I'll be bringing bedpans to the real nutters."

"Don't exaggerate, Ma." Not once at the hospital had she *ever* needed a bedpan. Or even a tissue. She hadn't cried, not a single tear, not even after five electroshocks followed by cold packings, and a misfired injection of something slimy that pooled into a painful lump beneath the skin on her arm. The inflammation lingered, along with a migraine that laid her flat for a week. Other than these mementos, she had no recollection of the treatments. They wiped memory right out, like chalk off a blackboard. One swipe and it was gone.

"You'd think if you couldn't wipe your own ass," Louise continued, "you wouldn't be getting up to shenanigans on a locked ward, but that's the way they are."

"After *they* go to sleep," Primrose told her mother, "you'll put your feet up and watch Lawrence Welk."

"I'd rather be in my own chair, watching him on my own TV, thank you very much." She turned her hands. Her fingernails flashed. "Isn't that nice?"

Primrose crooned, "It's luffly."

Norah grinned, and Primrose briefly felt okay about herself, her life, even her mother.

"I put the matching lipstick on layaway at Palma's. I'll get it on Friday, soon as I cash my check, so long as there's no strike."

Louise's job was union; for weeks, there had been talk of a walkout. Pamphlets explaining collective bargaining were stacked on a little table by the front door.

"Primrose, get off your fancy ass for once, and help me with my hair."

"Don't cuss," Primrose told her. "You're making Norah nervous."

"Don't mind me!" Norah shifted in her chair. To Primrose she looked beyond uncomfortable. In fact she looked ready to fall through the floor.

Dr. Addleman had advised Primrose to keep her mouth shut during these hard-to-gauge moments. *If you want friends*, he told her, *you're going to have to watch yourself.* She tended to overreact, he said, and she had trouble distinguishing transient awkwardnesses from other, more concerning interpersonal slips. It was important to hide her flaws, to respond appropriately to people, to avoid ostracism. It was important to be good, always.

Louise prised open a clear plastic clamshell case, exposing rows of white plastic curlers fitted on metal rods. As each rod heated up, a dot on the end of the curler turned from blue to red. Standing behind her mother, Primrose carefully rolled Louise's hair onto red-dotted curlers and secured them with U-shaped pins.

"Don't get burnt," Louise warned her. The curlers were hot on their metal insides.

"Yes, Ma." Smoke from her mother's cigarette billowed in her face, and she fought back another sneeze. A scrap of paper fluttered down from where it had been taped to the fridge.

"What's that?" Norah asked.

Primrose knew what it was: a list of chores that she was responsible for—wash the curtains, wax the floor, clean the bathroom. Dusting, of course. It had been stuck to the fridge since April.

"I wish you'd at least wash the curtains, Primrose," Louise complained. "Anyone driving by would think we weren't good people."

Anyone driving by, Primrose silently translated, re-pinning a hank of hair that had come loose, *would think Louise Tirocchi's daughter was a lazy* puttana *who can't be bothered to keep the curtains clean.* That's what her mother had meant, even if she hadn't said it.

There were advantages to being crazy, like knowing what people really meant by what they said. Though Dr. Addleman would tell her to keep her mouth shut on that score.

"Prim?" Norah said.

"What?" Primrose selected another roller, narrow as her pinky finger.

"You seem preoccupied."

"She's always like that," said Louise.

Primrose sneezed, jamming a pin into Louise's scalp.

"Easy!"

"Sorry."

When her hair was all rolled up, Louise padded to the bathroom. Every day before work, she locked the door against all comers and sat there smoking, flipping through old copies of *Redbook*, squirting herself with My Sin, and pouring bleach down the toilet, which she liked to do, she said, "for the sake of the septic system." Anyone who intruded upon Louise's time on the throne could expect an earful. If you had to pee during her bathroom hour, you were welcome to do your business in the yard.

Primrose and Norah were finally alone in the kitchen. Setting fresh rollers on the rods so the kit would be ready for the next night, Primrose racked her brain, searching for something to lighten the moment, to undo her mother's cussing and her mortifying comments about vaginas.

While Primrose squirmed, lost in these embarrassing thoughts, Norah retrieved Louise's list of household duties. "Let's see," she murmured. "Curtains, slipcovers... Have you waxed the kitchen floor yet?"

"I'll get to it. Right after I wax my mother."

"I heard that," Louise called from the bathroom.

They snickered, and there was a great rushing noise as Louise made a final attempt to clear out the septic tank.

"That's not how you do it," Norah said. "The flushing, I mean. It does nothing."

"Worse than nothing," Primrose said. "But who's going to tell her she's only wasting water?"

From her pocket Norah extracted a square of folded paper. "Never mind. Look at this."

Primrose unfolded the little packet. It was a handwritten copy of some pages from the *Kama Sutra*. She shook a finger at Norah. "Naughty!"

Norah grinned as Primrose re-folded the paper and stuck the wad down her bra.

"You are always so needlessly concerned with vulgarity," Norah said with exaggerated formality.

Primrose grinned, relieved to know that her mother's awfulness would not be held against her.

"Did you ever find Ovid's *Amores*?"

Keeping her voice down, now that Louise had ceased her noisy flushing, Norah said, "I saw the expurgated edition on the shelf."

"The expurgated edition of WHAT?" Louise shouted.

"*The Lives of the Saints*, Ma!"

Which weren't always so saintly, though Louise would be the last person with whom she'd share her thoughts on the ecstasy of St. Theresa, pictured on a prayer card tacked to the wall. "Transverberation," which is how the nuns had talked around it during catechism class, explaining that the word meant "pierced by an angel's grace." But if sexy Theresa had been pierced by an angel's anything, Primrose was pretty sure it wasn't his "grace" but some other, less abstract part of his anatomy.

"I have to go, Primrose. I'm late." Again Norah lowered her voice: "I'll look again for the Ovid, but forget the *Amores*. That's kiddy stuff. We want the *Ars Amatoria*—"

"The what?"

But Norah was already at the door.

"And we should think about how we'll go on if I can't find it."

***

Norah left, and Primrose escaped to her room. From her bra she fished out Norah's packet and hid it among the stuff piled on her nightstand. She still had art homework to finish. She changed into cutoffs and an old T-shirt. The *Kama Sutra* would have to wait. Her easel was already on the porch.

The assignment, a charcoal self-portrait, was giving her trouble. She had abandoned her first three attempts and was now beginning her fourth. Having roughed in the white space, her own face eluded her—as she'd feared it would. Nobody goes through electroshock without losing something, identity-wise— a sensitivity to where you ended and others began, or a talent for representing the boundary, or just the ability to pick your own face out of a lineup. Seeing her struggle, her art teacher, Joseph, had advised her to "drop back a level." She started a new, less challenging project, a sketch of the back yard. But even this had gone wrong. Before she knew it, she'd added a thumb-sized female figure frowning by the clothesline, like something out of Brueghel: *Landscape with Silver Lake Puttana*. Now there was a self-portrait, at least if her mother had anything to say about it.

She tore the sketch away and tried again. The line of the fence became perplexing—it was either too straight, and the landscape looked forced and mechanical, or it was wavy, as if the local gravity had gone haywire. Where did these strange influences come from? As if someone else—or maybe a whole host of someones—had invaded her imagination.

"Primrose!" Her mother's curler-covered head emerged from the window.

"*What*, Ma?" Her frustration was growing with the pile of discards at her feet.

"Don't you 'what?' me." Louise's voice rose in tandem with Primrose's irritation, their moods coupled according to a linkage she could never understand. "If Reggie gets into Mr. Shorty's crab apples, that goddamn cat's retching is going to keep your goddamn father up all the goddamn night. So you can just put down that goddamn crayon and find him."

Primrose's charcoal had disintegrated to a stub. If only it weren't two dollars a box.

"And take a bath, will you? You're filthier than my curtains."

"It all comes out in the wash," Primrose said philosophically. A show of equanimity was the one thing guaranteed to piss off her mother.

"I'll give you a wash. I'll wash that goddamn puss right off your goddamn face. Goddamn."

The window slammed.

Primrose's stomach was a balloon of acid, but she pushed herself to focus. She skimmed her palms along the surface of the paper, feeling her way in. So what if the cat was in the neighbor's yard. So what if the curtains were filthy. So what if her mother didn't like her face. As long as she could keep everything in her head under control, disorder—in curtains, in conduct—was the ticket, the way to go. The *redemptive possibility*, to use one of Joseph's phrases. She'd known this ever since her first date with Tino, which had been so humiliatingly chaotic he *had* to be The One.

They had gone to the movies. On screen, Marcello Mastroianni informed the leading lady that her hat looked just like *un petit escargot*—a snail! on her elegant head!—and Primrose, overwhelmed by giggles, had bumped Tino in the butter-fingered dark, sending his popcorn down the aisle. "Oh, no!" she cried, and then, running for the bucket, she'd tripped! Had gone sprawling, in fact, in her micro mini-dress. The theater erupted in wolf whistles, and she flew to the exit, expecting—or was it hoping?—never to see Tino again. But he was right behind her, wheezing with laughter or allergies or both. "From this day forward," he said solemnly as he embraced her by the dumpster, "you will *toujours* be my *escargot*." Which was exactly the sort of absurd commitment you could expect after tumbling ass-over-teakettle down a movie aisle instead of making a stately promenade, in a proper church, on your father's arm.

Primrose had smiled through her heaving shame: *Oh, Tino.* In the half-light, he even resembled Marcello—they had the same cleft chin and subtly lopsided mouth. He took her for hot wieners, and as they ate, her tumble down the aisle came to seem less déclassé than simply human, the result of being encumbered with an ordinary body vulnerable to mishap. He, too, was interested in ordinary bodily mishaps. He spoke earnestly about medical school where he intended to become a family doctor, someone you could see for a splinter or a cough or a mysterious ailment that turned out to be nothing, like the guy with the carrot problem in the *New Yorker*. It was then that the thought had first occurred to her: This Tino Battuta was *a good catch*. Those exact words. As if her mother had spoken them, approvingly, into her ear.

There were other reasons to marry Tino: to get out of the house, for one thing. To make sex less guilt-inducing, for another. Not to put too fine a point on it, though they'd always been careful, and Tino had never gone further than it was really safe to go. Also, she'd been with Tino for two years, and no one else was even remotely interested. Though it seemed her luck in this department was changing. When she'd accepted Lupo's invitation, it was as if she'd never heard of Tino. As if the night of the escargot had happened to somebody else.

The drawing still wouldn't come right. She set down her charcoal and stuck her hand in her pocket. It was heavy with tiny pieces of type, a gift from Lupo. Standing on the porch, the last of the day's sun warming her shoulders, she fingered the little blocks. He had left them in her campus mailbox in a velvet bag closed with a drawstring, as if they were a handful of jewels. Also in the bag was an article ripped from *Life* headlined "Atomic Theory Based on Indirect Evidence" on which he'd scrawled: THE FUTURE. On the flip side was a photograph of RFK. The gift reminded her of that strange SDS confab. It had been pretty wild, something between a space opera and a meeting of the school board, though it was hard to know for sure what to make of it because conversing with the guys who'd dominated the meeting was fairly impossible. Even bold Rosemary had been shouted down. To them, Primrose felt, she could only be—at best—a hanger-on. And weren't they right about that, too? They felt so comfortably right about so much. But then again, she had a brain and a mouth. Couldn't she use them? Well, but—

If she kept on with her drawing in this mood, she would ruin it, aliens or no aliens. That much she knew for sure. Better to take a break and look for Reginald. Make her mother happy.

The cat wasn't hard to find. Clumps of his fur were stuck to Mr. Shorty's chain-link fence. As Primrose knelt, examining them, something rustled overhead: Reginald, making his way along a branch. His tail swished as the branch dipped beneath his weight. He had a habit of whining for the oil from Louise's tuna fish, and Louise had a habit of indulging him.

"Psst! Reginald!" Something pricked the back of her neck, leaving a hot itch. She scratched, pushing her fingers underneath the thin chain that held Tino's class ring. The clasp broke, the ring bounced sharply off Primrose's toe—

"Shit—"

Reginald sailed through the air, caught the gutter, and clambered onto the roof where he began to wash his face, pushing his paws over his tattered ears in a gesture that Louise always said was a sign of rain.

At least he wasn't in Mr. Shorty's yard anymore.

Primrose knelt in the crabgrass. Tino's ring couldn't just disappear—not even if, for a moment, during that first conversation with Lupo, she had wanted it to. No, the world was more substantial than that. Nothing was ever truly created or destroyed. That was simple physics, the natural order of things. Tino had told her so.

The bathroom window opened. Louise's hand shot out, cupped around a quahog shell. She flipped it, and a flurry of fresh butts joined the drift beneath the window.

The screen door squealed, and Primrose's father emerged holding a beer. The pull-tab came off with a scrape and a hiss. A moment later, Louise charged out.

"Primrose! Why are you bare-assing around the yard like a *puttana*?"

Primrose picked at her shorts. There was no good answer to a question like that, which was, of course, exactly why her mother had asked it. Her father sipped his beer, his face unreadable, and shut his eyes as if to make them both disappear.

Louise huffed into her Maverick and roared backwards out of the drive, clearing the mailbox by a hand, her angry face just visible over the steering wheel.

Something glinted beneath the leaves of a skunk cabbage. There it was, Tino's ring. Primrose pocketed it, along with the broken chain. It would be nice to have a safety catch on her necklace. It would be nice to have a lock on her bedroom door.

When I'm married, she thought, *all my doors will have locks on them.*

Primrose made her way back across the yard, the crabgrass pricking her soles. On the porch, her father rested in an Adirondack chair, his head sunk on his chest, one hand wrapped around a can of beer.

"Reggie's on the roof," she announced.

Her father looked up and stared at her for a long, uncomfortable moment, then took another sip of beer. Did he think she was a *puttana,* too?

"He'll be down when he wants his supper," he said. And then: "Your mother's really got a bee in her bouffant about you and Tino."

"I guess so."

"I know it bothers you more than that."

Her father rarely judged her harshly, but this time he would only be telling the truth. She *was* letting Tino do things to her, and she was doing things to him, that were only covered in books like Ovid's, of which her mother definitely would not approve.

"It's all right," he said. "You can be bothered. She's bothersome."

Primrose relaxed. Maybe she wasn't such a *puttana* after all.

"What are you drawing?" He gestured with his free hand toward the easel.

"An experiment." She didn't want to talk about her homework, how she was failing at the larger project of finding herself, her *subject.* She pushed her hair out of her eyes. "We learned about Käthe Kollwitz this week."

"Never heard of her," her father said.

"Joseph showed pictures. Charcoal sketches. He asked us to see what we could do on our own."

Kollwitz had sketched dead children and their dead-faced, blank-eyed mothers, sentimental, obvious images that caught at her mind like tufts of cat hair on the fence and then blew away, leaving only the memory of her mother's voice, once upon a time, calling her by the name she used when Primrose was still her sweet baby doll. *Primrose-pi'*, she'd called her. *Primrose-piccola.*

"She has an exhibit soon."

"Who?"

"Kollwitz. At the museum." Where Lupo was taking her. Primrose brushed a gnat from her arm. Wasn't she allowed to have friends?

"An exhibit," her father said. "Fancy."

She squinted at her father and then at her unsatisfactory sketch. "You might do. For a subject, I mean."

"Better hurry. I'm about ready for the glue factory."

"Just act natural."

Her father pulled a pack of Camels from his pocket and lit up, his hand cupping the flame. As he smoked, he trained his gaze on Mr. Shorty's yard.

"Not to harp on a sore subject," he exhaled, "but your mother's got no right to talk to you the way she does."

Primrose didn't answer. She was already too far gone, lost inside her picture. Back and forth, she shifted her attention between her father and the paper, until its surface took on depth and contour. By the time her father's likeness emerged, the charcoal felt like something living in her hands.

Her father's monologue took a familiar turn: What was Primrose doing with her life? "You could teach kindergarten. You like kids," he argued, "and you're already getting a degree in childishness."

"Child development, you mean. Anyway, I'm getting a degree in art."

Which was another way of not saying her actual thought: *The doctor said I'll never hold a regular job.*

"Kindergarten teachers are union. Twenty years and out. A pension. Then you can go to all the exhibits you want."

Primrose frowned. If you couldn't be crazy and teach kindergarten, you could certainly be crazy and paint. Look at Van Gogh. Or Rosemary, who was probably at this very moment preparing for next week's class by slashing perfectly good canvases in pursuit of a more ideal perfection. Primrose wondered what her father would make of Rosemary. Not much, probably.

"It wouldn't hurt to have a skill."

"If you keep talking, the picture won't come right."

The pull-tab rattled in the can. "Get me another, will you?"

Inside, the sofa was heaped with laundry, dumped by her mother for Primrose to fold. But no one ever got into a gallery by folding laundry. Or washing curtains. Or getting beers, though this last task had advantages. In the kitchen, she peeled back the tab and raised the can to her mouth. She smelled charcoal on her hands, mixed with the odors of her mother's kitchen, cigarettes and cabbage, perfume and acetone. Her father's wallet lay on the table, his union card peeking out, its edges tattered as Reginald's ears.

Outside, she handed the beer to her father.

"Thanks."

"Look what Lupo Light gave me." She dug in her pocket until she came up with the blocks and poured them into her father's outstretched palm. Just saying Lupo's name brought a kind of relief. For some reason, her mother's hurtful *puttana* remark ebbed, too.

"Hot type," he said, impressed. "Who's Lupo Light?"

"Just a friend." Her father glanced at her. She broke his gaze, troubled, and smudged the cheekbone in her sketch, softening the line.

"Do you think Tino will go back to medical school?" Her father still hoped that whatever Tino had done could be undone.

Which was natural enough. Behind his bluster, Leon had felt the same way. Parents were all the same. They only wanted to keep you safe—no matter what that safety cost you, how it held you back.

"He's just not cut out for it, Dad." Which wasn't exactly false, but wasn't the whole story, either.

"But won't he get called up?"

"He'll find a way out. A lot of guys do." She turned the easel toward her father.

"Not bad," he said. Then: "He's really not worried about the draft?"

"I guess he's going to do what he wants, no matter what. It's his life."

"Don't you have some say?"

"I'm not sure." She remembered the boat. Tino hadn't mentioned it since the disastrous funeral dinner. Perhaps he'd seen her point about spending money on pipe dreams. "Maybe."

Down the hill, a haze hung over the spot where Silver Lake's rambling triple-deckers gave way to mills and factories. Reliable Button was down there, too, where her mother had worked before she landed her hospital job.

But Primrose hadn't known Tino then.

"Five o'clock," her father sighed, extracting another cigarette from the pack. "Quitting time."

He'd gotten off at three; he was only part-time these days. As the match flared, a boy in overalls scrambled across the yard.

Primrose blinked. The boy vanished.

Had he been there at all? Or was this one of her mind's tricks?

The noise of mating beetles rang in the air. Her father toyed with Lupo's letters, pushing them around with his fingertip until they spelled: PROMISER.

"You know I like Tino," her father said gently. "But he hasn't exactly rushed to put a ring on your finger."

"That's right," she replied. And just because she'd agreed to let Lupo take her to the museum didn't mean she was two-timing

Tino. Who didn't like museums anyway. Who only read the *New Yorker* for the cartoons.

Her father rearranged the letters: PRIMROSE. "You know, I think this Lupo Light is a little in love with you."

THE BOOK OF LOVE:
On Kissing
By Norah Thomas and Primrose Tirocchi

According to a sixteenth-century missionary, villagers on the western shore of an island near Nova Scotia kiss with their eyes crossed. Exogamy, too, is strongly marked.

Over a lifetime, an average person spends two weeks kissing. Extraordinary people—you know who you are—may spend rather more.

Kissing on Sundays is technically forbidden in Connecticut, which is a good reason to avoid weekend trips to Mystic Seaport, and explains everything we know, or have heard, about the young men of New Haven.

Kissing bug: Any of the various bloodsucking insects of the family *Reduviidae*, capable of inflicting a painful bite. AKA *cone-nosed bug*. Cf., infectious mononucleosis, AKA *the kissing disease*.

Why do we kiss? According a specialist at a European university, kissing began when prehistoric mothers spat chewed food into their babies' mouths, like birds. This theory neglects the obvious fact that these women, who weren't dumb, would have nursed their children until teeth appeared. Some people don't have the sense God gave a quahog.

A second theory, of unknown origin, holds that the soul lives in the breath; kissing fuses two souls forever.

Abstract kisses: of death, of life, of peace.

8. Lead a horse to water

Here's what no one tells you about having a congenital case of Ants-in-the-Pants: Sometimes they're *fire* ants. The following Monday, as Tino climbed the stairs to Reliable Button's business office, he tripped on a putty knife that some fool had left on the landing. As the knife clattered down, Tino nearly lost his lunch, and he expected his nerve to follow shortly. It had never been easy to ask the old man for anything. The more you needed something, the harder it was. No wonder he couldn't sit still.

By the time Tino reached the third floor, his eyes were running from the factory's atmosphere, a thick vapor of acetone and shellac. Images from organic chemistry invaded his mind: molecules changing valences, stepwise conversions of one thing into another. Transformations that, once started, were not easily stopped. If only his own life worked that way. But Pat had been right—you can't just sit around waiting for your future to arrive. You had to make it happen.

He opened the door marked BUSINESS OFFICE, startling Phyllis, his father's bookkeeper, at her desk. She motioned for him to wait and returned her attention to the ledger. After a half-hour, Leon called for Tino. His *agita* was a hot swarm in his chest.

Leon's desk was piled with onion-skin invoices and cardstock studded with beads in the next season's colors—lemon yellow, acid orange, a blinding high-gloss white. Tino squeezed himself into the only other chair, by the window.

"You won't apologize, then? And see if they'll take you back?" Leon asked.

"No."

"They *will* take you back, you know. Nobody wants to turn a smart young man into cannon fodder."

"Not true. That is not even remotely true."

"Now, Tino. People do make mistakes. And they do recover from them. Say, for the sake of argument, you changed your mind."

"I won't change my mind." Tino stared at the doorway. Through it was the corridor, the front office, the stairs, the blessed street.

"You don't have a skill, Tino."

"I know." Did he ever.

"You don't have a trade." His father leaned over him and shoved the window up. The room filled with the smells of exhaust, asphalt, wieners. The phone rang in the outer office.

Leon sighed. His gaze was level, serious, and, to Tino's surprise, not angry. "A bright young man with prospects and your whole life ahead of you. I just don't understand, Tino. How could you go and *do* this?"

Anger would have been easier to deal with. Kindly perplexity was something else. Tino stared at his hands. He had no job, no skills, no trade. So much for the Brindisi dexterity.

"Fine." Leon slid the plastic selector knob of his telephone index back and forth. "You don't want to explain. You just want to get on. I understand. I was young once too. You have a right to your own mistakes. Heaven knows I've made enough." At Leon's elbow, the squat black phone buzzed, signaling big news from the outer office, something Phyllis could not deal with on her own.

Tino spoke before his father could lift the receiver: "Maybe there's something I could do around here?"

"I'm afraid we won't have much work this summer. I might even have to lay off some guys. Let me tell you, Tino, the prospect doesn't thrill me. They have families to support." These words fell heavily, weighed down by all the more worthy people—worthier than him, certainly—who also relied upon Leon.

"What about around the office?"

"Don't tell me you want that women's work."

Phyllis appeared in the doorway, scowling. "Leon, it's *Joey*." Joey was the West Coast rep for Reliable Button. "He's on *California time*."

Leon looked at his watch. "It's 6 a.m. in California."

"I'm just telling you what he *said*." She clicked back down the hallway. "*California* time."

"All right," Leon called after her, picking up the phone with barely concealed distaste. "Put him through."

On the wall behind Leon, a painted horse followed a painted jockey to a painted trough. If you pulled the chain hanging from the corner, the painting, which was mounted on a hinged panel, would open, revealing a real bottle of J&B and a real pair of glass tumblers rimmed in gold. During important meetings, Leon would yank the chain and, with a flourish, offer his guest a drink.

Certainly Tino would never get the cabinet treatment by begging for work. Women's work, especially. The artist had left no doubt about the sex of the prize horse.

By the time Leon finished with Joey, the room was very warm, and the sun felt hot on Tino's scalp where the hair was getting sparse.

"We're all worried for you, Tino." Leon tangled his fingers in the phone cord. "I don't like what you've done, not one bit. But you know I don't like this war, either."

"I know," Tino said warily. He wasn't sure where Leon was going.

"Remember those three fellas at Poppa Tavio's wake? The ones who kept their backs to the wall?"

Tino nodded. With quick movements Leon wrapped the phone's cord around his fingers.

"Those so-called gentlemen are friends from way back. Not friends I particularly like, or even people I would care to share a meal with, but they came to pay their respects and to remind me of an outstanding favor which we, as a family, are owed. A debt," he said, "from a long time ago."

Leon's pulse moved through his hands, changing his skin from pink to white and back again, in those places where the phone cord was wrapped tight.

"I'd rather not deal with these people, Tino. Better to let bygones be bygones. But if we have to do it, I'll call it in. This favor, I mean."

"So what are you actually going to do, Dad? Whack some guy on the draft board?"

"That's not how things get done." He paused. "Not necessarily."

"So?"

"Family is family. That's all I'm saying."

Tino twisted inside like the fish he was, caught in a net of filial obligation, sticky warp and clinging weft going back for generations.

Swims with the fishes.

"Here's an idea." Leon brightened. "On your way in, you probably noticed the stairwell."

"Yeah."

"The painter quit just before Poppa Tavio's wake."

So that was why Leon had been so angry the morning of the wake, and why he had been late.

"All the hard work's done. It's even primed."

Tino wasn't sure he'd heard right, or if Leon really meant it. Apparently, his father was giving him a job. Turning the screws, too, by making him ask for it. The *agita* flared again.

"Well, maybe I could do final coat?"

"Attaboy," Leon said.

9. The *Sumac*

Tino arrived at Reliable Button at seven the next morning, a can of paint dangling from each hand. In the storeroom he found a mop, some rags, a dowel, a roller, a tray, and a bucket that he filled with hot water and soap. He set everything in the foyer, making several trips, and then stopped to rest on the landing, his feet planted wide apart, arms stretched so his fingertips grazed the wall on either side. A wingspan. Funny how you could measure everything by the body.

With a key he pried the top off a can and stirred the paint with the dowel. He poured paint into his tray and dipped the roller. Already his back was aching. But at least here, working for his father, the day would come to an end, and he would not have lost anything except his time. Which wasn't worth much, though his father would give him thirty bucks for this job. Hoisting the charged roller, he applied paint to the wall in smooth strokes. Leon had allowed him to choose the color. When he finished, the stairwell would be periwinkle blue, the color of Primrose's eyes.

Thirty bucks. Well, it was something. A start.

He worked his way down the stairs. When he felt the front door press his back, he planted the roller in the tray and left to buy a donut. Outside, the morning still seemed fresh. He checked his watch. It wasn't even nine. He had worked fast, and now he had the whole day ahead of him.

When he returned, he found Leon in the lobby holding his tackle box.

"Fishing today?"

"Gonna try." Leon leaned over to examine a spot where a dark scuffmark had been. Now there was just a shadow.

"Think it needs another coat?" Tino was beat, and the day beckoned, but he didn't want any special treatment from his father.

"I think you'd better. Another coat would eliminate that mark entirely."

"Or someone could come in first thing Monday and scuff it up all over again."

"That's the spirit."

"Sorry," Tino said.

Leon straightened, pressing a hand against his lower back, exactly where Tino had felt a twinge earlier. "Do us both a favor, Tino. Don't get old."

"I'll do my best." Tino crouched to pry the top off the second can of paint. "Assuming I get the chance to try."

"Well, about that." Leon paused. "I made some calls."

"You did?" he asked, then regretted it. It was bad to show how much hope he had pinned on his father's intervention. The truth was, he was slipping further and further into Leon's debt, with no clear idea how to repay him.

"Augie Maiello might have a line on something at the boat yard, contract work like I did for the Navy during the war." The other war, he meant, the world war—though you'd think, from the way Leon talked, it was the only war, and that the present mess was just some wrongheaded folly. "But I wouldn't bet the farm on it."

"Okay."

"If that doesn't pan out, the guys at the club always need caddies. The work won't keep you away from Uncle Sam, but it'll at least keep a buck in your pocket."

The guys at the club were like Dom Carcieri—beefy, insufferable. They'd tip a lousy dollar and expect you to act like you'd gotten the key to the Taj Mahal.

"Don't frown, Tino. It's not so bad. All cash, and you'll be out in the sunshine."

The stairwell spun. He leaned on the handrail.

"You okay?"

"Fine," Tino said, blinking back a blackout.

Leon pushed the door open and kicked the doorstop down. Hot air pressed in, mingling the smells of asphalt and hot weiners with the odor of the paint.

"Better?" Leon asked.

"Not really."

"Listen, Tino. What's done is done." Leon rested a hand on Tino's shoulder. "Tell you what. Come by Monday morning, and we'll see what else there is for you to do."

"Thanks." It was better than caddying at least. "I appreciate it."

It was only after Leon left with his tackle box under his arm that Tino noticed the bills tucked beneath the paint tray. Thirty dollars, as promised. A start.

An hour later, Chick strode in. He was wearing aviator sunglasses and chewing an unlit cigar.

"You're just in time," said Tino, who was taping a hand-scrawled WET PAINT sign to the wall.

"In time for what?"

"For lunch. Your treat."

"Forget lunch. The draft board does not stop for lunch. Are you in or out, Battuta? This deal won't wait forever."

"It's been waiting two weeks."

"The seller's antsy."

Tino knew the feeling. He smoothed the tape. "All right," he said. "I'm in."

"You didn't need much convincing."

"I guess not."

"Attaboy." Chick extended his palm. "Pony up."

From his pocket, Tino extracted two tens.

"That's all?"

Through the dark lenses, Chick's eyes were bloodshot. One eyeball was deep red near the inside of his nose.

"Christ!" Tino leaned in for a closer look. "I've seen better-looking eyeballs in the St. Louis ER. What happened?"

"Never mind." Chick added the bills to his money clip. "I'll cover you. *Andiamo*."

Chick had borrowed his mother's car, a custard-colored Dart. As Chick drove, Tino leaned out the window, trying to catch a breeze. No dice. The cool morning had given way to a hot, still afternoon. As they passed the cemetery where Poppa Tavio was buried, the traffic came to a halt. A hearse was approaching the turn into the cemetery parking lot. Some mourners had already arrived. Just like at Poppa Tavio's funeral, they were mostly gray-haired and stooped, the women stuffed into dark dresses and tightly laced black shoes.

"Age before beauty." Chick slowed, waving the hearse into the intersection. Behind it stretched an uninterruptible line of cars. "Damn it," Chick said. "We may be here a while."

"Seems like we're always here, doesn't it? Pretty soon there won't be any of them left."

"That's life," Chick quipped. "Get it?"

Tino groaned. Chick's jokes were all like that.

Past the church, the road sloped uphill toward the center of Knightsville. They passed a strip of mom-and-pops: the cobbler, the bakery, and the florist, who provided the same lilies for everyone who kicked the bucket, including Poppa Tavio and, no doubt, the duffer in the hearse they'd just left behind. Past the shops, the mill was shuttered. The river, sluggish now, flooded every spring. At least that much was reliable. Death, taxes, and the river. Traffic. The radio droned.

They turned into a waterfront lot where a motorcycle leaned against a tree. Chick parked the Dart. *Andiamo*, he muttered, as if in a trance. Prompted by what, Tino wondered. The funeral, maybe. A reminder of the old rituals, the old ways.

A dirt ramp led to a dock, to which an oblong boat was tethered, its name stenciled on the hull: SUMAC, NORTH KINGSTON, RI.

Tino followed Chick to the end of the dock, where they shook hands with the man who was standing there in a Harley-Davidson T-shirt. He gestured toward the boat.

"She's not much. Not compared to what you'll find at the Providence Yacht Club, as I'm sure you fellas know." Tino caught his glance and stared back evenly. The boat was, indeed, not much—at the very least, it needed a lick of paint, some caulk, a thorough washing. "But she's solid. Take a spin?"

Chick hopped aboard. The man went next. Tino held the rail, his insides going to jelly.

"Steady," the man said, extending a hand. Tino gripped it and levered himself over.

"Aren't you glad we didn't stop for lunch," Chick said as Tino sank onto a wooden bench in dire need of refinishing.

The man started the engine, which kicked up a cloud of exhaust as they pulled away. Could this *felucca* really take them to Canada?

They passed the fire station and the bakery. Behind the gleaming windows of the Miss Cranston Diner, a waitress leaned over a booth and pulled a cord, sending the blinds down in a wave. Tino continued to hold the rail, unsure whether to laugh or barf. One might easily lead to the other.

A rhythmic glunk-swoosh rose from the boat's core, like a heart with a murmur: she loves me, shh, she loves me not.

"What's that?" Chick asked.

"Just the bilge," the man said.

"The bilge," Tino repeated. "That sounds ominous."

"She's a lady," the man said. "You can't expect her not to need this and that."

Another lady also needed this and that. Tino could practically hear Primrose making the case for her priorities. Two hundred dollars could become a wedding ring, a security deposit, a nest egg.

"How'd she come to you, sir?" Chick asked.

The man told them that the boat had gone on the block when its previous owner had died at the helm. "Heart attack. The Coast Guard found her going around in circles."

"That's heavy," Chick said.

"Some say they saw a light in the sky when it happened, but you know how folks are. The more they talk, the less they know."

Back on the dock, Chick counted three hundred and forty dollars from his money clip.

"That's all?"

"Aw, shoot." Chick removed his glasses and rubbed the bridge of his nose. Under the best circumstances, Chick's burdened-man-of-the-world act was not convincing. Today's burst blood vessel didn't help. "I'm afraid we've wasted your time, sir. I thought she was going for one-forty."

"The offer was four hundred."

"Sorry." Chick returned the clip to his pocket. "My mistake."

"It's bad luck," Tino said, "to buy a boat if the captain died in it. He ought to have gone down with his ship."

Chick nodded sagely, as if this were an important consideration that he hadn't taken into account. "Yeah. Didn't expect to hear that at all."

"You boys look too clever for that malarkey."

"Well, we do like the boat. And we're here."

The man continued to glare. Chick shrugged. Not sure if he was disappointed or relieved, Tino followed Chick down the dock. The bilge sputtered and fell silent.

"All right, all right," the man called. "I'll take your three-forty."

Chick winked his good eye at Tino. "Deal."

There were papers to sign, a transfer of title and a bill of sale. Chick folded everything into his pocket and promised to register the boat first thing in the morning. In the parking lot, the man helped them hitch the trailer to Chick's car. The hitch was functional but rusty. Tino hoped it wouldn't have to be replaced too. They backed the trailer down the ramp. The man helped them maneuver the boat onto it and rumbled off on his bike.

"You were pretty good back there," Tino said after they were back in the car.

"Speak for yourself, Mr. *Rime of the Ancient Mariner.*"

Chick took an envelope from his shirt pocket and handed it to Tino. It was from the Selective Service, and it gave the place and time that Chick was expected to show up for his physical.

"Oh, no." All at once the whole day seemed lost. Tino sought words, encouraging words as befit the time, the moment, their friendship—and failed to find them. He passed the envelope back to Chick, who tore it into pieces and tossed them in the water.

"What are you doing?"

"Only what a million other guys are doing."

Tino was aghast. But he felt a twinge of admiration, too. He wanted to just the same thing with his dean's letter, but he didn't have the nerve. Not yet. For now it would stay in his wallet.

Chick pointed at his bad eye. "So I had a little beer and stumbled into a little something known as a telephone pole, and then I hit the ground, you know, a little bit. But now we've got the boat. O, Canada!"

The *Sumac* rocked, straining at the ropes. Its imperfections were more obvious now that it was out of the water: dented hull, warped boards. Not to mention the wheezing bilge. Forget Canada. Without a lot more investment, this boat wouldn't haul their asses to Conimicut.

On Cranston Street, a siren wailed. Chick pulled over, the boat a strange weight behind them. A moment later, a Brillo-haired cop leaned through Chick's open window and sniffed. Smelling for booze, Tino thought, or grass.

"How can we help you, Officer?" Chick asked. His bad eye was on Tino's side—a small mercy, and Tino was glad for it.

"You know you got a busted taillight?"

"We bought this boat a half hour ago," Chick explained. "We haven't had a chance to check the lights."

"Should have thought of that before." He wrote out a ticket and gave it to Chick, who handed it to Tino, who glanced at the charge. Another five dollars gone, just like that. "A boat's a big responsibility."

"Yes, sir." Chick reached for the ignition. The guy was still staring. "Sir?"

"You boys seen anything funny this morning?"

"Like what?"

"Some lady called the station, said she'd seen a flying saucer."

"Here?"

"You betcha." The cop cracked his knuckles. "Now that ladies got vacuum cleaners and self-cleaning ovens, they got nothing to do all day but make up stories about spacemen."

"We haven't seen any spacemen," Tino said.

"Definitely not," Chick added.

The cop let them go. "All right, boys. But keep your eyes open," he said. Sneering, he added: "If you can."

The neighborhood slipped past in a blur of storefronts— nothing here to tempt a visitor from outer space. A crowd had gathered on the sidewalk where another cop stood towering over a kneeling man. Tino couldn't think what law the man might be breaking. As far as he knew, it was not illegal to be strange in public. Though it might get you tossed into the loony bin, like Primrose. Tino flashed on a newscast he'd seen, years before, about a monk in a yellow robe who set himself on fire in some backstreet of Saigon. Who in the world would set themselves on fire just to make a point? Primrose sometimes mentioned it: "That's all that's left for them to do."

Chick stopped short. Watching the crowd, he'd nearly run a light.

"Damned rubberneckers," he said absently.

Tino shook his head, trying to rid himself of the terrible image. That sort of thing just didn't happen here.

When the light turned green, Chick hit the accelerator too hard. As he struggled to keep control, the boat yawed behind them. In the side mirror Tino glimpsed the boat drifting across the centerline.

"Jesus Christ! Didn't you lock the hitch?"

St. Mary's brick façade came into view. In the parking lot, three girls were skipping rope.

"What we should do," Chick said as he spun the steering wheel, "is throw a party. Christen our new baby."

Tino gripped the dashboard. "Christen it?"

"In the customary fashion. By breaking a bottle over its head."

"Over the bow, you mean."

Chick laughed. "I said what I said."

10. Thrift

Pressing the accelerator pedal to the floor, Tino thrummed up Unaconicut Hill. Tonight he had no time for anything as earthbound as gravity. What he wanted was an escape path. He wanted to crest the hill and vault himself into orbit like a satellite.

In truth he was in no shape for a party. He'd showered, but the paint smell lingered, giving him a headache; and he couldn't shake the queasy memory of Chick's bloodshot eye. At the summit, he kicked it into neutral to save gas, and a line came to him: *Thrift, thrift, Horatio.* An echo from an English class, maybe, something he'd half-heard while daydreaming about baseball; or, more likely, it was one of Primrose's adoring repetitions of something her art teacher had said.

Funny how a girl could get inside you, her thoughts becoming your own. Primrose seemed to have the same problem, but in a more general way that led to confusion. A stranger in the donut shop reading the newspaper out loud to himself could become, for Primrose, someone quietly trying to get inside her mind, wreak some havoc there. Tino would have to keep an eye on her if things between them got serious. Well, any more serious. Which they might.

He turned a corner, and the houses grew shabbier—roofs lacked shingles, gutters hung skew. The *Sumac*, too, would need attention—the bilge, all those dings in the hull. Money—that was the key. Drive. Ambition. Maybe he should caddy, like his father said. There were worse things than getting paid to walk around outside all day.

If the cash piled up fast enough, Primrose might get her wedding ring. She might also become a widow in short order. He remembered the *Sumac* yawing all over the road. He was like that, too, these days—inwardly all over the place, only intermittently in touch with reality, with what was straight and true.

Thrift, thrift.

Unless nothing was straight *or* true. He parked in front of Primrose's house and stared down the hill. Providence spread below him in the dusk, the city's lights glittering all the way to the waterfront. He beeped the horn, Primrose appeared in the doorway, and just like that, his headache was history.

Her father's voice followed Primrose out the door: "Be home before midnight or your mother will have a conniption."

Tino suppressed a groan. Good nights did not begin with reminders of Louise. But then Primrose was in the car, offering her cheek to be kissed. She was wearing the lemony perfume he liked, the one called Come, Summer, as if the season might be persuaded to visit, though it never stayed long around here. Some things you get briefly, if at all. It was important to recognize that.

Primrose had dressed carefully, in a red-and-white polka dot skirt topped with a red cardigan that she'd pinned with a cloisonné dahlia. The skirt, cut on the bias, swirled around her as she moved. She had put her hair up in some complicated way involving many hairpins and, this being Primrose, a yellow number-two pencil.

Tino touched the knot at the nape of her neck, brushing at the wisps that had escaped her up-do.

"Who'd you make yourself look so fancy for?"

"You." She smiled. "I dressed up for you."

Tino traced the curve of her shoulder with his index finger, making a trail down her arm that might have looped back and slipped under the cardigan, into what might have been a tickle or a caress, had she not grabbed his hand and pulled it to her nose.

"Paint thinner?"

"That was just the start of the day." He sighed, remembering his unexpected chat with Leon. "Which was a long one. I'll tell you all about it later."

"Promiser," she said distantly and settled into the far side of the long front seat, too far away for Tino to put an arm around her. It was his own fault; no doubt she'd already intuited his betrayal with the *Sumac*. The smog-shrouded town unfurled below, giving him a stifled feeling, like when he went to sleep in his clothes.

It was important to be patient at these moments, which were so dodgy, so full of potential in every direction, including the wrong one, the one that led to certain disaster. The only thing he knew for sure was that if he pushed, he'd lose her. She needed time, gentle handling. Once she warmed up, she'd be fine. Or so he hoped, rolling down the hill with his foot off the gas to save money he hadn't made yet. *Gravity*, as Chick liked to say, *is a gift from the Maestro*. Might as well shut up and bide his time, take the advantages within reach.

The drive was quiet, the silence broken only by a jet's overhead throb. It was flying at a low altitude, the wings shadowed deep purple to match the dusky sky. When the shops and tenements gave way to fields and vegetable stands, Primrose switched on the radio. Linda Lyndell's big voice filled the car. She was singing about a lost boyfriend, trying to lure him back with promises of domestic bliss, a whole pipe-and-slippers routine.

"She's not exactly liberated," Primrose observed.

"There's a place and time for everything, I guess." Primrose was not exactly what he'd call liberated, either.

"For pipes and slippers?"

"How about I'll bring you your slippers one night, you can get them for me the next. We can take turns. Isn't that equality?"

Primrose stared out the window. Again Tino was struck by how long he'd been away. A year ago, they'd have had an argument, something good-natured and lively. Maybe her passivity had to do with her new friends, who seemed to be the tune-in, drop-out sort. Or maybe it was the drugs she was on. What he wouldn't give now for a good fight, just for the contact—anything to pierce the folds of this sulky shroud into which she kept retreating, leaving him alone.

The motel was ultramodern, like something out of *The Jetsons*, all acute angles and huge picture windows. The sign said: BLAST-OFF BUNGALOWS.

"Here we are." He turned into parking lot and parked beside Chick's Dart.

At the end of the lot, behind a chain link fence, was a swimming pool. A girl in a bikini floated on an inner tube, trailing her fingers in the blue water. At the pool's edge, a knot of guys had formed around the barbecue. Someone had opened one of the motel room windows and threaded a bunch of extension cords through the gap. Feedback screeched through a speaker. On the other side of the lot, the *Sumac* was parked on the trailer.

"Oh, *you didn't*. Tell me you didn't, Tino."

"Well," Tino said as he watched her expression darken, "I guess I did."

"You did."

"I know what you're thinking. Wedding rings cost money."

"They do."

"And your mother has expectations."

"She does."

Primrose slipped out of the car before the fight could gather speed. Tino cut the motor and hurried after her into the party's scrum. Chick had planted himself slantwise in a doorway, a plastic lei swinging around his neck. Ray-Bans peeped from the front pocket of his aloha shirt. He shook the hand Tino offered, then led them into the dark bedroom he had reserved.

Every detail of the room's decor was space-themed, from the twin rocket-shaped beside lamps to the portrait of Buzz Aldrin, painted on black velvet, hanging on the wall behind the bed. Tino tugged Primrose's arm and pointed to the ceiling.

"It's mirrored!"

"The better to see you with," Chick cackled. His bad eye had cleared some; a sliver of white had interposed itself between the iris and the bloodshot remainder of the sclera. They followed

him into the bathroom where cans of beer were tucked into a tub full of Esso ice. "What's your poison?"

"What have you got?" Tino asked. "I mean, besides one hell of a shiner?"

"Too-shay," Chick replied, handing him a beer, "means 'Have a 'Gansett'' in Chinese."

"What you know about Chinese," Tino said, "fits on the tip of my finger." Which he wagged in Chick's face before cracking the can's tab and drinking deep. He offered the can to Primrose, who took a swig and set the can on the ledge beneath the mirror.

"Look!" She leaned over the tub, pointing to a shadow on the wall. "There's a picture in the paint. If you squint, you just can see it, right there. Looks like Jackie Kennedy."

Tino craned his neck to see, more for politeness' sake than anything else. In truth he did not want to look at any more paint. "I don't see anything."

She plucked the pencil from her chignon, stepped out of her shoes, and balancing on the tub's ledge, began to sketch on the wall.

"Careful," Tino warned.

"It's pencil. It erases."

"The manager's not going to like this," he warned. "Chick's going to get a bill."

"Nonsense. It's art."

She leaned on him as she worked, and this proximity, not to mention her lemony perfume, went straight to his head. That she could still do this to him, after everything that had happened, was astonishing. He rested his cheek against the cool fabric of her skirt. Primrose sketched until, sure enough, a woman's face emerged, wearing a pair of enormous sunglasses and a pillbox hat. If the image hadn't been in the wall in the first place, like the apparition at Lourdes, then Primrose had produced a more-than-decent original.

Had the image been there, or had she created it?

"Never a dull moment," Tino bleated from somewhere near her hip. "With you, I mean."

She smiled. "Thanks, I think."

Night had well and truly fallen. Outside, people lounged by the pool, the tips of their flicked cigarettes blazing arcs through the darkness. Someone picked out a melody on a guitar while someone else noodled on a bass. A few people swam, naked or nearly so, their wet suits piled on the pool's perimeter. The swimmers—so carefree, so secure—reminded Tino of his dream of life after medical school, the comfortable future he'd jettisoned in the space of a morning. Or maybe it was just the first time he'd been able to stop and think. How hard it could be sometimes to just stop. To think.

Oh, God. Not that.

The room's door could be locked, so he locked it. As far as Tino was concerned, the world beyond this tacky three hundred square feet could go to hell all on its own for a while.

Primrose rested one foot on a chair, her skirt hiked up, and unrolled her stockings. Tino watched from the bed, holding his breath. When she tugged at her halter, the knot refused to come undone.

"Help a girl out, will you?"

Tino worked the knot. In his fingers the fabric felt untrustworthy, cheap and slippery. When it finally loosened, Primrose clasped his hands to her face. He didn't like what he saw there. His fumbling with the knot had broken the mood, and now she was tense.

"You want another beer?" He pushed a hank of hair from her eyes.

She shook her head. "With my meds? I shouldn't."

"Are you okay?"

"I'm a little tired, maybe." She smiled, an effort to reassure that was not less charming for its reflexive, knee-jerk quality. "Sorry."

"Don't be." He took her hand.

"Promise?"

Promiser.

"Promise what?"

She kissed him. He couldn't say another word so long as her mouth was pressed to his. As he pulled her onto the bed, she murmured something he didn't quite hear. It sounded like: *Hey, hey baby. Turn out the light.* Or: *Maybe we should use something.*

She fiddled with her up-do until her hair came down all around him.

Outside Chick was shouting. "All the beer we've got is now out here in the cooler because Tino and Primrose have commandeered the room. And they've *locked the door!*"

Hoots. Primrose's dress slipped to the carpet, and then she was beneath the covers without a stitch. The air conditioning, set too high, pebbled her skin. She wrapped herself around Tino, and her embrace felt like the last trustworthy thing in a world that was pitching and roaring and about to go completely to the dogs. After a moment, it was hard to say how any of that mattered when Primrose, with her cool hands, sprung him from his undershorts.

Primrose parted the curtains. The moon hung like the last pellet on a candy necklace—pitted, nibbled, mostly gone. She tugged her dress on and sat beside Tino on the bed where she picked a bluish circle of dried paint on his arm. "What's this?"

"Macaroons," he joked. "Milk."

The pillow whuffed softly upon impact. "Tino. Listen. Can I ask you something?"

Tino paused. Where was this going? "Shoot," he said.

"What was St. Louis like? I used to think about it, writing to you. I tried to picture the landscape."

"The landscape?"

"Yes. What did you see?"

"What did I see?"

"That's what I'm asking! What did you *see*?"

The question felt strange, edged with threat. The road into St. Louis had followed a wide river through brown fields punctuated by silos and lopsided corncribs; later, amid blocks of tenements, the countryside's quiet gave way to the scream of the elevated train. That was the scenery. Nothing to write home about. Soybean fields forever.

"You know exactly what it was like," he said. "Who gives a shit about the scenery?" He was exasperated—with himself, for not knowing how to answer her question, and with her, for asking in the first place.

"I'm just trying to understand." She verged on a whine. "I've *missed* you, Tino. For a whole year now—"

She was trying to understand, yes, to draw a line from the past to the present, from his misadventures in St. Louis to this moment in a lousy motel room outside Providence. But the past was gone—like his dream of medicine, like Poppa Tavio in his grave. All that was left were shadows in the brain, dumb tissue falling apart beneath his clumsy scalpel. "What's done is done," Tino said. "Bygones. Let's let them *be* gone."

"I knew it." Primrose pouted. "Medical school made you cold."

His mind popped into a scary, brakeless gear, and for once, instead of braking, he let it roll. "You're the one who's cold," he snapped. "You don't want to get married, you just want to get your mother off your back. Why can't you admit it?"

She scooted away, across the bed.

"Be realistic, Primrose," he said, applying the conversational brakes at last.

"Realistic!" Primrose snorted, turning around. "What you know about realism would fit on my little toenail."

"I've got no job, and no prospect of one, either. I could be called up any day. Which might not be the worst thing in the world, considering my alternatives. But if we were married, where would you be?"

"So under these circumstances, with no job and no money, buying a broken-down old boat is realistic but getting married isn't?" She smoothed the sheet. "I know what you think."

That was one problem with Primrose, her paranoia: She *always* knew. Or thought she did. Tino willed himself to be silent. The temptation to mock was strong.

"You don't want to get married, Tino, because it's my idea. Because you have to think of everything first."

He stared at her collarbone, her freckled shoulders, her sundown hair. "We're close," Tino said sadly, "and then this happens."

Softening, she took his hand. "I'm not actually angry. I don't feel much of anything, to be honest."

How strange: The end of being angry was nothing at all.

He poked his legs into his shorts and flipped the dial on the television until he found the Red Sox game, now tied at the bottom of the ninth.

"If the newscaster starts the body count, turn it off, please," Primrose said.

He didn't respond; after a moment he realized that he simply didn't know how. If the news started, he'd turn off the TV, sure. Or maybe he'd throw it through the window.

"Tino?"

The music stopped. The lights went out. The air conditioner fell silent with a mechanical grunt. The blown fuse raised such a protest from the pool that, in the bedroom, Primrose and Tino rolled their eyes in tandem, smiling at each other despite themselves. Outside, Chick shouted for the manager. Silence followed, and then came the whoosh and tinkle of small glass shattering as a bottle hit the deck. "To the *Sumac*!" they cheered. "The *Sumac*!"

Feet pounded the roof. That was when the splashdowns started, one after the other. Cannonball mechanics: water displaced, distance covered.

Chick shouted: "Gravity! Our gift from the Maestro!"

The lights came back blazing. On the television, the Red Sox game went into extra innings. Tino kissed Primrose, hoping the gesture would say what he couldn't, about St. Louis, what was real. She traced the valley that ran from his sternum to his belly button, and he wondered if she were thinking about landscapes.

"Hey," he said.

"Shh." She pressed a finger against his lips. In the ceiling's mirror, he saw Primrose approaching through a snowstorm. Or was it the television screen, gone to static? The mirror—what was she doing to the mirror? Primrose shook her head, and the illusion was so perfect that he was astonished to feel something wet—snow, real, literal, honest-to-God *snow*—falling on his chest.

"You're crying," he said, surprised.

"You're dreaming," she told him. "Look at you, you're half-asleep."

It was well past her curfew by the time Tino brought her home. They kissed quickly in the car. A light burned in the living room.

"Hey," Tino said at the last moment. "Where's my ring?"

She put her hand to her neck, where his ring wasn't. "I still have it," she insisted. "The chain broke, that's all. Don't worry."

"I won't," he lied, feeling like a heel for noticing in the first place.

Primrose got out, wrapping her cardigan around her. Already she could smell Louise's Luckys, the ones she chain-smoked as she sat watching the clock and dozing at intervals, the cigarette's lengthening ash threatening the upholstery until she woke up, ashed, and changed the channel on the television. Whenever Primrose went out for the night, Louise kept the thing on at full volume, a proxy for her own prerogatives: *You will always come back, he will always have to give you back.*

***

Rice paddies rippled in the televised chopper wind. Beneath her mother's water glass, a white ring had formed on the coffee table. Primrose crossed the living room and switched off the TV. Louise jerked awake.

"So?" her mother asked, the rising tone slightly too shrill, the fist barely hidden in the glove.

"We had a nice time."

Louise's cigarette had burned almost down to the filter. "You don't know what it's like, Primrose, to wait for your daughter to come home from wherever it is you go with that boy in his fancy car with his fancy friends..."

"He isn't fancy—"

"He has his own car, he buys clothes on his father's fancy account at Harvey's downtown."

Primrose sighed. It was true: Tino did buy his clothes there on his father's account, and they were nice clothes. Fancy.

"Don't think I don't know about Harvey's."

He's got a boat now, too, Primrose thought. Not that she was going to give her mother more ammunition.

"Thanks for waiting up," she said. She'd only come home a little late, like a million other girls on a Saturday night. She backed toward her bedroom, the hallway just two steps away, then one—

"Don't think I don't know what you're doing in the back seat of that fancy car—"

Primrose undressed in the dark and slipped into bed. Something rustled in the corner where she used to keep her dolls, as if a tiny version of Primrose, Primrose *piccola*, had been stashed there and was angling to come out. But Primrose knew it was just mice.

THE BOOK OF LOVE:
"You Can't Hurry Love"
By Primrose and Norah

Desire: c.1230, from Old Fr. desirer, from Latin desiderare "to wish for." Its original sense is "to wait for what the stars will bring," from de sidere "from the stars," and sidus (gen. sideris) "heavenly body, star, constellation" (but consider consider). The noun desire, in the sense of lust, is first recorded in c.1340.

Desire may be hot, but nothing about it is necessarily mutual. This sad reality has given rise to so much inflammation of body and soul that we even have words for it. To wit: If you're in love with someone who doesn't love you back, and you persist long after reasonable people have urged you to give up, you are said to be carrying a torch, or torching, for your beloved. See also torch song, torch singer.

[Cue music: "When You Wish Upon a Star" (1940). We sense Jiminy Cricket in the wings, egging us on.]

Those unhappy with the slow progress of their amores would do well to consider (natch) the male Drosophila bifurca, who requires three weeks to make a single sperm; or the giant turtles of the Galapagos Islands, who only reach sexual maturity at the age of forty.

A single erotic encounter between stick insects can last as long as ten weeks, during which the female carries the male around. As he is one-fourth her size, he is no more burdensome than a roomy tote, though the tote may be more useful.

Coitus interruptus: Also known as "being careful" and "getting off at an earlier station"—which does not, of course, exclude getting off, so long as you remember that there is a time and a place for everything.

11. The mystique of older women

"Hello?"

"Lupo! Glad you're up."

It was McKee. You couldn't get the guy in his office for love or money, never mind a pressing dissertation question, but here he was, chirping on the telephone at eight in the goddamn a.-m. on a Sunday. Lupo rolled over, taking the sheet with him.

"There's been another sighting. It's all over the news."

The details were familiar: A housewife saw a flying saucer while driving. "I want you to check it out," McKee said. "Her name's Lola DiMaio. She's in Maple Bay. Give her a call. Tell her you're working for the newspaper. You don't have to say that it's *The Good Five Cent Cigar*."

"Okay." Lupo peeped behind the window shade. Already the sun was high and hot. "I stopped in this week, you know. My thesis—"

"Talk soon, Lupo." McKee hung up.

This wasn't how Lupo had planned to spend the day. But he couldn't afford to piss off McKee. He'd spent the past six years cultivating him. He'd started as a freshman with no interests beyond building radios and reading comic books, and finally, after years of classes and meetings, he had joined the ranks of McKee's graduate students in the astronomy department. McKee had assigned each of them a detail, and it was just Lupo's luck that his was UFOs. You'd think a tenured professor of radio astronomy would be above space aliens, but McKee had developed an interest. As if this stuff weren't absolute hooey. But Lupo knew better than to complain.

They'd only talked strategy once before, standing by the fence one afternoon during McKee's official "office hours," which, by special arrangement with the astronomy department, only took place at McKee's house. In warm weather, McKee met students while watering his begonias as the dolphin splashed and whistled. In the winter, you could shovel the front walk, and afterward, if you were lucky, he'd chat over mugs of hot cocoa in his kitchen.

Lupo had asked McKee for an incentive, something to make Mrs. DiMaio talk.

"If the prospect of getting her name in the *Cigar* isn't enough, you could say that you're doing research for your thesis. Her account could even appear in the *International Journal of Radio Astronomy*." He squirted water along the fenceline in an efficient stream. "She doesn't need to know that I'm the editor. Or that it has a circulation of fifteen. You might get a fellowship, tell her. Or a Nobel Prize. Yes, that's a good one. Definitely tell her that."

Reluctantly Lupo accepted the assignment. A job was a job, and a deferment was something not everyone had. Plus, he couldn't claim he didn't have experience. In addition to attending the meeting where he had met Primrose, he had interviewed several witnesses already. Today's would be like the others, a wife with a husband, children, a mortgage—someone whose responsibilities should have made her more skeptical. She would natter about what space aliens had done—or, he suspected, what she hoped they'd done—to her during the kids' afternoon nap. He would take notes, show polite interest, finish the write-up after lunch. One more day gone, just like that, and still no progress on the dissertation.

On the way to the police station, coming off the road that linked Lupo's neighborhood with the rest of Maple Bay, Lupo pulled over to take a closer look at the place where Mrs. DiMaio claimed to have seen her flying saucer. On the median strip, there was only a thick patch of grass in need of cutting. No scorch marks, no alien goo, nothing. Exactly as he'd expected.

In the station's lot, an officer sat hatless behind the wheel of his squad car, smoothing his buzz cut while peering into the side-view mirror. Lupo kept to the edge of the lot as he headed toward the entrance.

Inside, another cop—older than the first, but with the same buzz cut and distracted demeanor—waved Lupo into a windowless paneled room. A police blotter was on the table beside a phone. "Coke?" he asked Lupo.

"You got Dr Pepper?"

"Who's Dr Pepper?"

"Never mind." Lupo handed him a coin. "Coke's fine."

The jackass cop left, whistling. Lupo scanned the blotter. Fortune was with him: The report he wanted was on the first page. Down the hall, someone bellowed, and then the noise stopped and the quiet was broken only by the rattle of the machine dispensing Cokes. The cop returned with a bottle, which he uncapped with one hand and set on the desk, leaving Lupo to make his next move. Lupo took a deep breath, steeling himself, and dialed the number he'd found beside the entry in the blotter. After two rings, a woman answered.

"Mrs. DiMaio?"

"Who wants to know?"

Following McKee's directions, Lupo posed as a reporter calling about a UFO sighting. He said that that if she would grant him the interview, he would add her story to a piece he was writing about UFOs in Rhode Island.

Something crackled—a flaring match—and Mrs. DiMaio inhaled audibly. As she exhaled, Lupo did, too. Something about his imaginary article took wing in his mind, and he was surprised to hear himself babbling some nonsense about forcing the scientific community to stop discounting eyewitness reports like Mrs. DiMaio's and give the sightings the serious consideration they deserved.

"What you saw in your car must have been terrifying, Mrs. DiMaio," he said, almost believing that what was oozing out of him at this moment was sincerity. "I wouldn't want history to forget you."

Friendlier now, she gave him detailed directions to her house. He knew the area, of course, and could easily imagine what he'd find: a small ranch on a street lined with similar houses, each fronted by young maples planted with the expectation of luxuriant shade in two or three decades, just when the owners would retire to Florida.

Lupo arrived to find the side door open and the screen locked. When he rang the bell, a tow-headed boy and an equally fair girl jostled each other to the doorway, each wanting to be the one to undo the catch. Neither was quite big enough to gain the advantage. The struggle dissolved when Mrs. DiMaio appeared in a rickrack-edged housedress, her platinum hair styled in a motionless bouffant. She cuffed the boy and reached for the girl, who slipped away. The boy followed, wailing.

"My kids," she apologized. "Come in, if you can stand it. I'll warn you," she said over her shoulder as she led him down the hall, "not many can."

In the kitchen, she poured him a cup of coffee, set a spoon on the saucer, and retrieved a container of cream from the fridge. "Milk?"

Lupo smiled. It was so Rhode Island to call cream "milk," understating the richness of the offer, so you could never feel grateful in the right proportion or for the right thing.

She poured the so-called milk.

"Tell me *when*," she said—completely unnecessarily, since she seemed to know exactly when to stop pouring, thank you very much. Lupo sat back, intrigued. He had heard about the mystique of older women. Until now he hadn't believed it. Could it possibly consist in just this grace with the cup, the spoon, the milk?

Lupo set his tape recorder on the table, threaded the uptake reel, and pressed the button. Mrs. DiMaio regarded the machine warily, and Lupo worried that he'd have to shut it off, but he held his tongue, and after a while, she began to speak.

"It was the strangest thing I ever saw. Like an upended gravy boat in the air."

"A gravy boat?"

"As I came over the hill, it flew straight at my car. I pulled over, and a light came shining through the windshield. The light started to move all over me. I felt warm, and embarrassed, as if the light, or whatever it was, *could see through my clothes*."

The wheels on the tape recorder turned and turned. "Then what happened, Mrs. DiMaio?"

"Not a damned thing! The light went away. My radio, which had stopped working, came back on. My whole head was buzzing. I pulled off the ramp and went straight to the police station, where I made my report."

Lupo was about to tell her about the research he was doing for McKee when a thump from the second floor interrupted his train of thought. Mrs. DiMaio looked less concerned than simply annoyed, so he kept his mouth shut. No reason to burden her with McKee's half-baked theories. With those two hooligans underfoot, she had enough problems.

"So I'm not the only one?" Mrs. DiMaio asked.

"No." Lupo shook his head. "You're not."

"And what happened to me happened to the others?"

"Lots of the details are the same. Your story checks out."

Mrs. DiMaio took a deep breath. They exhaled in tandem. He smiled at her, wondering why he'd ever been reluctant to take this assignment. Their spoons went round in their cups.

"I just don't know what I'm going to tell him."

"Him?"

She gestured toward the counter, where a uniformed man stood at attention in a framed photograph tucked among the cereal boxes. Her husband was a Navy doctor, she explained, stationed on a hospital ship. He'd been about to start in private practice when he got called up.

"That's too bad," Lupo said hollowly. Hearing about her husband was like hitting a dead spot on a dance floor. Or maybe it just was that he'd realized he was dancing alone.

She reached for her cigarettes and offered him one. Lupo refused. He didn't smoke.

"It's a dirty habit, I know," she said, lighting up.

The tape recorder sputtered. Lupo toggled the switch until the tape ran smoothly. But before Mrs. DiMaio could resume talking, her children roared into the kitchen. The girl was holding a stick of gum. She cornered her brother near the fridge; he bumped it, hard. His eyes filled.

"When I say, 'Do you want to chew this gum?' you say yes," the girl told him.

"I want to chew this gum," he said, his forehead creased with the effort not to cry.

"No. Do you want to chew this gum?"

"YES."

"Well, today yes means no." She pushed the gum between her lips and chewed hugely. "Too bad."

The boy began to bawl. On the radio, someone said, "You know what they say, Ron: What doesn't kill us makes us free."

Mrs. DiMaio shooed the kids and switched the radio off.

"I'll fix you another coffee, if you want."

Lupo pushed his cup across the table.

12. Schlock

There were no aliens in Manhattan, but there were art galleries, dozens of them, through which Lupo's mother had dragged Lupo while he was still too small for regular school. He spent those long afternoons trotting after her, carrying her immense heavy purse and offering his own warm cheeks as needed to defrost her icy hands. Not to put too fine a point on it: A museum visit was not Lupo's idea of a good time. Not even the prospect of an afternoon with Primrose could offset his dread of wandering around a gallery reading small type off index cards and overhearing predictable arguments about whether Käthe Kollwitz's art was more valuable because it was created under communism or because it was made by a woman. He would have preferred to take Primrose to the observatory to see real stars. But the department of love was not like the department of astronomy, where he was at least on his home turf. When it came to romance, that alien planet, he would have to take what he could get.

Lupo rode the bus up to Calvary Street to collect Primrose for their date. He found the house and mounted the front steps, only somewhat alarmed by the jagged lines crazing the foundation of her house. On the front door, below a row of peek-a-boo windows, a rosary dangled from a nail, along with a gold tusk on a matching chain—added, Lupo supposed, just in case the rosary hadn't covered everything. He rang the bell, and a moment later, Primrose appeared like some hippie genie from an unprepossessing bottle, wearing her dirndl skirt. He smiled despite his anxiety. She had a way of making him dream.

"Come in." She receded into the interior, her skirt's hem fluttering around her calves. "I won't be a minute."

Lupo fumbled with the catch until it lifted. He stepped inside, into the living room where someone in a nurse's uniform—from her age and resemblance to Primrose, it could only be her mother—was stretched out on the sofa with her eyes closed, her stockings balled on the floor beside her white work shoes. Music—an operatic tenor voice singing in a language Lupo did not recognize—issued from a record player in the corner, while a pink conch puckered on the mantel, as if blowing an obscene kiss. On a small table near the door, a set of keys weighted down a stack of leaflets that bore the title, THE INDUSTRIAL WORKERS OF THE WORLD IN THEORY & PRACTICE. Also known as the Wobblies, he remembered from some now-distant history class. How appropriate to find them here, just when he was feeling so wobbly himself.

Primrose reappeared holding a pair of white plastic peas attached to u-shaped loops of wire. Lupo, in his continuing bewilderment, wasn't sure what they were until she hooked them, one at a time, over her earlobes. Earrings were usually too much for a hippie outfit. But on Primrose, they looked just right.

Without opening her eyes, the woman on the couch murmured, "Where are you going?"

Primrose grabbed Lupo's hand and led him out the door, slamming it behind them. The screen door's squeal followed them down the front walk. Lupo frowned.

"Shouldn't we tell her—"

"No." Primrose stopped suddenly, and Lupo stared as she wrapped a stray thread from her skirt's hem around her fingers and broke it off with a quick snap. "Forget her. Let's go."

"I saw Lola DiMaio this morning," Lupo remarked a moment later, slightly breathless from the pace she'd set. It was as if she couldn't get away from that house fast enough. "She thinks she saw a UFO."

"Oh, I've heard about Lola DiMaio," Primrose replied lightly, having seen the news report too. They slowed, picking a path down the uneven sidewalk. The bus stop was still a block away. "She thinks Ho Chi Minh controls the weather."

A sly grin. Grateful for the warmth, Lupo smiled back. Maybe Ho Chi Minh really did control the weather. In a world where a house could stand on a crumbling foundation that was apparently held together by rosary beads and bovine effigies, where a daughter could slam the door on her mother's questions as to her whereabouts of an afternoon with a young man, who could say anything for sure about Ho Chi Minh or the weather?

Primrose, he noted, took care not to step on cracks in the sidewalk. His walk fell in with hers, and he skipped the cracks, too. How charming she was, Miss Loony Tunes.

"Do you think SDS should change the charter? Address this alien nonsense?" Primrose asked, as if to ground them both in some shared reality, no matter how ridiculous.

He stole a glance at her. Was she making fun of him?

"You've got quite a poker face," he said. "I can't tell if you're serious or not."

"Well," she teased, "the details in each sighting *have* been amazingly consistent. It's almost as if there *might* be something going on here."

"Oh, there's definitely something going on." He paused, sensing that he was getting himself in deeper than he should. "I'm sure the new subcommittee will get to the bottom of it."

"Oh, RICUFOG, warehouse of oddballs. I suppose it gets them out of the way. But you'd think they'd be more interested in other things. Civil rights. The war. The bomb."

So she wasn't completely out of it.

"Yeah," Lupo agreed. "With so much else to worry about, why are aliens suddenly so attractive to them? And not only to them."

"It's always easier to think of other things," she said.

The downtown bus came into view. The driver pulled up at the curb, raising a cloud of grit that painted the inside of Lupo's already dry mouth. The doors opened, they stepped inside, the doors shut, and they were off. Lupo paid the fare for them both.

"It does seem weird, this UFO business," Lupo said, settling into the aisle seat of the two-seater she'd chosen. "Maybe it's a kind of popular mythology, no worse than astrology." He shrugged. "But also, no better. When Lola DiMaio sees a flying saucer, she's saying something about her life. About what she's afraid of. It's not just little green men."

McKee wouldn't agree with him—McKee had ideas about the nature of interplanetary travel and the level of civilization required to undertake it—but McKee wasn't here.

"What does she think aliens are going to do? Park a spaceship in her carport? Grow mutant tomatoes in her garden?" Primrose adjusted an earring.

"Something like that."

Primrose shook her head, smiling. "I don't believe you."

"This is a small place, Primrose. Nobody gets out the welcome wagon for folks who aren't from here." He paused, completing the thought in his head: *And I ought to know.*

"What does any of this have to do with astronomy?"

"I don't know. Yet." Although Lupo was tempted to natter about astronomy and McKee, to substitute his teacher's authority for his own, painfully sensed lack thereof, he stuck to the facts. "My dissertation advisor has ideas about UFOs and cosmic rays and dolphin language."

"But you don't."

"I'm more interested in radio astronomy. With modern technology, we can catch many new signals from distant stars. Well, new to us anyway. The stars themselves are as old as time, and the signals are ancient, from light-years away. Did you know the universe is getting bigger?"

"Bigger?"

"Yeah."

"And yet the world gets smaller and smaller," she mused. She didn't seem impressed by his line, which he considered a real killer, about signals from distant stars.

"Also, McKee—my advisor—keeps a dolphin in his swimming pool."

"You mean he's crazy."

Their eyes met, and she held his gaze with an electric intensity despite her disinterest in cosmic radio. His world, for a moment, went entirely to static: station break, no signal.

The bus stopped short. She flew forward, and he grabbed her just before she bumped the seat in front of them. "Thanks," she said.

Lupo kept a hand on her arm, as if maybe he'd forgotten that he put it there.

They reached the downtown plaza, and the bus disgorged them into the street. The museum was a short walk from the bus stop. He followed Primrose, who knew the area better than he did, as she snaked between the city's tall buildings and up the broad leafy thoroughfare to College Hill. Outside the museum, a small crowd had gathered, waiting for the doors to open for a talk on "The Maps of the Ancient Sea Kings," scheduled for that afternoon in one of the galleries devoted to ancient art. Some kind of clockwork device had recently been recovered from an old shipwreck off the coast of a Greek island, and a professor of engineering from the University of Rhode Island—someone he'd not heard of, with a foreign name, heavy on the consonants—was on hand to explain the find.

Primrose pulled Lupo toward a second, less obvious entrance at the side of the building. The door was open, and as no one was on hand to sell them tickets, they made their own way deeper into the building until they reached the modern art wing.

"This way," Primrose said, and presently they found the Kollwitz show. According to the leaflet, the curator was inspired by sketches she had done when her children were still small. The end of the nineteenth century was, apparently, a desolate time— if not for art, then at least for the artist. Primrose and Lupo stood before a sketch of a woman and five men at the edge of a grave. One man had threaded his arm through the woman's, and he was pointing with a thick finger at the corpse.

"What do you think?" Primrose asked.

"It's too doctrinaire for me," he admitted. "Not that my taste is anything to take seriously."

"I get the sense that these people are trying to explain this terrible thing to each other," Primrose said. "Maybe a little stridency is in order."

"Maybe." He wasn't convinced.

"Maybe," she scoffed. "Well, at least they're not fighting a war."

"But they are. Or were." Lupo showed Primrose the paragraph in the leaflet that explained Kollwitz's obsession with her subject. She had lost a son in the first world war, the leaflet said, and a grandson in the second. To Primrose, the exhibit's title, *Käthe Kollwitz: Sentimental Realism*, suddenly seemed maliciously apt. What a stupidity, to have an aesthetic—or worse, a sentimental—response to war, the one thing on everyone's minds these days anyway. And no one was sentimental about that. Yet they, like Kollwitz, seemed powerless in the face of it. All the big decisions were made elsewhere. No one could do more than Kollwitz had done; yet her earnest and intensive effort had produced such meager results. It was all schlock. Why hadn't she noticed it before? She bit her lip.

"I'm sure you saw better shows all the time in New York."

"I liked the planetarium, actually."

For a moment he was himself again, but younger, in a school jacket and tie, taking in views of the night sky in a darkened domed room while his mother trailed behind him, for a change, and so pretty in her stylish suit, her string of pearls. Being with Primrose was like that—she had the same glamour, unmistakable as a perfume.

He touched her arm, guiding her to the next room. The curator had titled this part of the exhibit "Small Oils."

"What a euphemism," Primrose muttered as they passed the sign. "They might as well say it outright."

"Say what?"

"What they mean. Minor art."

They stopped before a rough oil sketch of a woman in what appeared to be a shroud. Her eyes were closed, and her arms were crossed in front of her.

"Is she dead?" Primrose wondered, twisting one of her earrings. "Oh, Lupo. I'm afraid this whole trip has been a bust."

"I can't say my expectations were very high."

"Mine were, I guess."

He cleared his throat. A few minutes' worth of hand-holding was not enough and never would be. If he wanted to get anywhere with Primrose, he needed to do something. Fast.

"Rosemary Garrity's having one of her parties next week," he blurted. "You should come."

It seemed to him then that Primrose's tractor-beam stare had weakened, and was now suffused less with powerful gravitons than with ordinary, sad pity. Of course, *of course,* she would not come.

"Next time," she said suddenly, with a broad smile, "we'll go to the planetarium."

He was so surprised, he laughed out loud.

But the guilt. She could not outrun, outwit, outsmile *that.*

When they circled back to the lobby, Primrose excused herself and headed for the toilets. They were dark, and Primrose fumbled with the lock before giving up and pushing one foot against the door. As she washed her hands, she made a fast ugly face in the dark mirror.

"*Facciabrutta,*" she told her reflection.

The terrible face stayed in the mirror. Worse, its mouth gaped wide open. The canines elongated, becoming tusks.

From one of the stalls, a woman stage-whispered, "Masturbating!"

Primrose fled, only to stumble right into Lupo as he emerged from the men's room on the other side of the hall.

"Let's walk," Lupo suggested. "You look like you could use some air."

Lupo offered his arm, and she took it gratefully. This was just how it started last time, when she wound up in the hospital—strange sights in the mirror, strange words in her mind. She tried to forget what she saw, as Dr. Addleman recommended: "You are not to give these emanations more attention than they deserve. They are the products of your diseased brain." Her father had put the same point differently: "Your mind plays tricks." That's all it was, just a little trick, a game she played on herself, without knowing it.

And if you believe that— This was a different voice, skeptical, perhaps sane.

Or it was another trick. It was hard to tell sometimes.

She gripped Lupo's arm as they headed toward the park. Leaves blew upward on their branches, silvering the trees against a dense white sky. They detoured into a shop where Lupo purchased an umbrella.

When they arrived at the park, Lupo steered them past the children's center. The kids were out, their buttoned raincoats shining as they swung from the monkey bars and jockeyed to see who would be first down the slide. Their shrieks rent the air.

On a path fringed with blooming lilacs, Primrose paused to sniff a blossom. Petals fell all around. As she closed one hand around a blossom, she saw, as if in a dream, a child's plump hand sliding fingerpaint across slick paper. Maybe her father was right; maybe teaching kindergarten was what she was here on Earth to do. She tried to imagine Käthe Kollwitz minding children, washing curtains, curling her mother's hair, and keeping the household accounts, all the while also secretly trying to put marks on paper in a way that became something more than just, well, marks on paper. It couldn't have been easy, she had to admit. Louise's task list was still taped to the fridge at home, pricking her with guilt every time she fetched a beer for her father.

Lupo was humming a song she didn't recognize. There was a lot about Lupo she didn't recognize. She let go of his arm, guiltily forcing herself to wonder how Tino's afternoon was going. He'd taken his father's advice and was caddying at his father's club. What was it called? Oh, yes, now she remembered: The Matterhorn. He was out there carrying bags in all weather, bearing with the lousy tips and the insults.

Lupo plucked a lilac and tucked it behind her ear. She smiled at him, making the expected gesture. "You are rather beautiful, you know," he said nervously. On some level, he knew, she was already fading from him, already gone.

"Oh!" Primrose wobbled, and there was a snap as the heel of her shoe broke off. Lupo reached to steady her. Wincing, she picked up the busted shoe and brushed the gravel from her heel.

The road ended in a park with a stream crossed by a wooden bridge. Beneath it, orange koi jostled each other, their thick-rimmed white mouths like rolled-up condoms. Primrose gasped. The fish dispersed. Lupo asked if he could carry her shoes, and she handed them over without a word.

In a narrow passage set between rows of lilacs, wet branches scraped her face. A curl of her hair escaped her ponytail and fell over her nose. The errant curl smelled of lilacs.

In her mind, Louise hectored her: *This is not how nice girls behave*. Another voice, harder, foreign: *Facciabrutta*. The world was full of *scratch* and *tear*, of hurt that swelled until it burst in her mind like fireworks and the ash rained down as salt that burned and stank like her mother's My Sin.

She stopped. *Whose* sin?

"Hey!" Lupo pulled her awkwardly to the edge of the lawn and flopped down, sliding his feet from his loafers. He seemed so harmless, sitting there peeling his socks from his feet.

She closed her eyes and sank down beside him. Her breath came in little sucks of air. He smelled faintly of laundry soap, a homey, well-cared-for smell that immediately doused her mental fireworks, so much roar and flame.

"I bet you do a lot of laundry," she mumbled into his fragrant neck.

"We have washers nowadays," he said, stroking her hair. "The work involved is very minimal."

Admire him, she reminded herself, remembering an article she'd seen in *Redbook*. *Make him feel like he's in charge.* "Tell me what you do for McKee. Your UFO hunter."

He pressed her hand to his cheek. She was warm and solid, and so long as he didn't look into her eyes, he guessed that he was probably doing fine. For now, anyway.

"Well, it's complicated," he said. "Stuff comes into the atmosphere, our instruments pick it up. But the instruments are dumb, and the universe is noisy. Someone has to sort the signals from the noise."

"You mean, those are real signals? Messages? That someone sent?"

"Now you sound just like McKee."

"There are worse things, I guess."

"You guess." He smiled. "I really don't think anyone's sending signals. Things like cosmic rays just rain down, leaving traces for us to pick up. The universe is full of stuff like that."

"How much do you really care about this stuff?" she asked. It was hard to imagine what any of it had to do with anything she might know about. Her mother, for instance. Husbands. Tino. Sex. "It seems kind of irrelevant to ordinary life."

"Nothing's more relevant than the truth, which is what science aims to find out."

Primrose took his hand and turned it over, examining the fine fingers, the tendons and ligaments that stood out in relief. She could see him at work, turning a dial on a machine that spied on the stars; she saw the same fingers on her breasts, between her legs. Her blood whacked in her temples. This was not covered in Ovid. *I should end this now,* she thought, *before anything else happens. Before it's too late.*

"Are you going to marry him?" he asked suddenly. Nothing was more relevant than the truth.

"Lupo," she said. "I'm here now with *you*."

"*Are* you? I don't want any be-here-now bullshit."

"Yes," she answered, confused. Why was he angry? "I really am here right now with you."

"That's not what I meant."

"If you *must* know," Primrose said tightly, "Tino hasn't asked."

"He's just spinning his wheels," Lupo said, more to the sky than to Primrose, or so it seemed to her. "Come on, Prim. What are *you* doing with your life? You can't just waste it, hanging around Knightsville—"

"Silver Lake," she corrected him. "I'm from Silver Lake."

"Right," he said. "You still haven't answered my question."

She glanced at him. It wasn't good to wear your ambitions on your sleeve, especially if the ambitions were grand and the sleeve only homespun—and, in her case, raveled and twitching from a recent infusion of haloperidol. Besides, they'd just been to a museum where a woman's work was on full and humiliating display, its minority, its sheer *littleness,* pointed out for all to see. You'd have to be a moron to imagine the curator meant to celebrate the work of a major artist and not merely to point a bemused finger at some twee curiosity. If she told Lupo the truth, would he sneer at her, too?

"I suppose I could paint," she said finally.

"Sure, you could paint. You could also get a degree."

He wouldn't sneer, but he would give her an argument. Unsure which response was worse, she swept a stray lilac blossom from her skirt.

"I *am* getting a degree, Lupo. I can't go to school *and* work to pay for it *and* clean the house *and* have babies."

"Forget cleaning. Forget babies. Apply for a scholarship. Or is that too revolutionary a thought?"

"Let's go," she said, getting up. She took her shoes back, wondering who was the bigger kook, her or Lupo.

She hurried to the edge of the lawn. Lupo followed, lifting his umbrella over them both. The rain had started again. "What just happened back there?"

"I'm sorry," she said reflexively.

"*I'm* sorry."

Primrose limped beside him, so close he could feel the warmth of her. Her shoes swung uselessly from her hand. "How about *your* mother, Lupo? How does she manage?"

"Mom works in her garden. She reads. She doesn't clean or cook. She says these are jobs best left to the professionals."

"My mother cleaned houses before she got her hospital job," Primrose said. Louise had also worked, for a time, at Reliable Button, but Primrose didn't feel like mentioning that. It seemed even less respectable than housecleaning, to have your mother work for your boyfriend's father. "She'd tell stories about what she'd seen in the medicine chest. Sometimes she came home with cast-off things."

Sometimes, she didn't say, her mother made her wear them.

Lupo flushed, a tender pink spot at the center of each cheek, as if he felt called out by this difference between them, implicated in her private struggle.

Oh, God. Somehow he had come very close.

"How about your father?" she asked, to change the subject.

"He's a teacher. A socialist sociologist with a quantitative bent and plenty of opinions," Lupo said, talking fast around his discomfort. He wasn't proud of what his father had done. "He lost his job at Rutgers, in the math department, for shooting his mouth off. That's the reason we're in Rhode Island. Or one of them anyway. My mother has family here. She wants to reconnect with her roots, as she puts it."

"Your mother's from here?" Primrose hadn't expected that.

"Born and raised. She left after high school, went to Queens College to study acting in between auditions for the Rockettes. Then she met my father."

"So much for her career on the stage."

He shrugged. "She's not a serious person."

Neither am I, Primrose thought, though it was clear that Lupo had given her the benefit of the doubt in this regard. So far anyway.

"What does your father think of having someone come in to clean? I mean, with him being a socialist and all." She glanced at him, wondering if she'd gone too far.

Lupo replied easily, "I'm not sure he does think of it. Frankly, Mom needs the help. My father doesn't even know how the stove works."

They crossed the street. St. Mary's bell tower loomed over them; beyond it stretched the cemetery where Poppa Tavio was buried. A jagged flash ripped the sky, and Primrose's mind again flew to Tino. If he was still on the course, he'd be soaked. He might get hit by lightning. Not that she was wishing for it. Was she? Primrose sniffled again, feeling silly and ashamed, and wiped her nose with the back of her hand.

"I think I'm coming down with something."

"Whatever it is, I hope it's contagious," Lupo said, adjusting the umbrella so it covered Primrose more fully. "I don't mind having what you're having. But the only thing coming down now is the rain."

Past the church, the sidewalk dissolved to sand and broken glass. Primrose and Lupo exchanged looks. She couldn't walk over that mess; even going around it, she would probably get cut. Lupo handed her the umbrella. Then, without a word, as if it were the most natural thing in the world, he picked her up and carried her. When she looked at him to be sure everything was okay, he kissed her. Her tongue found his, and it got worse. Honks and wolf whistles. A man leaned out of his car window and bellowed AH-OOH-GAH as he whizzed by.

Primrose broke the kiss.

"That," she gasped, "was nice."

But what she thought was: *Puttana*.

Setting her down, Lupo spoke quietly. "Come with me to Rosemary's."

In the agony columns of *Redbook*, cheating was always a disaster. But might it not also be the opportunity of a lifetime? Maybe Lupo, not Tino, was *the one*, was *her ticket*. She could learn about astronomy. She could talk with Lupo about mathematics, about computer programs and cosmic rays. It would probably be better than eating chocolates and bickering with Lorraine Battuta. As for Tino—well, maybe Lupo was right. Maybe he really was just spinning his wheels, waiting for something better to turn up.

"Okay," she said. "I'd like that."

Lupo waited with her until the bus arrived. Primrose took a seat behind a fogged window. As the bus pulled away, she rubbed a clear patch in the glass. Lupo was still there, watching her go.

The ride back to Calvary Street seemed to take just moments. A mystery there, how an afternoon with someone special—new— could change your perspective. Lupo would probably say that their date had made a shift in the local spacetime, as if their being together could change the forces of nature. Strange how Lupo's voice was already in her head.

At home Primrose locked herself in the bathroom, filled the tub, and piled her clothes on the floor. A handful of lilac petals swirled on the surface of the water. She sank down after them, letting the water close over her head, and came up with a rushing exhale. One day she too would be a swirl—silicon, atoms, stardust. Tino, too. And Lupo. In the grand scheme of things, what difference did a kiss make?

The petals stuck on the tub walls, buoyed up on waves made by her breathing.

"Helloooo..." Her father's voice floated in.

"I'll be out in a minute, Dad."

THE BOOK OF LOVE: Dating Tips

By Primrose and Norah

You & me

Sittin' in a tree

K-I-S-S-I-N-G!

1. On a date, sit close. Pressed against him, you will easily compel him to acquiesce to your plans for the evening. Cat got your tongue? Say whatever people generally do say on such occasions. "The boxers are entering the ring," you might observe. It is important that the ambiguity remain unmarked: You both are and are not talking about his shorts. "Who's your favorite?" Whatever he says, reply: "Me, too."

2. If a speck of dust lands on his letter sweater, flick it off; if nothing's there, flick it off just the same. The idea is to show that you're paying attention.

3. While you might not get a yes to every invitation, everyone likes to be asked. If you scatter your Pez freely upon the waters, your Happy Face dispenser will never be empty.

4. Unexpected meetings may be managed as follows: Start a conversation on a subject that makes him feel like an expert: baseball, car engines, the possibility of intelligent life on Mars. Ask open-ended questions. Smile. He'll never notice your lack of makeup or your messy hair.

5. Don't let him go to the drive-in without you being there to admire him in all his masculine glory. Usually, if he's shaved and brushed his teeth, that's glory enough, or ought to be.

6. If, as they say, "faint heart never won fair lady," the same is true for fair gentleman: Poltroons of either sex are useless in love's service. If you've arranged to meet, arrive well before the appointed time. No wheels? Hoof it. Nothing should stop you—not rain, not your mother, not your insecurities, *nothing*!

7. We are not so moralistic as to condemn you to only one boyfriend. Just be discreet. People have trouble enough finding one person to love. Now here you are, enjoying the attentions of *two*. Of *course* you will provoke envy if you parade your luck. Go further in your discretion by varying the time and place of your assignations. If you get caught, deny everything and don't despair. Jealousy is the cayenne pepper of love: just a dash makes everything hotter.

8. Your lover has no defects. If you cannot convince yourself on this point, lower your standards—or find a different lover, someone you can admire freely. Dote. Pay compliments. And promise, promise, promise. Hope, duly fostered, holds out a long time.

9. Dim the lights. You know why. Like Saint Theresa, may we all be Pierced by Grace.

PART 2: SUMMER 1967

13. Spin cycle

"Tighter," Louise demanded. "You didn't roll them tight enough last time, and the whole thing came down just as I was emptying a goddamned bedpan."

"You and your bedpans," Primrose sighed, rummaging in the box for a smaller clip. Louise peered into her hand mirror, tweezers held aloft, menacing her chin.

"Pretty is easy when you're young. Then you get old, and it's work. Gotcha." Louise plucked the hair, wiped the tweezers with a tissue, and considered the result, a thick black filament. Satisfied, she returned to canvassing her chin for more unrulies. "I know you don't believe me now, Primrose, but just wait. Someday you'll have a hairy chin. Your boobs will fall down to your knees."

"Ma!"

"It's true." Louise set her tweezers down and lit a cigarette. "Your body betrays you. Your beautiful, innocent, *untouched* body."

Primrose re-rolled the troublesome curl and pinned it tightly. *Puttana, puttana.* Ever since her date with Lupo, the word had clanged in her mind. She'd begun to think the only relief might be to allow the word to tumble from her mouth and let her mother do her worst. But then the whole world would know what she had done with Lupo in the middle of Cranston Street while Tino was humiliating himself, caddying in the rain. Not to mention what she might do tonight, with Lupo, at Rosemary Garrity's. *Puttana.*

On the phone earlier, when Tino had asked about her plans, she told him she was going to an SDS meeting. "Those people?" he'd scoffed. She had no answer for him. She had considered telling him she was going to a meeting of RICUFOG, but if Tino strained at her lie about SDS, surely he would choke on one about a committee to deal with the status of space aliens in the charter. One problem with lying was the need to be good at it, to think through all the possibilities suggested by the reality you were manufacturing. Being organized enough to lie effectively was a lot of work.

She glanced at the clock. Soon it would be time to get the laundry. Economizing, she'd stuffed a week's worth of washing, including the uniform Louise needed for her shift, into a single dryer in the laundromat. The odds were about even that the whole load would dry. It was a risk, but she was running too late not to take it. Assuming her successful retrieval of a clean and dry uniform from the laundromat, Primrose expected to arrive at Rosemary's at seven, which meant she needed to be at the bus stop by six-thirty if she wanted to be on time. What she was doing with Lupo couldn't even be called a date, not technically, and certainly not now that she had coaxed Norah into joining them.

Louise's record spun on the turntable: *Ave Maria...* How awful, Christmas music at this time of year. When would her mother—

Primrose's stomach turned. Her mouth filled with spit. She ran to the bathroom.

"Primrose?"

She retched, bringing up a thin stream of yellow goo. The shadow in her mind shifted position, threatening. She took breaths, reminding herself to be calm. It was important to remain calm—so she'd been told, over and over. Her period was late, but it had never been regular. She opened the tap and splashed cold water on her face.

"Primrose!" Her mother thumped the door.

"I'm fine!"

"You're fine, you're fine," her mother mocked. "You don't sound fine."

The overhead light hummed. Primrose tucked her head between her knees to still all the world's turning, starting with her mother's stupid record player and its songs out of season. On the tile was a copy of *Redbook*. In need of a distraction, she picked it up and began to read.

Women's magazines were so confusing. You were supposed to avoid being a *puttana* until you got married, at which point all you did was try to *puttanize* yourself by following advice from magazines—how to apply makeup, what to do when your husband says he's bored. Did Lupo's mother read this stuff? Mrs. Battuta surely did not. In the rare moments when she was sitting, she was usually busy with something else—mending, cutting coupons, organizing the recipe box.

The nausea passed. Louise banged on the door again. Primrose opened it to find Louise standing before her in her slip, loops of her hair hanging down to remind Primrose of exactly where and how she had failed to roll anything tight enough.

"What kind of daughter locks the door on her mother?"

"Sorry." Primrose edged into the hallway, using the *Redbook* as a shield. "It must be the heat."

"Oh, the heat," Louise scoffed. "The *heat*."

Her mother followed her to the kitchen where the remaining rollers had cooled in their tray. Primrose pulled out the plug and put it back in again.

"Shit," Louise said.

"They'll warm up in a minute, Ma. You won't be late."

"It's not the time I'm worried about," Louise muttered. She resumed her place at the table, lit another cigarette, and directed a gimlet stare at Primrose. "Is there something I should know? It's not right to keep things from your mother."

"I'm fine, Mom." Sixty seconds until the curlers were warm. Fifty-five.

"So you're just fine, are you? Well, if you say so, Primrose."

"I do," Primrose said quietly. With a fingertip she touched a roller: lukewarm. Forty-five seconds. "I do say so."

The phone rang. Louise lifted the receiver and shouldered it against her neck. "Hazel!"

Hazel was a union big shot who worked with Louise. They didn't always see eye to eye. Even so, it didn't do to lose friends on account of politics. Thus it was writ, in the Book of Louise.

Hazel squawked, loud and fast. Mandatory overtime was her latest cause; she wanted to pressure the hospital to expand their full-time staff instead of pushing extra work on employees with forty-hour commitments already. Where was the extra work coming from? The VA hospital's roof had partially collapsed in a storm, and so the VA had to send its patients to area hospitals. Howard took the psychiatric cases, boys who'd been deployed and come back raving. Louise had attended one disastrous meeting where the nurse's aides had shouted at the hospital's administrators; they responded by shifting the ablest aides to another ward, leaving Louise's with the newcomers and the jerks. That was Louise's first union meeting. Afterward, over a jelly glass of Four Roses, she vowed to Frank that it would be her last. But she still took Hazel's calls, and Primrose knew why: They made her mother feel important.

"Calm down, Hazel." Louise swung her foot, taking agitated puffs on her cigarette. "Remember, you're on a party line."

At last the rollers were hot. Primrose plucked one from the tray. Louise leaned back, waving her cigarette.

"That's exactly right, Hazel. They've got no right telling us how much is too much, how much is enough."

No matter how carefully Primrose rolled it, her mother's hair kept slipping around the curler.

"Hold still, Mom!"

Louise ignored her. "The only way we're going to get them by the throat, Hazel, is by walking out. I just don't think it's worth it for this particular problem."

"You didn't say *why* your union wants management by the throat," Primrose interrupted.

"Little pitchers," Louise remarked to Hazel before putting her hand over the receiver. "I almost forgot you were here. Finish up, Primrose. I've got places to go, people to see."

"Forget I'm here," Primrose told her. Another copy of *Redbook* lay splayed on the table, opened to the horoscopes.

Peering over her mother's shoulder, Primrose checked the news for her sign. *Someone will do you a good turn, but beware of false friends.*

"Don't you dare sulk at me."

"I'm not sulking! My stomach's funny, that's all."

Louise sniffed, skeptical. "Well, if you must be a Nosy Parker—"

"I'm not, Ma. I swear."

"It's the *Negroes*," she continued. "The hospital's been hiring them without the union's say-so."

"Oh," Primrose said around a fingertip she was sucking, having burned herself on a hot roller. "The *Negroes*."

Whenever her mother got to talking about the *Negroes*, she always sounded dumb. As if the word were not a euphemism, as if the knife it concealed could not clearly be seen, glinting through the threadbare fabric of her words. But then Louise's mind was like that, a wide drawer full of knives.

Louise shook her head, ridding herself of some sharp-edged thought, and Primrose heard the clatter between her own ears.

"Of course they're short-staffed, Hazel. But if they're short, it seems the hospital has a right to bring new people in. Now, I know everyone who works there has to be part of the union. That's the rule. The union gets us and gives back a no-strike promise. But now that they're hiring *those people*, we're going to break our promise—is that right, Hazel?"

Primrose cleared her throat. Those people? Louise talked as if Norah had not been Primrose's best friend since forever; as if she had not herself learned to make *pastéis* from Mrs. Thomas, who was glad to translate the recipe from her mother's cookbook, carried from Santa Catarina do Fogo; as if Norah's father had not been forced from a job not so different from Louise's, just because his union could not, in the end, accept a Black man. Had Louise even noticed these contradictions?

"They can't be blamed for taking the work. I'd do just the same if I had to. As for the members, well, you won't be surprised to hear it, Hazel. The members don't like it one bit. 'They can start their own,' they say, and they strike to keep the place ours.

Meaning, theirs. Except it isn't theirs. It's a state hospital. Which means one thing: It belongs to the state."

"Which includes *them*," Primrose blurted, irritated. "*Those* people."

"Ouch, Primrose!" Louise gripped Primrose's wrist. "Not so tight!"

Hazel's voice rose, but Louise interrupted her. "Now listen up, Hazel. If we strike, you know what they'll do, don't you? They'll fire us all. Starting with the aides. And they'll call in the Reserves." Louise paused. "That's right. You heard me. The Army National Guard and its capital-R Reserves."

Hazel expostulated long and hard in response to this point. When she ran out of steam, Louise ended the call.

"I might not have the words exactly right," Louise told Primrose, "but Hazel knows what I'm talking about." She patted her curlers thoughtfully. "If they do bring in the Guard, at least those boys won't have to go fighting in that stupid war."

"Could that really happen, Ma?"

"It's an ill wind, Primrose, that does no one any good. Anything could happen is what I'm trying to tell you. But listen. You don't have to hitch your wagon to that Battuta boy."

Knowing this riff by heart, Primrose attempted to forestall another recitation. "We've been over this, Ma."

"You'd be better off getting a job, if you ask me."

"I haven't asked you." Primrose snapped the curler set closed and yanked the plug from the wall.

"Excuse *me,* Primrose, for telling *you* what to do." Louise stretched a net over her curlers and made her way to the bathroom. "But what the hell do I know?" she cried out at the threshold. "I'm just your mother!"

Primrose flopped onto the horsehair couch, the upholstery tickling her bare calves. From one perspective, her mother was right. Anything *could* happen. She didn't owe Tino anything. Her own life was not laid out in advance like a fairy tale or a story in *Redbook*. But then she wasn't like Norah, who had always been busy and active, always the girl with the plan—to study Classics at Pembroke, to teach Latin in a high school like theirs. What a task it was to turn an ambition into a reality—Norah's light often burned all night, and she had always looked wan and exhausted the next morning at the bus stop. Primrose played the sidekick, happy—or so she thought—to let her life take the course she expected, from love to marriage and the baby carriage. Which now seemed to be rolling straight down Unaconicut Hill. At a certain point, there'd be no jumping out. Wasn't that what she wanted? Shouldn't she want something more, something else, somewhere else? A line came to her from the *Kama Sutra*: *When the wheel of ecstasy is in motion, there is no order.*

Well, it beat *Redbook*. She hoped the clothes were dry.

14. Wild nights, wild nights

The Pocasset Avenue bus lurched through the rush-hour traffic. Nauseated again, Primrose nibbled a saltine from the sleeve she'd stashed in her bag. Her raincoat didn't fit as well as it used to, and because she was unable to locate her umbrella, she had been forced to knot one of her mother's plastic kerchiefs under her chin. She saw her dowdy reflection and regretted caving to her mother's pressure to cover her head. At least the clothes had been dry, and nothing had needed ironing. Yet for all her haste, the bus was now stuck in traffic. She sighed, brushing cracker crumbs from her lap. Effort so infrequently availed.

Norah was waiting at the library stop, her trench coat neatly belted at her waist. She stepped onto the bus and paid her fare, exact change. She glanced down the rows, and Primrose waved, moving over to make room. A woman with her hair pulled back into a kerchief cut her eyes at the two of them, and Primrose squelched an urge to spit. But Norah just smiled and said amiably, "Some weather we're having, isn't it?"

The woman scowled. The bus rounded another corner and headed toward the baseball field. The clouds broke, and a beam of late sunshine illuminated the pitcher's mound. The woman in the kerchief got off at the next stop. "Bye now," Norah cried after her.

"Bet she won't take this route again," Primrose said.

"More room for us. So who's coming tonight? Besides your *secret beau*."

"Some people from art class, I think," Primrose said uncomfortably, hoping Norah wasn't going to razz her all night about Lupo. "You'll keep this thing quiet, right? I don't know what's happening with Lupo. It might be nothing."

"You don't owe either of them anything. You know that, don't you?"

Them: Tino, Lupo. Her mother had made a similar point earlier. "I keep hearing this."

"So you do know."

Primrose sighed.

"What's Rosemary like?" Norah asked after a moment.

Relieved to field a question she could answer, Primrose responded, "She's been painting practically since she could hold a brush. She was in a group show last summer."

"What's she doing in your class if she's that good? I thought you were only taking intro courses."

"I am. She takes everything Joseph teaches, even if it's introductory."

"She's a disciple, then. Which would make him a guru, like they have on *the Coast*." She grinned, playing with the mythic sound of the place, the heavy landing it made in conversation. "Who knew this could happen right here on Calvary Street?"

Primrose shrugged. The relationship between Joseph and Rosemary was something she never questioned. They simply seemed good together, and the precise configuration—teacher-student, guru-disciple—didn't bother her. You could meet a husband anywhere, which was why you had to wear makeup everywhere. Thus it was writ, in the *Book of Red*.

"Is she any good? I mean, as a painter."

"Well, she had that show. Joseph lets her paint whatever she wants, which means he trusts her judgment." Primrose added in her fake Louise voice: "And that is a privilege not granted to many in this life."

"Maybe Rosemary is just a pain in the ass." Norah frowned, looking at her with a fresh intensity. "Are you all right?"

Primrose gripped the seat ahead of her. She trained her eyes on her knuckles as they went from white to pink and back again. It made her feel less nauseous to concentrate on that one thing. After a moment, the feeling passed. "It's okay," she said to Norah. "You can unfurrow your brow. I'm fine."

Norah didn't look convinced. But the bus squealed around a corner, and Rosemary's house appeared, a beige triple-decker ringed by a chain link fence. Primrose pulled the cord to signal a stop. Rosemary's street didn't look particularly different from theirs. It had the same triple-deckers, the same ruined sidewalks. A tall pine had dropped a dense carpet of needles near Rosemary's gate.

They came up the front walk, and Norah rang the bell. Someone pounded down the staircase, and the front door whipped open. Barefoot and wrapped in a towel, Rosemary stood before them, her hair slicked back wet. "Primrose!"

Primrose introduced her to Norah, to whom Rosemary held out one plump, damp hand while holding her towel up with the other. Norah did her part with the handshake, and Rosemary urged them both inside, apparently unconcerned that anyone might see her half-naked from the street. As they followed her up the narrow staircase, Primrose noticed a tattoo comet streaked across her right ankle.

The apartment, on the top floor, consisted of a single large room divided by a screen printed with an image of Mount Fuji. Rosemary took their coats and draped them over the top of a folded futon, then disappeared behind the screen. "Be right back," she told them. "Make yourselves at home."

In addition to the futon, the room was furnished with two sofas in mismatched chintz, a coffee table, and a record player. Cushions were piled on the floor beside a milk crate holding LPs. Thumbtacked to the walls were Klimt prints whose yellows and oranges matched the drips and blobs of paint spattered on the floor. Joseph said Rosemary used color "like a decorator," for "accents." That was his one big criticism of her work.

"Imagine," Norah whispered. "No parents. No curfew!"

The towel flew out over the top of Mount Fuji. A minute later Rosemary emerged wearing a pair of bell-bottom dungarees and a thin red T-shirt that announced *Je t'aime.*

"You've got a nice place," Norah said.

"Thanks. The light's great for work."

"Work where?" Primrose didn't see any paintings around, though the smells of turpentine and linseed oil were strong, and the paint on the floor was surely evidence of something.

"Out here." Rosemary made a gesture that encompassed the room. "I keep the canvases in the back stairway. My finished stuff bores me. The unfinished stuff is too depressing to look at all the time. Joseph, come meet Primrose and Norah!"

A lanky man, barefoot like Rosemary, with dark hair hanging thickly over the collar of his frayed button-down, emerged from behind the screen bearing martini glasses and a pitcher on a tray. As he poured their drinks, Primrose slipped her feet from her shoes. The chintz sofas were deep and soft. She took the brimming glass that Joseph offered, and Rosemary passed her a bowl of shiny green olives. Primrose took one and handed the bowl to Norah, who set the bowl down without taking any.

"I brine them in vermouth," Rosemary said. "Aren't they delicious?"

They were, in fact, delicious—like they'd been soaking in snow water and pine needles. The martini tasted like this, too. Soothed by the booze and Rosemary's chatter, Primrose's nausea receded. The bell rang, and Rosemary jumped up to answer it. She returned with Lupo, who stood awkwardly by the coat-piled futon clutching a bouquet of daisies.

Primrose stood, thinking the flowers were for her. Really, he was only too thoughtful.

But Lupo only pressed her hand and passed the bouquet to Rosemary. "I'm getting too old to show up to dinner parties empty-handed," he explained.

"They're perfect," Rosemary gushed. "Excuse me while I find a vahhhse."

Primrose sank back into the sofa, her cheeks hot. How could she have been so stupid about the destination of Lupo's flowers? The martini had gone straight to her head.

On the sofa's other end, Joseph pushed a box of toothpicks toward Norah, who attempted to spear an olive. Every time it slipped away, they both quaked with laughter.

A pang of longing shot through Primrose: *Tino.*

Lupo perched, straight-backed, on the sofa's edge, as if unwilling to give in to the cushions. He seemed confused and out of place, the only person present who was either too square or too wound up to remove his jacket. Moved by his awkwardness, and having decided to forgive him for the flowers, Primrose slipped to the floor and leaned against his leg. He pressed her shoulder. That was when Norah broke off her tête-à-tête with Joseph and coolly introduced herself to Lupo.

"I've heard so many wonderful things about you," he said.

Narrowing her eyes, Norah passed him the olives.

Rosemary reappeared carrying Lupo's daisies in a jug, along with a plastic tub of port-wine cheese and a plate of crackers. Everything was arranged on a red lacquer tray that, but for a few scratches, would not have been out of place in Mrs. Battuta's breakfront. To make room on the coffee table, Lupo pushed aside a stack of dog-eared paperbacks. Primrose caught sight of a few of the titles: *Ti Ho Sposato per Allegria*, which had just been released as a movie, *The Tin Drum*, *The Carpetbaggers*.

"Total trash," Rosemary remarked of the last one. The cover sported an illustration of a blonde with deep cleavage. She picked it up and handed it to Primrose. "Want to borrow it?"

Primrose shook her head. There was no way she could borrow Rosemary's racy book.

"Her mother will have a conniption just looking at it," Norah said.

"True," said Primrose.

"As well she should." With her legs curled beneath herself Rosemary smiled slyly at Primrose, who buried her reddening face in her martini. Would the whole night be this mortifying? Primrose took a big sip and set the glass on the table. There were no coasters, and from the rings on the tabletop, Primrose gathered that Rosemary was not fussy in this aspect of her housekeeping. Neither was Louise, who soon would be waiting up, her icy glass sweating a fresh ring into the coffee table at home.

Primrose hadn't told her mother about the party. This crowd wasn't like Tino's friends or his fancy family, but she was still sure her mother would not approve. Which was one reason she was there in the first place. It was like SDS, a secret realm where she felt like she might possibly, for once, get free of her mother.

The room darkened, and they talked of stupid things: course requirements, professors, classes. Rosemary brought out an armful of candles—the kind that came in glass cylinders adorned with pictures of the Virgin Mary and all the saints—and Joseph lit them with his Zippo. He extracted a joint from his pocket and lit that too. He took a hit, as did Lupo. He offered it to Norah, who shook her head, *no*. Joseph went to the record player and selected an album, Dave Brubeck's *Take Five*. No one objected, though Rosemary said she was having a hard time getting enthusiastic about Brubeck lately.

"He's so square," she complained.

"Speak for yourself," Joseph teased, cuing up the record.

The room filled with modest, reticent sound: a brush on cymbals, a breath insinuated through a horn. Tino often played the same record for Primrose in the Battutas' living room; usually his mother would interrupt to express her disappointment that Tino had failed to keep up with his piano.

Reaching for a cracker, Lupo touched her arm, calling her out of her thoughts about Tino. Lupo was something else—like Brubeck's music, he had a cool, electric vibe. As the candles burned down, she edged closer to him, or perhaps he was moving toward her. At this point in the evening, it was hard to know. She leaned on his shoulder; he clasped her hand. When the joint came around again, Primrose took a hit. She was moving faster now, in a direction that led irreversibly from Tino, their universe of study dates, root-beer floats and drive-in movies, and the oppressive Battuta household—which somehow poisoned everything with its atmosphere of silent expectation.

Lupo had started to talk about how cerebral Brubeck was and how for this reason he would always be misunderstood. "To understand him, you have to be able to match the time signature of 'Blue Rondo' in your head with some transcendent, singular Song. Why?" He glanced around, noted the general lack of interest, and hurried to make his point: "Because that is just what Brubeck wants, to make over the structure of Song itself."

Every time Lupo said "Song," Primrose heard the capital S. Rosemary heard it too, and it made her scowl, but everything made Rosemary scowl. For Primrose, it was just like when he talked about space aliens and popular mythology. He wasn't the world's most prepossessing guy, but in her presence, she realized, he took on a shine. Still, his point about Brubeck sounded familiar. She recognized it from an article in the *New Yorker* that she had saved for Tino. Lupo was repeating the idea as if it were his own.

Norah said, "Hmm," in a way that conveyed *bullshit*. Maybe she'd read that article, too, during a quiet hour at the library.

Primrose swallowed another olive, having decided to ignore Norah's pointed looks. Flirting with Lupo wasn't a mortal sin. And it wasn't like there was a ring on her finger.

Joseph said, "That kind of idealism might be all right for Brubeck. He gets the big bucks. He can play whatever time signature he wants. In the real world, though, we have to deal with messier things. Not just the what but the how and the why."

"What you want is Bessie Smith," said Rosemary. "Or Big Maybelle. An artist who isn't afraid of the grain of her own voice."

Lupo looked skeptical. The *New Yorker* article had not addressed these questions.

"You don't think Brubeck thinks about the how?" Norah asked Lupo.

"He knows how," Lupo said. "Listen to him."

"And the why?"

"What matters," Joseph said, setting his glass on the table with more force than necessary, "are effects."

Rosemary said, "Joseph, would you check if there are more olives in the kitchen?"

"Sure." When he got up, Norah followed him with her eyes.

"Norah," Rosemary pressed, "tell us about yourself."

Norah's face went briefly slack, wary and assessing. Primrose cut in: "She's going to Pembroke in the fall. Pembroke! It's only the best school in town."

"You must be very smart," Rosemary said to Norah.

"We'll see," Norah said with a rueful smile, "what the scholarship office says."

"She *is* very smart," Primrose insisted. "But let's not put her on the hot seat about it."

"I wouldn't dare," said Rosemary.

The atmosphere grew tense. Maybe, Primrose thought, she shouldn't have mentioned Pembroke or Norah's ambitions to study there. She looked to Lupo for help, but he had closed his eyes and was obviously trying to get lost in the music. Joseph brought out the rest of the olives in a tall glass jar and set it on the table. With a long-handled fork, he snagged an olive and offered it to Norah, who took it between her teeth. For a moment she and Joseph struggled, and then the olive popped off the fork. Norah lapsed back into the cushions, grinning triumphantly with the olive held between her teeth. Primrose gasped, Lupo warily opened one eye, and Joseph burst out laughing. Rosemary asked sweetly, "What were you saying, just now, Joseph, about effects?"

He waved her off. Miffed, Rosemary retreated to the kitchen. Cupboards slammed, pots banged on the burners of the stove. A few minutes later she re-emerged from behind the screen carrying shot glasses filled with a greenish liquid on another lacquer tray. When it was her turn, Primrose declined the glass Rosemary offered. It had a cloying wintergreen odor.

"What's this hooch?" Joseph asked, taking a glass from the tray.

"An aperitif."

He sniffed the contents of his glass. "Smells medicinal."

Norah forked another olive out of the jar and ate it, nibbling delicately around the pit, which she deposited in a napkin.

"Give me that," Primrose hissed. "I'll plant it between the sofa cushions."

Norah murmured, "You'll do no such thing, Primrose Tirocchi."

The doorbell rang. Joseph hurried downstairs and returned moments later with an armful of white boxes that he distributed around the coffee table. Chinese takeout—a first for Primrose. They filled their plates.

Rosemary, Joseph, and Lupo ate with chopsticks. Joseph tried to teach Primrose and Norah how to use them, demonstrating by holding Norah's hand, which made Rosemary scowl again. Norah, who didn't seem too comfortable with the pedagogy either, extracted her fingers from his.

"Let's keep it fun," she told him, taking up her fork.

While they were eating, the album ended. Rosemary reached behind the sofa and came up holding a record, brand new, still wrapped in cellophane. She hulled it, balling up the crackling plastic, and set the record on the player. It was by a band that Primrose had never heard of, called the Deferments.

"I saw them on the Coast," Joseph offered.

Primrose murmured, "Oh, the *Coast*."

"They're decent," Lupo said. "They're coming to the Hog House next month."

Norah asked, "What were you doing on the Coast, Joseph?"

"Organizing a demonstration. You can't imagine what's happening out there. One Saturday I was at Golden Gate Park. There's a crowd. A guy blows on a conch, someone else starts to chant, and then somehow it becomes a whole seamless experience—a thousand people present in the moment."

"But what do they *do*?" Norah pressed.

"Nothing. That's the point. It has to be right because it feels right. Everything flows from that."

"A song," Lupo ventured, "in four-four time."

"Ha," said Rosemary. "If Johnson could get this figured out, the war would be over in a minute. No one on either side would feel like fighting anymore."

Norah was skeptical. "You're gonna lift up the entire universe just by taking a hit and lying in the grass?"

"Lying on the grass," Primrose repeated.

Everyone was lying. Everyone was on grass. She clapped a hand over her mouth, stifling a fit of giggles.

"We thought we could use the show as a platform," Joseph explained, ignoring Primrose, "but it didn't come together."

"Too bad," Norah said. "A platform for what?"

"Think about it demographically," Joseph said. "You and me and everyone else our age—we're huge. Anything we do, the media covers it. We're the pig in the python. And we've got the tiger by the tail," Joseph said.

"Not to mix your metaphors," said Norah.

"I'll mix your metaphors," Joseph replied, winking.

"You can mix *me* another drink if you want." Rosemary held out her empty glass.

Joseph poured the dregs of his own drink into Rosemary's. Her eyes widened in surprise. "The point," he said, "is that our energy is good. Theirs is evil. Good is stronger than evil. We can't lose."

Norah said, "That's not activism."

"Don't harsh us," Rosemary told her. Harshly, it seemed to Primrose.

Norah shrugged. "Just my opinion."

"You've got a point, Norah," Primrose said. "So does Joseph."

"No, I'm sorry, but you can't conciliate." Rosemary's nostrils flared with irritation. "You can't promote peace while you burn down the White House."

"Unless you smoke a doobie in the Oval Office," Lupo said.

"Now we're back where we started," Norah said, laughing. "Maybe you're right, Joseph. Maybe Johnson's gotta get high."

Primrose regarded Norah through the smoke. She wasn't doing too badly for a girl who was afraid of being a third wheel.

"*À propos* of *àp*-solutely nothing—does anyone know how the Hog House got its name?" Joseph asked. "I've been to a few shows, and I've never understood it."

"Well, I know," Primrose offered. "One version of the story anyway."

"Oh?" Rosemary's favorite syllable sounded colder than ever, now that there was exactly zero male attention turned her way. "Do tell."

"I was there once, for a concert. Tino took me."

Beside her, Lupo receded into the chintz depths, leaving a cold space. To fill it, Primrose began to talk in a rush. "It's an old slaughterhouse. Used to belong to a local aviation club. The owners sold it to a friend of Mr. Battuta's from way back, by the name of Frank Clemente."

As she spoke, more and more of Tino's voice slipped into her own. It was almost as if, through her, he was making himself present in the room. Transmigration of souls, only living, not dead—a kind of metempsychosis.

Or maybe just psychosis.

Norah offered her a carton of fried rice. Primrose waved it away.

"So anyway, the club's original members bought the place for next to nothing after a town upriver dammed the flow that had sluiced out the slaughterhouse since I don't know when, and the owners decided to seek their fortune elsewhere."

Norah pushed the carton at her again. "Your plate's empty."

"No, thanks," Primrose said. It came out as one sharp word: *Nothanks.*

Norah sat back, her hands raised in surrender.

"So," Primrose continued, "the new guys thought they were little Lindberghs and that the old abattoir would make a perfect flyer's club, where they could smoke their cigars and theorize about the stock market when they weren't smoothing the kinks out of their landings."

Norah laughed, too loud, and shot Primrose a significant look, which she ignored. Lupo fingered the edge of the coffee table.

"Meanwhile, back at the ranch...," Rosemary said.

"And so how'd it get the name?" Joseph asked without looking up, prospecting with his chopsticks in the carton that held the kung pao chicken.

"Well, naturally," Primrose said, as it finally dawned on her that she was talking too much, "all went well enough until one afternoon a hurricane whirled off the ocean and splintered all the single-engine planes on the runway. The damage sent the guys packing. At which point, Frank Clemente bought the place, threw a coat of paint over everything, and renamed it the Hog House after a Parisian brothel."

"Oh, Primrose," Rosemary said sweetly. "What would you know about Paris? Or brothels?"

Or whores. Primrose knew about whores, of course, because she was one, and Rosemary knew it, and Norah, and Lupo, of course, and probably everyone else from here to Pawtucket. It was time to go, yes, past time. Her mother, at home, would be waiting up—

Rosemary began to collect the plates.

"We'll get those," Norah said. "You sit down. You're our host."

Mutely, Primrose collected the dishes and followed Norah into the kitchen.

"Are you all right?"

Primrose set the stack of dishes on the counter. Her tongue felt enormous. "I feel like I ate Lorraine Battuta's powder puff," she said.

"I know I've been giving you a hard time."

"I'll say."

Norah offered her a stick of gum. "Juicy Fruit?"

Primrose took the gum and was shocked by the flavor that exploded in her mouth. Had *anything ever* tasted *so* delicious? "It's like an *orchard*," she enthused.

Norah gave a half-smile. "That'll wear off soon enough."

They returned to the living room to find Lupo whispering to Rosemary. This new constellation seemed of a piece with the night itself, which had turned and turned again, triumph transforming into disaster and back again according to some unknown rota. Was it the martini? The joint? Psychosis? Through the window, Primrose watched a custard-colored car tow a yawing boat down Pocasset Avenue.

If they were going to take the *Sumac* out, surely Tino would have told her.

Surely.

At the intersection the car slowed, its directional blinking steadily; it turned a corner and vanished.

"I feel dizzy," Primrose said. Lupo pressed her hand. "It's like the whole world is shifting."

"Maybe it is." Lupo looked at her for what felt like a year.

"I should get along home."

"Let me walk you home. I'll get your coat."

"Would you get mine, too?" Norah called. "If you'll wait, I'll walk home with you both after I say my goodbyes."

"I'll be downstairs," Primrose said. Lupo might be unhappy about Norah's third-wheeling, but so what. The whole night had been such a wash.

Outside, Lupo walked Primrose into the shadow of the pine. His face was a pale blur, his eyes shining dark pits into which she might sink, if only she could let herself. "We should get out of town, Primrose. Just you and me. Go to New York, the way you want. We could take the train, be back the same day."

Queasily, she remembered his point about "Blue Rondo." Maybe originality was overrated, romantic, naïve. Maybe that's just what normal people do: take on other people's ideas, wear them like Trigère suits.

"I know it sounds crazy—" he began. "But people actually do this. They take the train. They go to the city."

She met his eyes and lost something there, something she'd been wanting to lose for ages without knowing it. She moved into his arms, and he kissed her. "Juicy Fruit," he murmured.

Someone was coming down the stairs. The noise startled Lupo, who took off down the walk. When Primrose turned around, Norah was standing in the entryway, opening her umbrella.

Lupo walked them as far as the foot of the hill, where Pocasset Avenue met Calvary Street, then hopped on the night bus that was going in the other direction, toward Maple Bay. On their way up the hill, Primrose told Norah about everything—the trip to the museum, the kiss on the grass, how that was as far as they went, how she kept wanting to go much further, but there was also Tino to think of, his lost deferment, all the humiliating jobs he had to do.

"And to top it all," she moaned, "I think I'm pregnant."

"Are you sure?" Norah's eyes were round as 45s.

"I'm worried."

"Wow. That's heavy."

Primrose sighed. She'd expected something more, or different, from Norah. But if the situation were reversed, Primrose wasn't sure she could have done any better.

"We'll talk tomorrow," Norah promised.

Inside, Louise was snoring. Primrose squelched the TV. She lifted the old conch, one of her mother's knickknacks, from the shelf and held it to her ear. She knew the shell echoed the movement of her blood, not the ocean like her mother said. Still, the roaring lulled her. Later, she drifted off to snatches of "Blue Rondo" and the noise of her own blood coursing through the pipes of her mother's house, echoing there.

THE BOOK OF LOVE:
Aphrodisiacs (Alphabetical)
Compiled by Primrose and Norah

Airplanes; alizarin crimson; artichokes, asparagus, and avocado; basil; caviar, champagne, and chanterelles; chili peppers, chocolate, and cinnamon; holidays, honey, hotel rooms; invitations; leeks and lobster roe; marzipan; mirth; oysters; peppermint; pistachios; rhinoceros horn, powdered; roses, red; saxophones, sea holly, and sleeping cars; snow, dreamed; Spanish fly, powdered; tiger penis, dried; tomatoes and turtle eggs; truffles, black; truffles, white; wine, red.

15. Boating

When Primrose spied Chick towing the boat down Pocasset Avenue, for once she had not been imagining things. The whole adventure had been Dot's idea.

"Everyone *says* you can't do anything without a functional hitch," Dot said. She and Chick lay tangled on the floor in the *Sumac*'s hold. A tired light, distinctly 40-watt, leaked through the boat's trapdoor, silvering Dot's bouffant. They'd managed to only minimally muss it. But it was early yet. Between licks applied to Chick's earlobe, she pressed: "But I say, what's already there is good enough. As am I. Functional or not. Sufficient unto the day and all that."

"All that?"

She stuck her tongue in his ear. "Love the one you're with."

"That tickles!"

"So does this. Ugh!" She brushed something from the back of her leg. "Are you aware the floor in here hasn't been cleaned since the Eisenhower administration?"

"The floor's not that bad."

"You have to do it."

"Clean the floor?"

"Well, you should do that, too. But what I'm saying is that you should take this baby for a spin."

"Why?"

"Because," she sighed, "you have to show how much you love me. Whether your love is true. If we should get married. Here comes the bride, et cetera."

"I'm supposed to take this boat on the road, *un*hitched, so we can find out whether we should *get* hitched?" He twined his fingers in her hair, which yielded with a soft crunch.

"Clever, yes?"

"You have your own way of putting two and two together," he muttered, his nose pressed to her shoulder.

"Like Noah, populating his ark."

"That's two *by* two, Dot—but never mind."

She'd yielded her bouffant, and so Chick, gentleman that he was, yielded reciprocally in his view of what was possible, given the hitch he had. And the girl. The boat needed moving, and so he would move it. It was stupid, but wasn't that just what you did for love? Of a person? Of a boat? Look at Tino, throwing away his get-out-of-war-free card just to come home to his true love, his brilliant loony piece of ass. Talk about hitched! With one dumb move, Tino had gone and signed his damned life away. He'd *better* marry Primrose.

At the corner of Pocasset and Dyer, Chick cranked down the window. Someone was blasting beatnik jazz from the top floor of a triple-decker, the one with a gutter hanging loose by the eaves. Those beatnik hippies were up there listening to their records, doing whatever beatnik hippie things they did, and they most likely had no idea that sooner or later, probably sooner, their house would need a new roof.

It was funny, when you thought of it, what life made you ignorant of. And how what you didn't know could surprise you. Like a roof coming down all of a sudden.

Could he really tie himself to Dot the way he'd hooked himself to the *Sumac*, which might at any moment roll through the rear window and kill him, most likely by decapitation?

Not to put too fine point on it.

But then again, look on the bright side: You couldn't send a headless guy to fight a war.

When the light changed, Chick checked his hair in the rear view and settled in, singing, "I went to the funeral just for the bride, just for the bride..."

The following day, Chick was still singing when he pulled up to the Battutas' house. Tino was sitting on the front step.

"Time waits for no man," Chick said. "Let's go."

"In a minute." Tino pointed at the sky. A shadow wheeled, high up.

"Space alien?"

"Barn owl. It's quartering."

"Get in the car," Chick told him. "The day's not so young, and neither are you. Since when did you become a zookeeper?"

"Since I started hanging around with zoo animals," Tino said, flopping into the passenger seat.

Chick looked at him for what seemed like a long time. "What's eating you, man? You look like you lost your best friend." He glanced in the rearview mirror and adjusted his Ray-Bans. "And yet, I am still here."

Tino ran his hand through what remained of his hair. Everything was bugging him: his father, his mother, his dean's letter, which was still burning a hole in his wallet, in lieu of the cash he needed. His draft status. Chick's call-up notice, floating out to sea. Not to mention Primrose, phoning this morning with her news. Her period was late. She was throwing up. Oh no, there was nothing on his mind.

"Where's Primrose?"

"She had a meeting."

"A meeting," Chick said slowly. "What kind of meeting?"

"SDS or something."

"You know SDS doesn't have an office around here. Not a real one anyway."

Tino lit a cigarette. "Since when do you know so much about SDS?"

"Since I started hanging around with zoo animals," Chick said.

Tino thought of Zio Zio, all the bootless work he did for his union, the money up front, the shoving on the picket lines.

"Never mind, Chick. That sort of agitation's never done anyone much good."

"You want something done right," Chick said lightly, accelerating now that they were on the Maple Bay Parkway, "you gotta do it yourself."

"What the hell does that mean?"

"It means we've got a boat! If I'm called up, I'll take this baby right across Lake Champagne—"

They headed up the hill, away from Tino's neighborhood. "Champlain," Tino corrected.

"Which I'll be drinking with my girl on the other side of the border." Chick slowed to a stop at an intersection. No one was coming. He let the car idle.

"You're really going to do it? Take the boat, get married?"

"It's an option." Chick pointed to an envelope Tino hadn't noticed on the dashboard. Tino opened it. Inside was a subpoena with Chick's name on it. His real name, in official, unpronounceable full: Cesare Bonanno.

"Jesus," Tino said. "Now you've really got to report for that physical."

"Or they're gonna throw my ass in jail."

They went to Miss Cranston's. It was late morning, and Dot's shift had just ended. Still in uniform, Dot brought plates heaped with food, lumberjack breakfasts with all the fixings. But when she joined them at the table, she only picked at a slice of toast. Chick's news was hitting her hard.

"Tell us a story about med school, Tino. Anything to take our minds off this." Chick waved his terrible document, and Dot pushed her plate away.

"I could tell you some stuff that would really put you off your food."

"Tino, please," Dot said. "I have a weak stomach."

"If you puke, I'll hold your hair. Not that you'd need it." Chick patted her bouffant. "You shellacked the hell out of this thing."

She swatted his hand away. "That's a talent."

"In gross anatomy," Tino began, "I was paired with the only girl in the school. She was amazing, with fingers like a pianist's. She could get inside a membrane and out again without leaving so much as a crease. You okay, Dot?"

"Go on," she sighed. "I'll be fine."

"This Elizabeth knows what she's doing. Her father's a surgeon. It's in the blood."

Dot paled. "Don't say 'blood.'"

"You thought you'd have it easy," Chick mused. "She'd do all the work, and you'd just sit back."

"What's wrong with that? Anyway, she got kicked out." Tino paused to take a sip of water.

"For what?"

"I'm telling you. The school rule was, only male students get male cadavers. So we got a female, an old lady." He paused, remembering his surprise when he noticed the woman's ankles, slim and finely turned, underneath the sheet. "So," Tino continued, struggling to return the intrusive memory to his mental cold storage where it belonged, "we go along, doing our dissection. You got to be careful because if you screw up, you don't get a chance to try again. But we don't have to worry because this girl is so good. She teaches me a few things, and just as I'm getting the hang of it, something happens."

"What?" Chick was leaning forward eagerly. Even Dot had taken her hand from her face.

"Well, the professor is impressed. He goes on and on about her. Which makes the guys in the class real pissed. They start to whisper, they laugh when they see her coming. But in front of the prof, they're all business."

"What's the point?" Chick wondered. "I mean, I know med students are competitive, but you're already in—what's the point of being mean?"

"There's getting in, and then there's staying in," Tino said.

"Oh?"

Tino drained his water glass. His mouth had gone cottony. Chick didn't really get it, even after Tino had explained. How you had to fight to keep your spot, how it wasn't simply yours for keeps upon matriculation.

"Well, our dissection prodigy has a few problems." As did they all. "For starters, she's far and away the best cutter in the room, and the professor doesn't curve. Plus, and I heard this from more than a couple of the guys, she's taking a place that might have gone to someone who's humping a pack in the jungle."

"I always thought girls should stay out of school in order to save our hides," Chick said, leering at Dot.

"I'll save your hide," Dot snapped. "Those boys sound terrible. What happened next?"

"One day, when I lifted the sheet, I found a hot dog tucked into the woman's—"

"Predictable," Dot said.

"The guys at the next table were snickering, so we knew who was responsible. My partner, to her credit, doesn't blink. She tosses the dog in the bucket, and that's the end of it. Except, one morning the next week, after I try to talk to her about what happened and she brushes me off, I come into the lab to find the guys just getting down to work. And what do they find when they remove their sheet? Someone had gone and made a precise, devastating, *beautiful* dissection—of the guy's dick. Everyone knew who'd done it. And so she gets kicked out. For mutilating a cadaver."

Tino paused, aware of veering into dicey territory. It was easy to slip from entertainment to confession.

"Heavy," said Chick. "Nothing happened to the guys?"

"Not a blessed thing. Would you want to be responsible for sending three of the nation's best and brightest to the jungle, just for a practical joke?"

"Boys will be boys," Dot said, "but girls better not be."

Behind Dot's head, there was a sign: FISH AND VISITORS SMELL AFTER THREE DAYS.

"What happened to the girl?" Chick asked.

"What could she do? She went home."

"Did she have a boyfriend?"

"I never asked," Tino said. "She seemed pretty serious about school."

The ignition caught, the bilge gurgled, and they charged toward Middlebridge, where the guy in the bait shop said the fish were biting. Leaning over the *Sumac's* port side, Tino flung out his line. It came back empty once, twice, a third time. Chick, who wasn't having any luck either, sucked loudly on a cube of ice. Dot was stretched at the front of the boat, her forearm slung across her face, her T-shirt riding up over her bikini. They were quiet, pensive, buttoning themselves against a future they didn't want but could not think how to change. At least not without becoming something else entirely—filial nightmares, *agita* machines. Tino set his rod down, lifted the cooler lid, and extracted two dripping cans of beer. He handed one to Chick and cracked the tab on the other.

"We could get married and have a kid," Chick said. "I'd get a year's reprieve. The war might end in the meantime."

"But if it doesn't, you'll be in the jungle with a wife and kid at home."

"Is that better or worse than being there and single?"

See double, Tino thought. *Feel single.* A slogan he'd seen once at the bottom of a pint glass in a St. Louis bar.

"Or I'll shoot myself in the foot. Or you can dissect out my kidney. They can't take a guy with one kidney, can they?"

"You scare me," Tino said. "Besides, I stink at dissection."

Chick grinned. Tino's rod bent and shook. The water roiled as a school surrounded the boat. Tino leaned out over the side of the boat and reeled in a fat bluefish. As he pulled the fish clear, a second one leapt from the depths and snatched the hook from the mouth of the first.

"Jesus Christ!" Tino caught the second fish with both hands and flipped it onto the deck.

"Nice!" Chick shouted back, reeling furiously.

A motorboat roared by, scattering the fish.

Later, Tino and Chick ate sandwiches while Dot, still not hungry, smoked a cigarette on the boat's prow.

"Where's Primrose?" Chick asked around a bite of tuna salad.

"I told you, she had an SDS meeting." Tino's sandwich was salami, slimed with mayonnaise.

"That's what she said?"

"Yeah." Tino wiped his mouth with his hand. "So?"

Chick rested his sandwich in his lap and stared at the water. "Look, Tino. There was no meeting. I saw her on the road with Lupo Light."

"What?"

"Sorry, man. I thought you should know."

"Jesus." Tino flung the remains of his sandwich overboard. "With Lupo Light. Jesus Christ."

Something phosphoresced in the water. Tino noted it blankly: phosphor, carbon, hydrogen. The oxygen he suddenly could not get enough of.

Chick squeezed Tino's bicep. "We've got bigger things to worry about. Uncle Sam, you know?"

"I know."

"Are you really not going back to medical school?"

"I'm not." Tino crumpled wax paper into a ball. Even Chick didn't know the whole humiliating story; he probably never would. Better to let that particular bygone be gone. "But that's not the worst of it."

Because Primrose, that bitch, the crazy bitch—

And with Lupo Light, of all people. Nerdy Lupo Light.

His breathing came in ragged heaves. He exhaled slowly through his nose, like he did before a big exam. Except this time there was no lecture hall, no proctor, no blue book. No cheat sheet, either. "Primrose says she's pregnant."

16. Incipit

One night they went out wearing bathing suits under their clothes, and Tino took the back roads to a beach they both liked, where no one ever bothered them. It wasn't much—just a few yards of pebbly sand and rotting dock that seemed to have been abandoned sometime in the preceding century. Beyond it stretched a gray length of sea that rolled up dark and greasy on the sand, reminding Primrose of the photograph of her parents that had sat for as long as she could remember on the coffee table. In the picture, Louise was posed like a pinup girl at Frank's feet, and Frank towered over her in shining black trunks, water running down the length of him.

In the Chevelle's passenger seat, she drew her legs to her chin. Her middle had thickened, and her breasts were swollen and tender. Although Lupo's invitation—a trip to New York!—warmed her whenever she thought of it, she was trying not to think of it. Louise would never have allowed herself to get into this position, pregnant, unmarried, *puttana*. Primrose curled around herself, making her body a tight circle. Inside, she felt hollowed out by shame.

Tino punched the radio's buttons, dissatisfied by everything on the air. Once upon a time, they'd both liked the same music—Dave Van Ronk, the Red Clay Ramblers, Chuck Berry, Linda Lyndell. But she was pretty sure he'd never heard of the Deferments. He probably wouldn't have too much patience for anything to do with *the Coast,* either. For the first time, she wondered about Tino. Maybe they didn't have all that much to talk about.

She tilted her head. Her long hair fell over his hand. He caught a curl and fingered it as if it were something apart from her.

"You're angry."

"No," he said. But of course he was. He wouldn't even look at her.

"Liar." She squeezed his hand. "Pants on fire."

"We can't stay here all night," Tino said. "The cops'll come."

"No, they won't. They never come."

He exhaled skeptically.

"Are you afraid?" Primrose asked.

"Of the cops? No."

"That's not what I mean."

"What *do* you mean?"

"Maybe I'm afraid."

"Of what?"

"I'm not sure," she lied. "There's the war, I guess."

Tino swallowed hard before he spoke, but his response was a verbal shrug: "Everyone's afraid of that."

Primrose tensed. "What about the baby?"

"People manage. They take out life insurance. They make wills." His tone was exasperated. Didn't she know anything about life?

"Life insurance only goes to your wife if you're married. Which we aren't."

"If it weren't the war, it would be something else. You're just a worrywart."

The way he spoke cut her. She turned away from him.

Maybe an abortion was the right thing. There must be someplace she could go, someone who could do the job. She'd heard other girls talk—whispers in the bathroom, girl to girl. She rolled down the window. The breeze smelled like fried food.

So this was how it was: two people in a car, and no one behind the wheel. She swallowed hard to rid herself of the lump in her throat.

"Here come the waterworks," Tino sneered.

She jumped out, shedding clothes as she went. Before Tino reached the dock, she was gone. The last thing he saw was her freckled back, crossed by the black straps of her swimsuit, curving into the water. She swam toward the horizon in rhythmic strokes.

On the dock, Tino hesitated. How far would she go? He shrugged out of his shirt and hopped from foot to foot, removing his shoes. When he dove, the water was colder and deeper than he expected, the undertow more insistent. She kept swimming: a flash of white, a flash of black. But he was the stronger swimmer, and he reached her quickly. She turned to him, pushing her wet hair off her face, and his heavy mood lifted.

"Nice that you came after me. It makes me think you're not likely to disappear."

"Even if Uncle Sam gets my number?"

"Even if." The corners of her mouth turned up, and she flashed him a smile so dazzling that the idea of Lupo Light shrank to nothing more than a mental irritant—pollen, a flea.

Chick could be wrong. Wouldn't be the first time.

She slipped down; Tino followed. Underwater, Primrose back-flipped in a ragged cone of light. They caught like gears and kissed briefly, eyes open, wondering. The hard energy between them softened. Tino surfaced, taking slow breaths, and glanced toward the beach, where a horseshoe crab, shaped like a tank with a long tail, sat quite still.

"Primrose," he said. They should get out of the water.

But she had slipped away again, beneath the surface. He wiped his mouth and thought, unaccountably, of his mother daintily wiping her lips with a napkin, one of the hundreds sliced in half for the sake of economy. In his mother's view, no adult ate in a way that required a whole two-ply napkin. But to hell with those petty economies. Whatever was here in the water was already their problem, and it was a big one. The solution was not going to be easy or cheap.

Primrose surfaced. Treading water, she looked at him steadily. "This water tastes bad."

"It's not just the water. It's all of it, Primrose. The mess we're in. All of us, people our age."

"There are things we could do. We could have a sit-in."

A sit-in. What a concept. As if sitting around, chanting and waving signs, was going to increase the value of their lives in the minds of those who were clamoring so loudly for the continuation of this indefensible war. But that's just what you got from hanging around with the students in SDS—those zoo animals, her hippie friends, who imagined their lives were worth something. Was Lupo among them? Of course he was. The anger resurged, a heat that flared from his core and failed to dissipate.

"What the hell difference would that make?" he snapped. "You make it sound like throwing a party."

"I know people who've done it."

"You know I'm not much of a joiner. Besides, if I tried any of that hippie crap, my father would wring my goddamned neck!"

"Tino!"

But he had already started back for the dock. The closeness he'd felt earlier was gone, and now he felt nothing. Less than nothing.

Behind him, Primrose swam with difficulty, taking tired, heaving breaths.

Let her gasp. Let her drown.

Slowly Primrose paddled back. Reaching the dock, she set her elbows on it, resting for a moment, before she grabbed the hand he'd grudgingly offered and clambered up. They sat on the dock for a while, as was their habit, drip-drying so as not to ruin the Chevelle's upholstery. Her wet hair was cold against his arm.

A barnacle colony had grown along the side of the dock. As if in a trance, Tino leaned over and scraped the shells away. As each dropped, it became something else: a windfall pear from his grandfather's tree, Primrose's dress heaped on the front seat of the Chevelle, a molecule slipping, like a charm, off a protein chain. He ran his tongue over a tooth he'd chipped, years before, on a stray shell fragment in his mother's garlic snails. Hope, then: The jagged tooth might be a blessing in disguise, a small, ordinary thing that might keep him from dying in a place he couldn't imagine except indirectly, through news reports, photographs, and other forms of gossip with no less questionable relationship to the truth. Could a broken tooth make you 4-F? Maybe it could.

"Let's go," Primrose said.

They walked back to the car, the last of the day's warmth rising up from the asphalt against their bare feet. Tino could see now that Primrose carried the future, right there in the new little potbelly that poked out when she bent to brush sand from her heels. Whereas he was something sadder, a drag on tomorrow, stuck to the past like a barnacle on a dock. So what if he took the easy way out? It wasn't even that easy. And so much else was so hard.

He sank into the front seat without bothering to dry off. Heading back to Silver Lake, Tino took a shortcut through a subdivision where new houses were sprouting up, fronted by spindly trees. As he drove, Primrose changed into her dry clothes under a towel.

"I'm going to tell Ma tonight."

"Right," said Tino. Louise had Friday nights off.

"She's already looking at me sideways." Primrose looked at her chest. "These boobs are a dead giveaway."

He flashed back to Primrose, turning underwater in that strange sea light. Within her floated a mystery he couldn't see, a future that was unfurling past him already, and whose value he would be tempted to pronounce upon, as his father's generation had pronounced upon theirs.

Unless something changed. Unless he did.

The forgiveness he'd felt earlier returned, stronger now. Maybe he really had done her wrong, believing what Chick had told him.

"You're upset," she said. "It's all over your face. What is it?"

They approached an intersection. The light went from green to yellow. He stepped on the gas.

"I heard something—"

A horn blared, and Tino swerved into the opposite lane. A car—large, white, and moving altogether too fast—veered around them and sped away.

"Jesus Christ!" Tino barked. Primrose stiffened.

After that, Primrose sat very still and didn't say anything.

As they approached Unaconicut Hill, Primrose asked, "Will you circle back around after you drop me off?"

"Sure." He pressed her hand.

"If I need you, I'll blink the lights. Louise might be apeshit, and you'll have to take me away."

She was talking like she'd rehearsed. He glanced at her.

"Do you honestly think—?" It was so dramatic, this idea she had of what Louise might do. Then the fear in her eyes made him scared, too.

"Okay," he said. But it was not okay at all.

Outside her house, he let the engine idle as he kissed her goodnight, trying not to add to her anxiety by doing anything that might communicate his own.

As she reached to open the door, he pulled her back and brushed the hair, still damp, from her eyes. She left without a word.

He cut the engine and slid down in the seat. Feeling sleepy, he closed his eyes. When he opened them, the house was dark. Something moved along the foundation—Reginald, out hunting mice, his body pressed close to the ground.

How long had it been? He couldn't see his watch. Had she blinked the light?

Tino released the brake and allowed the car to roll downhill. And so he went, gathering speed.

17. To arrive like an echo

The television ceased with a whine and a snap. Louise opened her eyes. Primrose sat carefully on the arm of the couch.

"Mom. I have something to tell you."

"So tell me something," Louise replied groggily. "I'm not getting any younger. Did he ask you to marry him? Did he, finally?"

Primrose stared at the crumbs in the rug. "It's not that."

"Well, then, what is it?" Louise yawned. "Speak your piece, Primrose. It's late."

Primrose exhaled slowly, clasping her hands in her lap. "I think I'm pregnant."

Louise stared at her, her face gone pale and slack. Then she reached for her ashtray and flung it through the picture window. The night air rushed in. *I said that I would slap your face*, her mother bellowed. Primrose stared at her hands. Her mother yanked her hair. *Look at me when I speak to you!*

Primrose closed her eyes. *You are not speaking.*

Louise hit her—twice. She'd have gone further, but Frank came into the room, and Louise began to scream at him instead.

Frank said, "That's enough."

Louise continued to shout. Primrose covered her ears.

"I said, that's enough, Louise!" Frank slammed his fist into the wall. The noise jarred Primrose, propelling her out of her stupor. She ran to her bedroom, closed the door, and leaned against it. Louise pounded the door so hard that Primrose's teeth clacked against each other.

"What are you doing in there, *puttana*? No, Frank, you can hit the wall all you want, I'm not through with her yet."

"Louise, you'll wake the neighborhood."

"I don't give a good goddamn. Everybody already knows we've got a whore for a daughter. It's not like it's news."

Primrose heard her father leading her mother away. Louise was still angry. But at least she wasn't shouting anymore.

I should flick the light, she remembered. *Tino's waiting.*

She looked out. There he was, leaned back in the driver's seat. She flicked the light and waited, but the car didn't move. He's waiting, she thought. He wants to be sure.

18. Midsummer

Primrose woke shivering, rolled out of bed, and pushed the window shut, the creak of the casements jolting her from a dream in which a radiant boy—not Tino, not Lupo—punched holes in a ticket and then handed it to her. She couldn't read what was written on it. When she asked his name, he told her, "Christopher Columbus," to which she replied, "You're not helping." He waved her toward the entrance of a cave. She hadn't gone in.

She rubbed her goosefleshed arms. The chilly weather reminded her of the first school days, with their mingled odors of crisp sour apples and sharpened pencils, and for a moment she almost convinced herself that it was the middle of August, and the chill she felt was just the end of summer vacation. But no, it was still midsummer, and she'd only awakened into the same old life, the same old problems. She changed into a clean sweatshirt and dungarees.

The bathroom was rank with bleach and Louise's loaded ashtray, which Primrose emptied out the window, grateful for the lungful of fresh air. In the kitchen, she found a foil-wrapped stack of pancakes—a peace offering—on the stove alongside a greasy pan. She ran hot water into the pan and set it to soak. The water was dark like the mouth of the cave in her dream, but the beautiful boy did not appear. Someone, probably her father, had swept up last night's mess and nailed plywood over the window. How had she slept through the hammering? Perhaps that was the source of the dream boy's ticket punching.

On the radio: the war, the war, the war. A riot. "We have received reports of an oddly shaped aircraft just off Point Judith. Residents within ten miles of the area are advised to avoid unnecessary boat travel until further notice."

Primrose silenced the radio and headed out. She could still feel her mother's palm against her face. The sting of it. At the end of the walk, she sat on the steps and shook a black ant off her foot. Norah came down the path in a fresh T-shirt and Bermuda shorts that looked to have been pressed about three minutes ago. Primrose sank down, her misery complete.

"I told Louise," she blurted. "Last night. Late."

"I did hear a noise." Frowning, Norah glanced up the walkway at the plywood-covered picture window. "I guess she didn't take the news very well."

"Not at all."

"I guess she wouldn't. What about your dad?"

"He was gone when I woke up. But she made me breakfast. So maybe she's sorry."

"Did she hit you?" Norah's voice was matter-of-fact. The matter was a fact, after all—Louise was a hitter. More than once Primrose had shown up at school with Louise's palm-print on her face.

"I felt like less than the dirt on her feet. After I got into bed, she shouted through the door to tell me I'd have to go see Dr. Addleman."

Norah grimaced.

"Yeah." Primrose shuddered. Dr. Addleman had chilly hands and eyes like tumbled stones, and he ordered electroshock as easily as Chinese takeout. He might even send her back to the hospital.

"Can I ask you something?"

"Sure."

"What's happening with Lupo?"

"I guess I'm exploring."

Norah murmured: "Two guys is at least one more than you want."

"I don't know what I want. And now it looks like what I might have wanted, once upon a time, doesn't even matter."

Once upon a time. The first words of any story, if you believed *The Book of Love.*

Norah looked at her, a forceful glance with a question in it.

"I suppose I have to marry Tino. But first he has to ask. And so here we are." Primrose sighed. "Meanwhile, I need something to wear to the Matterhorn. I've outgrown my prom dress, and I broke the heel on my new shoes. In a fairy tale, I'd get a visit from a fairy godmother and help from an army of magical mice."

"Fairy godmothers don't often get to this neck of the woods," said Norah.

"No, I suppose they don't." Primrose wiped her face with her hands. She might be humiliated, but she could still aim for resilience, for pluck. "But Atlantic Mills is just down the road, and I hear there's a sale on."

19. Pink sentiments

Primrose wrestled a hanger inside her new dress and hung it in the closet. The dress was two sizes larger than usual, and even so, there wasn't an inch to spare. But the price had been right—four dollars, minus forty cents because she'd found a tear in the hem that earned her an additional ten percent damaged-goods discount. She turned sideways and looked in the mirror. It wasn't an illusion. Even under her largest shirt, she was bigger, especially up front.

"What I don't understand," Louise said, having materialized in the doorway, a plastic turquoise ashtray in one hand and a burning cigarette in the other, "is why you can't get Tino to marry you."

Primrose squared her shoulders and turned to face her mother. Louise produced a handful of torn-out magazine articles from the front pocket of her housedress. "For your edification," she said as she set them on the dresser.

Primrose riffled the pages: "How to Win His Heart." "The Man Who Won't Commit." "So This Is Love." The title of the last one was printed in Pepto-Bismol pink on lighter pink paper.

"You can't force someone to marry you."

"*I'll* force *him!*" Louise snorted. "It takes two, you know. He bears some responsibility."

"What if I don't want to get married?"

Louise's eyebrows shot up. "You want to raise a baby by yourself?"

The truth was, she wasn't sure if she wanted to marry Tino. Lupo had shown her *something*. What? Deep inside her, a small weight shifted, no larger than a sparrow; she passed a hand over the spot and thought, *Not now, for God's sake. Let me think.*

Maybe she didn't want to marry Lupo, either, but at least now she knew that Tino wasn't necessarily the best she could do. She could look further afield, or she might not get married at all. She didn't have to go all the way to *the Coast*, either. As nearby as New York, things were happening—not at Bergdorf's or the Met, but at places like the Peace Eye Bookstore, where she had heard that people like Rosemary and Joseph were meeting every night to explore consciousness, the next new frontier. In her mind's eye, the girl who was wearing Pauline Trigère at the Met was now sporting bell-bottoms at the Psychedelicatessen. Sometimes she was, anyway. Other times, though Primrose didn't like to admit it, she was wearing the pretty suit. With matching pumps.

"Primrose?" Louise waved her hand in Primrose's face. "Earth to Primrose!"

"What I mean is, Tino could also help pay for the abortion," Primrose said, coming out of her trance.

"Paying up is not the same as bearing some responsibility. You want to play, you got to pay—and I don't mean cash, young lady."

Holding her mother's gaze, Primrose felt for the dresser and leaned her hip against it. The mirror shimmered.

"Tino can't avoid this. He can't run away."

"If I force him," she said slowly, gripping the dresser's edge, "he'll balk. You know how he is."

"He's a man. He should act like one. All I'm saying, Primrose, is that you're going to have to do something that you don't want to do. You'll have to change Tino's idea of his future as a big man on campus, you know, with prospects and completely without responsibilities to you or to that baby you're carrying."

"It's not a baby. And it's not your decision."

"Of course it's a baby!"

"Not yet!" It didn't have a name. It didn't have a history.

"You'll fry in hell. Like a pig on a spit."

Primrose flashed on an image of a girl running, running downhill through smoke and flame. Primrose knew the girl was screaming because her mouth was open. Her face contorted. Her hair on fire. It felt like a message from the future. Was it real, or had it originated in the firefight that only happened between her ears?

"There is no hell," Primrose told her mother. "Except the one we're in."

"What kind of hippie malarkey is that?"

Primrose pitched forward and grabbed the doorknob. As she tried to pull the door shut, her mother held on from the other side.

"Leave me alone!" Primrose screamed.

Abruptly Louise let go, her eyebrows lifting in two curves of surprise. Primrose slid to the floor and rested her head between her knees, trying to banish the vision of the girl with the burning hair. "Leave me alone," she told the burning girl. "I just want to be alone."

Louise laughed from the hallway. "You should have thought of that before you let him put his thing in you."

THE BOOK OF LOVE:
Family Romance
by Primrose and Norah

Love is fatal in certain situations, and for this reason it is important to think carefully before taking any irreversible steps.

Such as?

Fucking without a license. The consequences of unprotected sex are, as we have discovered, much worse than anything we could have imagined previously. Worse, almost certainly, than not fucking at all.

But let's be clear: By "unprotected," we mean something more than not wearing a rubber.

Consider, for instance, the mating habits of the praying mantis. Or the plot of *Oedipus Rex*. From nature to literature, all our stories of romance are patterned on the first one, or more precisely our fantasies of it: of mother and father, and whatever goes on beyond their bedroom's threshold, the mind's shut door.

20. News from the galaxy next door

"Most people would rather not think about the events that took place at Roswell, New Mexico, during the summer of 1947."

Otis Foreman, the leader of RICUFOG's subcommittee of student UFOlogists stood at a lectern in a basement classroom. He had distributed the meeting's agenda on mimeographed sheets, but the day was so humid, the papers were curling at their corners. The room smelled sharply of mildew, and the ceiling tiles were marked by water stains in which it was possible to see anything: daisies, mushroom clouds, mouths opened in screams or laughter. A box of donuts lay untouched on a table.

Lupo sat at a wobbly desk, trying to remember how he'd gotten here. McKee had landed a write-up in the campus paper, a loosely fact-checked piece linking recent UFO sightings to his research on dolphin vocalizations. Lupo had not seen the article. He didn't want to think too much about whatever his dissertation advisor was spouting in a non-refereed and not especially prestigious publication like *The Good Five Cent Cigar*. "Gonna shake some shit loose" was all McKee had said when Lupo asked him why he'd gone and published a thing like that. "Now go to the meeting," he urged Lupo. "See what you can see."

The items on the agenda were boringly normal: introduction of new group members; news from the recruitment drive; instructions for the distribution of flyers and leaflets. Boring, too, were the attendees. Unlike the SDS meeting where he'd met Primrose, which had been mixed in terms of gender but uniformly well scrubbed and even fashionable, the subcommittee's members were virtually all male, and in their obvious contempt for appearances, they resembled the speaker, with his zits and exuberant facial hair. The only woman in the room was sitting at the next desk, a blonde in pedal pushers who looked like she might have gotten lost on the way to a pep rally. Lupo didn't remember seeing any of them at the SDS meeting, but that had been a long time ago, practically ancient history. He barely recognized himself from those days; how could he possibly recognize anyone else?

"Most people would rather not know," Otis went on, "about Area 51, the place they call Dreamland, and what happened there just six months ago when a local paper went bust after reporting on strange lights in the sky." He glanced at the audience, gauging interest. "But we are not most people. We have questions—lots of questions. What *is* the practical feasibility of interplanetary flight? Are so-called flying saucers a corporate experiment by an outfit like Dow Chemical or Union Metallurgic? Could you really start and stop on a dime, at thousands of miles per hour, without violating fundamental laws of physics?" He paused. "How fundamental, really, are our laws of physics?"

The question hovered in the air.

Because if you could violate the laws of physics—Lupo continued the train of thought—who was to say you couldn't do something else? Like break up with your steady boyfriend, or finally finish your doctoral thesis, or otherwise turn the big flying saucer of your life around?

"Allow me to remind you of something," Otis continued, shuffling his notes. "I may be an engineering student, but that doesn't mean I don't know my history. Before Galileo, the Earth for most people—even educated and skeptical people—really did revolve around the sun, and they had all sorts of proof for that assertion. It was only decades' worth of accumulation of so-called anomalous data that convinced the naysayers. This reminder should be salutary. It should wake us up. It should, dare I say it, give us hope."

Lupo rubbed his cold hands. Heat didn't stay in basements. He imagined the heat-flow diagram, the red arrows showing the heat escaping, never to return. Maybe the SDS protesters were wrong. Maybe it was entropy, not freedom, that was on the march—which was, he realized, just a scientific way of articulating the truth that everything was always going to shit.

Someone had started the box of donuts on a trip around the room. He watched, distracted, as the box neared his desk. When it arrived, he extracted an old-fashioned and offered the box to the girl in pedal pushers. Favoring him with a wide smile, she chose a chocolate frosted.

"Our data may seem anomalous, but reports of alien sightings are accumulating, and they share intriguing similarities. Who is to say our understanding of the universe is invulnerable to subversion by a new Galileo?"

Primrose, Lupo doodled. *Promiser*. He remembered a moment from their day in the park: her fingers trailing along the pond's surface and the plants swaying in unison below. She never answered his question: Would she, could she, come with him to New York? For a day—or longer?

"Modern scientists think UFOs belong only on the pages of *Amazing Stories* and *Fantastic Fiction*, alongside articles about ESP, Sasquatch, and the Loch Ness Monster. But they, and their institutions, can be just as limited as their predecessors, who refused to recognize the reality of meteorites, continental drift, germs, and Neanderthal man."

The donut box circled back to its original position on the table at the front. A door slammed down the hall, sending a wind through the room that lifted the lid of the empty box and blew it to the table's edge. Would anyone bother to push it back? Lupo wondered. But no one else seemed to notice. There was the rub, the crux: Anything might happen, at any moment. While everyone awaited the catastrophe, the guy at the lectern droned obliviously on.

"We know the truth," Otis intoned. Lupo recognized the move, winding up a speech with a stark declarative. Someone from Toastmasters must have given him a lesson. "The political recognition of alien consciousness is the first step toward recognition of our own alienation. We must confront our aliens before we can confront ourselves."

A clever point, Lupo thought. But something about it sounded familiar. Had Otis lifted it from the Port Huron statement?

"The good news is, we're reaching people. Baby steps, yes, but we're making real progress on the public relations front. Sightings are getting more attention in the press. In fact, just last week, according to this article by the eminent astronomy professor Peregrine McKee," he waved the paper in the air, "the DiMaio sighting was covered by the journalist Lupo Light, who also provided a summary of recent UFO activity in the area."

Fucking McKee! What the hell. He was no journalist. Lupo saw his career slip away, down astrally projected tubes.

"Thanks to their work, everyone on campus knows what's in the air all around us, and they'll be on the lookout. We'll hear more stories as others, emboldened by the coverage, come forward. Incidentally," he said formally, "I believe Mr. Light is with us today."

Otis pointed at Lupo, and everyone turned to stare. They reminded Lupo of fish in an aquarium—dumb, unresponsive, floating at the mercy of a current whose source did not interest them. Shooting fish in a barrel—that was supposed to be easy, and perhaps it was.

"You should all feel free to talk to Lupo," Otis said.

Lupo smiled grimly. He hoped no one present would feel free. These people were not operating under any condition of freedom that he recognized. Except, maybe, that pedal-pushers girl.

Next on the agenda: new business.

Pedal Pushers stood up. She cleared her throat, and there was a pause in the room's white noise of disinterest. Feet ceased tapping; chairs failed to creak. She was there, she said, to report on a UFO sighting. Her voice came in and out, as if tuned to an ambivalent station. From what Lupo could gather, she had been counting egrets (she was a marine biology major, a fact Lupo also recorded) when something *huge* belly-flopped into the marsh. She had been soaked. She had felt shocked. But she'd also had the presence of mind to perform some experiments.

"First, I picked up a rock. It was about the size of a baseball, weighed about as much as a can of cranberry sauce. I came as close as I dared. I flung the rock at the hull. It bounced back," she said, "in a way that's hard to describe. As if it had hit an invisible armor or force field—"

Lupo shifted position, aware of a tension that had not been there before. His fingers were not so cold anymore, either.

"I got closer. I touched the hull. It warm. Like a quarter if you held one in your hand for a while."

Lupo sensed the edge of a coin in the palm of the hand that was not writing, but when he opened it, of course, his palm was empty.

"It felt like there was a lot going on, uh, underneath."

Around the room, mouths were open, as were notebooks. From the manic scratching of pens, Lupo surmised that no matter how loopy her story was, the subcommittee would soon be all over it.

She held up her evidence, the baseball-sized rock that hit the saucer. She pointed out the dent in the rock that its collision with the force field, or whatever it was, had made. Despite the lack of anything empirical or even tangible to ground her story, something about the experience had lit her up. She scribbled an equation on the blackboard, and Lupo forced himself to sit up straight. An equation! She knew some math, and *still* she believed in UFOs.

Someone asked, "How did it end?"

"I passed out. When I woke, the saucer was gone. But it had left dents in the grass about the size of roasting pans. They gave off a burnt smell. That was all. I packed up my stuff and went home."

Home. A silence while they thought of it and then ceased to think. Chairs scraped, knapsacks rustled. Acting fast, Otis adjourned the meeting. As the group filed out, he made a point of buttonholing almost everyone, reminding them to distribute leaflets advertising their next meeting, two weeks from today. "Don't leaflet on rainy days—the ink runs. We have a permit for leafleting at the Deferments concert on the twenty-third, but we still have to pay for printing. Remember to pass the hat."

The Deferments. Lupo recognized the name, but from where? Oh, yes: Rosemary's party. Where they talked about demonstrations, mass media, how they could, simply by being themselves, Change The World. Arguing the big picture over boxes of Chinese takeout.

But didn't everyone want to Change The World? The tools were all the same—shoe leather, mimeographs, the willingness to sit through boring meetings and pretentious Chinese takeout parties. The RICUFOG kids were both better and worse, engaged in an objectively futile project—or so it seemed to Lupo—yet admirable in their perseverance, the way they allowed hope to spring from nothing more than inexplicable dents in swamp grass and odd lights in the sky. He thought of Pedal Pushers, who had something risky to say and the wherewithal not just to say it, but to present reasons and evidence, to do the math.

She would have nothing but contempt for "Blue Rondo." Lupo was sure of that.

She was still there, packing up her gear. Her slowness seemed notable, perhaps deliberate. He might approach her. He liked her well enough. But did he need to ask her out today, when he still had Primrose on the brain and McKee's assignment to complete? The backlog of unfinished business seemed inauspicious. He pocketed his pen. Besides, Pedal Pushers had already done him a world of good. Without a single word, she had told him everything he needed to know about himself and Primrose, who wasn't the only cute girl in the solar system. Not at all.

Otis—he needed to speak with Otis. Among other things, Otis could connect him with the group's faculty adviser. Lupo hurried to the front of the room, where Otis was stuffing leftover leaflets into his beat-up knapsack.

"Got a minute?" Lupo asked him.

Otis looked up, squinting as if he couldn't quite place him. "Only just," he grunted.

"Do you have any more sightings to track down?" Lupo readied his pen. "I'd be happy to join you, if that's the case."

"No such luck. What I have are problems—well, problem sets. When you flunk organic chemistry, you're obliged to attend summer school. Wages of sin." Otis zipped his knapsack. "But I can give you a lift if you're headed in my direction."

Lupo followed Otis to the blazing parking lot. Sunshine bounced off dozens of chrome fenders, and Otis' glasses turned dark. Otis headed for a station wagon parked by itself at the lot's far edge. The parking lot shimmered, a vast black desert. Lupo hustled after him, trying to avoid the stickier-looking spots of asphalt.

"So, who's in charge of RICUFOG?" Lupo asked. "Who's your *leader*? You can't run a club without an adviser."

"So you're coming with me?"

Greetings, earthling, Lupo thought. "Who is your *faculty adviser*?"

"Oh, right. The guy you want is Misha Rodenko, in engineering."

Lupo hadn't heard of him. Had McKee?

"You said he's in engineering?"

"Not everyone's in astronomy. Besides, who do you think builds your telescopes?"

"Is he from around here?" Lupo was finally beginning to understand the importance of this question.

"No, he's Russian. Soviet. Defected."

"When?"

"Beats me. You're the reporter. Isn't that your job? To find things out?"

Lupo held his tongue, reminded himself to stay in role.

From his pocket Otis withdrew a ring of keys. He heaved the car door open and flopped into the driver's seat.

"Here's the thing, Lupo. You can't just waltz into Rodenko's office hours. For one thing, he doesn't keep any. If you want to meet him, you have to wait for an invitation."

"But that's absurd! All professors have office hours." Except McKee, of course.

"Rodenko doesn't. No office hours, that's the rule. You want to see him, you make an appointment. Sounds weird, but I guess that's how they do things over there in the US of SR."

Something didn't add up. A Soviet scientist, an engineer, sponsors the campus UFO club, but his office hours are invitation-only. What did he get out of the UFO club?

"Otis," he said, "why do you think these people are seeing UFOs?"

"You say 'these people,' but every sort of person sees UFOs. It's been documented. Housewives, bankers, scientists."

"Very different inner lives," Lupo offered.

"Who can say? An inner life is just that. Inner." Otis shrugged.

He'd clearly mastered the art of the shake-off. Might as well have been coated in Teflon, this guy. Nothing stuck.

"Why are they seeing them now?" Lupo pressed.

"You mean, when all the world's going to hell?"

"Exactly."

He turned the key, and the engine started with a bang. Lupo jumped.

"Quite an exhaust you have there," Lupo remarked, hoping to cover his skittishness with a hale-fellow-well-met jocularity. No such luck: Otis was grinning at him as if he intended to bang the exhaust for the next twenty minutes.

Engineers, man. It was hard not to envy their ease with the material world. That Teflon-coated persona surely had its advantages, too.

"I don't like to psychologize, and I don't typically like people who do," Otis said. "But do you want to know what I *do* like about you, Lupo Light?"

"What's that?" Though Lupo was pretty sure he didn't want to hear it.

"You go straight at things."

Which was a psychological point. Lupo pressed his lips together, willing himself to shut up for once. To let the smart-aleck opportunity go. For once.

The car lurched. Otis would be gone in half a moment, and with him, Lupo's next best chance to impress McKee, which was about as close to redemption as he could hope to get these days.

"Look, Otis. Can you get me in to see Rodenko or not?"

"You're persistent, too. Another likable quality, in moderation. I'm signing off now, Lupo. But you'll get your meeting. Stay tuned."

21. Mitose to the music

July began with ten straight days of rain. The runoff leached into the bay where it raised no alarms, although Primrose, who had sat out the storms eating saltines in her room, worried for the horseshoe crabs. She didn't feel pregnant apart from her odd, weepy concern for those ugly things—and of course, the omnipresent nausea that, as far as she was concerned, just *was* the baby, an alien force demanding something that only she could supply, and she would, if only she could figure out what it was.

The wind shifted, sending a draft through the open window. Primrose buttoned her sweater; crumbs rained onto the floor.

Despite her threats, Louise had not forced Primrose to visit Dr. Addleman. He couldn't tell her anything she didn't already know. The problem was, what to do next. Having a job, even a modest one, meant Tino presumably had money for an abortion, but he wasn't sure he wanted that. But in that case, would he marry her? He waffled on this point, too. Meanwhile, her paints sat in the corner, gathering dust. Life, it was true, went on—but it was hard to remember the point of painting in the midst of all this going-on. She half-hoped for a call from Lupo, but the phone stayed silent. Soon it would be too late. Shivering, she shut the window.

Meanwhile, Louise had shelved "Ave Maria" in favor of Louis Prima's "The Lady in Red," now in heavy rotation. She had memorized the lyrics, hitting her lines with an exaggerated emphasis. The lady in question seemed like a real piece of work, whose number was available for the asking. Whenever the song played, Primrose burned with shame. As much as Primrose had hated "Ave Maria," she now preferred it, with its intimations of mercy and forgiveness, to "The Lady in Red." Louise's deadpan sarcastic and mercilessly correct rendition had made it clear that, as a family, they were well beyond mercy, never mind forgiveness. *Marry in red*, Primrose remembered the schoolyard chant, *you'll wish yourself dead.*

A few days before, Louise had handed Primrose a wad of cash and ordered her to "do what needed to be done." She'd given up on God, she said. She didn't need Him or any other members of His Family, including Maria. Besides, what kind of trick was that, getting Maria pregnant without making her a *puttana*? It was simply too convenient. No, she didn't need that Family and their Holy Prevarications. All she needed was the music of Louis Prima, the layaway plan at Palma's, and to be left *strictly* alone during the hours before she left for work. After that, there had been no further word from Louise, apart from whatever could be inferred from her new taste in music.

That night, Primrose and Tino were going to the Hog House. They had tickets to see the Deferments courtesy of Rosemary, who was attending a last-minute gallery opening New York. Having never heard of the band, Tino hadn't wanted to go, but Primrose insisted, saying they were the next big thing.

Dressing for their date, Primrose struggled to tune out her parents, who were fighting all the time now. Tonight, for once, the argument had nothing directly to do with her. Hospital labor contracts were up for renewal, and Louise's union, sensing resistance to their new conditions, had abruptly broken off negotiations. A strike was planned. Louise wanted to cross the picket line, but Frank didn't like the idea.

"Even if they *don't* bust your head, what happens when it's all over and you go back to work? You'll get nothing but bedpans, and they'll run you right off your feet. No one's going to look out for you."

"I get nothing but bedpans anyway. Maybe they'll promote the strikebreakers."

"Don't be crazy. All you're going to prove is that you're disloyal."

"It's wrong, what they're doing."

"It's wrong to negotiate on your behalf? But what else are they there to do?"

"That's not what I mean, and you know it."

"What they're doing is none of your damn business. When you took that job, you made a promise."

"Some promise. I don't need to remind you, it's a union shop. It was join or no job."

"If you hate it that much, why don't you quit?"

"The money," she panted, tiring of the fight. "We need the money."

"We don't need it that much." Last week, Frank had returned to full-time work. It was the prudent thing to do, he said, with the strike pending.

"That's where you're wrong."

"I don't want to hear it, Louise."

When Tino pulled up, Primrose hurried to meet him. As she slipped out the door, the rain, which had been threatening all day, came down in a gray rush. In the car he turned to her, his face all concern: *But you're soaked.* As they pulled away, he cranked the heat and put his arm around her. He smelled like ironing starch and shaving cream, like the money he was making and not spending on abortions or wedding rings.

Puttana.

Primrose, feeling sick, switched off the heat. She rolled down her window and stuck her face out in the rain. By the time they reached the Hog House, she was feeling better. Her dress was nearly dry. The sound of someone noodling on a bass guitar wisped into the car. Droplets pattered on the car's roof, a quick burst of noise without commitment.

They hurried across the parking lot, skirting puddles. As they neared the turnstiles, the music grew louder.

"That's awful," Tino said as they gave their tickets to the person by the door. "I don't understand why everyone thinks this stuff is so great."

"Wait," she urged, brushing droplets of rain off his cheek. "They haven't even come on yet."

Tino fell silent; he was learning that silence was a tool for carving out space in which to allow Primrose to shift perspective, let second thoughts inform her first ones. He didn't need to help with that; all he had to do was let the process unfold. Inside, he headed for the bar, buying time, along with a beer for himself and a Dr Pepper for Primrose.

The darkened stage was dominated by an enormous castle with up-lit crenellated turrets. A huge papier-mâché falcon perched atop one of them; its wings opened and closed, casting weird shadows. The stage floor had been painted blue-green to suggest a moat. A catwalk stretched overhead. Key change: The piano receded, and the guitar picked up the melody. The stage lights swung down. On a screen hanging from the top of the castle wall, a circle of light appeared, then a black beetle-shaped figure that swelled, pulsed, and split in a sequence Primrose recognized from Tino's biology textbook—mitosis. A cell dividing, like whatever was now doubling and redoubling inside her, two becoming four, eight, sixteen, thirty-two—

Oceanic noise: bass, brass, ethereal guitar. The feedback was tremendous. Tino held Primrose close, steering her in and out of pockets of empty space. When the crowd rushed forward, she shook in his arms.

The drawbridge descended over the painted moat. A trio of cowboy-hatted fiddlers appeared. One was wearing a pair of green velvet shoes, the toes tipped with tiny bells; he walked with giant steps, stomping his feet to maximize the jingling. A lanky brunette, wearing a dress with a fringed hem, strode across the stage. The fringes stopped at the tops of her thighs. Her features were too sharp to be conventionally beautiful, but her sinuous movements had their own grace. She was gripping an electric guitar as if it might get away from her, and as she reached the stage's lip, she strummed the instrument experimentally.

Someone, not Tino, pressed against Primrose. She stepped away, surprised. Somehow she had lost Tino in the crowd. The music rose and swelled. As the number continued, the crowd began to sing along. Primrose shifted from one foot to the other, trying to ease into the beat. One song led to another, each more dissonant than the last. In the din, Primrose heard Tino scream.

Finally the band came to the end of the set. "Thank you," said the lead singer. She flashed a quick grin and dashed offstage. The lights went up. Tino was nowhere to be found.

But the scream—it had to have been him. Primrose felt sure of it. She drained her soda, sucked air noisily through the straw.

Then again, she'd felt sure of plenty of things that had never happened.

Tino materialized at Primrose's elbow. "I hate this stuff. Why did we come?"

Primrose frowned. "Is that why you screamed?"

"Jesus Christ, look at that."

Tino pointed out the window. On the far side of the parking lot was a building that had once housed a brewery. All the windows were dark; some were broken. "Once upon a time," he said, "those windows were lit up all night long."

Primrose crunched an ice cube, all that remained of her drink. "Things change, Tino. At least they still make Gansett. And some other things besides. They export."

"They sell to other states," he replied, irritated. "That's not export. Not at all."

Soothe him, she admonished herself, trying to remember the advice printed in *Redbook*.

"The unions are killing this country," Tino said, Leon-style.

Since he'd come home, he'd taken a turn. Now he really was becoming his father, aping his views on organized labor, the world as seen through the prism of Reliable Button. He rubbed his temples where the hair was receding. Soon he would look just like Leon, too.

"I'm not sure a union's to blame for the loss of this brewery," Primrose said.

"What?" Tino cupped a hand to his ear. The band was tuning up for the next set.

Her mother was probably at work right now, changing sheets or mopping the floor. If she hadn't gotten her head smashed for crossing the picket line.

She shook her head, mouthing the words: *Nothing. Never mind*.

Tino excused himself to look for the john.

Primrose stared out the window at the darkened brewery. What Tino thought didn't matter. What mattered was her life, here and now. It wasn't too late. She could still finish school. Her parents would help pay for it. Even nice girls got in trouble. It could happen to anyone. It could all be fixed. It would all, as Louise was fond of saying, come out in the wash. It might drain into the harbor and poison the horseshoe crabs, but maybe that too could be remedied, with time, determination, and the application of money, the universal solvent.

A man in a seersucker suit, too narrow through the shoulders, sidled up to Primrose and asked if he could buy her a drink. She waved him away, startled by the intensity of her own dislike: *You're a poor thing, buddy. A real sad sack*. The gleam of his oily brow was the last thing she saw before the lights went down again. The singer climbed onto a stool at center stage and curled her hands around a microphone. Her enormous mood ring, completely black, contrasted starkly with her mouth, which was painted so thickly with white lipstick that she looked like she'd just eaten a powdered donut. She raised her eyes to the ceiling, and the room went quiet.

"Let me tell you," she said, "about a little town called Patagonia, PA. Which doesn't exist anymore, if it ever did, except in the imaginations of a select few shining-pure souls like the ones gathered here at the Hog House tonight."

A man cheered. Someone else clapped. Hoots, whistles.

"Now, the reason Patagonia doesn't exist anymore is because of the racist imperialist policies of the United States government."

The audience fell silent.

"And the undeniable though sad fact of death."

A memory caught at Primrose, of footage she'd seen on TV: a trio of monks in saffron robes; a remote monastery whose ruined buildings jutted from the earth like neglected teeth; a whey-faced monk fingering gray stones. And then came more news of the war, familiar numbers and statistics, and then, there, on a chopper, was death itself, wrapped in plastic bags and offered up in neat military lines.

Someone shouted: FUCK 'EM!

Fuck the warmongers. Yes. Before they fucked you.

"Shut up," she said sweetly, "and let me finish."

She chanted for a good ten minutes, nonsense syllables that slowly sharpened into a paean to peace and love, "the twin solutions to the mushroom cloud." The fiddlers reappeared holding smoking sticks of incense. Primrose rubbed her smarting eyes as the band began again to play. The singer's mood ring had turned bright green, the same color as the carpet at the hospital where she'd had the electroshock, all five sessions of it, soup to nutty, nutty nuts. The fiddlers played louder while the singer stood on stage; the mood ring flashed, and she stroked her neck with the stone. When she turned her hand around, the ring had gone blood red. "Peace, brothers and sisters," she concluded. The music swelled. Encore.

Primrose wandered through the crowd. Someone clasped her hand: Tino. His eyes were dark, iris-less. He slung an arm around her and drew her away, pressing her shoulder awkwardly into his armpit. A beat came on, fast, staccato. People poured onto the dance floor. Someone yelled into a microphone: "Time to do the funky wallop, ladies and gents!"

A girl in pedal pushers swayed at the edge of the room alongside a man who looked familiar. Primrose squinted to get a better look.

Lupo.

He strode over, more than a little of the proud peacock about him, leading his new friend by the hand. They shouted introductions over the music. The girl stood slightly apart, watchful. Lupo explained that they'd taken a "direct action" by leafleting the cars in the lot in the service of some cause or other. He smiled in a way Primrose didn't like—too knowing, too sardonic. She thought: *He's not from around here.*

"What did you think of the show?"

She shrugged. "It was a little unreal."

"Oh, unreality! Well, I don't think that's *their* problem."

Was he sneering? Primrose couldn't tell. Unreality being, obviously, one of *her* biggest problems. But then again, she wasn't the one chasing UFOs.

"What about you, Tino? The Deferments aren't your cup of moonshine, I bet."

Something about the way Tino looked at Lupo chilled Primrose, as if Lupo were a specimen that Tino was about to dissect. "What would you know about my cup of moonshine?"

22. A mother's prerogative

Louise crumpled the leaflet Primrose had brought home, an advertisement for a meeting devoted to socialists and Other Unidentified Aliens. Just the sort of ridiculous cause Primrose was always falling for. The whole business put her in the mind of stray kittens. But Primrose was no kitten. She might have a baby or two, but she'd never have a litter, not with her weak nerves, and let us be thankful for small favors.

Louise tugged a tatty bedsheet over the chair she had ruined the night before, after falling asleep holding a lit cigarette that dropped ash on the armrest. It was a dumb thing to do. Dangerous, too. She was so tired. The ward was full of new faces, boys back from the war. Whenever the phone rang, every single one of those kids would start up from a sound sleep, shouting. She helped hold them down until someone else could administer a sedative, jamming the needle into whatever was available, thigh or fanny or upper arm. They were soldiers, for sure, and madmen, that could not be denied. You would be maddened, too, by a government that manufactured you into cannon fodder, treating your one life as if it weren't worth a hill of beans unless you spent it snuffing out every soul you could find in villages and paddy fields on the other side of the planet. But her patients were also just boys, the down still thick on their thighs and sometimes their cheeks, too. It was hard to know what to make of them, apart from lamenting the fact that each and every one of them had been born of a mother and was, therefore, somebody's precious baby. As they were on the other side, too, though she didn't have to rock those kids back to sleep on her shifts. The truth: The powers that be, whoever *they* really were, didn't see these kids the way she did, for what they most truly were: children born of mothers. As Primrose was born of her. Was *hers*, as much as Primrose hated to admit it. Well, she had been just the same with her own mother, and no harm had come of it. No harm should come to Primrose either. Which was why, in the end, she had handed Primrose a stack of bills in an envelope, greasy at the corners. She had made an exception—but wasn't that what a mother should do, being a mother? Though one couldn't make a habit of it. That's how kids got soft and useless. On the ward, people were going soft and useless all the time, scheduling one patient for release and letting a different one go. Without a doubt, they were understaffed. The union hadn't loosened its stranglehold on hiring. It was probably best to do just what her supervisor had been advising ever since those boys started coming in: Don't go looking for your own kid in their faces. It's the devil you don't know who'll surprise you.

23. Basic training

"The body," Joseph grouched, fussing with the model's shawl, "is basic." He draped a rectangle of brocade low on her shoulder, scowled, and pulled the fabric up again. The studio was hot. Sweat had dampened Joseph's collar, but the model was unmoved, cool. "A body, this body, that body. Anybody at all will do, it's not like we're particular."

The model held still, an illusion broken only by a minute, disapproving twitch around her mouth. The shawl floated to the floor. That's when Primrose felt it: *Whoosh*. The model had removed herself mentally from the room. Her body was all that was left. Basic.

Primrose bit her lip. Her mother's envelope was tucked in her handbag, a decision she had made and unmade at least ten times today, like a bed. Where her problems began.

"The sadness of the body," Joseph said, emphasizing *sadness*, as if this whole business of explanation was, in some way, deeply and personally expensive to him. "See if you can get this. The body has a language. You are its translators."

Joseph blamed them for being inept, but Primrose figured at least half the problem had to be his. Instead of selling into galleries in New York, he was stuck in Rhode Island, trying to get his students to do something most of them had never imagined—to make a mark on a surface in what he called "a condition of freedom," which to Primrose meant without the Louises of the world yammering in her ear.

But how free could you be if your body betrayed you, like Louise said? Freedom was abstract, but the body was not, not at all. The body might be basic, but it was also subject to circumstances, to politics—to what other people made of it. They might decide that your basic function was to pop out babies or to get shot up for nothing on the other side of the planet. Either way, you had no real say. No matter how Joseph went on about his precious demonstrations and the point of putting paint on canvas, the bit of the world was in his mouth as much as it was in hers. They were different people, champing different bits, but they had that much in common.

Tino had a bit in his mouth, too. He just hadn't noticed yet. Or maybe he still hoped it wasn't his, or that he could spit it out.

Joseph came over and leaned in to peer closely at her drawing. "Are you going to help with the Be-In? We're thinking we'll have it sometime in the fall."

The fall. For a moment, all Primrose saw was orange-gold: defoliants, a flaming hillside, a saffron robe.

"Sounds about right," she said, stepping back from her easel. Joseph leaned in to deepen a shadow she had too hastily blocked in. Amazing how little it took to go from surface to depth.

"What about that guy Lupo—do you have his number?"

"He's in the book," Primrose said.

"I see." He paused. "Will you think about it?"

"I will," Primrose promised, not at all sure that she would.

"Good. There's plenty of time," he said, moving on to the next easel. Sarcastically, he added: "So you can *think* about it."

So that was how things stood. Well, fine. She could live with his priorities; he was the teacher, after all. Setting priorities was his job. But she still wished he had said more about her sketch. The shadow he added was *exactly* right. What did he see that she could not?

Rosemary rushed in, sweat beading her upper lip. When she ducked out to visit the supply closet, Primrose peeked at her easel.

The canvas was washed in pale yellow and gray. Over this Rosemary had outlined, in charcoal, a sweeping area of squares and circles that she was slowly filling in, stippling the surface with tiny dots. She used different colors: burnt orange, emerald green, sulfur yellow. Whatever it was, the picture was most certainly was not the figure drawing that constituted today's lesson. Rosemary returned, catching Primrose before she could avert her eyes.

"Want to grab a coffee after class?" The words were out of Primrose's mouth before she could think twice.

"Sure," Rosemary said as she picked up her palette knife, unfazed by the scrutiny of her work. "Is Joseph hassling you about the Be-In, too? I'm getting tired of hearing it, listening to these guys yammer while they wait for us to fetch the drinks."

That night at Rosemary's house, Joseph had brought out the martinis. Primrose remembered that clearly. But she also remembered the way Rosemary had been shouted down at the SDS meeting. How a tendril of an idea had pushed up from Rosemary's mind, only to wither in the chill of a general masculine ignoring. Rosemary was talking about something bigger than who got the drinks.

Primrose touched charcoal to paper, just where she hoped the model's knee would emerge from the page like a miracle. She squinted at the model, at the page and back again, but nothing happened. She glanced around. The others were struggling, too. The model fidgeted, and a student groaned from behind an easel: the model was not supposed to move. But then many things that were not supposed to happen, did happen. The model scratched her nose. She swung her long foot. Her toenails were painted Paramour Pink.

THE BOOK OF LOVE: Abortifacients

by Primrose

A bad fall

Agent Orange

Ascorbic acid

Black cohosh

Brewer's yeast

Clothes hanger

Dioxin

Dong quai

Evening primrose (!)

Jumping up and down

Knitting needles

Mugwort

Nutmeg

Parsley

Peacock flower

Pennyroyal

Tansy

Wild carrot

24. The shakes

After class, Primrose and Rosemary went to Miss Cranston's where they ordered chocolate milkshakes. Primrose took one sip and pushed hers away—too rich. Rosemary followed with a long, reckless pull and then slapped her palm hard against her forehead.

"Ice cream headache," Rosemary groaned. "I always drink these too fast. Two hot coffees over here, please," she called out, flagging down the waitress. "These shakes are damn cold."

"What did you expect? They're made of *ice cream*."

The waitress huffed off and came back, still huffing, with two steaming cups. She set them down and pulled the milk and sugar to the center of the table.

"These are about as hot as the milkshakes were cold," she snipped. "So be careful. Despite what you seem to think, your mother doesn't work here."

Primrose regarded her. "I'm not so sure about that."

"Suit yourself. But don't make me say I told you so."

She flounced off, and Rosemary, who had watched the whole exchange with mouth open in amazement, asked, "What's gotten into you?"

"Well," Primrose said, stirring milk into her coffee, "I seem to be pregnant."

Rosemary scrutinized the sugar bowl, her mouth twisting with responses held back, thought better of. When she finally spoke, she sounded like a teacher who had taught the same lesson too many times.

"Look, this is not a big deal. I know you feel like it is—but it's not. You made a mistake, so what. You don't have to pay with the rest of your life. Certainly the father, whoever he is, doesn't think he's got to." She broke off her monologue to take a sip of coffee. "It's not Lupo, is it?"

"He's not the father."

"Who is?"

Maybe telling Rosemary wasn't the right thing to do after all. "You don't know him."

Rosemary shrugged. "I'm just trying to help."

"I want a baby someday," Primrose insisted. "I'm not generally against motherhood, though my own mother—well, never mind. I'm just not ready for it now."

"Relax," Rosemary said as she pulled a cigarette from the pack on the table. "I'm not the FBI. Though I don't mind telling you, you'd be more convincing if you didn't sound like you were choking on the whole idea. Of motherhood, I mean."

She lit up and offered the pack to Primrose, who waved it away.

"Listen, Primrose. You don't have to have it, and don't let anyone tell you otherwise. I know someone who can help. Plenty of other girls have been through this, and they're just fine. You will be, too."

So it might be true, then: She might wear a Pauline Trigère suit and go to an opening at the Met. She might sell her paintings in a swank gallery. She might work in an artists' colony; she'd been told such things exist. She would get her own doctor, someone her mother didn't know, and she would ask for a prescription for the Pill. Her life might not be all about Louise.

Rosemary patted her arm. "He's decent," Rosemary told her, passing a slip of paper across the table. On it, she'd written the name and address of a doctor across town. "He's clean."

The following afternoon, Tino took Primrose out of the house while her mother dressed for her shift. This was their plan, but still, Primrose couldn't look at him. Staring at the Chevelle's dusty dashboard, she said: "Thanks for coming to get me."

"I'm not doing much." He couldn't look at her either. The neighborhood went by in a blur. "That sounds very unromantic, I know."

"I don't need you to be romantic. I just need you to be here."

"Are you sure?"

Finally, she was able to look him in the face. He hadn't shaved in a few days. Reaching across the seat, she put her hand to his face, let his stubble scratch her palm. "I spoke to Rosemary."

"That girl from art class?" he asked, keeping his eyes on the road.

"She says there's nothing to it."

"So you're sure."

Primrose swallowed. "Yes," she lied. "I'm sure."

He was quiet for a moment. Then he sighed.

"We've got the money. You've done the legwork. If it's what you want, then I suppose it has to be fine with me."

"It doesn't *sound* fine."

Tino banged the steering wheel. "Goddamn it, it's fine!"

"You don't need to yell."

Passing the ballpark, Tino revved the engine. They looped off main road and sped onto the highway. "I know your reasons," Tino said tightly. "You don't want to get married. You want to run around with Lupo Light."

She forced herself to breathe slowly."

"It *is* my body, isn't it?" They were headed in an unfamiliar direction; the highway signs pointed to places she'd never been. The sky was blue and empty. But here was a new feeling: For once, even though she wasn't sure of Tino, she felt sure of herself, of her own resolve. "You *could* marry me, but you won't. So I have one other choice. Only one. And I am making it."

"I'm sorry," he said quietly. "I'm sorry this happened. All of it."

"Me, too."

Tino stretched his arm around her. She leaned into him, because that was the thing to do, the thing that was expected. She felt exactly nothing. As for Tino, his face was unreadable. Perhaps he felt nothing, too.

Outside the doctor's office, she kissed his cheek. The roughness surprised her again. Another surprise: how this feeling thrilled her even now.

"I guess if you really want to do this—"

"I do."

"Well," he said, "all right."

The doctor's office smelled of mice. A painting hung on one wall: A bright yellow path snaked through a dark green fairy-tale forest; kitschy flowers dotted the foreground, all the way to the cottage's rough wood door. On another wall, there was a large window with a view of the airshaft. Turned off by the painting and its obvious symbolism, Primrose took a seat near the window. Tino sat beside her.

"Are you okay?" Tino asked. "Your color isn't good."

Primrose smiled thinly. Her heart pounded. "I'm fine."

Two pigeons were fighting in the airshaft. Now and then stuff drifted past: ash, a dirty feather. Tino sneezed into his handkerchief.

You could only really sterilize things with an autoclave, as Tino knew from his shifts in the ER. This office would not contain an autoclave. From the state of the waiting room, the doctor seemed hardly aware of the existence of mousetraps. "Jesus," he whispered to Primrose. "You said this guy was clean?"

Primrose took slow breaths, trying to calm down. Her anxieties mounted: What if this doctor wasn't as skilled as Rosemary said? What if she got out and started to bleed? She'd be hunched in her mother's bathroom bleeding onto the linoleum, and Louise would say: *You'd think you could do just this one thing right.*

Primrose pulled her compact from her handbag and peered at her reflection; she powdered her forehead, blotting away the shine. It felt good to do these normal things. Primrose flipped the pages of an old copy of *Ladies Home Journal*, skipping over the stories that had to do with children, and settled on the beauty section, which featured seven ways to get better bouffants and a dozen tips for thicker eyelashes. These, too, were normal things. One could drink a tablespoon of cod liver oil daily. Or eat bowls of gelatin. If all else failed, you could simply fake it; laid out on the facing page were various options for doing so, complete with illustrations.

"They look like anchovies," Primrose said, her finger resting on one of the thinner, more natural-looking sets of false brows. Tino smiled, acknowledging the joke though he failed to find it funny. Nerves, she figured. She had them, too.

When her name was called, Primrose stuffed the magazine in her bag and followed the nurse. Tiny feet pattered in the walls.

The nurse wore the same outfit as Louise did on her shifts—a white polyester dress with cap sleeves and a zipper up the back, white nylons, and thick-soled shoes. She took Primrose's blood pressure and left her with orders to undress. There was dust in the corners and behind the trash bin, and a brown spot of something—Was it blood? Surely it was blood—on the floor.

That blood might be her own in an hour or two. And then what? There would be no trip to the hospital, no rescue by a smart doctor. No one would lay a hand on her. They'd just wait to see what would happen. Whether or not she would die.

How much less risky it seemed, just then, to have the baby. For three hundred days, she'd carry it. Then one day, it would be born. So simple. So natural. No dust, no mice. Millions of women did it all the time. Had done it. Through dust, through mice. Would continue to do it, even when they dropped the bomb or blasted the moon from its orbit or colonized Mars. That was life. It persisted. Like dust. Like mice, nesting in walls, squeaking and pattering in pursuit of their mousy objectives—love, food, avoidance of mousetraps.

Then it came to her: *They fucked us up. Our parents fucked us up.* To them it was all right to die for someone else's crazy schemes—Louise's scheme to make her a proper lady, Lyndon Big Jackass's plan to make the world safe for American business. It was just the same on Calvary Street as it was anywhere else. The worst part of it was how they could make you believe that certain actions really were in your own best interest. Like aborting a baby, or having one, making you pay with your life when all you'd made was a mistake.

If we let them, they will kill us all.

She leaned against the door and slid down, shutting her eyes. Tino would be out there, waiting for her to return without this burden inside her. This drag on the future.

Or had she missed something?

To keep this baby—now, that would be something. A love child, isn't that what they called it? They would be two, mother and child, standing together against this crappy world. They didn't stand a chance, but wasn't that all the more reason to fight? To say: We'll do it our way. We don't believe in your power.

And wouldn't they talk, all of them—the mothers, the fathers, the friends. Even Tino. She'd be *the talk of the town*, just like Louis Prima said, like they all said.

She shivered. Something was wrong, but what of it? So much was wrong. Let it be wrong. Let them talk. She would have this child. She would make love without Louise's hiss in her ear. That was the condition of freedom Joseph kept talking about. She would be a mother. If Tino wanted her, she would be a wife.

Above all, she would paint.

Primrose dressed, then retrieved her makeup kit from her bag and angled her face toward the mirror. With deliberate movements, she applied lip gloss from a pot, replaced the lid, and dropped the pot back in her bag. She was a normal woman doing normal things. Holding tightly to this idea of normality, she walked out of the procedure room and back to where Tino waited. As he stared, she gathered herself into her coat, turned on her heel, and rode the elevator down to the street.

Tino found her outside, standing by the Chevelle's passenger door. As Tino drove her home, she explained her decision. It wasn't easy. Familiar as it was, Tino's close presence seemed to exert a pressure, and she struggled to convey the same conviction she had felt so strongly in the doctor's office.

We can do this, Tino. If you won't help, I'll do it alone. But I hope you will. Help, I mean.

She was fighting, she said, for their life together. All three of them.

She thought Tino had listened. At least he had not scoffed at what she'd said. But he hadn't proposed on the spot, either, and later on, she realized that she had hoped he would. The plain fact was, he needed to be convinced. Even as he'd insisted—manfully, she noted, proud of him still, despite everything—on being with her when she broke the news to Louise.

They made their way together up the concrete walk, his warm hand clasping her cold one. Her breath came in spasms, and she wasn't sure how much longer she'd remain upright.

The important thing, she told herself, was to get through the next fifteen minutes. As for the rest—the baby, the money, a life together—they'd have to figure that out. Or she would.

The key shook in the lock. He put his hand over hers to still it. She knew he wanted her to be brave, to feel brave. But his face was white.

"After everything she's done to you, Primrose—"

"Shh, Tino. Let's not go in shooting."

In the living room, Louise was stretched on the horsehair sofa. Louis Prima was rotating on the turntable. Coming in from the kitchen, Frank did a double-take.

"Tino, what a surprise. Can I get you a beer?"

"Thank you," Tino said, "but I don't think I'll be staying long."

Primrose dropped his hand.

"Why don't you sit," Louise said to Tino, "and have something to wet your whistle."

"Tino already *said* he wasn't staying," Primrose snapped. "He *said* he doesn't want a beer."

Louise extinguished her Lucky. "And how did you enjoy your little trip to the butcher's?"

Primrose imagined herself disappearing like the Cheshire Cat, one piece at a time, until nothing was left but the fake smile pasted on to cover up her shame.

"Mrs. Tirocchi," Tino began, perching on the edge of the armchair just opposite Louise, "we have something to tell you about that. Mr. Tirocchi, you should hear this too."

Frank sat beside Louise on the horsehair couch. Primrose dragged a kitchen chair into the room and collapsed into it.

"So, what is it, Primrose?" Frank asked gently, his eyes creased with concern. "Are you feeling all right?"

"I'm fine. It's just—"

Tino interrupted. "We're keeping the baby."

Louise murmured, "Is that so?"

Frank slapped his thigh. "Well, that's wonderful!"

"Says you," Louise snapped at him. "And so now who's going to pay for formula? Snotrags? Diapers? Forget retirement, Frank. We'll both be on the job until the blessed day we die."

"Mom—"

"From the moment I laid eyes on you, Primrose Tirocchi, I knew you were a—"

"Louise," Tino said, cool as the surgeon he'd never become. If he didn't have the drive, the competitive urge, to succeed at *that*, at least he had the gumption to dominate Louise. "That's enough."

"Enough? I haven't even started, Tino."

"Primrose and I understand that we've made a mistake," Tino said calmly. "We intend to take responsibility."

Louise lit another Lucky, exhaled angrily. "No wonder you didn't make it through medical school. You're thick!"

Tino winced.

"You're damn right it's time to take responsibility!" Louise shouted. "Past time, if you ask me, which you didn't. What I meant was, I hope you plan to buy my daughter a wedding ring."

25. Daydream believer

"Dearly beloved," Chick began, "we are gathered here today because we have a slight problem."

The original quartet was together again, seated around a horseshoe booth at Miss Cranston's. They'd had their fun, a regular feast, but now the table needed clearing, the bill looking to. Though Primrose had devoured a grilled cheese and a milkshake, the food had merely dulled her appetite, whose edge she still felt, gnawing at her insides like a tooth about to erupt.

"My mother says the boat's got to go," Chick said.

"What's the problem with the boat?" Tino asked as he conveyed the last of his French fries to Primrose's plate. He'd seen her hungry look. "I mean, apart from the bilge, marina fees, and the lingering ghost of the dead captain?"

"It blocks her view, she says."

"Her view of what?"

"The driveway."

Dot pulled her smokes from the pocket of her work apron. She was just off her shift, and she looked like hadn't slept in a week.

"Dot, I only got a little pickle," Chick complained. He held up a dill spear the size of his pinky.

"So?" Dot shook a cigarette out of the pack and lit it. "Don't tell me you came here just to measure the pickles."

"I give up," said Chick. "What say I take you home, Dot?"

"Let me grab my tips. I need to make rent."

Dot had moved out of her parents' place into a small apartment. With bills to pay, she had a new way about her. She smiled less, and in conversation, she went straight to the point.

"You women's libbers," Tino joked. "You work your own jobs, you pay your own taxes. We ought to send *you* off to war."

"The war would be over by now, if women were fighting it," Dot told him as she got up. "And you know it."

The evening ended the way it usually did, in the front seat of Tino's car. But this time, Primrose turned away from Tino just as he went to kiss her.

"No," she said, putting a hand on his arm. "Tell me why you hate women's libbers and want to send us off to war."

"So you're a women's libber now, too?"

"I might have to become one. You haven't asked me to marry you." A passing car's headlights traced shadows on the dashboard, and a new possibility occurred to her. "Chick wants to get rid of the boat. If you sold it, there might be enough for a ring."

"His mother's on the warpath, but she'll calm down soon enough. She always does."

Primrose slipped out and shut the door quietly. Beyond withholding kisses, there wasn't much she could do. Tino had to make up his own mind.

Down the hill, red lights twinkled around the oil tanks, telling whatever was nearby not to get too close. Primrose strode up the walk, adjusting her clothes. Maybe the philosophy of those red lights was not such a bad one after all.

26. Lorraine

From the doorway to his mother's dressing room, Tino watched his mother set her hair.

"Stop hovering." She set her hairspray on the dressing table beside the bowl of Hershey's Kisses and turned to him. "Would you look at that. My *agita* is all over *your* face. What's going on, Tino?"

He rocked back on his heels, as if to gather some force he did not have. The sun sank inexorably. Night always came first to his mother's dressing room, as if it were necessary to check with Lorraine before slinking into the rest of the house.

"Mom," he blurted. "Primrose is pregnant."

She sat motionless. "She's sure?"

He nodded. She took a chocolate from the bowl. Through the soles of his shoes, Tino felt where the hardwood floor ended and the carpet began.

"Stop fidgeting, Tino. Let me think."

She unwrapped the chocolate and set it aside. Tino stuffed his hands in his pockets, willing himself to stand still for once, to listen.

"Some girls just manage to get in trouble," she said. "This won't be the end of it. There will be other messes. She had one breakdown last year," she reminded him. "She'll have another. That's how she's made. But you don't have to marry her just because she's fragile and makes bad decisions. Call it off. Tell her it's over."

"I can't do that."

"I know what you're thinking, Tino. You could do worse. She's a nice girl, very pretty..."

"She's beautiful."

She looked at him sadly. On her dresser, there was a framed photograph of her taken at his age, in a dress Poppa Tavio had made. She was smiling, her face smooth, her eyes luminous. She turned back to the mirror. "Pretty fades."

"It does not."

Lorraine unscrewed the cap from a little pot on the table and scooped out a small quantity of lotion.

"Trust me," she said over her shoulder, patting lotion on her neck. "You don't build a life on pretty. You can do better. You just need to put it all behind you—Primrose, St. Louis. Make a fresh start."

"I don't want to do better. I don't want a fresh start."

Lorraine turned her back to him and caught his gaze in the mirror. "*She is sick.* You're going to have to deal with that. Hospitalizations, pills, doctors. And you're going to make *us* deal with that, me and your father, for the rest of our lives. Oh, Tino. We've given you everything—"

"It won't be your responsibility."

"The *hell* it won't." Lorraine spun around, her eyes narrowed to angry slits. "You say a baby's on the way. Who's going to watch this baby while Primrose has another breakdown?"

"Since when did you start looking into crystal balls?"

"You're making the mistake of your life," she said. "And not for the first time, either!"

Trailing his hand on the banister, Tino toed his way down the stairs, lightheaded with the realization that Primrose had been right after all. His parents and all the rest of that generation really had fucked them up. But he could still make a life of his own. *Their* own. He would propose, Primrose would accept, and they would simply be happy—happier than his parents ever dreamed of, happier than they even could conceive of being. In nine months, he'd have his own family: mother, father, baby. His mother could take her nerves and her chocolates straight to hell. She didn't know the first thing about mistakes, how you could make them and still come out all right.

27. To every purpose under heaven

The night of the dance at the Matterhorn, both Primrose and Louise wanted to use the bathroom at the same time.

"Why can't you take turns?" Frank asked. He was running hot water into the kitchen sink, preparing to do the washing up.

"You're always so *reasonable*, Frank. One of these days you'll get a *spine*."

"Is that so?" Frank lowered a handful of dirty flatware into the water.

"No need to get pissy," Louise told him, though he'd only made a moderate splash.

"I'll need an hour at least," Primrose cut in.

"Oh no, you will not. I don't see you making any mortgage payments." Louise repositioned the napkin holder on the plastic gingham tablecloth. "And until you do, you will get twenty minutes in there, tops." She sighed. "Although I might not be making any payments, either, if I don't make it into work tonight."

"So you're joining the picket line after all?"

Louise stared at her. Frank plunged his hands into the suds.

"Now look what you've done, Primrose. You've gone and upset your father."

"Speak for yourself. I'm not the one who's being upsetting."

"What I do tonight is none of your business," Louise said. "I need my time alone, Primrose. I want to be prepared for whatever happens."

"Me, too," said Primrose. "I want to be prepared, too."

"Ha," Louise scoffed. "If only you'd thought of that before."

"For God's sake, let her go, Louise." Frank sponged a dish. "You won't be long, will you, Primrose? Besides, Louise, the last time your union threatened to strike, they made a deal with the management at the last minute, which is the only time any deals get made, and in the end, there was no picket line to join or cross. There's no reason to believe tonight will be any different."

"All right," Louise conceded.

"There's no need to get riled up."

"Fine."

Primrose hurried to her bedroom before her mother could change her mind. It was nice to get her own way for once. She laid her new black dress on the bed, along with a strand of pearls, fakes, from an odd lot Tino had unearthed in some forgotten drawer at Reliable Button. The late sun seeped a reddish light into the room, over the beads, lending them a melancholy luster. So romantic! Primrose shook her head. What crap. Sunshine on a set of cheap plastic beads. Though they didn't look half bad now, in the rich afternoon light. She picked up her notebook and began to jot a note for *The Book of Love*, but then smoke from her mother's cigarette drifted in. Right. Louise was waiting.

As Primrose scurried to the bathroom, she overheard her father pleading with her mother: "Tell me you're not serious about going in tonight, Lou."

Silverware rattled in the sink. "I'm just going to see what I can see."

"What you'll see is a bunch of angry nurse's aides about to lose their jobs. Just sit tight, Louise. They won't fire you. They don't have the nerve. Who else would give those people their sponge baths every night? You think the nurses would do it?"

"Please. They wouldn't know a sponge basin from a flying saucer."

In the bathroom, Primrose poured bubble bath in the running water, smiling to herself. Green glowing sponge basins with tiny humanoids inside them, reading computer printouts! And bedpans, too—making visitations, freaking out the likes of Lola DiMaio. *Greetings, earthling!* Too bad she wasn't talking to Lupo anymore. He'd have gotten a kick out of this.

"Yoo-hoo!" The doorknob rattled. "Don't take all night in there, young lady!"

Louise stomped down the hall.

Primrose soaked until her bath got cold, then ran more hot water into the tub. When she finished, she wrapped herself in her bathrobe and opened the door to find Louise glowering there, her back pressed against the wall and her up-do slipping from its pins. She pushed past Primrose into the bathroom and slammed the door.

In her bedroom Primrose tugged the new dress over her head. It fit too tightly across the chest, but it wasn't unwearable. From the jumble of her makeup box she extracted a compact of pancake makeup and smeared it on her face. Mechanically she applied powder, blush, eyeliner, mascara. For lipstick, she had a few choices, including the tube of Paramour Pink, a gift from Louise, who had recently decided the shade wasn't right for her after all.

"You aren't going to the Matterhorn all tarted up like that, are you?" Louise asked, startling her. She was standing in the doorway wrapped in a towel, blowing smoke.

"No one will notice," Primrose said. How long had she been staring into the mirror?

"Lorraine Battuta will certainly notice the way you've troweled on that foundation."

Primrose leaned toward the mirror and squinted at her reflection. She tweezed a stray hair near her brow, then another. Louise's face floated into view, coming over her shoulder through a cloud of smoke. "Be careful you don't tweeze your face off," she said. Trapping her Lucky between her index and middle fingers, Louise pinched Primrose near her waist.

"You're getting awfully thick around the middle. When I was pregnant with you, I didn't show until my seventh month."

"It's just the dress," Primrose snapped. "The way it's cut."

"If you don't watch out, you'll be a 4-H cow."

As if the answer truly interested her, which it didn't, Primrose asked, "Why are you so cruel?"

"Because I'm your mother, that's why."

Primrose heard the television snap on, the noise of her father settling in for the night. A distant roar, followed by a broadcasting voice. The Sox were playing at home tonight. Fenway Park, another world.

Primrose headed back to the bathroom. Louise followed. When Primrose tried to shut the door, Louise placed her hand on the knob. No one was going to shut a door in Louise's face tonight. Primrose flashed on herself, heavily pregnant and stuck forever in this house with her mother, who'd never let her have a moment's peace.

"You tweeze those hairs, they come back faster. And thick, like a man's."

"You're full of good advice, you know that, Ma?" Primrose yanked the doorknob from her mother's grip. "You should write a book. How to prune your face, how to avoid becoming a cow. You could call it *Future Farmers of America* and put a picture of Twiggy on the cover."

Louise shouted, "Twiggy's not even American!"

Noise from the TV welled up: a base hit, maybe, or a double play. As Primrose did her hair, she heard her mother pull out of the garage. The night stretched ahead of her, full of possibility.

When Tino arrived, she was out and down the walk in a flash. Relieved to be out of the house, she sank into the front seat, and he leaned over, smiling, crooning, "At last..."

She flipped the visor to check her makeup in the mirror. That was when she noticed Tino's parents in the back seat.

"Mrs. Battuta! Mr. Battuta!"

Tino hadn't told her they'd be driving to the Matterhorn with his parents. She flipped the visor back up and, squirming, pulled at her dress where it was tight across the chest. From over her shoulder she caught Tino's mother shooting her a funny look. She probably hadn't gained an ounce with either of her boys.

"How are your mother and father, Primrose?"

"They're fine, Mrs. Battuta. Thanks for asking."

As they pulled away from the curb, Frank burst through the front door shouting.

"Tino, wait," Primrose said. She cranked the window open as her father hustled down the walk.

"What's wrong, Mr. Tirocchi?" Tino asked.

"You hear about the strike?"

"Just what was in the paper," Tino said. "Did Louise go?"

"She drove off in a huff twenty minutes ago," Frank said, "saying she wanted to see the picket line. I don't know if she's going to cross it or join it or what. Probably she just wants to see the show. She's likely to earn herself a knuckle sandwich, if you ask me. Would you mind checking on her before you head out tonight?"

"No trouble at all," Tino said, even as his mother tsked in the back seat. "We'll just swing by and see that she's okay."

By the time they reached the hospital, the rain was gusting all around and Tino had to set the wipers on HIGH just to see ten yards ahead. Arriving at the parking lot, they joined a line of cars. State troopers in riot gear crowded the entrance, stopping each car as it went in.

"Riot gear," Tino scoffed.

"For a bunch of little old ladies?" Leon wondered.

"You know my mother," said Primrose.

"A force to be reckoned with," Tino said, flipping the dial on the defroster, "but maybe the riot gear is just a touch over the top?"

"Don't concede anything, Primrose!" Leon bellowed from the back seat. "Don't give him an inch!"

Primrose smiled, but her insides told a different story. Leon didn't seem to realize that her mother's job was on the line, or that she might be out there choosing between her livelihood and her conscience. Primrose was still angry at Louise—for the money, the abortion, the slap, sex, everything—but she also had to admit that she was proud of her, too.

Perched on the edge of her seat, directly behind Tino, Lorraine stared out the window, her lips pressed into a thin pink line.

One of the guards asked what they wanted. Tino explained that they were there for Louise.

"We just want to talk to her, to see that she's all right," he said.

A group of women paced back and forth outside the hospital's entrance. Their wet overcoats clung to their bodies. They carried signs: HOSPITAL CRISIS. RESPECT OUR JOBS. THIS IS A UNION SHOP.

Across the street, a pair of counterdemonstrators hoisted a banner: HEIL HOWARD!

Primrose glimpsed Louise peeking out from behind an azalea in full scarlet bloom.

"There, Tino!"

He beeped, and Louise hurried over, pulling a plastic kerchief over her head. A chant rose from the picket line as Louise approached the car. She leaned into Tino's open window and whispered in his ear.

"What?" he said. He couldn't hear anything over the shouting.

"Everyone's been fired," she said, louder now, but looking over her shoulder as she spoke. "It's all over. They're gonna bring in the Reserves."

Tino stared at her. "The Reserves."

"That's right."

"Hop in," he said.

Louise peered doubtfully into the car's interior. "Three's a real crowd in your front seat."

"Come on," Primrose said, scooting closer to Tino. "There's room up here, next to me."

Still, Louise hesitated.

"I'm not that big yet," Primrose said defensively.

"It's not that. I don't want to leave my car in the lot."

"You and Frank can come back for it," Tino said. "After the dust settles."

Thunder. Primrose counted—one Mississippi, two. There was a flash of light.

From the back seat, Lorraine piped up: "You'll get soaked, Louise. You'll catch your death."

Louise scurried around to the passenger side and slid in beside Primrose. They drove back to Calvary Street in a silence interrupted only by the scrape of the wipers on the windshield. Louise huddled against the door, her cigarette trailing sparks out the window. Primrose sat stiffly, feeling her dress getting wet where she was pressed against Louise.

At a stoplight, Primrose whispered to Louise, "Did you do it?"

Louise shook her head. "I was like Switzerland. I stayed neutral."

Tino pumped the brakes through a deep puddle. Primrose glanced at her mother. "I'm glad you didn't join them," she said.

Louise shrugged. "I'm no hero."

At the Tirocchis', Tino asked if he could use the phone. He wanted to call Chick and let him know what had happened before he saw it on the news. Louise invited them all in, but Lorraine stayed in the car, fussing with her compact mirror.

Inside, Frank sat at the table, sipping a beer and watching the storm. Primrose swept a pile of union leaflets into a drawer. She couldn't help noticing how Leon looked around.

"What happened on the line?" Frank asked.

"Turn on the radio, you'll hear all about it," Louise said brusquely as she hung her coat on a hook. "That reminds me. You better hurry up and enlist, Tino. Tomorrow morning, first thing. There'll be a line down the block if you wait."

Another clap of thunder, and lightning forked across the sky. The lights blinked out, the radio hissed, the TV went dark. Tino hustled across the room and lifted the telephone's receiver. He needed to talk to Chick.

"I take that back," Louise said, looking down the hill. "No one will get word of this for a while."

"I'll say," said Frank, fiddling with the antenna.

"Listen," Tino said into the phone. "If we get there early, we might have a shot at this thing."

He and Chick agreed to head over to the reserve board together the next morning at sun-up. Then Leon called the Matterhorn.

"Party's still on," he said after a few minutes of conferring with the maitre'd. "They've got candles and kerosene and a generator."

"Hot diggety," Louise said, flopping onto the horsehair sofa. "You go on now, Primrose. Have your night on the town."

Primrose stared at her, barely breathing.

"Do I need to spell it out for you, *cagootz*? We've all been fired. But we're essential. Someone's gotta empty those bedpans." Louise cackled. "What kind of society lets its hospitals fail? That's just the sort of catastrophe the Reserves are for. As long as Tino's first in line tomorrow, he's got a shot, a good one, at a stateside deployment. You and Tino—"

Such odd lights in her mother's eyes—

"You got a reprieve!"

A reprieve. The words ricocheted in Primrose's mind. *We got a reprieve.*

Off they went, windshield wipers thumping. In the front seat, Primrose nestled against Tino. Her dress was nearly dry. The Matterhorn was only a few miles away, but it might as well have been on another planet. The closer they got, the more abstract her mother's house became, until even its smells of nail polish and boiled cabbage were just things she might have read about in a fairy tale, once upon a time.

Leon shifted in the back seat.

"Your sciatica?" Lorraine asked him.

"You know how it kicks up when it rains."

"Wouldn't you know," Lorraine said. "I left the Fiorinal at home."

They turned onto the long road that led to the club—PRIVATE DRIVE, the sign said, MEMBERS ONLY—and rolled through a nave of evergreens. The clubhouse was off to one side, a low building whose main entrance was marked by a fountain where a stone maiden poured water from a stone pitcher. The storm had blown through, and blue-green waves of grass swelled all around. A man in coveralls disappeared into a distant stand of poplars. Tino got out and circled to the passenger door to help Primrose from her seat.

The quartet made their way toward the entry. Black-eyed Susans blossomed in clumps along a walkway lined with birches. Their trunks were peeling, as if sunburned.

"We started from nothing." Leon was in a nostalgic mood, gesturing expansively, taking in the clubhouse and the endless lawn. "In 1948, we were just a group of guys sitting around, wondering why we couldn't get into Quidnesset or Valley. Then it occurred to us—if they wouldn't have us, we'd build our own. And that," Leon concluded grandly, "is the American way."

"Oh, Leon," Lorraine said. Her tone was sweet, but her words conveyed a warning. Too much bragging was not good for anyone's prospects.

Primrose smiled politely. Leon made his way, yes, but on the backs of people who streamed out of the factories at quitting time and shopped the sales at Atlantic Mills. Women like her mother, all more or less faceless to Leon, who, even as he borrowed the phone in her mother's kitchen, had failed to remember that she had once worked for him.

The Battutas were good people, decent, hard working. And yet—

Primrose bit her cheek, stumbled.

"Easy," Tino said, catching her elbow.

Tasting blood, she suppressed an urge to spit.

"Once upon a time," Leon announced, "we were getting strung up from trees in Louisiana."

"You might still get strung up," Lorraine told him, exasperated. "I'll do it myself if we miss cocktail hour, no thanks to your running on."

In the ballroom, dozens of round tables were set with glittering silverware and gleaming china plates. White tablecloths complemented white napkins folded into swans, white roses erupted from crystal vases, and white paper lanterns hung down, lit from within. Girls in cocktail dresses sipped sparkling wine from flutes, while their dates managed outsized tumblers of Scotch and rye.

They found their table, and Tino ordered them both sodas. A waiter glided by with a platter of spanakopitas. Tino took one and put it on his bread plate. Nauseated again, Primrose waved the waiter away.

Wearing a white dress made of layers of chiffon, Fayrene joined them at the table. As soon as she sat down, she ruffled what remained of Tino's hair.

"I got a letter from Pat," she announced, clearly over the moon as a result of this development.

"Is that right?" Tino slipped an arm around Primrose's shoulders. Although his wool suit was itchy on her bare skin, his touch made her feel less nauseated. What was a little itch, anyway? She didn't mind Tino's cheeks when he didn't shave. She liked him a little rough around the edges.

"What did my brother have to say for himself?" Tino asked Fayrene.

"He says the beer's something special over there." She stared briefly into the distance. "When do you think he'll be back?"

"Two, three months. He's on short time now."

"And you, Primrose? How are you? It seems like ages since we last spoke."

"Nice to see you again," Primrose said politely, feeling clumsy and fleshbound compared to Fayrene, but then Primrose wasn't the one torching for an old flame who was three thousand miles away.

Maybe that flouncy white get-up wasn't so flattering. On closer inspection, Fayrene looked like a goose.

Tino excused himself. "I could use a beer. Doesn't have to be German."

"You go. I'll stay with Primrose. You know Aldo just made the law review, don't you, Primrose? Everyone says he has a great career in front of him," Fayrene opined.

"He's the Robert Kennedy of the family, isn't he?"

"That might be pushing it," Fayrene responded. "Oh, Primrose! Your skin looks so chic against the dark dress. I wish I had a long neck like yours."

"Thank you," Primrose said stiffly. Fayrene had kept her eyes strictly above the neckline. Her solicitude spoke volumes. *Puttana.*

Tino returned with a beer in one hand and a glass in the other. He set the glass down and took Primrose's hand. Meanwhile Fayrene kept prattling. "I was just telling Primrose how beautiful she looks—"

For the first time Primrose noticed that Fayrene, when she talked, sounded a lot like Tino's mother. No wonder Pat hadn't been too sure about Fayrene.

Under the table, Tino squeezed her hand. She squeezed back, letting him know she was all right.

There was salad, followed by roast beef and scalloped potatoes. Dessert, lemon cake with Chantilly cream, proved too rich for Primrose, who ordered a cup of Sanka and drank it black. Soon after coffee, the Battutas bundled themselves into their coats and made their way out with a clutch of others who were also calling it a night. Primrose thought she saw Dom Carcieri, the undertaker, in the group, but she couldn't be sure. All the men looked the same after a certain age. Someone slapped Leon on the back, dislodging his fedora.

A new band took the stage. Fayrene's eyes glittered. She grabbed Primrose by the hand. "Now we can really cut a rug!"

Primrose, entranced, slipped out of her shoes and followed her onto the dance floor.

Catching her from behind, Tino murmured into her hair, "This band is certainly not the Deferments. Though I suppose nothing is."

"Thank heaven for small favors," she replied absently.

"And large ones."

"Those too," she said, though his relief at possibly having secured a deferment did not quiet her own unease about their future. Turning in his arms, she got a jolt: Tino was wearing Poppa Tavio's top hat.

"Where did you get that?"

"I've been keeping it in the Chevelle's trunk," he said, grinning. "I never know when it's going to come in handy."

The band launched into a cover of "Whiter Shade of Pale." Tino pulled Primrose tight against him and dreamed—cruelly, Primrose thought, given the circumstances—into her ear. "We'd have our own house. It'd be just us, no one else. Every night."

"If you're going to talk like that," she said, unsure whether to sob or scream, "you had better mean it."

"I do mean it," he whispered. "I do."

Or was this another Brindisi prank?

"What do you say? Will you at least think about it?"

"Think about what, Tino?"

The room shimmered, candlelight on crystal. According to the song, a sizable contingent of vestal virgins was leaving for—where else?—*the Coast.*

Primrose sighed. "All I've been doing, Tino—"

"Is thinking about it," he said. "I know."

He was a good man. Loyal. Smart. He had flaws, but so did she, and hers, she feared, were more debilitating. She pushed back those memories—the locked ward days, the electroshock nights. His face, so close, seemed enormous and hopeful—not the face of someone who thought only of her flaws. One word and he was hers, her good catch: hook, line, sinker. She tried to swallow and found that she could not. Something bright—a flashbulb, or perhaps an exploding distant star—went off behind her eyes, and she saw her own history, approaching fast, in pictures. There would be gift registries, bread-and-butter notes, grocery lists. A diary, a few paintings, *The Book of Love* squirreled away in her hope chest. Above all there would be traceless time—years of listening to Leon natter on about the past and spinning into Tino's arms on the Matterhorn's dance floor. She felt a movement inside, a feather brushing against some interior membrane, and she heard her mother: *He's funny. He's smart. He's a good catch.*

"Come on, Prim. What do you say?" Tino's eyes were round, his voice imploring. His white dress shirt felt crisp, expensive. He loved her. The ring he'd produced from behind her left ear proved it.

There it was: Tino Battuta's familiar magic. His way with small objects.

"Oh, I don't know," she teased, giddy from hearing the question posed at last. He spun her out and around. From his face, she could tell he was disappointed; he didn't understand that she was only pretending to resist.

She flew hard into his arms and planted a kiss full on his lips. "Got it?"

"Got what?" He looked like a fish, gasping for air. A good catch, indeed.

She slipped his ring on her finger. "*Yes.*"

THE BOOK OF LOVE:
Tried & True Ways to Snag Your Man
Compiled by Primrose

1. Voodoo

2. Lasagna

3. Arranged marriage

4. Get yourself knocked up, not that

we'd know anything about it.*

---

* *I think you're being awfully hard on yourself, Primrose. —Norah*

Part 3: FALL 1967

28. Into the fire

By their third week in their new home, a two-bedroom on the outskirts of Maple Bay, Primrose was so heavily pregnant her bones ached. One morning she scraped her hair from her face and squinted at the alarm clock, unwilling to believe how late she'd slept. Needles of light pierced the hemstitched drapes, lighting up every dust mote in the room, all her little responsibilities.

So this was married life.

She sat on the edge of the bed, spelling out her breaths the way Dr. Addleman had suggested. Breath in: O. Breath out: K. The dust was O-K. She was O-K.

OK? OK.

O-K.

No need to panic. The days were long, and she was sufficient unto them—another mantra she had picked up, heaven knew from where. Her lazy *Redbook* days were over. But she had plenty of time for dusting and vacuuming, and plenty of tranquilizers from Dr. Addleman. She had her whole life ahead of her to keep house, to shop, to unpack boxes, to write thank-you notes for the wedding presents piled in the living room. All her books were still in boxes. So was her Royal. Even her *New Yorker* magazines had been torn up and repurposed as packing material.

O-K.

My kingdom, she thought, *for a clean house.*

The baby rolled inside her. She pressed below her ribs where the tiny rump was pushing out. She was sure it was a girl. The baby's ceaseless activity expressed something specifically feminine, a fussiness that would take a lot to blunt, if not eradicate. A boy would be easier, more agreeable.

Sufficient unto the day.

Tino's alarm blared. Primrose rolled over and silenced it. Tino had been up for almost an hour, awakened by the morning paper thumping against the front door. Now he was humming in the bathroom, a Sousa march, wildly off tune.

So this was married life! Listening to your husband noisily monopolizing the bathroom while the house dirtied itself *ad infinitum*. Joseph's classes, Rosemary's parties, Lupo and his ideas about life on other planets—all these seemed to belong to someone else's existence.

Primrose padded into the kitchen, which smelled sharply of pine cleaner. Louise had scrubbed it yesterday while Primrose lolled in the living room, calling out at intervals that her mother shouldn't bother. After all, it wasn't her house. But Louise wasn't having any of it. She'd mopped the floors and wiped down the cabinets and the long Formica countertop, refusing to leave before everything shone. But even this was not enough for Tino, who just last night was complaining about the general disorder— the dust on the television set, the unopened boxes of wedding gifts stacked in the living room, and her sloppy handling of the mail, which she'd been storing in Poppa Tavio's top hat. Having somehow landed on the entryway table, the hat could stay there forever, for all she cared.

Primrose pulled her bathrobe tighter and opened the back door. Though a warm day was forecast, the air was still cool, and the sky a hard, enameled blue. She hadn't gone three steps before she stubbed her toe on a large pot of chrysanthemums, a gift from Louise. Pressing a hand against the spasming small of her back, Primrose bent to check the damage. Pot, fine. Toe, not so much. Her mother had struck a similar pose the day before, her belly straining against her work uniform as she heaved the flowerpot into position. Primrose had stared, horrified, thinking, *Oh, my mother is getting old.* The thought felt like a revelation. News.

Her mother's flowers sent their sharp autumnal odor up her nose, a smell of funerals.

Dr. Addleman had warned her about this: *You can't be morbid, you can't allow yourself the luxury.* The prohibition somehow only seemed to reinforce the morbid thinking, like the chrysanthemums that, by covering the smell in the funeral home, only drew attention to it.

She was taking her medication. Tino made sure of it, lining up the bottles each night and pushing them toward her over breakfast. But she'd felt down since the wedding—a small church ceremony followed by a luncheon at the Battutas' house. She had worn a gown of ivory satin tailored by a seamstress Lorraine knew from her days of working at Poppa Tavio's shop; the seamstress, who understood what she was doing and surely had done it many times before, had shaped the dress so Primrose didn't look pregnant at all, but only like a somewhat thickened version of herself, or so she thought when she saw the pictures. Of the day itself, the only thing Primrose could remember was standing next to Tino at the altar, flanked by Norah in a blush-colored knock-off Chanel suit and matching pillbox hat and Chick in a morning coat with a pale rose pinned to a lapel, and at that moment she was rocked by foreboding. Their best friends were so different; how in the world would she and Tino ever manage to get along? How well did they really know each other?

Well, what they didn't know became apparent soon enough, and so Dr. Addleman doubled her dosages, presumably to soften her landing in what seemed, at least so far, to be a permanent janitorial position in a house as still and shadowy as a tomb.

Stop it, you goose, she told herself. *Just stop.*

But it was undeniable that everything tended toward death. The whole summer had been about death—the riots, the shootings, the fourteen hundred buildings that had burned down in Detroit.

She refilled the feeder, and in a flash the birds were back—a flurry of house sparrows, followed by the big robin who always scared the smaller birds away.

"I know you," she informed the robin. "You're the guy who shows up late and spoils the party."

Tino stood just inside the doorway, looking smart in fresh chinos and a clean undershirt that hugged his torso, newly lean from calisthenics with his Reserve unit. In his hands was a box of donuts. Their rich smell made her mouth water.

She lumbered past him into the dark kitchen. Awkwardly, he kissed her cheek. "That's nice," she said, taking a chocolate frosted from the box.

"Were you talking to someone just now?"

She sucked a blob of frosting from her finger. For a moment, Primrose pitied him, a man whose wife talked to birds.

"Well, if you must know, I was talking with the robin who ate all the birdseed. He shouldn't be so greedy."

"He's hungry. That's nature. It has nothing to do with greed."

Primrose shook her head. The question turned inside her. It had everything to do with greed.

"You're up early," she said.

"I woke up and couldn't get back to sleep."

"Will you have the graveyard shift?"

He shrugged. "It's better than the graveyard."

Primrose nodded. No argument there.

He made her a cup of tea and poured them each a small glass of orange juice. They performed the morning's medication theater. When he finished his juice, he got up and went into the garage. Through the window, Primrose watched Tino set the sprinkler by the back fence. As it spun, it sent arcs of water over the lawn.

Even though the little house was in the shabbier part of Maple Bay, it still felt a long way from Calvary Street. She hadn't been back to her parents' house since the morning of the wedding, when Norah helped her pack. Her clothes had fit in a suitcase, and there was still room for the *Amores*, the volume of poems by her teacher, her stapled copy of *The Book of Love*—which she and Norah had sworn to continue, though neither of them had done much since the wedding. All that stuff had come to seem so thin and contrived compared to the simple, direct way that she and Tino reached for each other, the mingled pulse of her blood and his. On good days, anyway.

But there were disappointments, too. Primrose felt awkward about the changes in her body, the thickness around her middle, how she was always sweaty with hormones, desire, shame. Tino, for his part, was a difficult husband, easily provoked to rages that were all the more frightening now that she had nowhere else to go.

The screen door banged. Tino came dripping into the kitchen and, without even stopping to towel off, ran water into the percolator for more coffee.

"Damn sprinkler's stuck again," he snapped.

"Oh," she said, finding it hard to get worked up about malfunctioning garden equipment.

While the coffee perked, Primrose made the bed and loaded a basket of laundry into the washing machine. By the time she'd come back to set the table, Tino had poured himself a cup. The coffee set was a wedding present from one of Tino's aunts. Each piece, even the creamer, was ringed with daisies, avocado on white to match the kitchen.

Tino drained his cup and pecked Primrose's cheek. "I'll be back around five. Don't worry about the sprinkler. I'll get to it tonight."

"See you later, alligator," she said, concealing her irritation at the way he spoke, as if she might actually bother with something so stupid as a lawn sprinkler. The lawn was his concern; she was fine with crabgrass, which didn't need anything except to be left well enough alone. "Have a good day."

The Chevelle thrummed briefly in the driveway, and then Tino was gone. The hours stretched before her. She opened a window and allowed the breeze to disturb the curtains.

On a scrap of paper she listed her tasks: dinner to cook, laundry to fold. Shopping, if her mother came by and was willing to let her borrow the car. With a pencil, she began a grocery list: milk, juice, onions. Onions!

She prayed: Dear God. Save me from onions.

She imagined an airplane heading out over the ocean, to Paris or London or wherever girls went when they decided to get divorced. Was it normal to think constantly about divorce once you were married? Or were these just the thoughts you had, waiting for the pills to kick in? Which they did, after a while. Hope was something she felt in her body, a visceral shimmer. The pills, at least, were on the job.

Thanks *ever* so much, Dr. Addleman. I feel so *tranquil* now.

Tonight she'd make a real dinner—spaghetti and meatballs, with gravy homemade, not from a can.

She found a head of garlic in the pantry and pulled several cloves from it. Mrs. Battuta had shown her how to slice them thin and cook them with the least amount of heat. It was a tricky problem. If the chop was too coarse, the sauce would be tasteless and studded with big pieces of garlic that were unpleasant; but if the slices were too fine, they would burn and make the gravy bitter. She hadn't yet been able to get it right. Failure tasted like a ruined gravy.

She poured oil into a pan and lit the gas ring beneath it with a long match. The phone rang, and she felt a pang in her chest that told her exactly who was calling.

"Ma?"

"That's spooky, Primrose."

"What is it, Ma? I'm making the gravy."

"Modern girls just open a can nowadays."

"Tino doesn't like that."

"Hang on," Louise said. "I need to find my smokes."

Primrose selected the smallest knife from the block and began to slice the garlic. The knife block had been a wedding gift from Chick. It was a very fine gift, featuring knives of many sizes and functions—hack, cleave, slice, pare, bone—slotted into a block of polished maple the exact shade of Louise's up-do.

Primrose heard the click of her mother's lighter, followed by an exhaled breath so long and deep, it seemed to blow right through the line. Holding the phone from her face with one hand and scattering garlic with the other, Primrose remembered with distaste the specific flavor of her mother's gravy, the onions that never quite masked the metallic flavor of the can. She pushed a wooden spoon through the sizzling garlic and turned the heat off. Onions. Right. On the table, piled in a basket. The topmost one looked fine, just fine.

"Is Tino at work?"

"He goes every day," Primrose snapped. The onion's papery skin felt unpleasant, too slippery. She rolled it on the counter, then set it back atop the pile. She couldn't take the risk of slicing it now, not with her mother on the phone, agitating her. She was likely to cut off her thumb.

"Well, I don't want to bother you, Primrose." Her mother's tone turned formal. Hurt. "I just called to hear your voice."

Louise said something else after that, but there was static on the line and Primrose couldn't make out the words. They might have been "I'm only your mother," but then again, it could have been "I'm your only mother," which was true by definition but the sort of thing one never said—except that it was the sort of thing Louise *would* say, being fond of solecisms that tied Primrose in knots.

"Goodbye, Ma."

Through open window came the sound of a door slamming, followed by the jingle of reindeer bells. Elsie Minetta emerged from her house, her yellow nightgown sagging below the hem of her belted trench. With one arm, she heaved her garage door open and disappeared inside. Primrose imagined the cool interior, its smells of Turtle Wax and motor oil. Primrose and Tino had only a pitted aluminum carport, but she'd overheard Tino telling Keith, Elsie's husband, about a house for sale on the corner that had a two-car garage. Owning it was a pipe dream, of course. In reality they could barely afford their rent. Elsie coiled the hose and left it on the grass, ready to strike.

The phone rang again, and Primrose felt the old pain.

"Hello, Ma."

"How did you know?"

"I always know."

"Are you doing your ironing?"

"Tino wears work clothes to work," she said. "And work's the only place he goes. I don't need to iron for him."

In fact this was not quite true. *Someone* needed to iron for him, so Lorraine came regularly to pick up the wash. Just the whites, that was the deal. She'd return the basket the next day, Tino's handkerchiefs starched and folded into neat squares. Primrose wasn't sure how much she liked this arrangement, but she was quite sure she hated ironing, and she felt she could not refuse Lorraine's help in any case. After all, Tino's father had given them the money they'd needed, not just for the wedding but for the first month's rent and deposit on the house. If Lorraine wanted to take care of the white wash, too, Primrose didn't see the harm in letting her. But Louise did.

"It's your house, Primrose. You need to run it. You have to put your foot down."

Primrose sighed.

"Listen, there's a coupon for a press in today's paper," Louise said. "Should I cut it out for you?"

"A press?"

"A *garlic* press, you *cagootz*. For the *gravy*. It makes shorter work of the chopping."

"I'm pretty sure my mother-in-law won't like that. She disapproves of shortcuts."

Louise spoke sonorously. "You'll *ruin* your *hands*. You'll work yourself into an *early grave*."

"Ma."

"Have it your way," Louise said. "I suppose now that you're married, you don't need your mother to tell you what to do."

"I'm sorry." Her mother really wasn't trying to ruin her life; this was just another one of her mind's tricks. "Maybe you could drop off the coupon on your way to work?"

"I've got to go now."

"Oh, I see. Now that you've gotten your zinger in, you have to go. Is that it?"

"Maybe you can come for Sunday dinner this week, Primrose? Tino, too. It would be nice."

"Let me talk to Tino about it. Now let me go. I need to chop an onion."

She hung up. An acrid smell rose from the pan. The garlic was burning. She lifted the pan and waved it in the air. More of the garlic turned brown. She set the pan down. With a wooden spoon, she fished out the burnt bits, which now smelled like bubblegum. When she sniffed again, they didn't smell like anything. "Oh, be that way," she said. "Be difficult. If you must."

In the cupboard she found a can of tomatoes—Contadina, the brand Lorraine liked. The can spun in the electric opener, the lid's sharp edge glinting dangerously. She dumped the tomatoes into the pan, turned up the heat, and left it to simmer while she sat at the table completing her grocery list: Ivory soap, beef bouillon, dried oregano.

Onion! How could she have forgotten the onion?

Swearing, she pulled the large knife from its slot in the block. With this gift, Chick had also given Tino an Indian head penny. Apparently this was traditional, to offer a coin with a gift of knives. The recipient then gave the coin back to the giver, so the knives were not a gift so much as a purchase. Otherwise the gift was unlucky. In the end, Tino had given Chick a quarter and kept the Indian head penny, which he liked too much to give back. Primrose suspected the innovation might have opened them up to fresh curses. The coin sat in a jar that rattled whenever she dragged a cloth over the counter, as if possessed by a one-cent ghost that would not settle until some obscure justice was done, some recompense paid.

The grandfather clock chimed. Knives and coins—an ancient pairing. She shivered.

The onion, where's the onion? Oh, yes. There it was, in the basket, just where she'd left it.

She picked up the knife and set it down again. She'd lost her oomph, her mojo. She'd lost her faith in onions. They seemed to belong to some other planet's ecology. She craved other things: chocolate, salt, and chopped liver. The doctor said the cravings were common, but Primrose knew better. The cravings told her that the child would be impossible to satisfy. Even so, she had to try. She added the new items to her shopping list.

Elsie reappeared, now wearing dungarees and carrying a hoe and a lopper. She set these on the grass and hurried away through the backyard gate. A station wagon rumbled into the driveway across the street, and a moment later the Avon lady emerged carrying a sample case. Elsie, meanwhile, came back with a plastic bucket so small it might have belonged to one of her boys, and a bag of weed killer. All this busy activity, to what end? Better to let things take their course. Didn't weeds have as much right to air and water and sunlight as any other living thing? Weren't they just as green as the perfect lawn Tino was always dreaming about? It was bigotry, really—this frantic gardening. Bigotry against the weeds, who were so persistent and had so much pluck.

Primrose finished her grocery list, determined to get out of the house before one o'clock. She could walk to the store if she had to. Or maybe Elsie could give her a lift.

She was standing before the mirror smoothing her blouse over her midsection when the phone rang again. This time, it didn't make anything hurt, so she answered cheerfully: "Hello?"

It was Tino. As soon as she heard his voice, she felt warm all over. "I've got no news," he said, "except the usual."

"Wait 'til you get home," she effused. "The kitchen smells delicious, like my mother's on a Sunday."

"You mother's kitchen smells like feet."

"It does not."

"It does so, Primrose." His tone was light, but something about the exchange suggested he would brook no argument on this score. She remembered her mother's invitation. Maybe now was not the best time to bring it up. In the background someone was yelling for Tino. She leaned on the counter to relieve the pressure on her back.

"Hang on," Tino said.

"I'm sorry," she replied to dead air. She truly was sorry: They'd almost had a stupid argument, thanks to her over-sensitivity, and unlike him, she was at home where no one was yelling at anyone.

When she told Tino about the garlic press, he scoffed.

"A modern girl needs modern equipment," she said, fingering the electric can opener. Her hands were filthy. Ink from the circular smudged the greasy plastic surface.

"Think about our budget. What we spend on unnecessary things we could just as easily put away to buy something we really need."

"Like wineglasses."

"I was thinking of a down payment on a house."

An offering. She knew she ought to say something, express surprise or gratitude, but she couldn't muster a response. That was the effect of the pills, maybe. How they baffled everything. Through the front window, the trees in the Minettas' yard waved their branches, sending down yellow leaves. "Let's talk later," she said. It was the best she could do.

"Okay. Love you."

She tore the shopping list from the pad, folded the ragged sheet, and tucked it up her sleeve. Then she rinsed her hands in hot water from the tap and dried them with a fresh dish towel. The procedure calmed her. She would talk with Tino later about the budget, the little things she needed, the bigger things they might save for. Meanwhile, though, she had the day. The shopping could wait. The gravy could wait. She picked up the pencil and began to sketch things she couldn't see through the window: a pussy willow, a rock wall, the bend in the creek, the reeds.

29. Stateside

As Louise had predicted, the Reserves had been called up to meet the hospital's urgent need for help, there had briefly been demand for new recruits, and Chick and Tino had successfully joined the US Army Reserve. Though it was hard to tell the difference that made, beyond the cessation of threatening communiqués from the government. Their first day on the job, the only real soldier they met was the guy who came to greet them. Sergeant Anthony Caldwell sported a salt-and-pepper buzz cut and reeked of Aqua Velva; his upright bearing made Tino's back ache in sympathy.

Tino shook the meaty hand he was offered. "Welcome to A-Pavilion," Anthony boomed. "I'm the PIC."

The Army bristled with acronyms. PIC stood for Person In Charge, though Chick had privately insisted that the P meant Prick. He might have been right, too, if the normal relationship between names and what they stood for could be said to hold in the Army. But nothing was normal in the Army.

Anthony led Tino and Chick down a corridor past a series of empty double rooms. The patients' lounge was quiet despite being full of young men in pajamas staring at the television or the linoleum. Just weeks ago, Louise had been on this ward, doing the job he was being trained to do now. She was out of work, but wasn't that better than him humping a pack in the jungle? Or grinding away in a medical school library? He pushed the thought from his mind—that damage was done.

At the end of the corridor, Anthony opened a door labeled "Staff Room."

"Staff only in here." That was another weird thing about the Army: When it came to news, one announcement was never enough. The door shut behind them with a click. Two brown sofas occupied most of the space, while a darker brown carpet, thin and utilitarian, covered the floor. A row of lockers took up the opposite wall. In the corner, a table was littered with an overflowing ashtray, a hotplate, and magazines.

"The room's comfortable enough, but the first rule is you don't sleep while you're on the floor. Not even for five minutes on your break."

Someone should have told that to Louise, Tino thought.

Chick picked up one of the magazines on the table. *Playboy.*

"Strictly speaking, this particular reading material is out of regulation, but you know how it is." Anthony shrugged, grinning. "Boys will be, et celery."

Tino peeked over Chick's shoulder. Flesh. Hair. He looked away. Anthony twirled the dial on one of the locks until it popped open.

"Come here," he said, motioning for Tino and Chick to join him at the lockers. Anthony opened one of them to reveal a framed photo of a doe-eyed, exhausted brunette, her arms wrapped around a passel of kids who ranged in age from a tiny baby to a knock-kneed boy of about twelve. "Mine," said Anthony. "Five of 'em, all boys. You can't imagine the expense. Everything we bring home, they eat up, use up, and wear out."

Tino smiled because he was expected to. It crossed his mind that he, too, was a married man now, a family man; he might mention Primrose and the baby, due in February. With any luck at all, he'd still be here when the baby came. There'd be some kind of announcement; he might be entitled to a few days' leave. But then, Anthony certainly seemed capable of counting backwards, and he was apparently quite the upright citizen. Tino and Primrose probably wouldn't even tell the kid about their shotgun wedding. They'd just say he or she—Primrose was convinced it was a girl—had been "premature." By about four months.

"Where's the john?" Chick asked.

Anthony pointed him down the hall. Chick left.

"You want a coffee, Tino?" Anthony asked.

"Sure."

"Watch and learn."

Anthony led Tino to the small sink inserted into the green counter over a row of cabinets, opened the nearest one, and took out a can of Autocrat.

"When you make coffee, drop a nickel in the coin can at the nurses' station. Used to keep it in here, but folks used it as petty cash. If this system doesn't work, it's back to BYO."

"Okay," Tino said, wondering when the actual work would start.

A cart clattered down the corridor. Someone shouted for a nurse. Anthony, unperturbed, filled the percolator at the sink and spooned some Autocrat into the receptacle. Then he extracted an Allen wrench from his pocket and used the long end to plug the steam hole at the top of the percolator.

"Now, look here," he said. "It's not plugged up all the way, just enough to keep the steam to a minimum." And sure enough, there was a tiny gap between the hole and the wrench. Anthony said, "I don't know if they told you, but we've got our share of crazies."

"I heard." Using an Allen wrench to make coffee was fairly insane, but Tino decided to keep his mouth shut about it.

"Well, my point is, some of them complain about the hiss from the percolator. Listen up. You hear that?"

"Hear what?" Tino asked. The place had gone quiet.

"My point exactly," Anthony said. "As soon as the hissing stops, so does the shouting."

"Oh," said Tino.

"The people in risk management don't like cooking in here anyway. They say it's a fire hazard." Anthony pointed to the fire extinguisher on the wall. "So we came to an agreement."

The percolator bubbled thickly. He hadn't been here minutes and already it was nearly time for a break. Anthony was certainly weird, but on the whole the job didn't seem so bad.

Chick returned, jingling his keys.

"No sleeping," Anthony reminded them as he left them to their coffee break. "Don't snooze on the job, and we'll get along just fine."

"Yes, sir," said Tino, who had exactly zero concerns about napping. The coffee was so strong, he wasn't going to sleep for days.

"We're on the job, man," Chick said affably as he poured out a cup for himself. "We're on the jay-oh-bee."

30. War work

From his time in medical school, Tino knew that hospitals were monsters of order and routine. A-Pavilion was no exception. Even the simple business of signing in and out, to mark the antipodes of a shift, required the negotiation of two sets of double-locked doors and the assistance of a guard.

Tino rang the bell, which summoned the guard, who led him though a locked door into an antechamber. While Tino signed the daybook, the guard unlocked the second door. Later, he and the guard would perform the same *pas de deux* in reverse. Tino was new to the place, but already he understood that the ritual border crossing helped to sustain the hospital as a place apart, with regulations and procedures designed to maintain what was already there—the culture of slowness, changelessness, and, above all, delay. There was always another form to fill out, another signature to obtain. Tino didn't mind. The routines were calming, and he'd been chasing a deferment long enough to see the utility of bureaucratic inaction, how red tape could, under the right circumstances, save your life—or at least preserve it for a bit longer.

At the nurses' station, a young man in an overlarge white coat parceled pills into paper cups in between pushing his cuffs from his wrists and his shaggy hair from his eyes. Tino could hardly believe this beatnik was the resident physician. On the radio, the Sox game was interrupted by news from the big antiwar march in Washington. The newscaster reported that Allen Ginsberg was there, speaking of beatniks. How did that guy pay his rent? You couldn't make much if you spent all your time marching in Washington and writing peace poems.

Tino wasn't marching, and he wasn't writing poems. That was for the college kids, who had plenty of time for that sort of thing. Here, there were patients to look after, lunch trays to collect, floors to mop, bags of trash to be humped to the incinerator. Today was bed day—the sheets had to be collected and taken to the laundry, and then the beds were made up again with fresh linen. Anthony could snap a bed together in minutes, the corners crisp as a pizza box. Anthony was impressed by the military and expected his reports to be impressed too. Sometimes, despite his newfound appreciation for rules and regulations, Tino couldn't help trying to screw up Anthony's local bubble of order. Instead of folding the sheets into tight corners, he would just stuff them under. The result, to Tino, was a *real* military product: bunched, shoddy, half-assed.

In the break room, Tino opened a window, hoping to expel the room's atmosphere of overcooked coffee. He ferried a load of sheets to the dumbwaiter and sent it down. He took a pile of fresh sheets from the cupboard and distributed them, making up beds as he went. He continued until lunchtime, when Anthony ordered him to the nurses' desk. A candy striper was slumped over the counter, holding her head with both hands. Reflexively, Tino wondered if she were pregnant. A year ago, he realized, that possibility would not have crossed his mind.

"Belinda here isn't feeling too spry," Anthony said. "Can you and Chick manage the lunch cart?"

A stubbled guy in a bathrobe shuffled up, wanting to know when he could buy more smokes. Another one, who liked to sit in a folding chair in the corridor, called for ice, so Tino brought him a paper cup full of it. The guy demanded a Dr Pepper, and Tino brought that, too.

"Alakazoo," said the man and raised a hand in salute. "Alakazam."

"Alaka-Seltzer," Tino told him. The man stuck out his tongue.

"That's a pretty healthy reaction, actually."

Tino spun around. It was the beatnik resident who'd been at the desk before. The guy was about his age. Some prodigy, no doubt. Condescending, too. Tino wondered where he'd trained, how much money he brought home, who was waiting for him when he got there, whether he got the pipe-and-slippers routine.

"Who's Dr. Pepper?" the guy in the bathrobe said, shuffling away with a cup in each hand. "Can someone please tell me who the *fuck* is Dr. Pepper?"

The doctor peered at Tino over his glasses. "Your first day?"

"Nope." Their eyes met, and Tino blanked his gaze defensively. Beatnik or not, a shrink could sneak up on you. Look what happened to Primrose.

At the nurses' station, the candy striper was back on her feet, but only just. Three steps, and she paled again, leaning against the wall. Chick offered to drive her home, she accepted, and Chick winked at Tino as he followed her out. Not that Tino had expected anything less. Chick always managed to do all right.

Tino rolled the lunch cart down the hall. To stave off boredom as he delivered the trays, he mentally catalogued the patients on the floor. Some were obviously injured, with missing limbs or bandaged heads. More often the wounds were harder to see—one man barked obscenities for no reason, another sat for hours holding himself and rocking. Had Primrose been like that too? My God, what a thought. Best to banish it, and so he did.

Back in the lounge, Tino emptied the ashtrays. Butts still smoldered in some of them. It was amazing the whole hospital didn't burn down.

The doctors, who'd seen it all before, just kept prescribing their pills.

An hour later, Tino retraced his steps through the ward, collecting the meal trays. When he finished, he rolled the cart back to the nurses' desk where he found Chick struggling with a mop and bucket full of steaming water.

"Anthony gave me mop detail," he complained.

"But you got to take a joyride."

"No good deed goes unpunished," Chick said. "But she only lives around the corner. "

On his break, Tino tried to dial his home number and had to stop for a moment to remember what it was. It was funny not to be dialing the number for his old house— his mother and father's house. Primrose picked up on the second ring.

"What's cooking?"

"Dinner!"

"I mean, how are you?"

"Mom called. Tried to start a fight." Now that she was unemployed, Louise occupied her days busting Primrose's ass, mainly by criticizing her housekeeping. "You know she asked us to dinner on Sunday."

"I know."

Attendance at Sunday suppers was a family tradition recently invented by Louise, who, in coming up with the idea, surely intended to ruin his one day off per week. Primrose disagreed, but for the sake of peace they'd left the matter unresolved. So far, he'd managed to beg off three Sundays in a row, citing a need for rest. "You know how tired I am at the end of the week," he complained, knowing his go-to excuse would not hold for much longer.

"A guy from the marina called," Primrose said, yanking him back to reality.

"Jesus." His mind lurched. Something had gone wrong, he knew it, and it was going to cost plenty to make it right again. "Why?"

"Something about the boat. You have to take it out."

"Take it out?"

"That's what I said."

"Did he say *why*?"

"The bilge stopped working," Primrose snapped. "It's taking on water. Don't get pissy with *me*."

Even after the wedding, Primrose had been giving him plenty of *agita* about the boat. Keeping it in good shape siphoned money from their already tight budget and took time away from her as well. But as much as the boat was costing Tino—in the form of Primrose's ill will, not to mention cash on the barrelhead—he remained reluctant to part with the *Sumac*.

Tino relayed the news about the boat to Chick, who promised to check things out after his shift.

Later, in the parking lot, Tino allowed his attention to be caught by odd things—the glint of a streetlight off a chrome fender, the rich blue October dusk, a handful of anthills in an orderly row. When he looked at his watch, thirty minutes had passed. He hurried to the car, hoping the boat was still afloat in the marina and that Primrose had remembered to take the gravy off the stove. Hope, my God—what a dirty drug. It hit all the wrong places as well as a few of the right ones.

31. It don't rain (but it pours)

Tino leaned forward, stretching the overworked muscles in his back, and surveyed the damage. They should never have left the bilge to run all night. The engine had burned out, and the news from the marina's front office had been accurate: The *Sumac* was taking on water. Chick had done the initial damage control, dry-docking her in the lot behind a catamaran. And so she'd sat until today, when Tino and Chick both had the day off, and Primrose could be sent for supplies.

Somebody was backing a boat down the causeway. If there was any justice in the universe, they should have been next in line to get out there.

So much had not turned out the way he hoped.

"You're looking mighty sorry for yourself," said Chick, looking every inch the sailor in a captain's hat and spotless chinos. He'd even popped the collar on his navy polo shirt.

"Where's the yacht club?" Tino teased as they wandered around the *Sumac*. Up close, the hull was full of gaps and cracks. "I told you that bilge wouldn't hold."

"It *was* holding," Chick replied. "So what were we supposed to do? Life's too short to worry about stuff that works."

He flipped his cigarette with his thumb and middle finger. It arced, still lit, toward the catamaran and fell to the gravel, trailing a wavy line of smoke.

"We can't run the bilge forever," Tino said.

"You'd be surprised how long some expedients last."

"Something tells me I would not."

"Besides, who says anything about forever? We just gotta run it long enough to find the next sucker."

Chick handed him one end of a hose. Tino carried the other end down to one of the docks and connected it to a spigot. In a moment, salt water was running out of the hose in Tino's hands. It splashed on the gravel and his feet.

"Let's get to it," Chick told him. "Run that hose into the boat."

"But you'll flood it."

"Just do it. You'll see."

Tino looped the hose over the rail and threaded it down the steps into the cabin. He let the water run everywhere, and then he watched it pool and slowly drain into a hole—perhaps fresh, perhaps not—in the floor. No, they couldn't run the bilge forever, though everyone from Lyndon Johnson on down seemed willing to try. Guns and butter, foreign debt—the slogans were all over. The sickness of the whole business was that, in the *real* world— if such a place could be said to exist anymore, a place where things were sane and logical—the only reasonable thing to do with a problem was to fix it at the root. But in the unreal world, there were no root causes you could identify and eliminate.

In medical school, he'd learned about diseases that ran mysterious courses, guerilla diseases.

They said the VC fought like this, always relying on a measure of surprise.

Chick crunched around the perimeter, marking potential leaks with a permanent marker. The hull was pocked with Xs. Tino returned to the deck and swung his legs over the edge.

"How did we get into this mess?" Tino asked Chick. The smell of his marker crowded out the smell of the sea.

"Is this a trick question? You know what they say. Permissive parents. A Soviet plot."

"I was thinking of the boat."

"You think too much. Did you hear? Dr. Spock is a communist."

"Stranger things have happened," Tino said. "I guess."

Chick marked another X. "The other day I heard that the whole war was being waged to protect US government–backed drug trafficking in the South China Sea."

"Imagine that."

"But you know, I'm not much for writing letters to senators. Or organizing a bonfire to entertain the draft board."

"It's hard enough just getting to the marina."

"Exactly. But the *Sumac* is one problem that's actually *ours*."

"Because we can do something about it?"

"No, jackass. Because we own it."

They caulked until the hull was pocked like the face of a first-time shaver whose father had neglected to remind him to use a fresh blade. Chick cracked open a beer and handed one to Tino, who drank half in a single swallow.

"You know, she's not bad," Chick said. "She'll never win Miss Nautical Universe, but once she's in the water, you won't even see the patches."

"We'll do what we can." Tino drained his beer. "You still think we can get across Lake Champlain in this thing?"

"Escape still on your mind?"

"Some," Tino admitted. They were unlikely to be deployed, at least not immediately. But the Reserves asked for a six-year commitment, which was a long time. Their luck wouldn't necessarily hold. Like it or not, as Reservists they were already in the shit. "Maybe that's our fallback plan."

"Got to account for the context, man. Now that we're Reservists, that's desertion."

"Maybe it was always that," Tino said.

Chick whistled. "Looky-loo."

Tino turned to see Primrose staggering toward them, a paper bag from the hardware store cradled over her jutting belly. She wore a denim skirt and her old Dr. Scholl's, which were the only shoes that still fit her swollen feet. Guiltily Tino took the bag from her. She shouldn't be carrying heavy things. In the bag were the supplies he'd asked for: paintbrushes, rags, sandpaper.

"Are these what you wanted?"

"Perfect. Everything's perfect," he said.

She smiled, and in that moment, it was. Perfect.

He rolled the ball of his thumb over a sheet of sandpaper. It was good and rough; the caulk would come off quickly. But they'd be here all night if they didn't get started. With a sheet of sandpaper, he smoothed a patch of caulk the size of his palm. Chick did the same, while Primrose used a house key to pry the lid off the paint can.

"Jesus, that stinks." The paint had knockout fumes. Tino came up behind her and drew his handkerchief around her mouth and nose. "Breathe through this, please. We want our kid to arrive with all his arms and legs."

"Or hers."

Tino fastened the knot. It was difficult with all her hair, but if he yanked anything, she didn't say. The polyurethane smell went right out of his mind, and instead he smelled her shampoo, familiar, sweet. "Right," he said, kissing her nape. "Or hers."

Someone had a radio on, and the sound of a crowd cheering blew past them.

"Sounds like a good game."

"Dad's got it on television. He'll tell you all about it later, if you want to make that visit."

Well, shit. The last thing he wanted to do on his day off was visit with her parents, as she well knew. Frank was fine, but Louise—

"Would it make you happy?"

"It might get Louise off my back."

But the whole reason they got married in the first place was to get Louise off her back.

The sun was warm on Tino's shoulders. The broadcast switched to an ad for Burma Shave.

32. The files of Otis

After the wedding was announced in the newspaper, Lupo had phoned Norah. She guessed his intentions right away.

"Maybe you shouldn't have taken that pep squad girl to the Hog House," she told him. "After all, Primrose knew you might be there. And you knew she knew."

He couldn't argue with her logic. "Point taken," he said. "Now what?"

"Baby steps," she advised him. "It takes a while to get over these things."

She asked him not to call again. Primrose's new life was going to be full of stress and change, and she wanted to support her. A friendship with Lupo was sure to conflict her loyalties. Lupo reassured her that he had no intention of making life hard for Primrose.

"So I'll see you around?" he asked.

"Sure," Norah replied. "There's the Be-In."

"Which might be a research trip for me," he mused.

Norah said, "That's none of my business."

A few days later, Lupo met with Otis. He lived in a rental cottage on a spit of land poking into the bay. When Lupo arrived, Otis offered him a mug of coffee. The small kitchen was cool and drafty; the whole place, which was just two rooms downstairs and one up, looked distinctly un-weatherproofed.

Otis had promised to show Lupo his case files. Lupo wasn't too enthused about spending an afternoon reading reports of what he now considered space-age hooey, but McKee wanted to know what Otis had. So Lupo had agreed to go, but only on the condition that McKee would write him a recommendation that could get him to the radio observatory at Penticton in western Canada. Deferment or not, he couldn't allow McKee's UFO obsession to end his career before he even had a chance to start. Naturally he said nothing of this when proposing the plan to McKee, who had cheerfully slapped his own forehead and exclaimed "Why didn't I think of that?" before reassuring Lupo that he would, of course, write that letter. Of course, of course. He was only too glad to help.

Mug in hand, Lupo followed Otis to the main room. It was dark, narrow, and even colder than the kitchen, but it had a picture window giving on to a wide water view. It was stunning, so long as you kept your coat on. From a cabinet, Otis extracted a shoebox filled with index cards.

"Everything I got," Otis said as he gave the box to Lupo, "is in here. Have at it."

Otis disappeared upstairs. Lupo perched on the narrow sofa, balanced the box on his lap, and lifted the lid. Inside, the cards were arranged in rows and covered with neat, close handwriting. Newspaper articles were clipped to some of them.

Of course, the files read like jokes. There was the one about the alien who asked for a glass of water and offered a pancake in return. The pancake was sent to the FDA, which confirmed it was indeed a pancake. (Scribbled in the margin: *No space plasma here!*) Another reported a flying saucer with the polka-dot sheen appearing near the Unisphere at the 1964 World's Fair. Though the sighting was unconfirmed, the polka-dot detail made it interesting, and Otis had clipped to the index card a series of articles about a girl in a polka-dot dress who'd reported a saucer sighting on the eve of JFK's assassination. Included in the clippings also were the lyrics to a song by the JFK Quartet called "Polka Dots and Moonbeams."

Through the picture window, sailboats dotted the water. The breeze came steadily through, lifting the curtains slightly even though the windows were closed. Lupo zipped his jacket and flipped the collar up. How did Otis manage over the winter? This shack would soon be uninhabitable.

On a side table he found a pamphlet: *Manual for Draft-Age Immigrants to Canada.*

The saddle stitching was inexpert. The pages didn't line up at the edge. So this was the life raft, the rescue line.

Otis thumped halfway down the stairs and leaned over the railing. "How's it going?"

"You headed north?" Lupo waved the pamphlet.

"My roommate's afraid he might wash out of organic chemistry and not get into med school."

Oh, these problems with med school.

"I'm set to graduate next June myself, but I'm not too worried," he said as he descended, tucking in his shirt. "My flat feet might be enough to make me 4-F. Or it could all be over by next summer."

Lupo nodded, not knowing what to say. His deferment had been so easy. And now there was the possibility of Penticton.

"Want to come for a swim? The beach is just down the road."

"A little chilly, don't you think?"

"The day's heating up. The water's still warm. Will be until October, at least."

Otis' car was hot from the sun. There was a ragged hole in one of the seats, and as they drove, Lupo absently pulled threads from it until Otis said, "Hey, man. I don't have so many car seats."

"Sorry."

Otis spun the wheel. The ocean flashed into view, gray-blue as far as Lupo could see.

"Wow."

"Lupo! Don't tell me you've never been to the beach. How *long* have you lived in Rhode Island?"

"Not long enough, apparently."

Two girls were on the boardwalk. One was pulling at her brown ponytail, making sure it was tight; the other, a willowy blonde, reminded him of Primrose.

Baby steps, he reminded himself.

The brunette's ponytail swung from side to side as she walked.

Ahead of him, Otis was turning handstands, eating up the distance to the water in a series of flips. At the water's edge he shed his clothes down to his shorts. Lupo splashed in the shallows, his chinos rolled to his knees. Otis had been right—the water wasn't so cold. But sky was already whitening against the gunmetal ocean. Some things you get briefly, he thought. If you got them at all.

Otis loped toward him, dripping.

"So when do I get to meet Rodenko?" Lupo asked, finally remembering the purpose of this excursion.

"You *are* persistent." Otis shook himself, favoring Lupo with a cascade of droplets. "He's got a big talk coming up, but after that he may have room in his schedule. I'll talk to him."

"How do you know so much about his schedule, anyway?"

Otis's ears pinked under his wet curls. "We're not all rich like you, you know. I'm on work-study. In exchange for tuition, I keep track of his appointments."

"Sorry," Lupo said. "I didn't mean to be—"

Otis waved him off. "Forget it."

33. Still living

One day, while Tino was at the hospital, Primrose mustered the energy to return to art class. It hadn't been much fun. Her feet hurt from standing after just fifteen minutes, and she came home with swollen ankles and an unsatisfactory still life.

She considered the mess not entirely her fault. That day, encouraging what he called *nature morte*, Joseph asked the class to "connect with something that might just possibly unsettle your complacency." He then presented them with a large bird, borrowed from the taxidermy cabinet, that looked as moth-eaten as one of her father's sweaters. Beside the bird he set a handful of turnips. "Have at it," he told the class and retired to a corner to read the newspaper, which he rattled once in a while for no reason except, Primrose supposed, to break her concentration. He had even stopped trying to interest her in the Be-In. Could it be that, just because she was married and living in Maple Bay, he no longer found her interesting? In this anxious mood, her output was terrible: The bird was overdone, with tail feathers like a peacock's.

"What do you call it?" Joseph asked.

Primrose said, "Thanksgiving."

Joseph sighed. "What you have here, Primrose, is an exercise in pointless aestheticism. You're denying what's actually there."

Well, maybe. Meanwhile life was going on, making other plans for her. She returned home and stashed her exercise in pointless aestheticism behind the door in the breezeway. Louise was in the kitchen, as she had been every afternoon this week. Colonizing Primrose's kitchen had replaced Louise's pre-work bathroom hour. Instead of smoking out the window of the house on Calvary Street, Louise would make a big, noisy production out of some kitchen task that she felt Primrose ought to be more on top of. Today it was the fridge. Along with the milk and the juice, the clear glass butter dish was on the counter, a witness to Primrose's slovenly housekeeping, for inside was a half-stick of butter furred with toast crumbs. Louise was going at the fridge's interior with rag that stank of bleach.

Louise slammed the fridge door shut.

"Easy, Ma." Primrose said as she lowered herself, wincing, into a chair. "I need an aspirin."

"You shouldn't be taking anything in your condition." Louise rinsed her rag and applied it to the counter in long strokes. "I can't believe Dr. Addleman still has you on those pills. Heaven knows what they're doing to your little passenger." She gestured at her belly. "But doctor knows best, I suppose."

Despite her mother's insinuating tone, they had reached a sort of détente about Primrose's "condition." It was as if Primrose, as the bearer of a new focus for her mother's solicitude, also required loving attention despite her sluttishness. For the first time, Primrose had some sort of power in their relationship, a fact that alternately frightened and amused. In a few short months, all this would be different, of course. Primrose had no idea, none whatsoever, what would take its place. Nature abhors a vacuum, that's what Tino was always saying. But she only dimly sensed the contours of this new life. It was a kind of rippling in her mind, like a stage curtain that was about to go up. Showtime.

"I got you a present." Louise gave the rag a vicious final twist, hung it over the sink's edge, and began to rinse her hands, reddened from the bleach. "There's a box on the bed."

Primrose plodded to her room. On the bedspread she found a long, thin box sealed with Scotch tape, a yellowed bow stuck to one equally yellowed corner. This was not a new gift. It was one of Louise's recycled presents.

"Come on, bring it out," Louise called. "What's taking you so long?"

Primrose ferried the box to the living room. Louise wedged herself beside her on the loveseat, her mouth bunched with avidity. Primrose shifted the throw on the sofa's arm. There, beneath the artless camouflage, was the dark hole of a cigarette burn.

"But this sofa's brand new!"

"I'm sorry," Louise said. "Truly, I am."

"Tino isn't going be happy about that," Primrose said, replacing the blanket and also, not coincidentally, tucking the corners of her own irritation.

"What's done is done. Least said, soonest mended. Et cetera. Let's open this. Do you need help?"

Without waiting for an answer, Louise ripped the box out of Primrose's hands and pried off the top. Primrose lifted the tissue paper to reveal a length of yellowed satin that turned out to be a nightgown, long-sleeved and high-collared, with paste jewel buttons. It was perfect—for Miss Havisham.

"I wore this for your father," Louise confided, "on our wedding night."

Louise was smiling shyly like she'd just shared a secret that she'd nursed for years, as if the presentation of this heirloom had finally redeemed Primrose as an acceptable object of a mother's love. Which, in her mother's case, greatly exceeded the bounds of good taste and propriety.

"Oh, Mom."

Primrose sighed, re-tucking those irritated psychological corners. After all, who was *she*—pregnant and married in haste, with a filthy kitchen—to say what good taste was?

"What a thoughtful present, Ma," Primrose said as she folded the nightgown back into the box.

Louise said, "I want you to take Reginald, too."

Her mother was full of surprises today. "Oh, Ma. I couldn't."

"I can't stand the sight of him anymore, and Mr. Shorty is threatening legal action for scratching all the bark off his goddamn dogwood tree." Her mother chuckled. "But cats and dogs never did get on, did they? Can't you do your mother one small favor, Primrose?"

"But you know Tino's allergic."

"Keep him in the yard."

"Tino?"

"If you want!" Her mother laughed again. "Of course I meant the cat. Tell Tino he needs to learn to compromise. You don't want to be the sort of woman who lets her husband boss her around and not let her have anything, even a lousy cat." She paused to catch her breath. "What do you say, Primrose? Will you take him?"

Would she take him. Of course she would—despite Tino's allergies, the sad gift in her lap.

"If it makes you happy, Ma."

Louise patted her hand. "I knew I could count on you."

THE BOOK OF LOVE: Gifts

by Primrose

Magic gifts: glass slippers, ruby slippers, enchanted mirrors, invisibility cloaks.

Tragic gifts: diamonds, verse.

Trad gifts: chocolates, roses.

Bad gifts: A dress that burns the wearer. An oversized toy horse filled with one's enemies.

If sumptuous enough, gifts of property can stand in for paradise, but we have noticed that such extravagant quotations of Eden often have a melancholy aspect suggestive of some prior loss. The Hanging Gardens of Babylon were a gift from Nebuchadnezzar to his wife, who missed the verdant landscape of her childhood. The Taj Mahal was a gift to a dying princess from her husband; she wanted a mausoleum, and so she got one.

The soul, reaching, throwing out for love,
As the spider, from some little promontory, throwing out
filament after filament, tirelessly out of itself, that one
at least may catch and form a link, a bridge, a connection
... Whitman

After the death of Marilyn Monroe in 1962, her ex-husband Joe DiMaggio sent long-stemmed roses to her grave three times a week. The deliveries continue to this day.

34. Chasing professors

Lupo hurried up the steps of the engineering department, a Victorian brick pile fronted by a flagstone path. In the foyer, he peered at the mail cubbies, but he didn't see Rodenko's name. A few had labels in Russian. Lupo stared at them. He didn't know Russian.

But I know you, Rodenko, he said to himself. *You're the type of guy who would never put your name on a mailbox. Who refuses all mail, no forwarding address. Who—*

Lupo made his way upstairs, running his hand over the polished banister.

You're the type of guy—

On the landing, where the stairs ended, all the doors were locked. Lupo retraced his steps to the entryway where he lingered once again by the mailboxes. That's when he saw it: a cubby tucked behind the radiator with a label typed in English: RODENKO. NO PACKAGES PLEASE.

I know you, Rodenko!

Inside there was a paperback titled *Gears from the Greeks* and a thin white envelope. The envelope wasn't sealed. Lupo glanced around and, confirming that he was alone, opened it.

The results were disappointing. The envelope contained an overdue notice from the library. Professor Rodenko was six weeks late returning *Aquatic Environments that Work: A Practical Guide* (Berkeley: Bathymetry Press, 1963) and *The Use of Sea Mammals in Underwater Archaeology*, new rev. ed. (New York: Bell & Boom, 1955).

It was amazing what these guys got away with, failing to show up to their offices and to return their overdue library books. No wonder he couldn't finish his dissertation.

But what did dolphins and archaeology have to do with UFOs?

Lupo replaced the envelope and left. It was time to talk with McKee.

"Lupo! Over here!"

As usual, McKee was outside; today, as befit the season, he was raking leaves into a pile. In the pool beside him, Ted was a gray shadow turning circles in the murky depths. Scum floated on the surface. This semester, McKee had a full teaching load, and he was struggling to keep up with his usual responsibilities.

"Did you know, Lupo, that the East German government makes its spies drive taxicabs? They can't be tracked, and they can receive instructions all day on the radio. No one suspects a blessed thing."

The dolphin emitted a series of clicks. Lupo, for his part, didn't know what to say. What did he know about taxi drivers in the Communist bloc? McKee always managed to charge him with anxiety, keeping him off balance so he could hardly remember his own name, never mind his scientific interests.

"Got time for a chat?" Lupo ventured.

"Sure." McKee leaned the rake against the fence. He passed a hand over his face, as if to force his expression into something less put-upon, and blinked a few times, as if to be sure he'd really arrived in the right reality, in his back yard with his dolphin and his graduate student. "We should catch up. It's been too long."

McKee led Lupo into the house. In the kitchen, on the counter, was a copy of the book Lupo had seen in Rodenko's mail cubby: *Gears from the Greeks*.

"What's your interest in this?" Lupo blurted. "Erm—properly speaking, it belongs in the classics department."

"Says you," McKee grinned. Lupo steeled himself. More mysteries, no doubt, were on the way.

McKee opened the book to an article about something called an "Antikythera mechanism," a clock-like device that had been found off the coast of a Greek island.

"It seems to be quite old. Maybe a hundred years before Christ."

"And?"

"Well, it's missing a few parts. It's the damnedest thing. No one can figure out what it does without the extra pieces."

"Which are not so extra."

"Exactly so."

"What does this have to do with UFOs?"

"Well," McKee said, "according to this article, the Greeks simply couldn't have had this technology. Nor would anyone in the Islamic world. It's too advanced, verging on industrial. Possibly, *just* possibly, a descendant of Archimedes might have put it together way up north, but only if Archimedes had himself been part of an engineering tradition in that area, and not the historical one-off he is now believed to be."

"How do you know so much about Archimedes?"

He shrugged. "You pick up things, living your whole life at school."

"And if Archimedes didn't do it?"

"It's pure speculation, but where else could the mechanism have come from? Take a guess." McKee looked at him expectantly. "We only spent all summer working on it."

"It comes from outer space?"

"Bingo," he said. "Now get along home. I've got midterms to correct, memos to write, fish to feed."

"Have you read my dissertation prospectus yet?"

"I will, Lupo. Cross my heart, hope to die."

Stick a needle in your eye. The thread of Lupo's patience verged on snapping.

"What's your rush, Lupo? The whole point right now is to stay in school."

"All right," said Lupo, though nothing was right at all.

The following week, Lupo made another trip to Rodenko's office. This time the doors on the landing were wide open. Through one of them, a long-haired young woman festooned with love beads lounged behind a typewriter.

"Is this Professor Rodenko's office?"

When she spoke, she sounded just like Janis Joplin. "Who the hell are you?"

"A friend of one of his students. Otis—" Lupo groped for Otis' last name and was surprised to discover he'd forgotten it.

"Oh, Otis," she purred, lighting a clove cigarette. "Of course."

"Can I see him?"

"Otis?" She exhaled a plume of fragrant smoke.

"Not Otis! Rodenko."

"Professor Rodenko holds office hours on Tuesdays from nine to noon."

No, he doesn't, Lupo thought.

"But I had an appointment," he protested. One lie deserved another.

She flicked ash into a beanbag ashtray, then shifted it to get a better view of the big paper calendar on her desktop. "I don't see anything on the schedule."

"Maybe you forgot to write it down."

"Never," she said. "He's not here."

"He isn't?"

"Look, I'm not a magician. It's not like I can snap my fingers and make him appear."

"May I wait? He might stop by."

"Suit yourself." She pointed to a chair in the corner. "But I'm not expecting him in the office this afternoon."

After a while, the woman left. Seeing his chance, Lupo shut the outside door and engaged the lock. Then he went to the door marked PROFESSOR RODENKO and turned the knob. To his surprise, it gave.

He poked his head in the room, half-expecting to find Rodenko. But the office was empty, and the desk was bare except for a telephone and a handful of dusty comic books featuring the usual heroes—Flash Gordon, the Green Lantern, Spider-Man. On the bookshelf were volumes with Russian lettering down their spines; old journals, in English and French, on rocketry, field surveying, and land conservation; and textbooks on engineering. The Naugahyde recliner in the corner was still indented from the weight of its last occupant. Rodenko, no doubt.

And, in the corner, a small object wrapped in paper and covered in a layer of dust. Lupo slipped the wrapper off, and flakes of something white and ancient drifted to the carpet. Beneath the rime were hints of a mechanism, wheels with meshing teeth. Whatever it was, it was heavy. Old. Lupo thrust it in his pocket and left the way he came.

35. Bringing it all back home

The little house filled rapidly with Primrose's clutter: glasses of ice water from which she had taken only a sip; hairbrushes tangled with long strands of her yellow hair; paper clips and safety pins and hairpins and lipsticks; pens, pencils, paintbrushes; books stuck with bookmarks or dog-eared and left on the floor or under the bed, including her diary, which was unlocked—and which Tino left exactly where he found it, alarmed by the possibility that her inner life might be not just fully available to him but on promiscuous display. Not to mention the messes she left on the countertop, ads for no-iron sheets and eau de cologne, coupons for sanitary pads and frozen peas, handwritten lists of items to buy, foods to eat, and foods to be consumed when one wanted other, richer foods ("skinny substitutions," as Primrose had titled the list). He even found an op-ed that proclaimed, "There is no Great Society," accompanied by letter from a woman whose sons had been drafted. She had a lot of trouble with the antiwar movement, the SDS kids and their slogans and matches. Primrose had underlined this part: "I could not rest as a mother, witnessing the attempted emasculation of my sons by a society that no longer appreciates unquestioning loyalty, undying commitment, or the worth of a man for what he is, rather than for what certificates he can present to show that he is a man."

A person of value, she meant. Beyond cannon fodder.

What did he, Tino Battuta, have to show that he was a man? His pregnant wife?

He thrust the clipping aside. His wife might be queen of the castle, but that didn't make him her housekeeper.

On Sunday morning, his day off, he shook her awake. "Wake up, sleepyhead. Today's a good day to clean house."

She rolled away from him. "You do it."

He patted her arm. "It's not a big place. It won't take long."

"I'm nauseous."

"Have a cracker. A pickle."

Primrose pulled the covers over her head.

Tino dressed and drank his coffee. Primrose was still fast asleep by the time he'd cleaned up the breakfast dishes. It was high time for a little revenge. The bathroom wasn't going to clean itself, after all. So he poured some bleach in the toilet and swished it with one of her paintbrushes, which he left to dry on the windowsill. He felt better.

There was still hair in the sink and dust on the floor, but as he thought it was only fair to share the tasks, he wrote those items—clean floor, clean sink—on a list, which he tacked to the fridge with a piece of tape. When she got up, around noon, he directed her attention to the list.

"I didn't know I'd married my mother," she sniffed as she filled the teakettle.

"Did it ever occur to you, Primrose, that she might have had a point?"

"Never," she replied.

Tino went outside and started the lawnmower. When he looked back, the part of the lawn that had passed under the mower unrolled in a long green strip. He attacked the lawn's perimeter with his clippers until the margin was just so. The work made him feel loose and manly, the furthest thing in the universe from cannon fodder. So this was married life. Inside, sweaty from exertion, he leafed through the mail and waited for Primrose to ask him what he wanted for lunch.

A half-hour later, when the only sound in the house was Primrose's snoring, Tino sat alone in the kitchen slapping peanut butter onto slices of bread and wondering how the hell he was going to get the house cleaned on a regular basis. Nobody could live like this.

"Hire someone," his mother advised when he got her on the phone.

"We don't have that kind of money. You know that."

"I can take the rest of the washing. It's nothing to do another load every week."

Tino thanked his mother and hung up. He'd explain it to Primrose somehow. Helping out, that's all his mother was doing. Wasn't that what family was for?

36. Paper dolls

There were other visitors. Elsie stopped by regularly, at least once a week, to criticize what Primrose ate for lunch ("Cottage cheese is full of fat, you know"), how she dressed ("Are you a hippie or a red? It's as if you can't decide"), and the way she let Tino do whatever he wanted with their money—by which she meant spending it on the *Sumac*, about which Primrose had stupidly and indiscreetly complained—instead of saving for a down payment on a house. After years of living with Louise perpetually on her back about something, Primrose didn't mind Elsie's barrage of advice. Elsie meant well, and truth be told, Primrose was glad for the company.

One morning Elsie showed up covered in dirt. Standing on the front step, she kicked mud from the soles of her boots.

"Excuse my mess, Primrose. Maintaining that yard is a full-time job. Got any stamps?"

"Don't worry about your mess. As you can see, I'm no stranger to it." Primrose gestured toward the kitchen. It smelled of burnt coffee and long-ago toast, but surely Elsie's was no better. "I'm afraid I don't have any stamps, Elsie. Tino used them to mail the bills. But can I make you a cup of coffee since you're here?"

"Oh, all right," Elsie said after a moment, as if she were doing Primrose a favor. "But only for a few minutes. The day's backed up already, and I still have a dozen thank-you notes to write. Henry got such nice gifts at his birthday party last weekend," she continued. "All Fisher-Price. Except for one. It's just unaccountable. Someone, I don't even know who, gave him an old box of paper dolls. Remember those?"

"Of course. They were fun."

"I like to think Keith and I are fairly liberal in our views, but you have to draw the line somewhere. Paper dolls are not for little boys."

"But, Elsie, what if he's the next Christian Dior?"

"When you have yours," Elsie huffed, "you'll see."

"I think it's a girl."

"In that case, you can have the paper dolls."

While Primrose put the water on, Elsie opened drawers and cupboards. "There's nothing like being just married, is there, Primrose? I remember when we had room like this. But now? Oh, Lord. Now all we've got is a house full of junk." Elsie ran a finger over the new garlic press in the dish rack. "I'll bet this thing's a real work-saver."

"You'd think so. But the garlic burns faster when it's all crushed up, so there's more work watching the stove."

"You know, this house was a complete disaster before you got here. We were so glad to see those folks go. Not their fault. They just couldn't keep up. You can't be pushing a lawn mower in retirement. You'll give yourself a heart attack. But young people, that's different. You really give the neighborhood some juice."

"Young people? But you yourself can't be a day over twenty-five," Primrose flattered her. Elsie was probably closer to thirty. Her concern for property values made her seem old.

Elsie waved off the compliment. "Oh, please! Did you see Lola DiMaio this morning in her Avon lady getup?"

"I thought I saw her drive by yesterday."

"She'll hit you up eventually. Take it from me, you'll want to watch your petty cash."

Primrose placed three cookies on a plate and set it on the table with her everyday cups. It was a pleasure, really, to do these things, to handle familiar objects and make proper use of them.

"I was thinking I might like one of those pots of solid perfume," Primrose said. "I could keep it in my bag and not worry about breaking it."

"The things these Avon people dream up!" Elsie's laugh was like a bark—short, hard, brittle. An electroshock laugh. Primrose had no idea what was so funny.

When the percolator finished burbling, Primrose lifted the pot and filled Elsie's cup.

"Maybe I shouldn't call it petty cash," Elsie said. "Given the importance of our position, it's not actually petty at all."

Having filled her own cup, Primrose set the pot on the trivet. "Our position?"

"As mothers. As wives."

"What would you call it, then?"

"Mad money."

"Mad money?"

"For the times you get so mad you have to blow the joint. Bail money. Get-out-of-jail money."

Elsie's words meshed poorly with her chirpy exterior. But then everyone had secrets. You never knew what other people were carrying around.

Elsie riffed on. "Bail-yourself-out money. Money like a sump pump."

"I'd settle for a bucket," Primrose said, thinking of the *Sumac*.

"If only we had buckets of money," Elsie mused. "Then we wouldn't have to settle for anything."

A school bus rolled up the block. "I didn't think anyone got bused to Maple Bay," Primrose said.

"Maple Bay is full of wonders. Stick around long enough, and you'll see what I mean." Elsie pushed her glasses up. "Haven't you noticed the odd shit that goes down around here?"

"Odd?"

"I keep seeing black limousines. Guys in suits come out of them. You know, Primrose, if your husband or son or brother is killed in combat, you get a visit from men in suits. They arrive in black limousines."

A bright pain flared behind Primrose's left eye. "It's not just a telegram anymore?"

"Nope." Elsie looked meaningfully at Primrose's midsection. "Been meaning to ask you. I've got a trunk full of outgrown baby clothes—sailor suits, rompers, even Dr. Denton's. Everything's in great shape. You want it?"

Primrose didn't know what to say. "Well, we *are* on a tight budget."

"I have a car bassinet, too. You strap it to the seat, stick the kid in it, and off you go. If you have one, you can take a drive by yourself now and then—you don't need anyone to hold the baby."

"Sounds wonderful." She hadn't even thought about who would hold the baby while she ran her errands, but now of course the problem seemed obvious. Even if Tino was home, he'd be busy with his own things—the yard, the grass, the sprinkler. "Thank you."

Elsie smiled, a little wistfully. Or maybe Primrose imagined this. It was hard to be sure. Elsie was not someone she would ordinarily befriend. She had a weird vibe: bitter, unlikely to be surprised by anything.

"Do you have any more milk? Whole milk is such a treat these days."

"It is?" Primrose only ever drank whole milk. She was surprised to hear there were other kinds. She got the milk from the fridge and offered it to Elsie. It came out so fast the coffee overflowed the cup. Elsie lifted it out of the way and drank the overflow straight from the saucer.

"Excuse my manners," she said, setting the saucer down.

"My father does just the same," Primrose replied. "We're not fancy."

"There's stuff in the whole milk that's bad for our hearts. I read it in the paper."

"In the *milk*?"

"Yes!" She refilled her cup. "Keith needs to be extra careful. Heart disease runs in his family. His father died not two years ago of a massive heart attack."

"Like *agita*?"

"Not *agita*," she scoffed. "Nobody dies of *agita*."

"Well, that's a relief. Everyone I know has *agita*."

"It can get worse. You have to cut out butter, whole milk, ice cream, cheese, red meat. We don't eat that poison anymore. What happens," Elsie went on, her eyes fixed on some unfinished task beckoning over Primrose's shoulder, "is the fat builds up in the arteries and causes a blockage. It falls to us—the wives, the mothers—to prevent the problem."

"Oh."

"We have such *power*."

Primrose nodded, believing and not believing. It was a struggle to hold onto her own point of view. Others seemed to do it so easily, like breathing. If only Elsie would go away and take her dietary proclamations with her.

"Whatever you do, you have to be *stealthy*."

"Stealthy?"

"Don't argue with Tino about what you are or are not feeding him. Because stress from arguing can make a man sick, too."

Elsie opened up worlds, that much was clear.

That afternoon Primrose bought chicken cutlets at the All-Mac and served them to Tino *à la Milanese* with lemon wedges. "Not bad," was his verdict. "Mom does them with homemade bread crumbs, might be good to try that."

"Right," said Primrose. She would have to ask Lorraine how to make bread crumbs. As she was adding this item to her to-do list, the doorbell rang. By the time Primrose opened the door, the bell-ringer had vanished. But on the step was the promised car bassinet pinned with a note from Elsie: "Happy trails."

After dinner, Primrose and Tino sat on the back porch. Tino smoked his pipe, a new affectation. The smoke smelled pleasant, masculine. Lightning bugs flashed in the bushes; the trees were dark against the sky. It wouldn't take much to plant a new tree in the garden, one that would grow straight and true for twenty-odd years, just as she had before her marriage, that first division, that branching.

37. Another social call

One morning not long after Elsie's visit, Lupo materialized on the doorstep holding a box of donuts. Too surprised to say a word, Primrose led him into the kitchen where she gathered plates and cups, stopping to adjust her bathrobe, one of the few items of her wardrobe that still fit.

"Coffee, Lupo?"

"If it's no trouble."

"It's no trouble," she said.

She filled the percolator and plugged it in. He set the donuts on the counter. Numbly she assembled the usual items: coffee service, napkins. A plate for the donuts.

"How are you?" he asked. "How's married life?"

"It's all right."

"Just all right?"

"It's fine," she said.

But it wasn't. Everything was the opposite of fine. Their gazes met, but she looked away, her lips pressed tight against everything she could not bring herself to say. The percolator perked on, filling the silence. How awkward and disappointing it was, this business of growing up.

When the coffee was ready, Primrose poured them each a cup. Her movements seemed practiced, if not quite relaxed.

"How's your research going?"

"I've been chasing down a mysterious professor. Name of Rodenko. Soviet defector. His students have also formed a group for the study of UFOs." He selected an old-fashioned from the box.

"Far out." She scuffed a slipper on the linoleum. "Really far, even for you, Lupo."

Provocation enough. Before he could think the better of it, he was reaching into his pocket. The object he'd stolen from Rodenko was there, wrapped in his handkerchief. He set the thing on the table and unwrapped it.

"What's this?" Primrose ran her finger over its surface. Flakes fell onto the tabletop, joining the crumbs.

"I'm not sure. Rodenko thinks it's from outer space," he explained around a mouthful of donut.

She picked up the object and turned it over. "Are you still in touch with Joseph? I'm still going to his classes, but he's kind of distant and mean."

Lupo shrugged. "As far as I know, his Be-In is still happening. He calls me now and then to tell me how it's progressing. Looks like it's going to take place in the ball field near your mother's house."

"Ma's not going to like that. All those hippies and their trash."

"I don't know if anyone who lives there will. But Joseph said he had no trouble getting permits."

Primrose folded her napkin in half and tucked the packet between her cup and saucer. A dark stain spread to its edges.

"It's scheduled for when?"

"Early spring. I'm not exactly sure of the date."

"Good music?"

"Apparently."

She refilled his cup. "Will you let me know when they settle on a real date?"

"Of course. I'll call you." He paused. "So what's new around the neighborhood? See anything strange?"

This, apparently, was the million-dollar question in Maple Bay. "Strange?"

"You know, kids with three heads, dogs that talk. That sort of thing."

"It's Maple Bay, Lupo! Nothing is strange in Maple Bay. That is the whole *point* of Maple Bay." She paused. "Well, maybe there's something. You remember Lola DiMaio?"

He nodded. How could he forget the talented Mrs. DiMaio, not to mention her wild kids and her husband on that hospital boat in the South China Sea?

"Well, she's an Avon lady."

"New line of work?"

"She never seems to sell anything. She walks around with her case of samples, ringing doorbells. No one ever answers."

"It's probably innocent," he said. Actually, he didn't think anything was innocent anymore, not after his visit to Rodenko's office, but he didn't want to skew the results of this conversation by unduly biasing the witness. "Probably she's just trying to keep busy. Make extra money."

"Yeah," said Primrose. "It gets a little dull around here in the afternoons."

"I'll bet."

Her eyes shifted through their colors: first gray, then blue. Lupo, who'd nearly forgotten the debilitating effects of this dazzlement, looked away. "Will you keep an eye on her?"

"Sure. Why?"

"Probably, it's nothing." *Play it low*, he told himself. "Something McKee said. It could be related. He told me about this East German project of putting spies to work driving taxi cabs where their paths couldn't be traced or monitored. And they could transmit messages over CB radios."

"I doubt Lola DiMaio has a CB radio."

"Me, too," Lupo said. "But you never know."

"Should I keep a log?"

"Nothing so fancy. I know you're busy. Just notes would be fine. Mail them to me after a few weeks," he said. "I don't want to put you out of your way."

He set his dirty cup in the sink and left. From the window she waved as he backed out of the driveway, her other hand clasping shut the front of her robe.

She shivered; it was time to turn up the heat, but Tino had ideas about that, about home economics, about *thrift*.

She sighed. Her new life in Maple Bay came once more into focus, and it was Lupo's visit that now seemed unreal. But he'd left evidence: His precious mechanism was still on the table. She wrapped it in a dishtowel and stowed it in the junk drawer alongside the handful of hot type he'd given her the previous spring.

In the living room she found her old *New Yorker* on the coffee table. As she riffled through the pages, a subscription card fell out—another relic from her former life. Oh, the future she'd imagined for herself! Well, perhaps not all was lost. The card offered six free issues; she could always cancel if Tino objected to a subscription. She filled out the card and tucked it in her purse, vowing to mail it later.

38. Errors and omissions

Tino pushed the mop down the corridor, trailing a thick stripe of water. In the staff room, the percolator puffed coffee-scented steam into the air. It was a perfect morning on A-Pavilion, and everything was running just the way Anthony liked it: orderly, controlled, efficient, deathless. The signs posted all over attested to his commitment to this state of affairs, as did his written and verbal directives, like the one taped to the grunting percolator: THE WRENCH YOU MORONS DON'T FORGET THE WRENCH.

The Army expressed exactly the same impulse in massive, uniformed, institutionalized form.

Every so often a guy left A-Pavilion in a box. The cause of death varied. Bad reactions to a drug, a burst appendix, an aneurysm. Some guy figured a way onto the roof, pitched himself off, and shattered himself on the sidewalk, six floors down. Tino hadn't seen it, but Anthony had told him about it later, his eyes blank and haunted over a cup of his overworked coffee. "You wouldn't think a body would do that," he said. The coffins were military-issue, lined with stainless steel.

There had been rumors that Reservists were getting called up in different parts of the state. Tino asked Anthony about it.

"You'll see a lot of the world, you know, if you go. Parts you wouldn't see otherwise."

"Yeah," Tino said. *Like hell.* There was plenty Tino didn't want to see. Had no interest in seeing.

Someone had left the door to the courtyard open. The wet spots on the floor paled as they dried. Across the courtyard, a man in scrubs struggled out of the double-doors that led to B-Pavilion, where they housed the amputees. Over his shoulder, he'd slung—could it be? this whole place was so absurd!—a muscular, hairy human leg.

The amputated limb was draped in a sheet, but Tino could see the foot and ankle, both black with gangrene.

Oh, there was enough to see right here at home. More than.

The man in scrubs was heading for the incinerator. His itinerary gave Tino an idea. He felt for his wallet. Today was a fine day to rid himself of a burden he'd carried for too long.

WHOMP of minor explosives, shattering of small glass. Chick bellowed. "Thar she blows!"

Someone had fucked up with the Allen wrench. Anthony shoved past, shouting about protocol.

Protocol! What happened was simple physics. Mother Nature laughed at protocol.

Tino plunged the mop into the bucket, pushed the assemblage into a corner, and slipped out the door.

39. Nutrition

One morning in November, Primrose woke to Tino's shouting. Reginald had pissed on the kitchen floor, and Tino, barefoot, had stepped in the puddle. "Goddamn *cat*."

A thump, followed by the noise of claws scrabbling for purchase on the linoleum.

Primrose willed her pounding heart to slow. If only she'd been awake, she'd have found the mess before Tino and cleaned it up. But lately it seemed she was always asleep. Her mother said it was the baby making her so tired.

In the kitchen, Tino slammed the refrigerator door. The milk bottle rattled against something else inside the fridge, and Primrose held her breath. But there were no further causes for alarm. *No cause,* she sang nonsensically to herself, *no cause.* She padded into the kitchen, filled the percolator, and left it to boil. *Time to face the music,* she thought.

"When my mother was first married," Tino said, splashing milk into a bowl of raisin bran, "my father woke her up that first morning and told her to get to work. And she did. She hemmed his pants and darned his socks. She made him breakfast every morning—eggs and toast, *pizza fritte.*"

"Is that supposed to hurt?"

"Does it?"

"You want me to get up at the asscrack of dawn to make you fried crap that will give you a heart attack? No wonder your father has a heart condition. Your mother has devoted herself to giving him one."

Tino grunted. Maybe she *should* fry his breakfast every day until he keeled over.

The words were out of her mouth before she could think. "What if I left?"

"You can't leave," he said reasonably, infuriatingly. "We're married."

He disappeared behind the newspaper. She sighed. There was no leaving, and they both knew it. She'd be seeing the back of a newspaper first thing in the morning for the next fifty years.

The coffee was finished. Primrose poured herself a cup. The cat mewled outside the door.

"That cat," Tino announced, rattling the paper as he turned the page, "pisses the floor out of spite."

"He might be onto something." Primrose opened the kitchen door to find Reginald clawing the screen. "Shoo," she told him. "This is not your house, you only live here." To Tino, she said, "Maybe we should get a dog."

"I like that idea. He could eat the cat."

"I could eat a horse," said Primrose. Tino glanced at her over the newspaper, some comment, probably mean, already at his lips. "Don't," she said. "Just don't."

The paper rose, shielding his face. Primrose rummaged in the fridge until she found an apple in the vegetable drawer. She straightened up, bracing the small of her back with her free hand. The lower-back twinges were the worst.

His face, when she looked at him, was creased with concern.

"Look," he began, relenting. "Let me go to the store, get you some proper breakfast." In quick gestures he folded the paper into a neat package and set it on the table. Then he approached her, all gentleness, and rested a hand on her back where the pain was bad. "It's my day off. I've got time. What would you like?"

"Cream," she said, the desire hitting her all at once with extraordinary clarity. "All I want is a pint of cream."

He returned with most of the dairy case: ice cream, whipped cream, half-and-half, light cream, heavy cream, and, amazingly, a tiny jar of crème fraiche that Primrose gasped to see. "We'll have to save this for a special occasion."

"Nah," said Tino. "You eat it. It's good for you."

She ate it all, thinking of his heart, her own.

Later that afternoon, pushing her cart around the grocery store, Primrose noticed that clams were on special, twelve for a dollar. Primrose got two dozen, some frozen spinach, and a waxed paper envelope of bacon. On the drive home, the clams rustled in their thin box.

She had promised Lupo his letter today, the one with the log of Lola DiMaio's movements around the neighborhood. As far as she could tell, Lola was doing nothing out of the ordinary. She walked her kids to the school bus, she went to the grocery store, she puttered in the yard. But maybe Lupo would see something different in her results. What did she know about UFOs anyway? All she knew was if she waited any longer to send the note, she risked leaving Lupo high and dry, and the world of research was waiting. She was halfway home when, glimpsing the envelope peeking out of her handbag, she remembered her promise. Bad luck: she had perishables in the car. But she turned back anyway and headed for the post office, only to find that there'd been an accident near the loading dock and the line to get into the parking lot stretched for blocks.

Inside the post office, she stood in another long line for the clerk, and when she returned to the car, its interior had a fishy odor. Tino would not be pleased about this. Groaning, she rolled down the windows and sped home, where Tino was waiting for her.

"I'm not eating this," he said as he pulled the soggy package of formerly frozen spinach from the bag.

"You need B vitamins," Primrose said. "You'll get dandruff, and people will wonder why your wife doesn't take better care of you."

"Green vegetables make me throw up." He sniffed the box that contained the clams. "Jesus, these stink."

"They're fine," she said. "What you're smelling is the ocean."

"All I ever want for dinner is a steak and a bucket of J & B on the rocks. Chocolate ice cream for dessert. Don't you have any idea what food *is*?"

She glared at him, her hands on her hips, her belly slung and jutting toward him, two against one. "How dare you."

"How dare I what?"

"How dare you criticize what I cook. You think it's easy to keep a man alive?"

"Oh, come off it. When you've got your martyr's face on, you look just like your mother."

"Is that so? Well, I'll tell you what, Tino Battuta. Since you already know what you want for dinner, you can cook it yourself!"

She returned the groceries to their bag, grabbed her pocketbook, and headed out the door. "I'll be back tonight," she snapped. "Maybe."

"I'll be here," he replied breezily.

Fifteen minutes later, she was in her mother's kitchen, sweating onions for clam broth. Louise stomped around in her bare feet, angry for some reason or perhaps for no reason at all. She slammed into the bathroom and flushed the toilet; the radio came on. Frank wandered in, and Primrose smiled at him, pushing her fight with Tino to the corner of her mind along with Louise's sour mood, her slammed doors and manic flushing of toilets. All the sad things.

"It's nice to have you home," Frank told her. "You sure Tino doesn't mind?"

"He's out with Chick," she lied. "He doesn't even know I'm gone."

She thought: *I am barefoot and pregnant in my father's kitchen, exactly the way my mother always said I would be.* Of course, *of course*, this was her story's end.

She put the wilted spinach in a serving dish and crumbled bacon on the top. The clams she ladled into a bowl along with the hot broth and set everything before her father. He pulled out the inside of a clam with a fork and conveyed it into his mouth. "Good," he said.

From the bathroom, Louise roared, "Quahogs, Frank? You know they're all polluted."

"They're not quahogs, Louise. They're clams."

"Same difference. Don't say I didn't warn you."

To Primrose, Frank muttered, "I don't know what gets into your mother."

Frank ate a bowlful of clams under Primrose's beaming face, then sopped up the broth with the heel of a loaf that Primrose found in the breadbox. Primrose swallowed mouthfuls of spinach, not tasting them, wondering what awaited her back home in Maple Bay. When they finished, Primrose cleared the dishes from the table. Frank set the last fork on the last plate and doubled over, groaning. The fork clattered on the floor.

"Dad!"

Primrose rounded the table, banging her hip on the corner, and stood helplessly over her father. He pushed her aside and staggered down the hallway toward the bathroom. Primrose followed close behind.

"Open up!" she cried. "Dad's sick!"

Frank slumped against the wall, pale. She pounded on the door.

"Serves him right! Where'd you get those quahogs, Primrose? Your fancy mother-in-law's fancy grocery store?"

Primrose imagined her mother perched on the crapper, her cigarette burning down as she luxuriated in their extremity, in the power she had over them, sitting on the house's one toilet behind a locked door.

Frank unbuckled his pants.

"Mom!"

"Lou," Frank pleaded. "Let me in!"

"Their money won't save the Battutas, you know. God doesn't care what you got in your pocket."

"MOM!"

The door stayed shut. Shit gushed from Frank. The mess was unspeakable.

"GODDAMN IT FRANK WHAT IS THAT SMELL?"

"Don't look at me," Frank said. "Primrose, please. It will be all right. Just don't look."

Louise flung the door open, stepped over the filth, and stomped toward the kitchen.

"You crapped on my floor! On my clean floor, Frank! Goddamn you straight to hell, Primrose! With your rotten quahogs! Jesus God, what did I DO, what did I EVER do—"

Primrose fled.

The following morning, the police found the car parked by the river, and they discovered Primrose shivering on the bank, her eyes trained blankly at the cemetery across the water, in the direction of the Battuta family plot. They took her to the station, where she refused to speak except to give Tino's name and their phone number in Maple Bay. He came for her, but instead of going home, he drove straight to the hospital, because that was what you did when you had a crazy person on your hands.

Later, when a woman in her mother's spongy nursing shoes forced the pill of quiet down her throat, Primrose gagged and begged for water. She spilled most of it down her front, but the tepid mouthful she managed to ingest tasted of the weeds that choked the Pocasset and very nearly swallowed her up too.

40. Better all the time

Recovery, Dr. Addleman had once told her, is what you do for as long as it seems you might not recover. After that, you're on your way.

At first she clung to this. Later it occurred to her that she might have asked: Where to?

She reminded herself to bathe, to eat, to dress. By bedtime, she was wrecked, drained by the regimen of reminders, but despite her exhaustion, she often woke two or three times during the night, from hunger or discomfort or both. It was easier to sleep if she went to bed as soon as she finished with the dinner dishes. All her nights were early. Tino, exhausted by his shifts at A-Pavilion, did not complain. They never spoke of the night she went to the river.

Once, she asked him what was on his mind.

"I'm just glad you're home," he said. When he put his arm around her, she wondered at its solidity, the deadness of its weight.

41. Adjustments

Lupo groaned. It couldn't be later than seven o'clock, but the sun was already pouring in through the skylight. He twisted in damp sheets.

He had been waking up to a ruckus every day for the past week. After much bickering with his father, his mother had determined that their new house was decoratively insufficient and threatened to renovate. His father called her bluff: *Go ahead. Be my guest.* As a result, Lupo woke every morning to some new and invariably noisy invasion: wallpaper guys, plumber guys, lighting guys, guys to hang curtains and lay carpet.

"Turn it, turn it, a little more, STOP. You're gonna take out the gutter, you pinheaded freak." Lupo rolled over and raised the shade. A beefy guy held one end of a sofa, the spare-lined Danish modern kind his mother liked, while another one stood behind him on the truck, directing. "I mean that in the nicest possible way."

The dolphin next door had not yet attracted notice, but surely that was only a matter of time. And then, who knew what might happen if the news got around? Well, in truth, probably not much: titters, gossip, and then the wagging tongues would be onto the next curiosity. UFOs were already kind of passé. This was the peculiar magic of the suburbs. Anything that could happen, would happen—so long as it was unlikely to result in anything actually changing.

"Easy, easy, just, you know, oonch it—GOOD."

The couch was dark brown, a near perfect match for the new shag rug, soon to be wrecked because no one ever remembered to take off their shoes before coming inside.

One of these days he was going to come home from a sighting with space plasma on the soles of his shoes, and that would really fuck up the shag rug.

Space plasma! Clearly he was spending too much time with RICUFOG.

In the mirror, though, he discerned no sign that he was going native or, more precisely, alien: no space plasma, no unfamiliar cranial ridges, no new moles or freckles. He turned on the shower and zombie-walked into the spray. Primrose owed him a report; today might be a good day to pay her a visit. Warm water sluiced down his body, dissolving the edge with which his morning had begun. Now that Primrose was a married lady, alone in the house all day, he couldn't see the harm in cheering her up. He would stop when Tino was working, and they'd have coffee—an exciting ritual, yet chaste. He was sure Primrose appreciated the company. Hadn't she said as much that first day?

THE BOOK OF LOVE: Ten Foolproof Rules for Writing Romance Novels

by Primrose

1. All romance novels are written from the heroine's point of view, which should be as conventional as possible, the better to facilitate the reader's identification.

2. The heroine should not be old, rich, previously married, or with her own children.

3. The heroine should not be too smart. For the hero to be plausible, the reader must feel that he can teach the heroine something.

4. All heroes are tall, dark, handsome, and preferably wealthy.

5. Clothing should be removed in the first hundred pages. For better results, make it the first fifty.

6. Bosoms are for heaving.

7. For a Gothic touch, add ghosts, phantoms, and/or mysterious noises emanating from an attic, closet, shed, and/or a wintry heath.

8. Expense accounts, private jets, Italian-from-Italy shoes, and Pauline Trigère suits are wonderful details that keep the reader completely out of touch with reality.

9. No one should die or wind up in a mental hospital, with the exception of the hero's first wife, who should be hidden in the attic/closet/shed under inconsistent security conditions until needed to complicate the plot.

10. Don't talk about contraception. No one ever gets pregnant in a romance novel. People read these novels to avoid thinking about the relationship between cause and effect. If this bothers you, romance is not your métier, and you should write a different book.

42. Talk of the town

The doorbell again. Primrose lumbered to the door and peered through the glass. Lupo stood on the step, one hip canted in expectant contrapposto, sweating twin blots into the armpits of his shirt.

"The place is a mess," she said as she opened the door. "I'm a mess."

Tino's robe covered the indifferently bathed and groomed basics. She was large and round everywhere; her matted hair and spotty face could not be helped.

"Not at all." He repositioned his backpack. "I should have called."

She led him to the kitchen, put the coffee on, and dropped heavily into a chair. He stood awkwardly, not sure what to do with himself, until she gestured that he, too, should sit. She couldn't find much to say; the baby was large now and seemed to move all the time, keeping her attention turned inward. She wanted to sit alone and dream; failing that, she intended to let Lupo take the conversational lead while she listened, trying discreetly to keep her bathrobe closed.

Lupo relayed an update from McKee. "He thinks the dolphins might be ahead of us somehow—evolutionarily. They sense emotions and infer thoughts from them, rather than the other way around."

Primrose stared at him. "We infer our emotions from our thoughts?"

"That's the idea. Like, right now, you're confused."

She raised an eyebrow. He grinned. In the bubbly atmosphere of his flirting, she felt herself shrink slightly, as if she were returning to her usual dimensions.

"It's a theory," he said.

"How could you possibly test it?" A reasonable question, her first in days.

"I think we just did."

Primrose ran a finger over the tacky tabletop, willing herself into her identity as upstanding Mrs. Battuta who did not flirt with other men or allow them to see her half-undressed in her messy kitchen. "Why is McKee so excited about dolphins anyway?"

"He says they hear things we don't. Like dogs, only smarter. Communications from—"

"Outer space?" With a fingernail Primrose scraped at a particularly sticky spot, then swiped the debris to the floor.

"Maybe. We have instruments to pick up the traces of the invisible space particles that are perpetually falling through our atmosphere. Why can't dolphins also pick up traces—audio ones?"

Primrose was tempted to tell Lupo about the voices she'd been hearing, about the next breakdown she sensed looming, like a change in the weather. But he talked too much and to too many people: that little cheerleader bitch from the Hog House for instance. And Lola DiMaio. As far as she knew, at this point he probably even talked to aliens. Probably adored them, in fact—for their free-spiritedness, with their promises of life on a new planet, of a fresh start with swell new neighbors who smoked their reefer with space-age bongs and enjoyed unconventional family arrangements. Free love. Good times.

"I'm not sure how much this stuff about space aliens has to do with me."

"You?"

"Me. Here, in Maple Bay. With my neighbors, the garden, this house."

"Well," Lupo conceded, "probably not very much." He frowned, confused. "Does it have to have anything to do with you?"

She let the question hang. "Yes," she said finally, "I think it does. It should somehow be relevant. To this." She gestured broadly, as if to encompass everything—the dirty floor, the grimy curtains, the overflowing sink.

"The UFO story is coming along," Lupo said. He seemed not to have registered her point. Perhaps he couldn't. "It's more complicated than anyone expected."

He talked on and on. Barely listening, Primrose maneuvered herself around him and started rinsing dishes.

"I spoke to Joseph," Lupo said. He continued peevishly: "That fact might interest you."

Primrose turned to face him, letting the water run. "What did Joseph tell you?"

"He agrees with McKee," Lupo said. "He thinks it's all related—the UFO sightings, the dolphin research. He thinks the Be-In should be staged as a way to communicate with them."

"With whom?"

"Whoever's trying to signal us from outer space."

"Six months ago I would never have pegged you for a true believer."

Lupo reddened, hurt. He stammered: "I'm not. Not really. These guys, McKee, Rodenko—"

"Rodenko?" The name was unfamiliar.

"New guy," Lupo said. "From Engineering. Anyway. They're all waiting on news from Mars, and I can't even get reliable reports of UFO sightings from Pawtucket. Look at this."

From his backpack he withdrew a pamphlet and set it on the counter by the sink. Leaning over, Primrose read the title.

"Easy Journeys to Other Planets?"

"If going to Mars is easy," Lupo said, "I don't know what's hard."

"Life on earth." Primrose turned off the faucet. "That's what's hard."

She crossed the kitchen and rummaged in a drawer until she found the little flaking mechanism Lupo had brought on his last visit. She touched the gearwheel lightly, dislodging grit.

"Careful with that," he told her, returning the pamphlet to the depths of his backpack.

"This thing's been around for a zillion years, Lupo. My fingertip poses no threat."

"Just hold onto it for a while longer for me, okay? I promise I'll explain everything."

The baby kicked. Primrose passed a hand over her stomach. A car drove by, the radio turned up so loud she felt the vibration in the kitchen. Primrose and Lupo looked out the window. Primrose didn't recognize the woman who was driving.

"What's she keeping under that bouffant?" Lupo wondered. "It's huge."

"She could keep a loaf of bread in there."

"A bun in the oven?" When he glanced at her, her face was still. Same old poker face. Not getting the joke, or else it was just unfunny. "Or an alien."

"Lupo!"

In the spaces between the baby's kicks, Primrose imagined living with Lupo in Maple Bay, doing the grunt work of science in his odd way—calling on lonely housewives, peering over fences into back yards as if, at any moment, some profound revelation might occur. But there was nothing out there beyond the fences and lawns, the vegetable plots, the daffodils and roses. What was Lupo really after? And what in the world—this world, not another one—did it have to do with her?

After Lupo left, Primrose found the first issue of her *New Yorker* subscription in the mailbox. She turned the glossy cover to check the address. No mistake—it had come to the right place. But *Primrose Battuta*, who was that? Riffling the pages, she imagined life in the magazine's glamorous elsewhere, light years from Maple Bay. There was an ad for Pauline Trigère; there was another for Mercedes. "Talk of the Town" included a review of a Picasso show at the Met. She sighed at these dispatches from the gorgeous elsewhere of New York. Now *that* was another planet.

Unless it was all a media creation anyway, a fantasy cooked up in some hot city office where underpaid staffers punched the keys on their typewriters and picked at canned tuna for lunch. What was the point of living in New York if all you did was type up fantasies of that life—a life you *weren't* living—for export to the likes of her? So that kids, like the one she had been, oh, three or four lifetimes ago, could grow restive under their parents' roofs, straining against their narrow viewpoints, their unsettle-able old hash. That old story, again and again. Apparently no one ever got tired of it.

A limousine rolled past, its windows dark. Was it packed with federal agents, bearing their bad news? Or was it another car from Dom Carcieri's outfit, taking the relatives to the last hurrah of yet one more oldster? At the corner, the limousine signaled. Primrose lost sight of it round the turn.

43. The chairman

Behind the wheel of the Dart, Chick pulled up in front of the little house in Maple Bay. From the front door, Tino emerged bearing a ceramic pot of chrysanthemums. Primrose followed slowly, spade in hand. She was carrying high, and she moved awkwardly in her waders, another charity item from Elsie. Tino set the pot by the rhododendrons and kissed Primrose goodbye, a quick peck that just missed her cheek.

In the front seat, Tino found several hoses, a can of WD-40, and a tube of caulk.

"Did you hold up a hardware store?"

"Boat's not gonna fix itself," Chick said. "Our summer repairs were strictly stopgaps."

"We stopped quite a few gaps, as I recall."

They passed a new elementary school shaped like a protractor, two arms splayed wide, embracing a circular driveway and a patchy lawn over which lawn sprinklers threw water in scintillating arcs.

"We might get a rainbow," Tino remarked. "Trout, I mean."

Chick didn't answer.

"Why so pissy?"

"You'd be pissy, too, if you'd heard the news this morning. The strike's over. The nurse's aides are coming back."

Tino slumped in his seat. "Shit. We'll be redeployed."

"Is what I'm saying. We're back to Plan A."

"The *Sumac*."

"We need to make our wreck seaworthy, fast."

Benny Goodman's "The Glory of Love" twittered from the radio. Tino flashed on his parents, his mother in the living room teaching his father to jitterbug. How his parents loved the standards—so easy to dance to, easy to learn. Nothing like the Deferments or even beatnik jazz. Chick reached to turn the dial.

"Don't," Tino said. Maybe it was just his time on A-Pavilion, but it seemed to him that standards were among the most important things you could have.

Low tide. The marina reeked of seaweed and motor oil. The *Sumac* was berthed toward the marina's front, near the ramp that led to the water. The place was crackling; everyone was hustling to stay ahead of the weather and exchanging grins and handshakes. Comfortable in their identical khaki pants and white-soled deck shoes, the guys at the marina reminded Tino of the ones he'd fled in St. Louis. They also knew exactly how to wear the uniform of ordinary life. It was so important to look like you weren't trying, even if you were. Especially if you were.

Chick's idea was to finish the most pressing repairs while the *Sumac* was still in the water, so they could more easily test their results. The rest of the work, mostly cleaning, could be done on land. Following their plan, Tino replaced a hose in the bilge line, while Chick caulked and painted whatever he could reach. Tino moved on to the prow, where Chick had installed a gag bust of Chairman Mao. Notwithstanding the rumored call-up and pending general heavy weather, it was a glorious day to be outside. Tino smeared some NO-CRAK on his hands, which were taking a beating. With another palmful, he brought out the shine on the Chairman's bald head.

They'd been working for an hour when Primrose arrived with a paper bag stuffed with grinders wrapped in butcher paper. She wanted to make things work. He was trying, too. The grinders perfumed the air with the smell of meatballs, which made his mouth water while drawing dirty looks from the preppy contingent, who obviously knew nothing about good eating. The thought pleased him, and he felt himself loosen. Everything would be okay—even another breakdown might be okay—so long as she kept bringing his favorites for lunch, so long as they both kept trying.

Tino pushed up his glasses, leaving a streak of caulk on his nose.

"Cute." Primrose wiped the caulk away with her fingers.

The boat rocked on its moorings as a motorboat rumbled up alongside them. The man at the helm was what Tino privately called a *yacht-club punk*, decked out in a madras shirt and a gold-trimmed captain's hat. The woman beside him shivered in her cable-knit sweater.

"We've got this berth in five." He spun the wheel, letting the motor idle.

"Aye, aye," muttered Chick.

"We're just about done here," Tino added, just to be clear.

While preppy Captain Ahab tapped his foot, Tino stowed their supplies. Chick jumped onto the dock, and Primrose knelt to unravel one of the two ropes tethering the *Sumac* to it. She yanked the knot so the loop disappeared around the other side.

"Shit," she said. "I lost it."

"Madame," Chick said, taking the line, every inch the gentleman that Ahab was not. "Allow me."

Tino turned the key in the ignition. The engine sputtered. On the fourth try, it caught. Tino backed out by inches, craning his head to be sure he wasn't in danger of smacking into Ahab's *felucca*. The engine's whine rose in pitch and kept going. As did the *Sumac*. There was only so much room to move. Tino pressed his whole weight on the accelerator, trying to reverse direction. Ahab honked. The engine hit a still more urgent note. The wheel bucked in Tino's hand.

"Boy!" Ahab shouted. "Something's stuck in your works!"

The *Sumac* cracked into Ahab's boat and caromed off. The prow tilted steeply, and the deck slipped under Tino's feet. Ahab unleashed a stream of obscenities. Chairman Mao sank to his nose, to his eyebrows. Tino clambered up the deck rail. At the last moment, when it was clear that the boat had passed the point of no return, he leapt for the dock. The *Sumac* rolled over and sank.

"As the Maestro giveth, so He taketh away. Nothing to do now," Chick opined, "but cry in our beer."

Late afternoon was not a bad time to find a booth at Bradley's, which was as good a place as any to lubricate their grievances. Chick drained his glass and emitted a burp so communicative the waitress immediately set a fresh glass under the tap. Primrose sipped a Dr Pepper.

"You're not crying," Tino said to Chick. The statement was more like a warning, though Tino's own eyes were red.

"Not yet." With a finger, Chick traced the rim of his pint glass. "You're not crying, either."

"I'm relieved," Tino said, catching Primrose's eye. "Just think, no more boating expenses."

Chick leaned back in the booth, his hands stuffed deep into the front pockets of his chinos.

"So much for Canada," he said glumly. "There's still no guarantee we won't get called up."

Someone had made a gash on the wooden tabletop. Tino picked at it.

"Don't," Primrose urged quietly. "You'll just make it worse."

Chick drained his glass, the second one, and slammed it on the table.

"I don't know about you, but I for one am not going to spend all night moaning over a little boating accident!" he roared. "Besides, you didn't really think we'd have made it, do you, Tino? That colander wouldn't take us further than Block Island."

"Then what the hell did we buy it for?"

Chick said, "Hope."

"Excuse me," Tino said, sliding out of the booth. "I need some air."

Newspapers were stacked by the door. He pulled one out and turned the pages. When he found the AP, he scanned the items on the list, but they were full of the same old stuff: the body count, the latest diplomatic effort come to zero, a protest or a concert where someone had died or someone famous had shown up. Then, toward the bottom, a tiny item: ANOTHER RHODE ISLAND WOMAN REPORTS UFO ABDUCTION.

"Christ," he muttered. The world's craziness had well and truly reached Rhode Island, and it seemed safe to conclude that the whole world was loony tunes.

44. One fish, two fish

The day before Christmas, Primrose didn't leave their bed. She was too big now to do much of anything beyond leaf through magazines in between bathroom visits. Eight weeks from her due date, she needed to go all the time.

That night they were expected at the Battutas' traditional Seven Fishes supper, to be followed by Midnight Mass at St. Bartholomew's. All she had to wear was a maternity version of the little black dress—a little black tent she'd found on markdown at Goodwill. Oh, she'd let herself go, all the way—but what could you expect? Letting Tino go all the way was the first sin; this development was the next logical step. The sin, in both cases, was the same. Letting go, losing control.

While Tino was at his mother's house helping to trim the Christmas tree, Lupo had called to say that McKee had won a grant to go to Greece. There was a shipwreck he wanted to explore, and he wanted to use the dolphin to do it. Lupo was to accompany him. Primrose didn't bother to ask how long before he had to leave. Tino could be called up at any time, and with the baby coming, her life was about to change in ways that had nothing to do with Lupo Light. She wasn't fooling herself about that anymore.

The doorbell rang. Through the curtains, Primrose spied her mother on the steps, her finger headed once again for the buzzer. Shit *and* shinola. Solitude was hard, but it was preferable to *this*. Primrose made her way to the door as the summons came again, shrill, inexorable.

"What took you so long?" Louise grouched when Primrose opened the door.

"Look at me, Ma. What do you *think* took me so long?"

"You're out of shape, that's all." Louise propelled herself into the house. In one hand, she carried a sack filled with gifts wrapped in red and green foil; in the other, a beribboned potted poinsettia in full and mocking scarlet. Primrose followed, hating the plant already. In the kitchen, Louise set it in the sink and opened the tap.

"This plant needs a drink," her mother said, "and so do I."

Louise plopped into a chair, shooting Primrose an expectant look. Apparently even advanced pregnancy did not excuse lapses in hospitality. Primrose filled a glass with water and placed it on the table before her mother. As Louise drank, Primrose dragged the bag of gifts into the living room. She unpacked the bag quickly, scattering the gifts beneath their spindly tree, which she had attempted to brighten with a few decorations—a box worth of tinsel, a felt dove on a clothespin, a set of bubble lights that Lorraine had brought over. Most of the gifts were labeled FOR THE BABY.

Just as Tino never again mentioned her night by the river, her mother acted as if the floor-shitting incident had never happened. The day was just another stitch dropped from her family's collective memory. Of course, Primrose remembered it all.

It had been her fault, and now it was indelible.

Louise wandered into the living room. "What an anemic tree."

"That's what happens when they dip it. All the needles fall right off."

Louise tapped a fingernail against a bubble ornament that had stopped bubbling. As the fizzing resumed, she rummaged in the pile under the tree until she came up with a small package.

"For you. Open it."

Primrose removed the wrapping carefully, folded it, and set it aside. She could, at times, be mindful of the budget, of opportunities for reuse. The gift was a tube of waterproof mascara.

"You're a Battuta now," Louise said. "Soon you'll have all sorts of weddings and funerals to go to. Fancy affairs where everyone cries a lot. I found it at Palma's."

When Primrose pulled the wand from the tube, the mascara stuck to it in clumps that suggested even cold cream would not be enough to budge it from her lashes, if she could risk applying it in the first place. She screwed the wand back into the tube.

"It's not like people in our family don't cry at weddings and funerals, Ma."

"Oh, sure. We cry. But no one minds if our makeup gets smeary. You try the smeary look at the next Battuta affair and see how far it gets you."

Primrose held the gift in her lap, struck dumb as usual by her mother's combination of forethought and hostility. The square of folded wrapping paper drifted to the floor.

"What I meant to say is that, now that you're married, you'll be going to all sorts of important family events. Look at the label. This mascara is so tough it doesn't even run in the rain."

"Thanks, Mom." Primrose, relenting, pecked her mother's cheek.

"Wear it in good health," Louise intoned.

Primrose reached under the tree and came up with a small wrapped box. She gave it to Louise, who refused to open it.

"But Mom," Primrose said, "you let me open mine!"

"Not until tomorrow," Louise said firmly. "At my age, a body can't let herself go too much."

Primrose sighed. There was so much she'd love to let go—the housework, the budget, her obligatory attendance at traditional Battuta family events like tonight's Feast of the Seven Fishes.

"Oh, don't look at me like that, Primrose. Of course I'll open your gift if it means that much to you."

"Do open it, Mom," Primrose said. *Open it,* she thought, *and let's get this over with.*

In the box was a faceted glass perfume decanter, something Louise could fill with whatever scent she liked. Not a useful gift, by any means, but pretty. Primrose had found it in Palma's sale bin.

Louise set the gift aside and busied herself with repositioning boxes under the tree.

"You don't like it?"

"Oh," she said airily, "it's fine."

So she'd seen it in the bin. Or maybe it was a mistake to suggest your mother needs perfume, despite her love of bathing in it.

"Let me," Primrose said. "You'll hurt your back, all bent over like that."

"You," Louise said sharply over her shoulder, "shouldn't lift a finger in your condition."

"All right." Primrose gave up. She would never understand her mother. "I'm going to shower."

"In that case," Louise said, "I'll just make myself at home."

Go right ahead, Primrose thought resentfully as she hurried to the bathroom. *It's only what you're going to do anyway.*

After her shower, Primrose opened the window and pressed her cheek against the screen. The fresh air, seeded with snow, pricked her skin.

In the bedroom, she tugged the little black tent over her head, then puffed her way into a pair of nylons, queen-plus. They bagged at her knees, which were not pregnant, but refused to budge over her belly, which most definitely was. She wedged her feet into her pumps, relieved that they still fit despite her late and swollen stage of pregnancy, and applied her makeup, finishing with the special mascara. Maybe her mother was right. She was a Battuta now, and this new identity would require her to do and be something new as well. She wondered how long this requirement would last, and shuddered to think: *the rest of my life.*

In the mirror, her face was her thinnest part.

Louise called out to say she was leaving.

"Have a good night," Primrose called back.

The front door banged shut, but not before a piece of the night's mystique slipped in and stopped Primrose short by the picture window. It was Christmas Eve, after all. Maybe the animals would talk at midnight, the way that old wives' tale said they would. Louise's taillights disappeared in the snow.

These old wives' tales always seem to trail after her mother, and as always Primrose struggled to keep her head in their wake. Sanity, always so precarious, seemed even more so now that she, too, was an old wife.

Primrose sat down by the lamp and picked up *Doctor Zhivago*. Norah had loaned it to her ages ago. At first it was a slog. But now that her life had narrowed to a small house in which it was all she could do to make herself a cup of coffee, the book was more interesting. Pogorevshikh had just offered Zhivago a dead duck wrapped in a revolutionary poster when Tino burst in. The cold air streamed off him. Excited, he levered her up off the couch.

"Come on, Mom wants to show you how to make *struffoli*."

"Ave Maria," Primrose muttered. A night spent on Lorraine Battuta's *struffoli* assembly line was not her idea of a good time.

"Why the long face?" he asked as he helped her into her coat. "It'll be fun. Candy canes, mistletoe, the priest doing the Midnight Mass in his Christmas getup... You know he gets all his clothes from Liberace."

"That's just ridiculous." How rudely Tino seemed to effervesce, regardless of her mood. "Have you been drinking?"

"What makes you say that?"

"Your cheeks are red."

"Baby, it's cold outside!" When she didn't smile, he snapped at her: "Don't be such a wet blanket. It's the night before Christmas, for God's sake."

She pulled her coat around herself. She hadn't been able to button it in weeks. Softening, Tino fussed with her collar. He made minute adjustments to her scarf. His attention was too much. The tears that had been threatening all afternoon finally arrived. She swallowed hard, not wanting to ruin her makeup— though, thanks to her mother, the mascara would hold.

***

By the time they arrived, preparations for the Feast of the Seven Fishes were well underway. The smell of frying onions reached to the front door, and Primrose's ears filled with their sizzling.

In the kitchen Erma was managing the groceries, matching ingredients as they arrived to those listed on Lorraine's recipe cards.

"Roasted eel," Erma said, placing a card on the counter. She shuffled the other cards in her hands. "Baccala." Another card. "Angel hair with anchovies. Stuffed sole. Shrimp cocktail."

"That's only five," Tino observed. He opened the fridge. Inside were rows of containers sealed in plastic wrap and labeled in Lorraine's careful hand: Gravy, 12/21. Minestrone, Use Immediately!

Even though she'd seen the inside of Lorraine's fridge many times, its relentless orderliness never failed to take Primrose's breath away. If Lorraine Battuta had been running the war, it would all be over by now, and everyone would have been sent home with leftovers.

Tino poured a glass of seltzer for Primrose, who sipped dutifully. Erma came around the counter and counted the fish again with the same result. "Shoot," she said.

"You can't have a Feast of the Seven Fishes with only five kinds of fish," Tino complained. "It's not traditional."

"Don't I know it. Is it too late to send you to the store?"

"Try the freezer," Tino said. "Mom always keeps things in reserve."

Right: The *contadina* with her basket of *pomi d'oro* was probably still in the basement. But that was eons ago, ancient history.

Erma opened the freezer and disappeared headfirst into a dense cloud of vapor. Zio Zio passed behind her carrying a long knife. He said darkly, "Lorraine's upstairs."

"What for?" Tino asked.

Primrose wedged herself into a chair at the kitchen table and flipped through the cards in Lorraine's recipe box. "Shepherd's Pie." Primrose replaced that card and pulled out another. "Pigs in Blankets."

Zio Zio announced, "Tino, your mother has a headache."

Erma chimed in: "She took two Fiorinal and went to lie down."

There was a distant barnyard sound. Primrose caught Tino's gaze: *Gobbling?* she mouthed. Tino put a finger to his lips, shushing her. Meanwhile Zio Zio opened the basement door and leaned into the darkness. The noise grew louder. That was definitely gobbling. Zio Zio flicked the light switch and thumped down to the basement.

"He's just grinding the blade," Tino said as he shut the door. He was trying not to laugh. "Nothing to worry about."

"Who's worried?" Primrose mustered a smile, hoping to cheer herself up by joining Tino in his mischief.

"*I'm* worried!" Erma cried from the freezer's depths. "We have only five fishes."

Primrose had found a pencil and was doodling a catfish with long whiskers on the back of one of Lorraine's recipe cards. She gave the catfish a microphone, then showed the drawing to Tino, who grinned. She turned the card over. It was the recipe for escarole soup.

"Let's just take that one out," Tino said, slipping the card into his pocket.

Lorraine appeared in the doorway, wrapping herself in her apron. "It looks like the fish counter at Ruggieri's out here."

Erma's head appeared in the pass-through. "And *how* it does."

Lorraine continued: "We always do the desserts first, Erma."

"Take it easy, Ma," said Tino. "The problem is, we have only five fish."

"No, we don't!" Erma cried. "Tino is just being silly, as usual. Isn't that right, Tino?" She glared at him, and Primrose laughed, which only further confused Lorraine. Erma pointed at the packages. "Auntie, look. We have the shrimp, the sole, the anchovies for the angel hair. The eels are in the bucket in the breezeway; Zio Zio will clean them just as soon as he's done with whatever he's doing in the basement—"

"I don't want to *know* what he's doing."

Tino asked Erma, "Find anything in the freezer?"

"Coupla small filets. They look like your father wrapped them. The paper was falling off."

"A little freezer burn never killed anyone," Primrose remarked.

"Nothing burns in *my* freezer," Lorraine said stiffly.

"So we're up to six," Tino cut in.

"Says you." Erma smiled, unwrapping the filets and laying each one on its own plate. "One fish," she counted. "Two fish."

"Erma! Now don't you go handling the fish!" To Primrose, Lorraine added *sotto voce*, "She'll go right ahead and forget to wash, and the next thing you know there's a fishy smell on the *cuccidats*." Then, firmly, over her shoulder: "Desserts *first*, Erma."

"Sounds like you have a plan." Erma was miffed.

"*Susamels* first, *then* the *cuccidats*." Lorraine extracted a brick of butter from the fridge door. "Fayrene said she'd bring butterballs. We'll see how she does. I'm not sure how they make butterballs at her house. Then, Erma, we'll make the dinner. Now be a good girl and help me put the rest of this fish away. Primrose can't do a thing in her condition, nor should she."

"All right," said Erma, pulling plastic wrap over a dish. "I hardly touched them anyway."

In the parlor, snacks had been set out: dried figs and dates, a bowl of smoked almonds. A rectangle of snowy *torrone* lay on a narrow lattice-edged platter alongside a tiny silver hammer. Suddenly starving, Primrose crammed a handful of almonds into her mouth. They were very salty; she regretted leaving her seltzer in the kitchen. The radiator hissed and then, through the pipe, came once again that faint *gobble-gobble-gobble.*

Zio Zio had gone and done it again, buying a live turkey for Christmas dinner. This year, like every year, Lorraine had begged for a grocery-store turkey, which was simpler to prepare and did not make such a mess. But Leon, being who he was, was always going to carve the turkey. In which case Zio Zio, being who he was, needed to find some other use for his knife. If Leon, as head of the household, put the meat on the table, then Zio Zio would do his bit by slaughtering it. To rebuff such thoughtfulness would dishonor both Zio Zio and Leon. Lorraine, being who she was, always got stuck with the cleanup.

The Battutas' big tree winked at Primrose, and the lights reflected off the bottles clustered on a side table: raspberry brandy, Cherry Heering, an *eau de vie* that, when Primrose unstoppered it, smelled like pears. Christmas stockings dangled from the mantelpiece, lumpy with oranges and walnuts. She touched keys on the piano and listened to the notes fade.

"You look lovely tonight, Primrose."

She started at the sound of Leon's voice.

"Sorry. I didn't mean to surprise you." Leon looked festive, decked out in a red cardigan patterned with candy canes. He poured himself a brandy and offered her a sip.

"No, thank you," she said. "The baby."

"In our day, Lorraine could have a little something now and then. The doctor said it was good for her." He positioned his drink on the mantel and pulled his violin case from underneath the wing chair. "I suppose it was a different time. Mind if I play?"

"Not at all."

He set to work, running the cake of rosin up and down the bow, then lifted the fiddle to his shoulder and tucked one edge under his chin. He played "Ave Maria," which brought a lump to Primrose's throat, and then he sang along to his favorite, "Santa Lucia."

Con questo zeffiro, così soave
Oh, com'è bello, star sulla nave!

Su passegieri, venite via!

Santa Lucia! Santa Lucia!

She could only guess at the meanings: a sweet wind, a pretty boat ride. His mother's name had been Lucia, Primrose remembered, and shivered.

"Ah," Leon said. "How about something more cheerful."

The first bars of "Winter Wonderland" brought Erma running from the kitchen, wiping her hands on her apron. While Erma shimmied around, distracting Leon, Primrose edged from the room. How had Leon known about *her* mother and "Ave Maria"? Why did he play a song with his mother's name?

Maybe it was her pregnancy. She was so much more noticeable now. But what had she been to them—any of them, all of them—before?

There was no time to chase the question. In the kitchen, the dessert-making was in full swing. Lorraine cut butter into a bowl of flour. Pots and pans were scattered all over, and a fine dusting of powdered sugar covered every horizontal surface. Primrose pecked Tino's cheek and came away with sugar on her lips.

Erma returned, flushed from dancing. Lorraine turned the paste of flour and butter out onto the counter and flattened it with her rolling pin.

"Should we do a spumoni?" Erma asked.

"Forget it! We're late enough as it is. Let's finish the struffoli and call it a night."

The doorbell rang. When Tino opened the door, Fayrene stood in the breezeway, a tray of butterballs balanced on one hip, a Ruggieri's bag dangling from her other hand. Tino took the plate of cookies and whisked them into the dining room before Lorraine had a chance to criticize them. Fayrene set the grocery bag on the counter.

"I brought stuffies," Fayrene announced. She pulled out several plastic-wrapped packages of large quahogs on the half-shell, each filled with a fistful of stuffing.

"That makes *eight*!" Erma, weeping, ran from the room.

Fayrene hurried after her. "What did I say? What?"

Lorraine set a golden pyramid of fried dough balls—the famous *struffoli*—on the counter, muttering, "You modern girls are all so *sensitive*."

Primrose clapped her hand over her mouth, stifling her laughter. But it was useless. Tino had caught the hilarity as well, and in a moment they were both laughing. Primrose wiped the tears from her eyes, glad for her waterproof mascara.

The *struffoli* needed a final shellacking. Lorraine poured a jar of honey into a saucepan, attached a candy thermometer to the side, and set the pan on the stove. "Come over here, Primrose, and keep an eye on the thermometer while the honey cooks. What you want is a soft ball."

As the thermometer's mercury edged toward the "soft ball" mark, Tino excused himself to look after Erma and Fayrene. He was gone before Primrose could say *cuccidat*. And so the worst had come to pass: She was alone with Tino's mother in her kitchen.

Primrose gritted her teeth, resolved to make the best of it. "How hot is too hot again?"

"Hard crack!" Lorraine cried, pushing Primrose aside to snatch the pan off the heat.

"Whew," said Erma from the doorway. "Close call."

Against the far wall, the radiator clanked beneath the picture window. In the back yard, Tino was gesticulating with something that looked an awful lot like Poppa Tavio's gray top hat. Primrose looked again: Yes, that was indeed Papa Tavio's top hat, and Tino was using it to encourage a large turkey toward the road.

Primrose said, "Would you look at that."

But Lorraine and Erma, engrossed in pouring hot honey over the pyramid of dough balls, did not respond. The turkey disappeared behind the hedge.

"The *struffoli* is going to be too hard," Lorraine lamented. "We'll break our teeth on it!"

"Everyone likes it chewy," Erma said.

Later, when Primrose asked Tino about the turkey, he grinned. "I got nothing to say about that."

The party was, at last, in full swing. The house grew loud and hot, crowded with relatives. Primrose recognized some of Tino's extended family from Poppa Tavio's wake. Others she had met at the wedding. She picked at antipasti laid out on a platter: cubed salami and provolone, sliced capicola, a pale green pile of pickled peppers. Mrs. Battuta sipped a Cherry Heering from a silver goblet. Everyone toasted each other. Then they toasted old Tavio. "To his memory!"

Lorraine took Fayrene back to the kitchen. Primrose lingered in the doorway, hoping to overhear. Lorraine opened the fridge and pointed to the quahogs.

"You call this a fish?" Lorraine asked her.

Fayrene looked nervous. Tino hurried in, pushing past Primrose.

"Excuse me," he said. "My mother smells blood."

"It's a quahog," Fayrene said to Lorraine.

"I know very well what it is. But is it a *fish*?"

"Ma—" Tino warned her.

"Because if it isn't, we've only got—" Lorraine counted off with her fingers. "One, two..."

"It's a fish, Ma," Tino insisted. "It counts as a fish."

"It's a shellfish," Fayrene said. "Shell. *Fish*."

Aldo came into the kitchen, looking for an extra fork.

"Aldo," Lorraine called. "Come over here and tell me, is that a fish?"

"That quahog? I don't know, Auntie. Maybe."

"What would a priest say?"

"It can't be a fish. It has a foot," Tino said. "A pseudo-foot," Tino corrected himself. "Not a real foot. It's a pseudopod. Which means fake foot—"

"I'll give you a fake foot," Lorraine interrupted.

"If it has a foot, how can it be a fish?" Aldo asked over his shoulder, digging in the silverware drawer.

"Fish have feet," Tino said. "Some fish."

"I've never heard of a fish with feet."

"Still reeling from Intro to Litigation, are we?"

"Tino!"

"Three, four..." Lorraine was counting again.

"A coelacanth has feet."

"A seal-o-what?"

"Tino, why do you always have to use those big words?"

"Seals have flippers, not feet." This from Pat, who had just arrived, late as usual, and was still in his overcoat.

"It's extinct. The coelacanth."

"It doesn't exist. So it doesn't count."

"Five, six..."

"It's extinct, I tell you."

Pat kissed Fayrene under the mistletoe, then it was Primrose and Tino's turn.

After supper, on their way to the car, Primrose asked Tino about the turkey. "All the animals talk on Christmas Eve. Don't they?"

Tino laughed. "Well, if they do, I know one turkey who'll have something to talk about."

"It was a good deed," Primrose said.

"It won't go unpunished."

"They never do."

Inside the church, the nave glowed, lit by dozens of candles, and altar boys patrolled the aisles swinging thuribles of incense. There were songs and chants and prayers and readings; the priest gave his homily; the choir sang for fifteen minutes straight, hymn after hymn, concluding with "Ave Maria," which by this point only gave Primrose a little twinge.

"They get this once chance," Tino whispered to Primrose, who was leaning against him, lulled by the music. "And then it's back to the choir room for another year."

Primrose passed her hand over her stomach where she felt the baby turn. Then came communion, bells, and more incense. Primrose did not get up to join the line; neither did Tino, who just sat quietly beside her, watching the second hand sweep the face of his watch. Midnight struck. Mass ended. The snow Primrose sensed earlier had not come. It was a clear night after all. In the next town, her parents were asleep, dreaming of ballgames and nail polish, strikeout stats and layaway plans. As Tino helped her into their car, she squeezed his gloved hand. He closed the door gently. By the time he got behind the wheel, she was asleep.

THE BOOK OF LOVE: Commitments

by Norah

Commitment; n., late 14th century, "to give in charge, entrust," from Lat. *committere,* "to unite, connect, combine; to bring together."

Some etymologists break the word into parts supposedly constituent: *com* meaning "with, together" + *mittere,* "to release, let go; send, throw." As if *commitment* were something like a hasty meal or a tossed salad.

The Latin verb *committere* carries a whiff of criminality. From the fifteenth century to the present day, the word has also connoted—as we know all too well—a state of being cast away, institutionalized, committed. (*Ed. note, PT*: Ouch.)

45. Red zinger

Three weeks into the new year, Primrose brewed herself a mug of Red Zinger and at last sat down to investigate the object Lupo had left in her care. The gearing mechanism reminded her of an old watch, something her father might once have owned and broken and stashed in a drawer. Crumbling and clearly ancient, a device to keep the time someplace where time was for keeping.

As for her, she couldn't spend time fast enough. The days dragged by. She'd been feeling small contractions for a few days. Her mother said these were her body's way of getting ready, and Elsie had concurred, but her due date was still weeks away.

At three-thirty she rinsed her mug and packed Tino into the car. She dropped him off at work and then got on the highway. Tonight's art class was a make-up of another class Joseph had cancelled sometime in prehistory; if she wanted the class credit, she was obliged to attend. The radio blared a weather warning: heavy snow, whiteout conditions, a screwball blizzard pitched from Montréal. But the sky didn't look threatening. A snowflake or two, that was all.

The snowfall thickened as she drove. She slowed, trying not to outrun the Chevelle's headlights. All the way downtown, she thought about turning around but didn't. She took the exit, slid into the lot, and parked. The classroom building was open, but all the windows were dark.

There was a note on the studio door: CLASS CANCELLED DUE TO STORM.

By the time she returned to the car, the temperature had dropped so much that ice had formed beneath the car's wheels. Revving the engine just spun them. She couldn't get a purchase.

She trudged back inside, fed a coin into the public telephone, and dialed Tino at work.

"I'm stuck," she said.

"Thank God Chick showed up tonight. Give us half an hour. The freeway's sure to be a mess."

Primrose hung up the phone and wandered down the hallway. In a classroom, a man stuffed papers into a briefcase.

"I didn't know anyone was here," she said.

"I was just leaving," the man replied in an accent Primrose couldn't place.

He shoved the last paper into his briefcase, pushed on the top, and attempted to turn the latch. No dice: A full inch of paper came between the top and the bottom. Primrose came over and leaned on the case. "Now try," she said. Her bulk had to be good for something.

The gap diminished, the latch turned.

"Thanks," the man said. His thick glasses made his eyes seem absurdly small, currants set into a doughy face. "I'm Misha."

"Primrose," she told him. "Nice to meet you."

"Are you student?"

"Sort of."

"Sort-of students," he mused, "are more interesting than the other kind." He reached in his pocket and pulled out a pamphlet. His eyes bored into her. "Perhaps you might like to know about some research I'm doing."

He hit the second syllable hard. Re*search*.

"Re*search*?" She was already part of Lupo's so-called re*search*. It wasn't much fun. The baby kicked, hard. She put a hand on the spot. "Oof."

"You missed my lecture," he said accusingly. "Usually I teach at URI. Tonight I talked here. But students are exactly alike, no matter where I find them. Always missing lectures."

"I didn't know about your lecture."

"Of course not," he said. "But soon you will! Right now," he continued, dropping his voice to a whisper, "I'm working on history."

"*A* history?" she asked, unable to resist correcting him, to prick the smooth surface of his self-importance.

The man nodded rapidly. "Exactly so, exactly so. History of—how should I put it?—real estate in America, where you have so much. From Thomas Jefferson to the present, with special attention to desires for exotics."

"Exotics?"

"Fears about aliens, uncertainty about what is native."

"Aliens?" This was familiar ground.

"I'm sorry, I'm sure I'm making not much sense. Aliens are not so much part of your discourse in America."

"Actually—" Actually there was Lupo. Elsie Minetta. Lola DiMaio. "If you're thinking of real estate..."

"I am thinking of soil and water."

Was something in the soil? In the water?

She tried to stay calm. Where was Tino? Snow was piling up, inch after inexorable inch.

"So what's the situation?"

"My dear." He handed her a pamphlet. "It's ancient history."

Primrose stuffed the pamphlet in her bag, exhausted from the effort of listening, trying not to think about Tino and Chick on the snowy highway or the rage that was surely building as they drove. "Thanks."

"Don't mention it." He paused. "Is right expression?"

She forced a smile. "Exactly so."

It was only after she'd returned to the lobby that she noticed the author's name on the pamphlet's front page: Mikhail Rodenko. Misha. Lupo's guy. Small world.

46. The pamphlet

EASY JOURNEYS TO OTHER PLANETS

by Mikhail Rodenko, Department of Engineering,
University of Rhode Island

DRAFT—NOT FOR CIRCULATION OR QUOTATION
[*Ed.*: Too late!]

No national sovereignty rules in outer space. Those who venture there go as envoys of [the] entire human race. Their quest, therefore, must be for all mankind, and what they find should belong to all mankind. –LBJ

Any historian will tell you, apocalypse is [*Ed.*: an] idea whose time comes and goes; we are perpetually besieged with hints of catastrophe in [the] form of news. Uncle Walter Cronkite furnishes rapt viewers with reports of disasters made fresh daily:

- College students refuse jobs to preach "peace" and "love" in [the] streets
- Assassins pick off leaders one by one
- Johnson inexplicably escalates [an] already inexplicable war

Mere bagatelles! Sooner or later comes [a] crisis truly insuperable. But do we prepare? Not at all! Like [the] fabled grasshopper who saves nothing for winter, important opportunities pass by us. Resources dwindle, and imagination desiccates to [a] husk—adorned, of course, with stars-n-stripes.

Cemetery Plots: Our Need for Space Does Not Die with Us

[The] so-called Space Race, in which nations spend vast sums competing to be [the] first to send pets into orbit, is merely [a] moonshot distraction, loaves and circuses for [a] technocratic age. The real problem is growth of populations—living *and* dead. Here is [the] true Space Race.

Everyone knows [the] troubles we will soon face as [a] result of [the] exploding population. What is less well understood is [the] constraint on available space imposed by our dead—whose numbers are ever increasing. But their spirits remain with us on [the] material plane insofar as, like us, they require home comforts.

Let me be clear: There will not be room enough for all of us in [the] afterlife, not to mention room for all our *stuff*. With no place to house our dead and their effects, our planet will shortly be overwhelmed.

Historical and cultural antecedents are many. Scientists have discovered ancient tombs dug in [the] tundra, mummies buried with all earthly goods. Why do peasants fight to death for land? Because ancestors are buried there; we, [the] living, need places to house our dead. But if we, too, are to enjoy the same thing, we must first overcome the problem of [the] cemetery plot. To wit: On earth, there is no endless space. Landfills and cemeteries have no frontiers.

Soviets already understand. This law is encoded even in their language, which has no use for unnecessary articles — *the*, *uh* [Ed: *a*], *an*. English, on [the] other hand, is replete with such frivolities; no surprise there, of course, as such profligacy is only what can be expected from capitalist imperialists of [the] Anglophone persuasion, including my editor, [a] running-dog lackey whose bourgeois intrusions remain marked [like this]. [*Ed.: As the author refused to accept or reject my suggestions, they remain as bracketed insertions.*]

Why lies Lenin's body permanently in state? Because his tomb is [a] *shrine*. Incidentally this observation, based on nothing but obvious facts, ought to decimate [the] myth of "nonreligious" Soviets. In fact, they are completely religious.

While [the] United States miracles up strategies for containing irreligious "communism," indulging in "domino" theorizing and "kremlinology," Soviets busily create heavens on earth, palaces for their dead who have no other place to go. But simple logic dictates [the] inevitable outcome: Eventually live Soviets will run out of room for dead ones. The resulting pressure will intensify [the] so-called Space Race, which Soviets are winning because they understand [the] real problem: Space is exactly what we need more of. Of course we should race for it, as fast as we can! (*N.B.*: Cremation will not work; burning does not eliminate material but only shoots it into [the] atmosphere, making earthly life even harder to sustain.)

Who Are [the] Exhumen?

All we now know about [the] Exhumen is gleaned from fleeting sightings; all accounts are necessarily anecdotal. Of course they are. Touching down in Times Square would draw too much attention. Perhaps these creatures dislike bright lights and crowds, as many humans do.

Flawed as they are, these accounts share certain features. Alien aircraft are usually sighted in open spaces at dusk. Exhumen reveal themselves only to solitary people or small groups. Their spaceships leave deep tracks suggestive of aircraft of great weight that are nevertheless capable of changing direction "on [a] dime," to use [a] capitalist metaphor, in defiance of all known laws of physics. Observers report trance-like feelings of paralysis when caught in [the] lights of spacecraft, and radio transmissions are disrupted.

Of these reports, [a] sampling: Mr. Løthar Salgurssen, of Oslo, was driving one evening in October 1960 when blinded by [a] bright light "like a ball of fire" coming toward him. [A] mysterious force pulverized his windshield, and [the] fireball sped away. In September 1958, Pvt. Gerard McIntyre was sounding reveille at Tacoma AFB when [a] bullet-shaped object as big as [an] airplane flew through [the] nearby forest at [an] altitude of 200 feet, leaving [a] half-mile of broken branches. In 1960, [a] Venezuelan driver saw [a] flying metallic disc overturn [a] milk truck. Four years later, [a] similar object landed in [the] bed of [a] pickup on [the] Al-Can Highway. It flew off, leaving long scorch marks. According to another report, a similar aircraft lifted roof tiles off [a] Kodiak Island monastery. [The] Soviet counterinsurgency was blamed, but there is another explanation. These few examples I have culled from thirteen linear feet of files devoted to such reports. Much more could be said, but space does not permit it. This is my point. It never does.

Exhumen Technology

Far from being [an] exotic technological marvel, [these] UFO are machines with recognizable hardware, e.g., retractable landing gear and UV radiation capability. How is this possible?

Thanks to colleagues in classical archaeology, we have recently uncovered evidence to support advanced technological knowledge among the Exhumen. Off [the] Greek island of Kythera, divers using trained dolphins have discovered objects lost when [a] trading vessel sank in 80 BC. Among the coins and amphorae was found one bronze clockwork mechanism. Although it has been cleaned, it has defeated all attempts to restore functionality, due to [the] fact that it is operated by [a] *key*—which seems to be [a] miniature model of [the] Kythera mechanism itself. All that remains is to fabricate this key, but this cannot be done because no mechanism can be replicated *in nuce* if not found first in [a] state of wholeness. (There are many lessons here.)

What we do know: Archeologists assure us that such technology could not have been known to any civilization existing in 80 BC unless, *perhaps*—and this is [a] big *perhaps*—there was [a] colony, possibly started by Archimedes, of engineers of whom we have hitherto been unaware. Another possibility: [The] Exhumen were here even earlier than [the] ancient Greeks, and [the] mechanism is [a] first-century copy of [a] much older original. Either way, we suggest that [the] existence of this Kythera mechanism—original *or* copy—may be explained by recourse to alien intelligence.

Exhumen Consciousness: Varieties of Planetary Experience

Current forms of consciousness are clearly insufficient for communicating with sophisticated aliens. Yet [the] need to learn from them is pressing. We must speed our work using all means at our disposal, including techniques of so-called mind expansion, [the] only source of new real estate now known. Not only must we educate ourselves about intelligent life on other planets, but we must open ourselves to new forms of experience, including mass activities known as "be-ins," in which we signal to Exhumen that we are ready to hear whatever they have to say.

47. Dust-off in Maple Bay

When it was all over apart from the public relations, the official story ran something like this: One afternoon, while Keith was at work and the boys at an afterschool program, Elsie Minetta set a serrated knife alongside a casserole on the counter, lodged a stack of bills, carefully stamped and return-addressed to Keith, in the outgoing mail, and brought a potato into the garage where her car was parked. She stuck the potato into the exhaust pipe, installed herself behind the wheel, and turned the key in the ignition. On returning from work, Keith found Elsie slumped in the driver's seat.

A siren summoned the neighbors, including Primrose, to the perimeter of the Minettas' property. Paramedics conveyed Elsie's lifeless body to the waiting ambulance, her slack face the color of an eggplant. Keith slammed himself into the rear compartment, and the ambulance pulled away. A pair of police cars idled in the street.

"Calling all cars," Lola DiMaio sniggered as she sidled up to Primrose. "Dust-off in Maple Bay."

Stung by Lola's callousness, Primrose returned home. Her mind felt spongy as a loaf of Wonder Bread. In the next days, she could focus on only small things. It might be nice to do something for Keith and the boys—bring over a lasagna, offer to collect the mail. But the baby moved inside her, a stunt pilot doing barrel rolls, and she remembered her mother's advice, that expectant mothers were supposed to avoid bad, ugly, and even just weird things while pregnant, because these things might imprint upon the baby. If you so much as looked sideways at an eggplant, for instance, the baby might have an odd-shaped head.

At the kitchen window, Primrose folded her arms over her chest. She'd taken a risk, seeing Elsie's dead face. She could not draw any closer to the tragedy unfolding in the house across the lawn. But try as she might, neither could she tear herself away.

THE BOOK OF LOVE: O, Pomodoro!

by Primrose

According to our sources, sixteenth-century Spanish travelers introduced tomatoes to European eaters, having brought them from their travels in the so-called New World.

The first written reference to the tomato in Europe appears soon after, in 1544, when the naturalist Pietro Andrea Matthioli listed the *pomo d'oro,* apple of gold, among his favorite fruits and vegetables. He believed the tomato belonged in the same botanical category as the mandrake, touted for millennia as an aphrodisiac. (On that subject, see our list.)

The French reaction was similarly rapturous. When the French got ahold of the tomato, they called it *pomme d'amour*, apple of love.

From North Africa, a plainer moniker: *pomo dei mori,* "apple of the Moors."

Pomo d'oro, pomme d'amour, or pomi dei mori? Clearly no one can agree on the source of the name. But if you say them all five times fast, the differences dissolve, like the tomato itself, into a nice red gravy. Hold the onions.

To remind consumers of what it's like to eat a fresh tomato, today's commercial canners market their products using illustrations of the same sort of buxom young women who also feature heavily in novels of romance.

The tomato is a member of the nightshade family, and everyone knows what *they're* like. You have been warned.

48. Goes to motive

The sky was cyanotic, and Primrose could not stop thinking about Elsie.

The neighborhood hummed with gossip, each postmortem report stranger than the last. Some said she stuffed the exhaust with a beefsteak tomato, while others advanced a theory about an avocado; still others favored a tennis ball. The tomato-fanciers also overwhelmingly claimed that she'd left the car windows open and the garage door closed, but those who believed the tennis-ball version said both the garage door and all the car windows were closed, but the garage window was open just a crack, so her death was inevitable but also, tragically, not as quick as it might have been, owing to the extra oxygen. The avocado faction was impressed by none of this but could not muster a better alternative account. A fourth school of opinion about Elsie's death concerned itself less with the object used to stuff the tailpipe than with the state of completion of certain household duties. For instance: Did she leave the casserole assembled but raw, or was it waiting for Keith on the counter, fully cooked and covered in tin foil?

"What difference does *that* make?" Primrose asked Lola, who had called to share the latest news.

"Goes to motive," Lola said. "If the casserole was already cooked, the death could not have been an accident."

"I don't think it was an accident. How could it be an accident?"

"You never can tell," Lola said, "with some people."

There was, eventually, an official service at the church. Few attended. As it turned out, Elsie was not generally well liked. In fact, the resentment of Elsie was such that by the time she had checked out, everyone who lived within five blocks of the

Minetta residence was, on some level, relieved by her death—but also burdened by the necessity of keeping that relief a secret out of politeness. Not to mention the sad situation of the sons, "those poor motherless boys," as Lola liked to call them. Elsie may not have been beloved, but she was still a mother. To be rendered motherless was the worst thing that could happen to a child in Maple Bay.

Norah stopped by one morning not long after the funeral. Exams were coming up, Primrose realized with a twinge. It had been so long since she thought about things like that. She felt another twinge when she saw the books—thick volumes of Proust, Joyce, and Faulkner—peeking out of Norah's new canvas school bag. All Primrose had read lately was Rodenko's absurd pamphlet, and it was a far cry from fine literature, what with all the missing parts of speech and editorial intrusions.

She poured Norah a cup of coffee and told her about what had happened to Elsie.

"You must be freaked out. I know I am, and I've only been here five minutes. This place stinks, Primrose. These twisty little streets, with the houses all the same..."

"It's not that bad."

Norah held her gaze a little too long. "I've got news for you, Primrose. The Be-In's actually going to happen." From her bag she withdrew a flyer. Primrose recognized the design. The spirograph adornments, the freehand lettering—it all screamed Rosemary. "In two weeks. At Unaconicut Park."

"Who told you about it?" Primrose asked jealously, taking the flyer. "Was it Lupo?"

"Joseph called. He must have looked me up." She shrugged. "I'm in the book."

Norah seemed like a stranger. Norah's life had gone in one direction, hers in another. They hadn't talked about *The Book of Love* in ages.

"Speaking of books! That section on commitment was really good," Primrose ventured, spinning out a thread for Norah to catch. "I took it too personally at first."

"'O, Pomodoro!' had its points, too," Norah replied politely. "It's not the same, though, is it."

Once upon a time, they had traded ideas like marbles, snickering and giggling over the awkward bits, egging each other on. Now it was kid stuff, virtually undiscussable. Primrose sighed.

"So, have you been to a tailgate?"

"Tailgates are sort of déclassé," Norah said.

Primrose blushed. She'd only finished a handful of semesters, and she had lived at home, not in the dorms. What did she really know about college life?

"Honestly, Primrose, that surprised me, too."

"How is it, really? Pembroke, I mean."

Norah took a deep breath. "Well," she began, "I guess I'm glad to be there. *I guess*. But there's a lot I don't understand. Not school-wise. Socially."

"You? I find that hard to believe."

"I had to go to a tea. For my scholarship. The rich people who pony up want to meet the ponies, you know. See what they paid for. I was paraded around like some exotic new addition to their collection. A fine lady in a Swiss-dotted dress poured me a cup of tea and asked if I took lemon or milk. Lemon or milk! I hadn't slept in forever, and in class I kept getting hung up on the dative of possession. You know I don't drink tea. I couldn't choose, so I said both, which was the wrong answer."

"Oh, *no*."

"To her credit, Swiss Dot acted like it was the most natural thing in the world to take your tea with curdled milk." She paused and looked away, caught up in some emotion Primrose couldn't parse. "Live and learn, I guess."

Now it was Primrose's turn to look away. The scholarship tea sounded awful, but maybe Norah was exaggerating so she wouldn't feel left out. With the baby coming, it was hard to know whether she would ever have time to study again, and she was many credits short of a degree.

"Are you all right, Primrose? You don't seem like yourself."

"It's the pregnancy. Hormones." A lie, but the truth of her situation—that she was now on another path entirely, her life hemmed up as neatly as a pair of her father-in-law's trousers—was not something she felt comfortable discussing with Norah, or anyone else for that matter.

"It's not Elsie?"

"When people die, you aren't supposed to talk about how vile they were. Even Tino has clammed up."

"You didn't like her?"

"She was creepy. Always so busy in the yard, clipping branches, wrestling the hose. I couldn't look out the window without seeing her."

"Maybe she wanted to be noticed."

"No one notices much around here except for the state of your exterior paint and whether the lawn's mowed. It's all about property values. Despite appearances," she added grimly, gesturing all around, "*this* is not a house. This is a hot commodity."

"Oh, Primrose."

Tino set down his fork. A smear of red gravy clung to his chin. His mother had filled the freezer with plastic containers full of the stuff so they could have easy dinners of boiled macaroni. No matter how many times Primrose served this meal, Tino ate it all and failed to complain. She'd solved her cooking problem, but she couldn't help feeling that she'd lost something, too.

"Her soul is *damned*, Tino."

Tino rolled his eyes. "Stop it."

"She was a *suicide*. How could she possibly *deserve* a Catholic funeral?"

Which, deserving or not, was just what she got, complete with grimly tolling bells, drops of red wine scattered on the casket and a funeral line that snarled traffic for blocks. The dolly tipped, and Elsie's casket slid into the earth.

"There is such a thing as mercy, you know. She wouldn't have done it if she hadn't been suffering," Tino said. "She was like a sick dog that goes into the woods to die."

Primrose picked at a cuticle. "I work my fingers to the bone keeping this house, and you don't see *me* putting potatoes in the exhaust pipe."

"Primrose."

"Don't 'Primrose' me. I *do* work," she insisted. "I do my level best around here. Every day I don't put potato in the tailpipe is a victory."

"Well, most days I take the car. Plus, we don't have a garage."

"You know what I mean. Don't be fresh."

"You sound just like your mother."

"*My* mother?" To herself, Primrose had sounded just like Lorraine.

Huffing, Primrose took the dishes back to the sink. The Minettas' house was dark. Fine snow had turned the neighborhood into a moonscape, coating everything with a gray, icy dust.

Was happiness *this*?

At the table Tino took a long pull from a glass of milk, and all Primrose could think of was Norah, standing awkwardly at the horrible tea party, watching a moment of thoughtlessness curdle in her cup. Imagine going all the way to Pembroke, only to deal with fine ladies and their baloney. Might as well stay on Calvary Street, where at least folks looked out for each other and didn't go setting you up with impossible choices, like that milk-or-lemon trap.

"This milk doesn't taste as good as what we had last week," Tino said.

"It's fine," Primrose replied. "Don't act like I put a lemon in it."

"You call this fine?" Tino took another sip. "It's awful."

"It's low-fat. It's good for you," she said, enjoying his scowl. "Well, it is."

49. Girl Baby Battuta

Primrose surfaced from shallow sleep. As she turned in search of a cooler spot on the mattress, something snapped deep inside.

"Tino."

Snoring. She felt around, taking deep breaths. She was cramping now, the pain threatening to outrun her breathing.

"Tino!"

"What?"

"My water broke. Feel," she said, putting his hand to the wet sheets.

The pain ebbed, but she knew the reprieve was only temporary, and much worse was in store. In the semidarkness Tino moved around the room, gathering clothing, a hairbrush, baby clothes, and tossing these items in the open suitcase that had been positioned by the door for the past week. She'd been meaning to pack it, and now it was too late.

She slipped yesterday's muumuu over her head and pushed her feet into a pair of sneakers. Something dribbled down her legs.

"Help me up, Tino. Please."

Leaning on the arm he offered, she made her way toward the front door. While she waited, Tino hurriedly buttoned himself into his winter coat and grabbed the car keys from Poppa Tavio's hat. Outside the night smelled of earth melting. By the driveway, snowdrops were pushing up beneath the hedge.

Maple Bay was shuttered, ghostly. As they drew closer to the hospital, neat yards gave way to tenements, picket fences to chain link. At a stoplight, a car rolled through from the other direction. Tino slammed the brakes. "Jesus Christ!" he shouted, leaning on the horn. The car stopped, blocking the intersection, and for a long moment, nothing in the universe moved a blessed inch.

Tino sucked in his breath. "I can't fucking believe this."

"We're going to be shot," Primrose panted, gripped by a fresh contraction.

The driver's door opened. A green bottle fell out and rolled into the gutter. As if in slow motion, the door closed, and the car rolled away. Tino let out a high-pressure sigh, and they continued over the rutted road. Another contraction overtook her.

"Ow. Ow." Primrose gripped the dashboard. Tino drove more carefully, swerving to avoid the bumps.

When they arrived at the hospital, the intake nurse put Primrose on a gurney and hooked her up to an IV. Flat on her back, she stared up at Tino. He'd never seen anyone look so scared. So trapped.

"Get my mother," she said. "I need my mother."

On the phone, Louise let Tino call the shots. "When should I come? What should I bring?" Tino made suggestions, hearing his own voice as if from miles away. He was about to become a father.

"Don't worry," Louise said. "They'll give her an injection. She won't feel a thing."

When Louise arrived, the nurses took her straight back to see Primrose. Tino followed, hoping to be allowed to come along, but Louise turned just before they reached the double doors to the maternity ward.

"You stay here," she said firmly.

"But she's my wife!"

"There are some things a husband shouldn't see," Louise said ponderously. "There," she continued, pointing to an alcove where rows of chairs were arranged before a television tuned to a test pattern, "is the fathers' area."

Tino waited, trying not to think about the things a husband should not see and seeing them all the more vividly for that. Other men, looking equally bewildered, tried to make small talk. But no topic of conversation stuck, and they soon lapsed into silence. Which was just as well. Tino didn't want to say he was in the Reserves, to explain that he had an exemption thanks to that. Though for how much longer, he had no idea.

One by one, the men were called back to meet their newborn children. The television droned with the day's offerings—soap operas and game shows. Tino's mind went slack. It had been hours since he'd seen Primrose. Was she dying? What was going on? Just as he was sure he'd never see her again, a nurse poked her head into the room.

"Come meet your daughter, Mr. Battuta."

A girl!

In the nursery, under the fluorescents, Tino stood at the bassinet holding his firstborn, his own little girl.

Her mouth was a perfect scarlet bow; each of her miniature pink fingers was capped with a miniature pink-and-white fingernail. She was swaddled in a pink blanket, from which she had pushed one arm out; she was wearing a striped knit cap. Her wrist tag said: GIRL BABY BATTUTA.

He crooned at her, a soft noise that escaped him before he could form it into words. She opened her eyes, and he gasped, astonished at the recognition there. Her irises were dark, enormous, infinitely knowing: two long nights he hoped never to see the end of.

He bent his head to hers. She smelled of summertime, fresh-cut grass. She began to fuss, and her swaddling came undone. Tino, helpless in the face of this development, said, "Uh oh." The nurse hustled over, her spongy shoes squeaking, and wrapped her up once more. As she pulled the last corner tight, the baby poked an arm out. The nurse tucked it back in. Out it came once more. The nurse sighed. Tino laughed. That was his kid, all right.

The nurse took the baby from him and rolled her away in the bassinet. Tino watched them leave, wondering how much of the rest of his life would consist of just this—standing around, watching his baby girl go. Quite a bit, probably.

Primrose was still groggy from the anesthesia. Louise, who had been hovering, left for a smoke.

"How was it?" he asked, glad for the privacy.

"I didn't feel a thing. I'm all ripped up though." Primrose was nearly flat on her back, her hair spread loose across the pillow.

"Hurts?"

"The nurse gave me something. How do I look?"

"How do you look? You just had a baby!"

"Ma said I should put some makeup on. People might want to take pictures."

People. Her mother, his. They could hardly bear the sight of her pregnant, but now they all wanted a piece of the action. And here she was, barely able to sit up.

"Don't worry about what your mother said. You don't have to smile for anyone's camera if you don't want to."

She gave him a grateful, exhausted smile. "Did you see her?"

"I did. I did. Oh, Primrose. She's lovely." He paused, looking at her, then laid his head on her chest. "Thank you."

She passed her hand over his face. "No need. No need."

He kissed her. She tasted of mouthwash. "We have to name her. She can't go through life as Girl Baby Battuta."

"I'm way ahead of you," Primrose murmured, her eyes half-shut. She was almost asleep. "Her name is Brenda Nicole."

Even with Poppa Tavio's hat standing sentry in the hallway, the empty house unnerved Tino. He didn't like how the rooms echoed, and for the first time he noticed how dark they were. Light struggled through the small windows, set high on wood-paneled walls. A lick of white paint would brighten things up considerably. The landlord wouldn't like it, but as far as Tino was concerned, the guy could kiss his ass. He didn't have to live here, and what else was the damage deposit for anyway?

He collected the trash and took it out to the curb. He swept the breezeway. The sun hoisted itself into the sky. He was a father! Somebody's Dad. Daddy. Daddy-O. He smiled, liking the sound of it. Brenda Nicole—he liked the sound of that, too.

In the mail he found a letter addressed to him from his Reserve office. He tore it open, his mouth going dry as the dust he'd just brushed into the pan.

His Reserve unit had been called up. He was to report to Fort Polk, in Louisiana, near Baton Rouge, in one week.

50. Hurry up and wait

The rain had turned the road out of Baton Rouge to mud. The bus squelched onward anyway. Inside it, fifty-five silent guys were sticking to their clothes and to the absurdly small vinyl seats.

"What time is it?"

"Who knows?"

The military moved in two speeds, slow and slower. The bus turned a corner, and rain streamed in where the roof gapped.

"Shit." Chick brushed water off his arms. "I feel like a goddamned duck."

"Quack," Tino said. It was all he had to offer.

Somewhere, out there, people were doing real, productive work. At Cape Canaveral, someone was assembling a rocket. At Quonset, someone else was building a submarine. At Reliable Button, paint was drying on plastic beads, and in Maple Bay, Brenda's bottles were drying on the rack. Not that he would have any way of knowing any of these things for sure. But he had to believe that life, real life, was still going on elsewhere, and he might yet be part of it. These were his articles of faith.

The bus pulled into the compound. Along the road, signs greeted them: FORT POLK, BIRTHPLACE OF COMBAT INFANTRYMEN. FORT POLK TESTS THE BEST. One billboard featured an illustration of some people harvesting rice in a paddy field. Each wore a conical hat, and some sported ridiculous drooping moustaches. *This* was the enemy? What in the world was this war about anyway? Tino groaned, holding his head as if it might explode.

***

After they were marched off the bus, they lined up in formation, someone called the roll, and then the commanding officer introduced himself to each guy personally with a firm handshake and a brief hello-how-are-ya. Hungry from the trip and made anxious by the handshake business, Tino fidgeted through the formalities. The officer's manner didn't fit with anything Tino had seen so far in the Army, but then, things in the Army were never what they seemed.

Like everyone else, he was issued a pile of gear, and then they were marched off to their barracks to await their assignments. Hurry up and wait—at least that was familiar. He'd already done a lot of that on A-Pavilion.

All afternoon they waited for someone to come and tell them what to do, but no one did.

Over the radio came news of a massacre, by Americans, at a place called My Lai, and reports of massive breakdowns of military discipline in training units across the country.

"You aren't a CO, are you?" The guy with the radio was talking to Tino, staring fiercely at him with tiny eyes set in a broad, pale face. He didn't look like he would last a day in combat.

"No," Tino said. "I'm not conscientious. I don't object."

The guy snorted. "That's good, 'cause they send you anyway. You just don't get a gun. They make you a medic, and you have to drag people off the battlefield screaming."

"Is that right?" Tino wasn't sure he liked this guy with his non-regulation radio and his way of asking personal questions.

"And if they know you're a CO, they send you in *first*."

The door to the barracks opened. Someone yelled, "Battuta!"

"Yes, sir!" Tino jumped off the bed and stood at attention. He wasn't sure if this was the right thing to do, but he figured it wouldn't hurt.

"At ease. You got a phone call."

In the office, he took the telephone from the guy behind the desk. His mother was on the line. "I told you that girl would be trouble."

"Mom. What happened?"

"And now she's really gone and done it, Tino. She's taken off for some stupid party in a field somewhere. Something called a 'be-in.' I haven't any idea what that is, but I think it must be something the young radicals do—"

"Where's Brenda? Mom! What did she do with Brenda?"

"Well, that's just it. We don't know. She left a note—"

"A note?"

"Yes, she says she's going to this be-in, whatever that is, that she expects an alien invasion any day, and somehow this has something to do with the baby."

"The *baby*? What in the world could it have to do with the baby?"

"Oh, Tino, you know I don't understand any of this—"

"Keep searching," Tino said. "I'll be there as soon as I can."

Back in the barracks, he crammed everything he had into a duffel while relaying the whole story to Chick.

"You gonna run your exit by the CO?"

"Nope," Tino said. "I don't think you get leave just for having a crazy wife."

What he didn't say: a crazy Maple Bay housewife, not three weeks out of childbed, with primary responsibility for a newborn baby, who needed regular feedings, and diaper changes, and clean clothes, and walks in the fresh air, and cooing and patting and bouncing and singing and whatever else babies needed—

Hat in hand, his duffel slung over his back, he raced down the dirt path in the dark, expecting at any moment to be stopped and maybe shot. Once he reached the main road, he could hitch to the bus stop in Baton Rouge. His boots were heavy, but what he felt was worse. Not twenty-three years old, and already he felt like a dead man. AWOL.

A distant buzz became a roar. The noise was familiar. Steeling himself, Tino glanced over his shoulder. It was just as he thought: An Army jeep was hurtling up the road. There was nowhere to hide—the shoulder was narrow and hedgeless; beyond it was another freeway. Tino froze, waiting for the jeep to pass, knowing it wouldn't. Instead it slowed and came to a stop beside him. This was it, game over. Nothing left now but the court-martial.

Tino turned to face his future, resigned to whatever punishment the Army intended to mete out. The driver leaned over the passenger seat. Who else would it be but Chick, grinning from the interior darkness, his face smeared with camouflage paint, his teeth bright white.

"What the *hell* are you doing?"

"Come on! Hop in!"

They sped along the road to Baton Rouge, the woods dark all around them. "Where did you get this jeep?" Tino asked when he could breathe again.

"I liberated it. Isn't that what it's all about? Liberation?"

He was grinning, a broad cat-ate-the-canary smile opening out like a wide, welcome vista.

"We're gonna catch it. As if being AWOL weren't bad enough!"

"Only if *they* catch *me*."

"Where did you get the keys?"

Chick leaned over and wiggled his fingers in Tino's face. "The old five-finger Louie!" They bounced over a rut. He glanced sidelong at Tino. "You see, I've learned a thing or two from you."

Tino swallowed hard and sat back, resolved to keep quiet so as not to make himself a blubbering fool. What had he done to deserve such a friend? All the million things he'd do for Chick if they managed to get out of this, if they both made it back, somehow, to civilian life. Some day.

"Thanks for this," he said brusquely. "I mean—"

"Don't mention it." Chick grinned. "Not to anyone."

51. Activism

All night she'd been up and down, tending to little Brenda who needed this and that, and that and this. Good Lord, what babies needed. Brenda's fussing joined the rhythm of the hours, each crabby outburst initiating a sequence: diaper, feed, burp, rock. And then, if she was lucky, there was a blessed interlude, never longer than thirty or forty minutes, in which they both slept, Primrose dreamlessly. As for Brenda, who knew what babies dreamed?

At dawn, while Brenda napped, Primrose made herself a cup of coffee. The day stretched before her, its rhythms exactly the same as the nighttime's, dull as her own mind became after her initial round of Dr. Addleman's pills, which she gulped down with cold coffee, sour juice, whatever was around. When she ran out of clean glasses, she drank straight from the tap. Everything tasted foul; she couldn't remember the last time she'd eaten. As usual the kitchen floor was gritty beneath her bare feet; in the bathroom, a pink ring of mildew had formed at the toilet's waterline. She doubted she had whatever it took to remove the brush from the closet and swish the bowl with bleach, the way her mother did. And what *did* it take—strength, courage, will? Never mind. They were all just words now, and she hardly remembered the differences between them. Regardless of whatever you wanted to call it, it always took a whole lot of effort to do things just the way her mother did. And yet for so long now, there seemed to be no other way.

Someone knocked at the door. When Primrose opened it, Elsie was standing on the doorstep in her trench coat, the one Primrose had admired that first day in the breezeway. The coat was mud-caked, and one of the buttons had cracked down the middle; someone had sanded the gleam from her eyes.

"Primrose!" Elsie cried, filling the silence with the fake cheerleader enthusiasm that was, despite its falsity or perhaps because of it, nevertheless identifiably Elsie's. So here she was, back from the dead, and not overly changed by the experience, it seemed. "Give a gal a drink, would you? A gal needs a drink!"

"Of course," Primrose murmured. Madness was so strange. No matter how far she descended into this brainstorm other people called her illness, in one small, distant corner of herself, she never quite dissolved. And from this vantage point, she knew she should invite Elsie in, for there was no fighting with a ghost or a hallucination or a side effect of Dr. Addleman's pills. "Come in, come in!"

"Do I stink?" Elsie asked. Her face was dusky. "They say we stink."

In fact, Elsie reeked. Like the bottom of a trash can at the airless, lightless bottom of the sea.

"You smell fine to me," Primrose told her.

Elsie tossed her matted hair. But it was too much movement, or Elsie had been too long underground. Her right earlobe crumbled onto her shoulder. Primrose tried not to wince as fragments hit the tabletop, the counter, the floor.

"Ugh," Elsie said, brushing the bits away. "Been a while since you've gone at it with the mop and duster, eh? Well, you're entitled, what with the new baby and all. Can I see her?"

Defensively Primrose said, "She's sleeping."

"Well, aren't you just the mama bear!" Elsie laughed, a short bark that sent a foul blast into Primrose's face. "What a maternal instinct! I honestly didn't think you had it in you."

Primrose poured a second cup of coffee and set it before Elsie, alongside the sugar bowl. She took a creamer of milk from the fridge. "It's skim," she said, setting it on the table.

"Attagirl. You do catch on fast. That's an asset around here, let me tell you." A bitterness in that last sentence, or maybe Primrose imagined it. In her mind's eye, she saw herself at her kitchen table, pouring coffee for no one, talking to the wall. She hadn't had much sleep; the pills did funny things to her head; and her head did its own funny things, too. Dead people did not come back to life. Not even dead, unhappy housewives from Maple Bay.

"Do you know the story," Elsie mused, absently stirring another fragment of flesh into her coffee, where it dissolved like one of Primrose's pills, "of what happened on the road to Emmaus?"

Was Elsie reading her mind? Of course she knew the story. Thought to be dead and gone, Jesus reappeared to two of his disciples, who both knew and did not know that the stranger beside them was their reincarnated guru. He had that effect on people—you knew and you did not know, until he did something to make the truth incontrovertible, and that was called a miracle.

Or a hallucination.

Primrose said, "You know I'm not religious."

Elsie hooted and slapped her leg, which rolled grotesquely from the hip. "My funeral must have been quite a stretch for you!"

"It must be tough," Primrose replied soberly, "being dead."

Elsie shrugged, and her remaining earlobe fell away. Primrose clapped her hand to her mouth.

"A mere bagatelle, Primrose! You need to be less sensitive. Don't let these Maple Bay Avon ladies get to you the way they got to me."

Elsie lifted the lid from the sugar bowl. A spider escaped down the other side.

"Got a spoon? A clean one, I mean."

Elsie wanted Primrose to accompany her to the Be-In, scheduled for that afternoon in the ball field by Unaconicut Hill. "If we leave now, we'll be just in time to catch the main event. Some ex-KGB scientist is going to be talking about how to connect with people in other planes of being."

"Ex-KGB? Other planes of being?"

Elsie stirred her coffee and, as if taunting her, licked her spoon before setting it down. "I'll bet you know where I'm coming from. Don't you?"

The ex-KGB scientist had to be Rodenko. How many Soviet defector astronomers with an interest in astral travel could there be in Rhode Island?

What else had Lupo told her? She couldn't recall. Norah had invited her to this hoo-hah; that she did remember. If she went with Elsie, she'd likely run into them both. How could she face them in this state? Lupo with his earnest energy, Norah with her frank, open face and her sack full of books. They were coming up, they were coming through. And where did that leave her? They would be polite, trying not to notice her flabby body, her matted hair. The whole scene would be awful.

"Well, Elsie, now that you're back," Primrose said guardedly, wanting to change the subject but not so forcefully that she agitated Elsie into flinging more of her body parts around the kitchen, "don't you think you should spend some time with your boys?"

"They're going to boarding school in September," Elsie said. So the rumor was true. "Those boys don't need mollycoddling." Sadness scudded across her face, the shadow of a cloud. "They grow up so fast! But never mind that. What do you say? Let's go!"

"I should get Brenda."

"You new mothers! You should do this, you should do that— do you believe everything you read in Dr. Spock? How many kids has *he* pushed out? None, that's how many."

Primrose had to admit, Elsie had a point.

"Lupo will be there," Elsie taunted. "Bet you didn't know I knew about him."

Primrose's cup clattered in her saucer. Trembling, she put the whole thing—dish, cup, utensils—in the sink. When she turned around, Elsie was by the front door, sifting through the bills that Primrose had been storing in Poppa Tavio's top hat. Dr. Addleman's was among them, a small and thin envelope addressed to *Mrs. Tino Battuta* in his reticent, antiseptic hand.

Primrose took the mail from Elsie and shoved the pile in a drawer.

Elsie scowled at her reflection in the hallway mirror. She pulled Poppa Tavio's hat down onto her head and tucked her hair underneath it.

In the mirror Primrose saw nothing that she didn't also see standing before her, right now, in real life. If you could call it real. If you could call it life.

Elsie tapped the hat. "Mind if I borrow this?"

"Go ahead, Elsie. Why the hell not?"

"You know, Primrose," Elsie said as she adjusted the hat, "no one will call the cops if you leave Brenda for ten minutes. She'll be fine in her crib. Besides, what babies really need is to learn how to fend for themselves. You don't want to raise a spoiled brat, do you?"

Primrose said, "She'll cry."

"So let her cry. Sooner or later, she'll go back to sleep. That's what babies do."

It was a warm day, unusual for so early in the year. All over the muddy ball field, people were stretched out on top of blankets or lay writhing beneath them. With Brenda in her sky-blue sleeper squirming in her arms, Primrose picked her way along, following Elsie, whose muddy trench coat swung open over her dirt-streaked funeral suit. Flesh on flesh, that's what was happening underneath those swarming blankets, bodies pushed together for whatever they might get in the permanent now that the *carpe diem* crowd loved so much: warmth, fleeting companionship, the illusion that, even at the boundaries of the body, no one is alone.

Listen to the music
Off the pigs
It's spring...O dammit
I'm free

"The military's going crazy," a young man in a tie-dyed T-shirt was saying, speaking from behind her in an excited rush. "It's madness all the way up and down the chain of command."

Nervous laughter, the snap of a Zippo, the smell of marijuana smoke, a breath noisily taken and held.

Tino was out there, somewhere. A link in the disintegrating chain, holding up a plasma bottle attached to some poor bleeding alternative version of himself, because gravity still worked even if nothing else did—he was out there, perhaps thinking of her, almost certainly thinking of Brenda, and most likely going to pieces, talking to himself, saying *there but for the grace of God*, believing in neither prayer, nor grace, nor God, somewhere near Baton Rouge.

People were chanting:

Ho Chi Minh

Ho Chi Minh

From across the field, Primrose glimpsed her friends: Lupo had his arm around Norah, who was leaning against Joseph, who was clutching Rosemary about the waist. Rosemary caught Primrose's eye and waved, but Primrose was already gone, caught up in a movement of bodies. The crowd solidified into a single entity. Nobody—not Rosemary, not Lupo, not Joseph, not even Norah, so poised and organized, with her eye trained calmly on her future—could be there for her now. Not in the way that she needed. Only Tino was that person, and he was far away.

Atoms danced. Electrons existed if you thought they did, if they were the sort of thing that bothered you. If you cared. At the field's edge, Elsie sank down into the mud; a moment later she was gone, all but for Tavio's top hat; then the hat disappeared as well, and a clutch of white flowers pushed up in its place.

It was all her own fault, Primrose was sure of it.

All but the snowdrops, anyway.

She'd handed Brenda off to someone, just for a moment. Even though Elsie was nothing now but a mound of snowdrops, she had been right about one thing: Every so often, a mother needed a break. But then something had gone wrong, and Brenda was nowhere to be found.

Primrose made her way to the bleachers and climbed up to get a better view. She caught sight of the baby in her blue sleeper being passed from hand to hand, headed for the center of the crowd. No one wanted to hang on to the baby, that was clear from the anxious reluctance with which each person took her from the one before, and the relief that spread across the giver's face—a relief that Primrose recognized at just the moment something less comfortable, shame perhaps, spread across her own.

Primrose sat down hard on the bleachers, breathing in ragged gasps. A mother needs a break, she reminded herself. As for Brenda—

Primrose shut her eyes.

Brenda would be fine, and what a good girl she was, already making Primrose's life easier by making her own independent way in the world.

When Primrose opened her eyes again, a little girl had clambered up beside her. The girl, about six years old, was barefoot, her cheek smudged with peanut butter. Her gaze was piercing and magnetic, like a spaceship's tractor beam.

"Where's your mother?" Primrose asked, disoriented by the way the girl seemed to see right through her.

"Nice to meet you," the girl replied with a fierce politeness that reminded Primrose of Lorraine, who often said nice things when she meant just the opposite.

In the girl's arms, Brenda began to fuss. The girl rocked her too forcefully, her resentment plain as the peanut butter on her face.

Primrose said, "Let me have the baby."

The girl seemed not to hear. She reminded Primrose of some hinterland creature—small but unpredictable, skittish.

In the ball field, the center of the crowd had opened up and a man was speaking into a bullhorn: *Dolphins, angels, extraterrestrials—today we are witnessing the unification of every sentient life form in the universe.* Some people were listening closely; others, Primrose could tell from their faces, thought it was horseshit. Still, no one moved or spoke out; the man with the bullhorn kept talking, but now his words were unintelligible.

When Primrose looked again, the girl in the overalls was holding squirming Brenda out for her to take. "Here you go, ma'am," she said, with the same icy politeness as before. She pressed the baby into Primrose's arms.

"Thanks?" Primrose faltered. A stillness overcame her, falling from the crown of her head like a bucket of warm water. She couldn't have moved if she tried.

The little bitch bounded down the stairs and away.

Brenda fussed. She needed a diaper change, and of course, what Primrose hadn't brought, leaving the house with Elsie, was a supply of diapers. Further evidence, as if anyone needed it, of the unremitting spoiledness of babies: shit, piss, crust on the scalp, sour regurgitations. Brenda arched her back and kept fussing, making just the sort of noises that ill-tempered babies make when they want to spite their mothers.

"Oh, all *right*," Primrose muttered, the paralysis dissipating as mysteriously as it had come, leaving behind only a twanging exhaustion that emanated from the marrow of her bones. "You are just like your father."

The baby sought her gaze and held it, her eyes light brown—indeed, just like her father's.

Clutching Brenda to her chest, Primrose hurried back down the steps and back onto the ball field. Where would she find a clean diaper at a Human Be-In? The assembled crowd looked to Primrose more or less just out of diapers themselves. Surely there was more to life, to real life, than this. But before she could make up her mind, she was swirled into the crowd again, the stench and bones of it, bodies, smoke; at the far edge, a lanky, serious-faced young man wearing jeans and a flannel shirt pushed a hank of brown hair out of his eyes as he swayed to some music only he could hear, systole, diastole, *hum*.

52. Friendship

They drove all night and through the next day, stopping only for bathroom breaks and to buy gas and smokes. After their initial conversation, neither Tino nor Chick could find much to say. Tino was nearly out of his mind with anxiety. The whole time they were heading north, Primrose seemed to be whispering to Tino just out of earshot, a long, desperate monologue he couldn't quite hear. Except that, as they sped over the George Washington Bridge, with Tino looking out the window alternately holding his breath and gasping at the sheer size of the thing, he heard her speak as distinctly as if she were sitting beside him, her voice as usual ever so slightly aloof, sardonic: *Funny, isn't it? I mean, that it should come to this?*

At dusk on the second day, they crossed the Rhode Island border.

"Almost there, Tino," Chick said.

Tino had been dozing in the passenger seat. He sat up, rubbing his eyes. "Will you stay for a while, since you're in town?" He had no idea why it occurred to him to ask this.

"I might," said Chick. "Or I might just drive back to Louisiana. Return the jalopy, take my lumps."

The lumps: a court-martial for being AWOL, abetting a desertion, stealing a jeep. Tino knew he might be able to talk his way out of his trouble because Primrose was having what was, technically, a medical emergency. He didn't want to think about what would happen to Chick though.

"Or I might see Dot," Chick said.

"That seems like the better option. But you know I'm not one for doing things by the book."

Chick nodded. "You can say that again."

"How come you never asked her to marry you?"

"Well," Chick said, smiling sly, "we talked about it."

"And?" It was a relief to talk casually about everyday things. Normal life. Girls.

Chick reached over and withdrew their last pack of Parliaments from Tino's breast pocket. "Neither one of us was up for it," he said, shaking out the one cigarette that remained. Tino flicked open his Zippo, offering a light. "I'm not wild about marriage. Look at what's happening to you."

"You think this happens when you get married?"

"No," Chick said. "But I do think it's the sort of thing that can happen when you—well, I hate to sound sentimental but—when you love someone."

53. Into the wilderness

The empty house gave Tino the creeps. He willed himself not to panic as he searched the stale rooms. In the kitchen, he found a pamphlet advertising something called the "Exhumen Be-In" at the ballpark near the Tirocchis' house, by Unaconicut Hill. In the hallway, the house keys were still on the table, but Poppa Tavio's hat was gone, and a pile of mail had been shoved awkwardly into one drawer of the console table. The phone rang.

"Tino Battuta?" A man's voice, vaguely familiar, boomed at him through the receiver.

"Speaking," he said. "Barely."

"This is Dr. Addleman. A bed just opened up at Lesser Memorial. I can hold it for another hour, tops."

"Okay," Tino said. Someone must have called the doctor. Lorraine, maybe, or Louise.

"Don't 'okay' me, son. Get off the phone and bring me your wife. Clock's ticking."

Tino set the receiver in its cradle, irritated by the peremptory way the doctor had demanded Primrose's delivery. As if Tino had been the one to fail her, as if the doctor, too, had not had a hand in this catastrophe.

Brenda.

Not in his wildest nightmares had he imagined that it would come to this.

Outside, Chick leaned on the horn. Tino rushed back to the jeep. "To the park," he told him.

Chick reversed the jeep out of the driveway, and they sped across town.

Too late. By the time they got there, the demo was over. The grounds were strewn with trash. As they stood in the ballpark's stands, surveying the mess, Tino's thoughts wandered to geography; when he tried to remember where the Pocasset went underground, he found that he couldn't. But it had to be nearby. The printworks weren't so far away, and neither was the cemetery.

The cemetery. The river behind it. Where Primrose went last time.

"I know where she is," he said to Chick. "Let's go."

They rushed to the church, and sure enough, the Chevelle was at the far edge of the parking lot, near the edge of the woods.

"Bingo!" Tino jumped out and then, remembering, turned back. "Thanks a million, Chick."

"Don't mention it."

Tino stood there, not mentioning it, wanting more than anything to mention it.

"You're kid's in there, Tino. Go!"

Tino ran.

He didn't think she'd be hard to find, and in fact, she wasn't. Crazy ladies with newborn babies didn't just disappear into the woods—they left trails of crushed grass and broken branches, a pair of sandals, a bottle half-full of baby formula, a tube of lipstick that he picked up and examined: Paramour Pink. He grabbed the bottle and the sandals. Hearing a wail, he advanced toward the sound, dread double-thumping on the downbeat, diastole, deep within his chest.

She sat on a rock near the water's edge where the river broadened to a still pool. The riverbank was crowded with dogwoods blooming pink and white; the willows had sprouted their tender yellow-green first leaves. Beneath one of these willows Primrose sat holding the baby. She kept trying to jam a bottle into the baby's mouth, but the baby refused to take it, whimpering and turning her head away.

Her sandals hanging from his hand, Tino approached on tiptoe, trying not to spook her. He stumbled, and for a moment, he was sure she'd bolt—and then he was beside her, whispering, cajoling: "Here, let me take her for just a minute while you rest, we don't have anywhere to go, we can just stay here."

She handed him the baby, and he offered the bottle, twirling it lightly between her lips until she clamped her mouth around the nipple and sucked. He rubbed his finger along her hairline, which was caked with a waxy substance. Cradle cap, he guessed. It fell away in flakes.

He had the other bottle in his pocket, which meant he had about twenty minutes to get them all out of here. As if sensing his panic, Primrose laughed a husky, dry laugh with nothing inside it. Tino shivered. *Clock's ticking.*

"Look," she said, pointing at the water's edge, toward the shuttered mill. "There's a dead fish right there. Can't you smell the stink?"

"No."

"That mill is a menace to us all."

"The mill's been closed for a year at least."

"That doesn't mean the water's clean." She crossed her feet in her lap and positioned her hands, palms up and fingers touching, on her knees. She closed her eyes. After a few seconds, she pulled her knees up and wiggled her bare toes. When she smiled, lipstick was smeared all over her front teeth.

"I didn't know you went in for that yoga stuff," Tino said for lack of anything better. *Just keep talking,* he thought.

"I learned in the hospital." She shrugged. "We never had a honeymoon. I have to take my vacations where I can."

J'accuse, he thought dully. Some line he'd picked up somewhere, probably from Primrose, something she'd said years ago. Before—

Focus, you asshole.

"Will you take me to Paris someday?"

"Anywhere you want," Tino said, not saying that once he got her in the car, the first stop would be Lesser, where Dr. Addleman was waiting with a syringe of Haldol.

"Everything's blooming." Primrose trailed her finger down the baby's cheek. She was still sucking strongly, but her eyes were closed. "Maybe she'll fall asleep."

As if in reply, the baby stirred and fussed, spitting out the bottle. Tino caught it in midair, knowing somehow that tossing bottles was exactly the sort of thing Brenda would do. Parenthood was going to be a long fight, and he wanted nothing more, in that moment, than to have it. He resettled both baby and bottle into their previous rhythm, suck-swallow-suck, like bobbing in the ocean on a calm day.

"You'd think she was an easy baby. She does look like a daddy's girl."

"Is there any other kind?"

Primrose laughed her old laugh, and for an instant, it seemed like everything still might be all right.

"Let's get something to eat," he said, suddenly ravenous. It had been a long way back from Baton Rouge. "Meatball grinder, eggplant parm, you name it."

"I am not your dog," she snapped. "You can't get me into your paddy wagon by offering me that dog chow."

Her gray eyes flashed, a signal: Forget taking me to lunch. Take me to someone who can help.

"Oh, Prim." The waves lapped softly on the bank. "I'm sorry."

"You don't sound sorry."

And she was right; he wasn't sorry. He was only trying to restore their family, and he would say anything, anything at all, to make that happen. His head felt enormous. How long had it been since he'd last slept? The baby was a soft weight in his arms.

"Even if you *are* sorry, you shouldn't patronize me."

What was that signal, that flashing sign? Help—she needed help, she wanted it. He had to believe—

"Pig," she said without emotion.

No way he was going to dignify *that* with a response.

Primrose went to sit on a tree stump, playing with the ends of her hair. He gave the baby's bottle another half-turn to keep her sucking. She would eat until she nodded off, soothing herself to sleep according to some rhythm only she knew, keeping time with the whole world—the river, the robins, the trees, the wind. His heartbeat. Keeping time—it's not just the musicians who do it, he reflected. We all do it. Our hearts do it.

He rose with the baby in his arms and walked back up the path. Primrose rustled behind him. It was now or never.

He held Brenda to his chest and ran. Her bottle fell away, and Primrose shrieked.

You're taking a little girl away from her mother.

Brenda wailed.

He was a terrible person. A terrible father.

Primrose sobbed, taking ragged choking breaths. There was a thud, and Primrose howled as she fell.

Run.

The car door was unlocked, the bassinet in the front seat, the pacifier hanging on a ribbon from the handle. He slipped into the car, settled the baby. The engine came to life at a touch. He gunned it, knowing he should not wait, not even for a moment. But then he did wait, scanning the tall grass along the ridge for any sign of Primrose.

She limped into view, her face streaked with dirt and tears.

The baby fussed in a minor way, as if she was just trying him out, this daddy thing, seeing what he would do. Without looking, Tino stretched a hand into the bassinet and stroked her stomach. She quieted.

Primrose rapped the driver's side window with her wedding ring. Tino slipped into reverse, and the car bucked a bit, but she didn't let go. He rolled down the window.

"That's my *baby*," she said, pointing. Her hand was scratched and bleeding.

"You want your baby, get in the damn car!"

She held onto the door. Tino let the car roll. Not far, just a few inches—first three, then six. One foot. Primrose teetered.

The baby wailed. Primrose hung on, craning her head into the car's interior, her eyes locked on Brenda.

"Damn it, Tino."

"Are you coming?" Another inch. Her head cracked against his teeth.

"Tino!" She leapt back, her eyes fierce. He kept going. At the last moment—it happened so fast—she ran around to the passenger side, let herself in, and slammed the door. He reached over and gently, carefully, definitively brought his palm down on the lock.

"Goddamn it, Tino," she said, her voice rough with surrender. "Goddamn."

54. Bigger, muddier

The Huey banked, sank, and finally rose straight up, a clumsy metal spider on a filament of well-intentioned American know-how and can-do and yes-sir and aye-aye. The valley below was green on green, threaded with silver where the Canh Doc caught the light. Chick fought back a puke.

"What do they call you?" The pilot's voice came over in a staticky burst. The silver dollar–sized patch on the pilot's shoulder was embroidered with a bald eagle grafted onto a dragon. Underneath, in silver thread: *Inter arma silent leges.* Chick adjusted his headset.

"Cesare Bonano," said Chick.

"Cheesy banana?" The pilot scanned the horizon.

"Cesare," he repeated, knowing it was useless.

"Chest x-ray? Cheese soufflé?"

The bastard grinned, enjoying himself. Chick had kept his given name on his dog tags, a decision he now regretted. Tracer fire arced below them. Who knows how they might screw up his ID at Graves, should it come to that. Which, he had to admit, it might. Meanwhile, here he was, fighting a war in which exactly no one could pronounce his name.

"Chick," he said. "I'm Chick."

The pilot flashed a thumbs-up.

Chick scratched under his collar, consoling himself with the thought that to most of the guys he'd met in the Army, his name didn't matter anyway—he'd just been "the Italian fella."

"Holy moly," said the pilot, banking again. "Look at that hillside. Green as green can be, like some coconutty island."

He surveyed the instruments and abruptly yanked a lever. Chick's harness cut hard into his chest. The valley floor came up beneath his feet, and they hung there for a moment, wavering from side to side. The pilot righted the chopper and hovered, waiting for the flak-jacketed guy standing in a field of silver smoke—the LZ, the Landing Zone, Chick recognized it from what he'd learned, despite everything, at Fort Polk—to wave the signal to land.

"You'll see," the pilot said, easing the throttle. They descended fast. "It's nothing but shit on the ground. But from up here, man, it looks like fucking paradise."

Paradise? No way. Chick Bonano begged to differ, sir. Paradise was located elsewhere—in Maple Bay, to be precise, where Tino Battuta, the luckiest unlucky guy in the world, was on compassionate leave until his new bride got her shit together. Which was to say, indefinitely.

Chick reminded himself: *Breathe, you asshole. Breathe.*

55. A note from the road

Chére Primrose,

Greece! What a disappointment. There's nothing in Kythera but rocks to dash your brains out on—& squid, lots of squid. Here is the land of calamari. (As a Rhode Islander, you will appreciate.) To pass the time, I played chess with a guy who taught me restaurant Greek—*metzedes* (snacks), *bira* (you figure it out). Saw a bit of the country. Goats & ruins. The goats eat whatever they find & don't give a damn about ruins, not to mention the junk at the bottom of the sea.

The goats have much to teach us.

Speaking of junk, remember that little *objet* I gave you? It's not what I thought it was, but still—Well, I'm running out of space. Take good care of that thing. And you. Take good care of you, Primrose.

Best regards,

Lupo Light

April, 1968

Penticton, British Columbia

PS. Thanks for Rodenko's manifesto. I'm sorry the Be-In didn't work out.

THE BOOK OF LOVE
The End
by Primrose

When we were girls, the whole world believed in love. Our mothers told us, "No matter how smart you think you are, love is the most important thing in a woman's life." Marry for love, they told us. Love makes you whole. Love makes you real. Love makes the world go 'round. Love is all you need, all you need.

Well.

We now understand the extent to which we have, as *they say*, put the cart before the horse. The cart is, in fact, light years away from the horse, and the horse is chafing at the bit, wanting to forget the cart entirely, and instead to visit Paris, London, Rome, Barcelona, all the celebrated European destinations—so as to "find herself" or, failing that, to "explore her options."

The horse does not understand that there are no other options. It is April 1968, and the best have been taken from us. The best are already gone.

Perhaps: Love is not all you need. Love is not what it's all about.

There can be only one aim now: to finally set the horse ahead of the cart, to make the world ready for whatever's coming next. Ready, set—

Oh—

Acknowledgments

My parents, who came of age during the Vietnam War, filled my childhood with arguments about the meaning of that war and the opposition to it. While their predicaments have informed my premises, this novel is about something else—a group of young adults who, confronted by social and political forces that threaten to upend their lives, discover that they can no longer pretend to be immune, excluded, or exempt from those forces.

I grew up in Rhode Island, where the novel takes place, and I have incorporated details of locale that Rhode Islanders of the Sixties may remember. (There really was a bar called the Hog House and a boat called the *Sumac*; local newspapers did print reports of UFO sightings; and although it did not begin publication until 1971, *The Good Five Cent Cigar* is still the University Of Rhode Island's student newspaper.) Other details I gleaned from primary and secondary sources as well as from conversations with family and friends who shared memories with me. For the purposes of the story, I have simplified and modified the geography of the neighborhoods of greater Providence; I have changed the names of some landmarks and used others fictitiously. All errors are my own.

Violence has always shaped American foreign and domestic policies. I believe this violence begins in, and is sustained by, a repressive ideology of the family that's especially hard on women and children; capturing echoes of that ideology and its devastating effects was one of my intentions in writing *Ready, Set, Oh*. Because representation, while important, is not enough, a portion of the proceeds from sales of this novel will be donated to the National Network to End Domestic Violence, a nonprofit organization in Washington, DC, that works to end this scourge through effective practical and policy interventions.

I wrote the first draft of *Ready, Set, Oh* while a student in the MFA program at Columbia University. I'm grateful to my fellow students who read my work with care. Nicholas Christopher encouraged me to shape my material into a thesis and secured a grant permitting me to write through one particularly important summer. I am grateful to Nic and to Columbia for this essential support. I'm thankful as well for my other teachers: Binnie Kirshenbaum, John Glusman, Patricia O'Toole, Richard Howard, David Plante, and Alan Ziegler. At Columbia I was additionally supported by a teaching fellowship in the University Writing Program; I thank Nicole Wallack and Joe Bizup, program directors, for that opportunity. I thank Linda Josefowicz, Robin Kirman, James Pasto, and the late Ellen Tinsman, who advised me on early drafts.

I owe the chapter title "We arrive like an echo" to Will Duncan, whose song by that title is part of *Vanishing Point* by The Carpetbag Brigade; I thank Will and the company for permission to use it, and my cousin, Kristen Greco, for introducing me to their beautiful work. "Wild nights, wild nights" repeats, of course, the title of a poem by Robert Creeley.

I feel very lucky that this book has found a home with Flexible Press; thank you to Bill Burleson and Ed Sheehy for their visionary support and to Vicki Adang for her attentive copyediting.

Although my mother, the late Elaine Friden Greco, did not live to see this book's publication, she is present on every page, encouraging me to find my voice and use it.

None of this work would have been possible without the steadfast support of Linda and the late Michael Josefowicz, in whose Brooklyn home I wrote the book's first draft, and who looked after my infant daughter while I did.

Matthew Josefowicz, to whom this book is dedicated, relieved me of significant domestic responsibilities, freeing me to write under economically and emotionally secure conditions, and he still found time to read nearly every draft.

Our daughter, Jane, was scarcely a year old when the story of Primrose and Tino came to me on the corner of Union Street and Third Avenue. She was asleep in her infant carrier as I stood in a doorway absorbing the first reports of military and civilian casualties of yet another American war. The wars have continued, and I don't know what to say to her, except that this book, which grew up alongside her, is my effort to reckon with those wars, to do as the poet and activist Muriel Rukeyser urged in 1968: "To reach the limits of ourselves, to reach beyond ourselves / To let go the means, to wake."

About the author

Diane Josefowicz's fiction and essays have appeared in *Conjunctions, Fence, Dame, LA Review of Books*, and elsewhere. As a historian, she is the author, with Jed Z. Buchwald, of two histories of Egyptology, *The Riddle of the Rosetta* (2020) and *The Zodiac of Paris* (2010), both from Princeton University Press; and a novella, *L'Air du Temps (1985)*, forthcoming from Regal House. She serves as reviews editor at *Necessary Fiction* and director of communications for Swing Left Rhode Island, a progressive political organization focused on electoral work, voter protection, and voting rights. She holds an MFA from Columbia University, a PhD from the Massachusetts Institute of Technology, and a BA from Brown University. She grew up outside Providence, where she now lives with her family. *Ready, Set, Oh* is her first novel.

CPSIA information can be obtained
at www.ICGtesting.com
Printed in the USA
LVHW011638120922
728178LV00001B/121